TRANSHUMAN

Tor Books by Ben Bova

BEN BOVA

TRANSHUMAN

TOR®

A Tom Doherty Associates Book

New York

This is a work of fiction. All of the characters, organizations, and events portrayed in this novel are either products of the author's imagination or are used fictitiously.

TRANSHUMAN

Copyright © 2014 by Ben Bova

A Tor Book
Published by Tom Doherty Associates, LLC
175 Fifth Avenue
New York, NY 10010

www.tor-forge.com

Tor® is a registered trademark of Tom Doherty Associates, LLC.

The Library of Congress Cataloging-in-Publication Data is available upon request.

ISBN 978-0-7653-3293-6 (hardcover)
ISBN 978-1-4299-6542-2 (e-book)   JUL 31 2014

Tor books may be purchased for educational, business, or promotional use. For information on bulk purchases, please contact Macmillan Corporate and Premium Sales Department at 1-800-221-7945, extension 5442, or write specialmarkets@macmillan.com.

First Edition: April 2014

Printed in the United States of America

0 9 8 7 6 5 4 3 2 1

To darling Rashida

She walks in Beauty, like the night
Of cloudless climes and starry skies;
And all that's best of dark and bright
Meet in her aspect and her eyes.

LORD BYRON

Humanity is just a work in progress.

Tennessee Williams

TRANSHUMAN

University Hospital, Boston

I T OUGHT TO be raining, thought Luke Abramson. It ought to be gray and miserable, with a lousy cold rain pelting down.

Instead, the hospital room was bright, with mid-December sunshine slanting through the windows. In the bed lay eight-year-old Angela, Luke's granddaughter, frail and wasting, her eyes closed, her thinned blond hair spread across the pillow. Angela's parents, Luke's only daughter and his son-in-law, stood on the other side of the bed, together with Angela's attending physician. Luke stood alone.

He'd been playing tennis in the university's indoor court when the phone call from the hospital came. Or, rather, doggedly going through the motions of playing tennis. Nearly seventy-five, even doubles was getting beyond him. Although the younger men tried to take it easy on him, more than once Luke had gloomily suggested they start playing triples.

And then came the phone call. Angie was terminal. He had rushed to the hospital, bundling his bulky parka over his tennis shorts and T-shirt.

"Then there's nothing . . . ?" Luke's daughter, Lenore, couldn't finish the sentence. Her voice choked in sobs.

Norrie, Luke called to her silently, don't cry. I'll help you. I can cure Angie, I know I can. But he couldn't speak the words aloud. He watched Lenore sobbing quietly, her heart breaking.

And Luke remembered all the other times when his daughter had come to him in tears, her deep brown eyes brimming, her dear little form racked with sobs. I'll fix it, Norrie, he had always told her. I'll make it all better for you. Even when his wife died after all those painful years of battling cancer, Lenore came to her father for comfort, for protection against the terrible wrongs that life had thrown at them.

Now Lenore stood with her husband, who wrapped an arm protectively around her slim, trembling shoulders. Del towered over little Lenore, a tall, athletic figure standing firmly beside his diminutive, grief-stricken wife. He's being strong for her, Luke knew. But he could see the agony, the bitterness in his clenched jaw and bleak eyes.

The physician, Dr. Tamara Minteer, replied in a barely audible whisper, "We can make her as comfortable as possible. I'll contact Hospice and—"

"It's all right." Angela's tiny voice cut the doctor short. She had opened her eyes and was trying to smile. "It doesn't hurt. Not at all."

Lenore and Del leaned down over their daughter's prostrate body, both of them in tears. Dr. Minteer looked as if she wanted to cry, too, but she held herself stiffly erect and looked straight at Luke, standing on the other side of the bed.

I can cure her, Luke told her. He didn't have to say it aloud. He knew Minteer understood what was in his mind. She knew it. And she rejected the idea.

GLIOBLASTOMA MULTIFORME IS a particularly pernicious form of brain cancer. Stubbornly resistant to radiation and chemotherapy, it usually kills its victims in a matter of months. It rarely strikes children, but eight-year-old Angela Villanueva was one of those rare cases.

Luke Abramson was a cellular biologist at the end of his career. Approaching seventy-five, he had been under pressure for some years from the university's management to accept retirement gracefully and go away. Professor Abramson was well liked by his students and practically adored by his small laboratory staff, but his associates on the university's faculty found him cantankerous, stubborn, frequently scornful of his colleagues, and totally unwilling to go in any direction but his own. His retirement would be a blessing, they thought.

Cancer had been the curse of Luke's family. Both his parents had been cut down by cancers, his father's of the lungs and his mother's of the ovaries. His wife, good-natured and health conscious, had succumbed to bladder cancer despite a lifetime of carefully watching her diet and faithfully exercising to keep her weight down.

It was if some invisible supernatural monster haunted his family, Luke thought. An implacable enemy that took his loved ones from him, year after year.

Luke had anxiously watched over his only daughter, and was thankful to a deity he really didn't believe in when Lenore grew up cancer-free. But deep in his consciousness he knew that this was no victory. Cancer was out there, waiting to strike.

It devastated him when it struck, not his daughter, but her child, Angela. Glioblastoma multiforme. Inoperable brain cancer. Little Angie would be dead in six months or less. Unless Luke could prevent it.

L EAVING ANGELA WITH her grieving parents, Luke followed Dr. Minteer as she strode determinedly down the busy hospital corridor. The hallway bustled with people hurrying to and fro; it seemed to Luke more crowded than Grand Central Station.

He was puffing. First tennis and now a freaking foot race, he thought. We must look comical: a lean, bent old man with bad knees and what was left of his hair shaved down to a whitish fuzz, chasing after a slim, dark-haired oncologist. God, look at her go. Sleek and lithe as a prowling cheetah.

"Hey, Doc, slow up," he gasped.

Tamara Minteer stopped altogether and turned to face him. Slightly taller than Luke, she wasn't exactly beautiful, he thought: Her nose was a trifle too sharp, her lips on the thin side. But she was elegant. That was the word for her: elegant. She moved like a cat, supple and graceful. Almond-shaped green eyes set above high cheekbones. Glossy raven-black shoulder-length hair. At the moment, though, her lean, taut face was set grimly, her brilliant emerald eyes snapping.

"I know what you're going to say, Professor, and—"

"Luke," he wheezed. "My name is Luke."

"It's no good, Professor," Minteer continued, her voice low, throaty. "You can't wave a magic wand and cure your granddaughter."

Don't lose your freaking temper, Luke commanded himself. You need her. Don't turn her off.

He sucked in a breath. "It's not a magic wand and you know it. It's manipulating the telomeres, and I've got solid experimental evidence for its efficacy."

"In lab mice." Minteer resumed walking along the corridor, but at a slower pace.

"And chimps," Luke said, hurrying to keep up with her.

That stopped her. Minteer looked surprised. "I hadn't heard about chimpanzee experiments."

"One chimp. NIH won't let us have any more, something about the mother-loving animal rights activists. As if we were hurting them."

"You got positive results in a chimpanzee?"

Luke waggled a hand. "Sort of. We haven't published yet."

Minteer shook her head and started along the corridor once again. "I can't let you use your granddaughter as a guinea pig."

"She's going to die, for God's sake!" Luke barked. Several people in the corridor turned to stare at him.

Minteer kept walking, her soft-soled shoes squeaking on the tiled floor. She reached her office door and yanked it open, Luke two steps behind her.

He followed her into the office and closed the door tightly, then leaned against it, puffing. "You ought to be in the Olympics, Doc," he said, breathless.

"And you should be retired," Minteer snapped as she headed for her desk, her body as rigid as a steel bar.

It was a small office, windowless, efficiently lit by glareless light panels in the ceiling. Everything in its place, except for a bilious green spider plant that had overflowed its pot and spread halfway across the bookcase in one corner of the room.

"Let me try to save her," Luke pleaded. "She's my only grandchild, for God's sake."

"It's a totally unproven therapy. How can I let you experiment on an eight-year-old child?"

"So you're going to let her die? Is that what you call practicing medicine?"

"Don't tell me what I should be doing," Minteer snapped.

"Somebody's got to!"

Glaring at him, she said, "You know I can't approve it."

"Yes you could."

"I don't have the authority."

"But you could recommend it."

"How can I recommend a therapy I don't believe in?"

"What freaking difference does it make? Angie's going to die unless you let me help her!"

"You can't help her. We've tried targeted bacterial vectors and immunotherapy. Nothing's worked. She's going to die, whatever you do."

"And you'll be killing her mother, too. This'll kill Lenore."

That hit home. He could see it in her face.

"I'm no good at begging," Luke said, hating the whine in his voice. "But please. For God's sake, please!"

Her rigid stance softened a little. She looked away from him, then slowly sank into her swivel chair. Luke remained standing in front of the desk.

"Recommend it to the executive committee," he urged again. "Please. It's Angie's only chance."

Minteer locked her eyes on Luke's. For an eternally long moment she said nothing, just stared at him. At last she nodded slowly and said, "I can't recommend your therapy, Professor. It's just a lab experiment."

Before he could protest, she added, "But I can ask the committee to hear you out."

"Thanks! Thanks a lot," said Luke. Then he abruptly turned and left Dr. Minteer's office. He desperately needed to find the nearest men's room.

Executive Committee Meeting

THIS IS A waste of time, Luke realized.

It had taken two days for the executive committee to agree to hear him out. Two days taken from Angela's lifetime. Luke watched them as they came into the conference room and took their seats along the table. They've already made up their minds. He could see it in their faces. They resent being here. They won't listen to anything I say.

Twelve men and women, like a jury. Senior members of the hospital staff and the university faculty. They were all younger than Luke; four of them had been students of his, at one time. But they had stopped being active research scientists years ago. They were administrators now, paper shufflers, decision makers—who had already made their decision.

All right, he told himself. You've got to change their stupid hidebound minds. Stay cool. Don't get angry with them. Don't let them see what you really think of them.

He went through his presentation carefully, using his best lecture manners. No jokes, of course. Totally serious. Life or death. His slides flicked across the screen at the head of the room. His words bounced off the walls. The committee members shifted in their chairs, waiting for the end.

At last Luke showed his final slide. "As you can see," he said, working his laser pointer down the list of test results, "by activating the controlling gene set we increase the body's production of telomeres, which rejuvenates the subjects and alleviates the symptoms of aging."

He thumbed the button on his remote that turned off the projector and turned on the ceiling lights.

Luke's legs ached, and he desperately wanted to urinate, but he remained standing at the front of the conference room. The committee members glanced back and forth at each other. No one spoke.

Finally, one of his former students, now head of the university's grant committee, cleared his throat noisily. "Luke, your work with telomerase is very interesting, but I don't see how it could possibly apply to Angela Villanueva's case."

A better reaction than he had expected. Luke made a smile as he replied, "Glioblastoma multiforme is a form of cancer."

"A very dangerous form," said one of the women, halfway along the table. She was plump and gray-haired, wearing a stylish slate gray dress and a pearl choker beneath her double chin.

Nodding, Luke went on. "Cancer cells multiply wildly, they don't stop proliferating. But if we can inhibit their production of telomerase, we can kill them."

"Wait a minute, back up a bit," said the committee's chairman, Odom Wexler, a small, roundish black money manager with a fringe of silvery beard and wire-rimmed tinted eyeglasses. Frowning puzzledly, he asked, "Inhibiting their telomerase will kill the cancer cells? How's that work?"

Christ, Luke snarled silently, didn't you listen to *anything* I told you?

Patiently, he explained. "All normal cells reproduce a certain number of times, then they stop reproducing."

"The Hayflick Limit. I understand that."

"Cancer cells don't have a Hayflick Limit. They just go on reproducing, making more of themselves, building tumors that just grow and grow."

"Unless we intervene with radiation or chemotherapy," said the dean of the psychiatry department, a handsome man dressed in a navy blue three-piece suit. He had a leonine mane of silvery hair and a smile that had reassured countless wealthy wives.

"There's also surgery," added the surgeon seated down at the foot of the conference table.

"Surgery, of course," the psychiatrist muttered.

"All of those interventions have serious side effects," Luke said. "In Angela's case, surgery is impossible, and both radiation and chemo have been ineffective."

"And your intervention doesn't have serious side effects?"

Ignoring the snide tone of the question, Luke continued explaining. "Telomeres control the cells' reproduction rate. Each time a cell reproduces, the telomeres at the ends of the chromosomes shrink a little."

"Telomeres are sort of like aglets at the end of a shoelace, aren't they?" asked a balding man seated across the table from the chairman. He was a financial guy, a glorified accountant, neither a physician nor a scientist.

"Like aglets, right," said Luke. "Telomeres protect the ends of the chromosome strings, keep them from unraveling. But they shrink every time the cell reproduces."

"And when they get small enough the cell stops reproducing," said one of Luke's former students. "Everybody knows that."

You always were a smug little prick, Luke said to himself. Aloud, he replied, "And when your cells stop reproducing, you begin to get the symptoms of aging. Your skin wrinkles. Your eyesight fades. Your muscles weaken. When enough of your cells stop reproducing, you die."

His former student, almost smirking, said, "Telomeres were a hot subject for a while, back in the nineties. The cure for aging, they thought."

"They were right," Luke snapped.

"Inject telomerase into the body," the younger man continued, "and you regrow the cells' telomeres. The fountain of youth."

"It works," Luke insisted.

"In mice."

"It works on genes that mice and human beings have in common. It will work on humans. I'm sure of it!"

Before the back-and-forth could grow into a really bitter argument, Chairman Wexler interrupted. "But what's all this got to do with Angela Villanueva's case?"

"As I explained before," Luke said, trying to hold on to his temper, "by inhibiting her telomerase production we can kill the cancer cells."

"But what about the other cells of her body?" asked the gray-haired woman.

"We'll be inhibiting their telomerase production, too, of course. But the cancer cells will die long before her somatic cells become endangered."

"How do you know that?"

"I showed you my experimental evidence—"

"But that's with lab mice!" said one of the younger men. "You can't expect us to approve a human trial with nothing more than mouse experiments to go on. The FDA would shut us down in two seconds flat!"

Luke stared at him. He wasn't much more than forty, and he'd made his way through the political jungles of academia by smilingly agreeing with almost everyone but then going ahead ruthlessly with his own ideas. He never stuck his neck out, though. He always had underlings do his dirty work, and he had no compunctions about chopping their heads off when he had to.

"If you told the FDA that you approved the therapy and wanted to do a clinical test—"

"No, no, no," said Wexler, wagging his bearded head back and forth. "Luke, you know as well as I do that it takes years to get FDA approval for any new procedure. Then there's the state medical board and at least three other federal agencies to get through."

"There's an eight-year-old girl dying!"

"That's regrettable, but we can't put this hospital in jeopardy by going ahead with an unapproved therapy."

Luke exploded. "Then you pea-brained idiots might just as well put a gun to my granddaughter's head and blow her freaking brains out!"

He strode angrily down the length of the table, past the stunned committee members, and stormed out of the room.

Beacon Hill

LUKE SAT ALONE in the living room of his darkened top-floor apartment. Through the uncurtained window he could see the gold dome of the state capitol shining in the moonlight. He swished a tumbler of Bushmills whiskey in one hand, wondering what to do now. Maybe I should turn in my resignation after all, he thought. What the hell good am I doing anybody?

No, he told himself. I won't give those pinheads the satisfaction. Let them carry me out feet first.

He realized that the big recliner he was sitting on had become shabby over the years. The sofa, too. All the furniture. The place needed a paint job. It had needed one for years. The only new thing in the apartment was the flat-screen television that Lenore and Del had given him last Christmas, sitting there on the lowboy, dark, dead.

So many memories. Lenore had been born in the bedroom, down the hall, four weeks premature. His wife had died in the same bed. Luke had closed her eyes. He had wanted to die himself, but then Lenore gave birth to Angie, and the gurgling, giggling little baby had captured Luke's heart.

And now she's dying. And those freaking idiots won't let me even try to help her.

Well, screw them! Each and every one of them. I'll save Angie. I will. I'll save her or die trying.

The phone rang.

He glared at it, a flare of anger at the intrusion. Then he realized he was being stupid and picked up the handpiece before the automatic answering machine kicked in.

"Dad?" Lenore's voice.

"Hello, Norrie."

"Aren't you coming over? It's almost eight o'clock."

Luke remembered he had agreed to have dinner with his daughter and her husband.

"I'm not very hungry, Norrie."

"You shouldn't be sitting all alone. Come on over. I made lasagna."

He grinned despite himself. He heard her mother's tone in his daughter's voice: part insistent, part enticing.

"Del can drive over and pick you up," Lenore added.

He bowed to the inevitable. "No, that's okay. I'll come. Give me a few minutes."

Del and Lenore lived in Arlington, across the Charles River from Boston, in a big Dutch colonial house on a quiet street that ended at a two-mile-wide pond. The trip from Beacon Hill took Luke less than twenty minutes; during peak traffic hours it could take at least twice that.

Del opened the door for him and tried to smile. "We heard the committee turned you down."

They didn't get a chance to, Luke said to himself. I walked out on the stupid brain-dead morons.

As he took off his overcoat Lenore called from the kitchen, "Lasagna's on the way!"

The two men sat at the dining table as Lenore toted in a steaming tray. Del poured red wine into Luke's glass, then filled his own. Lenore sat down with nothing but water at her place.

"How's Angie?" Luke asked.

Lenore's dark eyes widened slightly. "She was sleeping when we left her."

"Dr. Minteer says she'll sleep more and more," Del added.

"Yeah," said Luke.

"We had a meeting with the grief counselor from Hospice," said Lenore. "She's very sweet."

Luke could see that his daughter was straining to hold herself together, to keep from blubbering. Grief counselor, Luke thought. Fat lot of help a grief counselor can be. He remembered when his wife died and they sent a minister, then a grief counselor, and finally a psychologist to him. Can you bring her back to life? Luke demanded of each of them. Finally they left him alone.

"Dr. Schiavo—he's the head of the oncology department—he wants to try nanotherapy," Lenore said, her voice flat, empty.

"It's a new technique," said Del. "Experimental."

Luke said, "Now that they've given up on Angie, they want to try *their* pet experimental ideas on her. Get another datum point for their charts. But not my idea. I'm not part of their team, their clique. I'm off their charts." He gritted his teeth with anger.

"Isn't that what you want to do?" Del challenged.

"No! I want to save her."

"We told Schiavo no," Del said. "Let her be."

"She's resting comfortably," said Lenore, almost in a whisper.

Luke stared at the lasagna on his plate. He couldn't touch it.

"She's not in any pain," Lenore went on. Like her father, she hadn't even picked up her fork.

"We're the ones in pain," Luke muttered.

Lenore burst into tears and pushed her chair back from the table. Before Luke could say anything she got to her feet and ran out of the dining room.

"Why'd you have to say that?" Del snarled. "Can't you see she's holding herself together by a thread?"

Luke didn't answer him. He got up and went after his daughter.

Lenore was sitting on the living room sofa, next to the end table that held Angela's kindergarten graduation photo, racked with sobs, bent over, her forehead almost touching her knees. Luke sat beside her and wrapped an arm around her quaking shoulders.

"Norrie, it's going to be all right," he crooned to her. "I'll fix everything. I'll make her all better."

"That's a helluva thing to tell her." Del stood in the doorway, fury radiating from his tall, broad-shouldered form.

"I can do it," Luke insisted.

"The hell you can! The committee turned you down flat. You can't do a thing for Angie."

"The committee's a collection of assholes."

"But without their approval you can't do a damned thing," Del repeated, advancing into the room and standing over Luke.

Luke rose to his feet. "I know what I'm doing. I can save her."

"Don't!" Lenore screamed. "Don't say it! Don't even think it! Angie's going to die. She's going to die."

Luke stared down at his daughter's tear-streaked face. "Norrie, don't you believe me? Don't you believe I can save her?"

Lenore took a deep, shuddering breath before replying. "Dad, I know you want to help. You believe you can. But everybody else says you can't. Even if they gave you permission to try, it'd never work. Angie's going to die, and there's nothing you or anybody else can do about it."

Luke felt shocked. *Norrie doesn't believe in me? My own daughter doesn't trust me?*

Without another word, he got up and brushed past Del, went out to the front hall, and pulled his overcoat out of the closet.

Del came up behind him, still obviously simmering with anger. "Luke, I don't want you telling Lenore any more of this crap about saving Angie. It's tough enough for her without you telling her fairy tales."

Luke looked up at his son-in-law's grim face. "Don't worry," he said. "I won't bother either of you again."

University Hospital

EITHER THIS WORKS or I end up in jail, Luke said to himself as he strode through the front entrance of the hospital. It was eight A.M., the hour when the administrative offices officially opened for business.

The door to the admitting office was open, but no one was at the counter. The desks beyond the counter were unoccupied, the computer screens dark. Luke could smell coffee brewing and heard voices chatting through the open door to the back room. Frowning, he hollered, "Is anybody here?"

He had spent the past two weeks preparing for this move. He had gutted his bank account and used part of the cash to buy a used Ford Expedition SUV, blood red. Then, in the garage beneath his Beacon Hill apartment building, he had done his best to turn the van into a makeshift ambulance.

Stocking the vehicle with the equipment and medications Angie would need wasn't easy, but the grad students who staffed his lab were willing labor. He answered their questions with gruff half-truths.

Now came the big hurdle: springing Angie out of the hospital. I signed her in, he told himself, I ought to be able to sign her out. He hoped.

At last one of the administrative staff came into the room in answer to his call. She looked nettled to see someone there so early in the morning.

"Can I help you?" she asked, unsmiling. She was a Latina, considerably overweight, her skin the color of milk chocolate.

Three hours later, Luke realized that these paper shufflers would have allowed Godzilla to check out a patient, as long as he could fill in all the forms. They didn't recognize Luke; they hardly looked at him. All they wanted was for him to check each and every box on the stack of papers they handed him. Consent forms. Discharge forms. Insurance forms. Lots of insurance forms.

Doesn't matter to them who's doing what to whom, Luke told himself as he waded through the paperwork. As long as all the i's are dotted and the t's crossed, their asses are covered.

Halfway through the papers his bladder started sending distress calls. The joys of an enlarged prostate, Luke grumbled to himself as he got up and headed for the men's room. He urinated, washed his hands, then returned to the administrative office and sat down to finish the seemingly endless forms.

"Just what do you think you're doing?"

Startled, Luke looked up from the papers and saw Tamara Minteer standing over him, fists on white-coated hips, her expression halfway between suspicion and anger.

Damn! he thought. I should have known these bureaucrats would contact the attending physician.

"I'm taking my granddaughter to a different facility," he half-lied.

"You can't do that."

Luke saw that several of the administrators on the other side of the counter were staring at them. He pushed the papers aside and got to his feet. In a lowered voice he insisted, "I got Angie admitted to this hospital. I can get her discharged."

"Her parents—"

He smiled grimly and pawed through the pile of papers until he found the form he wanted. "They waived their consent when we got Angie admitted. It's all here." He held the form under her nose.

"You can't take her out of this hospital!" Minteer hissed. "I won't allow it."

Don't get angry at her, Luke commanded himself. She's trying to do what she thinks is best for Angie.

He grasped her elbow and said, "Let's go down to the cafeteria and talk this over."

Minteer looked uncertain for a moment, then nodded minimally.

Luke carried the papers back to the counter. "I'll be back in a little while," he told the Hispanic woman. "Would you hold these for me, please?"

The woman took the papers, the expression on her face sullen, wary.

Luke and Dr. Minteer threaded through the busy hospital corridors until they reached the cafeteria. It was crowded with doctors, nurses, visitors, relatives of patients, office workers, all grabbing coffee, sticky buns, scrambled eggs, fruit juices. Not much noise, just the buzz of low voices and the clink of flatware on dishes.

He led her to a table as far from the serving counters as possible and sat wearily, his back to the wall.

"Where do you want to take her?" Minteer demanded, sitting across the table from him.

Luke hunched forward, kept his voice down. "To a facility where she can get the treatment she needs."

"Your telomerase inhibitors?"

"That's right. I'm going to kill her cancer."

"You're going to kill *her*!"

"So what do you want to do? Hand her over to Hospice and watch her die?"

Minteer hesitated.

"Do you have anything better to offer?" Luke pressed. "I can save her. I know I can!" Before the doctor could reply he added, "And even if I'm wrong, what difference does it make? You've given up on her. You and the whole goddamned establishment."

She slowly shook her head. "Professor, you can't just wheel a patient out of this hospital because you want to experiment on her."

"I want to save her!" he growled. "She's my granddaughter, for God's sake!"

"You can't get her discharged without the attending physician's approval."

"Which is you."

"Which is me."

"Then you'll have to sign off on it."

Minteer stared at him for a long, silent moment. Then she asked, "Where is this facility you want to take her to?"

"Oregon."

"Oregon? That's completely across the country!"

He nodded. "There are several places along the way we can stop off, check her condition, renew her meds."

"Several . . ." She blinked with confusion. "You're not flying? You're going to *drive* all the way out to Oregon?"

"That's right."

"But why drive? Why not fly?"

Now Luke hesitated. Hell, he thought, might as well tell her.

"Because," he said, "once my daughter and her husband find out I've taken her, they're going to go apeshit. They'll call the cops, the FBI, God knows who else."

"They don't know you're doing this?" Minteer's voice rose a register and a half.

"No, they don't," he admitted.

"Then I'm not signing anything!"

"You've got to!"

Dr. Minteer shook her head stubbornly.

"If you don't help me," Luke growled, "you'll be killing my granddaughter."

Tamara Minteer

S HE WAS BORN on a small farm near Blue Hill, Maine, not far from Bar Harbor. The family, of French Canadian ancestry, had been there since the American Revolution. Her father was an electrician who sometimes worked in the boatyards of nearby Southwest Harbor. He was a doggedly stubborn man, a hard worker who tolerated no laziness in his children, stern and gruff. Yet he slipped quarters under their pillows while they slept and told them that the Tooth Fairy had done it.

Her mother raised their nine children, tended the family's little vegetable garden, milked their cows, and occasionally took in laundry. Always smiling, she taught her children the songs of her own childhood.

Tamara was a bright and independent child, the next-to-last daughter in the family. She grew up strong and tall and healthy, and won a partial scholarship to the state university. She worked part-time during the school semesters, full-time during summers, and went on to medical school. Since childhood the only profession she had ever wanted was to be a physician.

It was in medical school that she fell hopelessly in love with a charming young scoundrel who had too much family money and too little sense of responsibility. He took her heart and, soon after, her virginity. Despite her mother's warnings and her father's misgivings, she married the young man. Tamara saw the good hidden beneath his lazy, self-centered ways, and knew that she could transform him into a wonderful, heroic healer.

She couldn't. Love turned to bitterness. They quarreled. They fought. She couldn't divorce him; that was unthinkable in her family. One day he sailed off alone into the calm and bright Atlantic and never returned. No word of him. Searches by the Coast Guard found nothing, not even his boat.

Tamara threw herself into her studies, feeling guilty to be free of him, wondering if he was alive or dead.

She went into oncology, determined to help cancer patients to combat their dread disease. Over the years, she learned that most of her patients died. The best that she could do was give them a few extra years. Death was her implacable enemy, and death almost always won.

She didn't become bitter. But neither did she become resigned to watching her patients wither and fail. She held on to her faith and kept herself on the cutting edge of new therapies, new concepts, new hope.

Angela Villanueva was an especially trying case. Eight years old. Glioblastoma multiforme. A death sentence for the little girl, despite every technique of modern medicine.

Then the child's grandfather insisted that he could cure her, with a treatment never tried on human beings. It was impossible, Tamara knew. The hospital's board refused even to consider it. The FDA and other government agencies would not countenance it.

But Professor Lucas Abramson pointed his finger at Tamara and told her that unless she helped him, little Angela would die. In his stubborn black-or-white ways, he reminded her faintly of her father.

"There's no maybes about right and wrong," her father had often told her. "There's right and there's wrong. One or the other."

One or the other. Abramson insisted that if she didn't help him to treat Angela, she would be killing the child.

No maybes.

Decisions

LUKE STARED AT Tamara Minteer, her high-cheekboned face set in a rock-hard expression of obstinate refusal, her green eyes locked on his own.

"If you don't sign the release forms," he said, very softly, "you'll be killing Angie. Not the hospital. Not the system. *You.*"

Minteer's eyes wavered.

"I'm the only chance the kid has," Luke went on. "You know that. Even if I'm completely wrong, I'm the only chance she has."

Clasping her hands together on the tabletop, leaning closer to Luke, she said, "Professor, you can't take a sick child across the country without a physician to attend to her. That'd be murdering her right then and there."

Before he realized what he was saying, Luke shot back, "Then you come with us."

"Me?"

"You're her attending physician. You come along with us."

"I can't!"

"You mean you won't."

She looked torn. "I can't just take a week or more off from my job. It's just not possible."

Luke reached into his shirt pocket and pulled out his cell phone. "All you have to do is call your department chief and tell him you have an emergency on your hands and you'll be gone for a while—a few weeks, at the most. He'll find somebody to fill in for you."

"She."

"What?"

"My department head is a woman: Dr. O'Shaughnessy."

Luke said, "I don't know her."

"She's not a bad sort."

He nudged the phone to her side of the table. "Call her."

Minteer froze, although Luke could see a flood of emotions in her deeply green eyes. Do it, he urged silently. Do it.

She pushed the phone back toward him. Before Luke could say anything, she pulled her own smartphone from the pocket of her white coat.

He held his breath as she thumbed the phone's keyboard. She could be calling security, he realized.

"Dr. O'Shaughnessy? This is Tamara Minteer." Her eyes met Luke's, then flicked away. "Look . . . I've, uh, I've got a personal emergency and I'll have to leave town for a few weeks." Luke heard a voice gabbling from the phone's speaker. "Yes," Minteer said. "Two or three weeks. It just came up all of a sudden. I hate to take off on such short notice . . . No, it can't be helped. It's . . . personal. Very urgent. Life or death, literally."

From the tone of the voice squeaking from the smartphone, Luke could tell that Dr. O'Shaughnessy was very upset. But at last Minteer gave a tentative smile and said, "Oh, thank you for understanding, Bridget. Yes, I'll stay in touch with you. Of course. Thanks again."

She snapped the phone shut and glared at Luke. "I hope you realize that I've just put my career in the toilet."

"No you haven't," Luke said. "When Angela's cured, you'll be on top of the world."

Minteer shook her head. "The child isn't a lab mouse, Professor."

"But it's the same genes!" Luke insisted. "Don't you see? Our genes for controlling telomerase production are the same as the mouse's. We share those particular genes in common."

"But that doesn't mean . . ." She left the thought unfinished and said instead, "You're right. You're the only hope that Angela has."

He reached across the table and took both her hands in his own. "Thank you, Tammy. Thank you from the bottom of my heart."

"Tamara," she said. "My name is Tamara. Not Doc and not Tammy. Don't ever call me Tammy."

He nodded, grinning. "Okay, Tamara. I'm Luke."

EVEN WITH ALL the paperwork filled out it wasn't easy to get Angela out of the hospital. The child was deeply asleep when Luke and Tamara got to her room. An IV was in one frail arm.

"We'll need a gurney," Tamara said.

"And an orderly to manhandle it," said Luke, knowing he was not physically up to the task.

"I just hope O'Shaughnessy doesn't pop in on us," she muttered as she went to the door and headed out into the corridor.

Luke looked down at his granddaughter.

I'm going to save you, Angie. I'm going to save you. Or die trying.

Two orderlies pushed a gurney into the room and, under Dr. Minteer's direction, transferred Angela's sleeping body to the wheeled bed. She tucked a pair of blankets around the child as one of the orderlies pushed the gurney and the other guided the IV stand alongside. Angela stirred and mumbled but didn't wake up.

Luke raced ahead and went to the parking lot for the Ford Expedition, his heart thundering. It was bitingly cold out there; his lungs began to rasp painfully. For an agonizing few moments he couldn't find the SUV, couldn't remember where he'd parked it. Then he fished in his trouser pocket and pushed the remote key. Halfway up the line a red van blinked and beeped.

Angie, Tamara, and the two orderlies were waiting just inside the hospital's entrance when he tooled the van up the driveway. It was a lot bigger than the sedan he'd left at his apartment building, but it steered easily enough.

They bundled Angie into the makeshift cot Luke had built into the back of the van. Then Minteer climbed into the right-hand seat, and Luke slid in behind the wheel.

She gave him an odd look. "I feel like Bonnie and Clyde," she said.

"Yeah. Me, too." He gunned the engine to life and put the van in gear.

"We'd better stop at my apartment and let me throw some clothes into a suitcase."

"Right."

And they drove away from the hospital with Angela sleeping peacefully and Luke feeling, not like Bonnie and Clyde, but like the guy who had kidnapped the Lindbergh baby.

Chelsea

FOLLOWING TAMARA'S DIRECTIONS, Luke drove across the Tobin Bridge over the Mystic River toward the town of Chelsea.

"Where's Old Ironsides?" he asked as he steered past a big semi rig belching black diesel fumes.

Tamara waved vaguely. "She's docked at a pier over in Charlestown someplace."

"I've never seen the ship."

"Me neither."

She guided him through a maze of streets and up a hill that was crowned by what looked to Luke like a small, rather shabby hospital.

"Soldiers and sailors retirement home," Tamara explained. Pointing halfway down the street to a modern-looking four-story redbrick apartment building, she said, "That's my place. You can park in the back."

Once Luke slid the van into a parking slot and turned off its engine, she ducked out and hurried toward the building's rear entrance. "Give me ten minutes," she called to him over her shoulder as she unlocked the door and stepped through.

Luke got out, too, his legs already aching from a twenty-minute drive. I'm too old for this, he told himself. How the hell am I going to drive all the way across the country?

Shaking his head, he walked to the rear of the van and pulled its back hatch open. Angela was sleeping peacefully, on her back, breathing regularly, the IV still in her arm. He tucked the blankets around her more snugly.

This is crazy, Luke told himself. I ought to have my head examined.

For December, it was a beautiful day. Cold, of course, but the sky was bright blue, and the wind coming off the harbor wasn't too bad. Luke pulled his woolen watch cap from the pocket of his windbreaker and pulled it over his nearly bald head.

Squinting up at the apartment windows, he realized that Minteer could be calling the police instead of packing a bag. He considered taking off without her. No sense letting her turn me in, he thought. Even if they can't arrest me for kidnapping they'll take Angie back to the hospital, and that'll be the end of her.

Gently, he closed the rear hatch, then went back to the front of the van and climbed in. He started up the engine, to get the heater running again. Then he pulled off his cap and stuffed it back in his pocket. He glanced up at the apartment windows onced more. I can't get through this without her, he realized. I'm an old man who's trying to make believe he's some kind of superhero. Who am I trying to kid? And he knew the answer. He was kidding himself.

But Angie's life depends on me. I've got to do this, got to get through it somehow.

The back door to the building opened and Tamara came out, wearing a long, warm-looking dark blue coat and pulling a roll-along bag with one gloved hand.

Luke popped out of the van again and helped her wrestle the bag onto the backseat beside his own well-worn suitcase.

"What've you got in there, concrete?"

She glared at him. "A woman has to pack a lot more than an extra pair of socks, Professor."

They both climbed into the van, and he revved the engine. "I thought Chelsea was nothing but a bunch of junkyards," he said as he steered up the driveway and back onto the street.

"It used to be," Tamara said, "but this section of the town is really rather pretty. You can get a wonderful view of the whole city of Boston from the park in front of the veterans home."

Nodding, he asked, "How do I get to I-95?"

"North or south?"

"South."

"You'll have to go back into the city, then down to Quincy. Follow I-93."

"Okay."

As he threaded through the streets, heading for the interstate, Tamara asked, "Where do you intend to go, Professor?"

"Luke. Call me Luke."

She nodded. "Okay. As long as you don't call me Tammy. My name is Tamara."

"You made that clear back in the hospital," he said.

"So where do you intend to go?"

"Philadelphia."

"Philadelphia?" she echoed, surprised. "I would think you'd head for Canada, get over the border."

Luke shook his head. "I've got friends at the University of Pennsylvania. Former students of mine. They'll take us in and help us get the meds and other chemicals we need for Angie."

"Oh. I see."

"Besides, you have to go through a customs station to enter Canada. I don't want to be stopped by some guy in a uniform with a missing-person alert in his hand."

Tamara nodded. "That's right," she said, her voice going hollow. "We're fugitives, aren't we?"

"Not yet, maybe. But as soon as my daughter finds out I've taken Angie, we will be."

University Hospital

B UT SHE CAN'T be gone!" Lenore insisted.

The head of the hospital's administrative staff sat stiffly behind her desk, Angela's discharge papers spread before her. She was a large, gray-haired, motherly figure, inured to the emotional eruptions of patients' relatives.

"She was discharged this morning in her grandfather's care," she said softly, placatingly. "All the forms are correctly filled out."

"But we weren't told!"

Shaking her head, the chief administrator pawed through the papers and pulled out the consent form that Lenore and Del had signed.

"You gave the power of discharge to your father, Mrs. Villanueva, when we admitted Angela."

"But he didn't tell me he was taking her out of the hospital!" Lenore screeched. "Where's he gone? Where's he taken my baby?"

The door to the administrator's office burst open and Del strode in, his face a thundercloud.

"I got here as soon as I could, Norrie," he said, rushing to her and kneeling beside her chair.

"Dad took Angie out of the hospital," she bleated.

Getting to his feet, looming over the administrator's desk, Del demanded, "How could this happen? We're the child's parents, for

Christ's sake. You can't just let her be taken away without notify-
ing us."

The administrator could see that nothing she might say would
placate these two. The hospital's in the clear, she thought. All the
forms are correctly filled out. If the grandfather took the child
without telling her parents, there's nothing we could do about it.
It's not our problem.

But Del Villanueva was standing in front of her desk, furious,
radiating dangerous rage.

Looking up at him, the administrator reached for her phone.
"Let me call the hospital's chief executive; he's the man in charge."

ODOM WEXLER'S MAIN job, as chief executive officer of University Hospital, was to talk well-heeled donors out of their money.
Hardly a week went by when he wasn't leading a small parade of
potential benefactors through the hospital's wards and labs and
gleaming, efficient treatment centers, all smiles and pleasantries as
he pried open their wallets.

But this morning he felt genuine pity for the couple who sat before his handsome desk, a mother in tears and a father who looked
as if he wanted to wreck the building.

"This is terrible," he said, focusing on Lenore. "We'll do whatever it takes to get your daughter back here, Mrs. Villanueva."

His chief administrator raised a cautioning finger. "Technically,
sir," she said, "Angela Villanueva is no longer a patient here."

Wexler absently stroked his beard, then shook his head. "This is
no time for technicalities. A child is missing. She's been abducted."

Del nodded vigorously. "Call the police. We've got to find Angie
before it's too late."

"I'll do better than that," said Wexler. Punching the intercom
button on his desktop phone console, he called, "Amanda, put
me through to the FBI's Boston office."

IT TOOK MORE than two hours for the FBI to send an agent to the hospital. Del had tried phoning his father-in-law's cell phone, then his university office, finally his home. No answer, only canned messages.

"Where is he?" Lenore cried. "Where's he taken Angie?"

Wexler kept the Villanuevas in his office, ordered lunch for them, tried to get them to relax a little.

"He can't have gotten far with her," he soothed, as they sat at the round conference table in the corner of his office, over lunch trays. Lenore hardly touched the sandwich in front of her. Del tore at his like a tiger dismembering its prey.

"Mrs. Villanueva, please try to eat something," Wexler coaxed. "You must keep up your strength."

Lenore reached for the plastic bowl of salad on her tray. "We're taking up so much of your time . . ."

"Don't worry about that. Finding Angela is more important than my morning's regular agenda." He knew it was true, although he also fretted that he'd had to cancel the meeting with a committee of bankers that had taken him several months to arrange.

The intercom buzzed. Wexler excused himself and hurried to his desk.

"Mr. Hightower is here," his secretary's voice announced. "From the FBI."

"Show him right in!"

Jerry Hightower filled the doorway as he stepped into Wexler's office. He was big, in every dimension, like a professional football lineman. Yet he seemed light on his feet as Wexler led him to the table where the Villanuevas were sitting.

The FBI agent's face was almost a coppery color; clearly he was a Native American. Unsmiling, black ponytail hanging down his back, eyes like onyx.

He sat heavily between Lenore and her husband as the two of

them poured out their fears to him. He listened patiently, letting them talk themselves out.

Then he looked across the table to Wexler. "How was he able to take the kid out of the hospital?"

Wexler gestured helplessly, both palms up. "It was a strictly correct procedure. He filled out all the proper forms."

Hightower made a sound that might have been a grunt. "All the proper forms. But he's taken the child away from her parents."

"That's kidnapping!" Del snapped.

"Maybe," said Hightower.

"What are you going to do?" Lenore asked.

Hightower looked into her red-rimmed eyes and said simply, "Find them."

New Jersey Turnpike

PULL OVER AT the next gas station," Luke said.

He had let Tamara take over the driving once they crossed the Tappan Zee Bridge and entered New Jersey. Now, nearly half an hour later, soft wet flakes of snow were sifting out of the gray sky.

"I'm okay," Tamara said. "I don't mind driving."

"I've got to make a phone call," Luke explained.

"Use your cell."

He shook his head. "Pay phone is better. They can't trace it."

"Are you sure?" Tamara asked.

"Pretty sure," Luke said. "Anyway, I'll make it real quick, so they won't have time to trace it."

She glanced at him uncertainly, then turned back to watch the road. The turnpike traffic was light, mainly because trucks had their own lanes, separate from automobiles.

Luke turned on the van's radio and fished through blaring rock music and twangy country tunes until he found a weather report.

". . . snow accumulation expected to be six to eight inches through tonight," an announcer was saying cheerfully. "Tomorrow will be fair and cold. Temperatures at sunrise will be in the twenties for most of the region."

Luke clicked the radio off.

"We'd better find a motel for tonight," he said.

"Why?" Tamara asked. "Philly's only an hour or so away."

"I don't want to take any chances driving in the snow. By tomorrow morning they'll have cleared off the roads."

She nodded glumly, then pointed to a sign announcing a service area five miles ahead.

When they reached it, Tamara pulled up to a gas pump. "You make your call, I'll fill the tank and check on Angela."

Luke nodded tightly, ducked out of the van, and sprinted through the falling snow to the service center's restaurant. A trio of pay phones hung on the wall just inside the entrance. He suddenly realized that he didn't have much change in his pockets and went to the restaurant's cashier to ask for a couple of dollars' worth of quarters.

Once he fed money into the phone, it took a few moments for the connection to go through. Luke peered through the building's glass doors to watch Tamara leaning into the van's rear deck.

Is Angie all right? he wondered.

Then a voice in the phone's handset said, "Hello?"

"Van?" he replied. "It's Luke Abramson."

"Prof? Good to hear from you. How are you?"

Van McAllister had been one of Luke's graduate students six years ago. Now he was an assistant professor at the University of Pennsylvania's department of cellular biology.

"I'm okay, Van. But I need your help."

"Sure, Prof, what can I do for you?"

Three minutes later, McAllister's voice was distinctly less eager. "Gee, I don't know if I can get all that together for you on such short notice."

"It's important, Van," Luke urged. "Vital. My granddaughter's life depends on it."

"The kid is with you?"

"I'll explain it all to you tomorrow."

"Well . . . okay. I'll see what I can do."

"Fine. I'll see you tomorrow, in your lab."

"What time?"

"The sooner the better."

"Let me check my calendar . . ."

Luke pictured McAllister poking at his computer keyboard.

"Could you make it at seven thirty? Before my students start coming in."

"Seven thirty. Fine. In your lab."

"In my lab. Room four-oh-eight in the biology building."

"Four-oh-eight at seven thirty. Got it."

"Uh . . . Prof . . . is your granddaughter with you?"

"Yes. With her attending physician."

"Oh. Okay. Yeah. See you tomorrow, then."

The phone clicked dead.

IT WAS SNOWING harder by the time they pulled onto the driveway of the Cherry Hill Inn and Suites motel. Luke asked the sleepy-eyed young woman behind the registration desk for two adjoining rooms and peeled off four fifty-dollar bills from the roll he had brought with him.

Cash transaction, he told himself as he went back to the waiting van. No credit card needed, no way to trace us. The room clerk had asked for an ID, so Luke showed her his driver's license. She peeked at it and that was that.

He carried the sleeping Angela in his arms past the surprised-looking room clerk and into the elevator, with Tamara trudging behind him, dragging both roll-along suitcases.

Once they had settled Angela in one of the double beds and wedged her IV bottle between the headboard and the wall, Luke turned to Tamara.

"Okay. You sleep in the other bed, I'll take the room next door." Before she could reply, he asked, "Do you have any aspirin?"

"What's the matter?"

Rubbing the small of his back with both hands, Luke said, "My back's killing me. Goddamn arthritis. Carrying Angie."

"Osteoarthritis," Tamara said.

"Yeah. One of the benefits of old age. I need some aspirin."

"Ibuprofen's better," she said.

"You have any?"

"Downstairs, in the lobby. There's a little store there. They'll have it."

"I'll go down and get a bottle."

She nodded, then asked, "What about dinner? I'm starved."

Stretching his back, Luke said, "After I've taken a couple pills I'll go out and find someplace that serves takeout. What would you like?"

"Anything. Meat. A salad, too."

"Wine?"

She shook her head. "Soft drink."

Angela stirred. Luke sat on the edge of the bed and leaned over her.

Forcing a smile, he said, "How're you feeling, Angie?"

She blinked several times, turned her head, saw Dr. Minteer standing behind her grandfather. "This is a different room."

Luke nodded. "We're taking you to a place where you can be treated. In a week or so you'll be feeling a lot better."

"I feel okay now, Grandpa. Just kinda hungry."

"I'll get something for you to eat."

"Hamburger?"

Luke glanced up at Tamara, who nodded, tight-lipped.

"Okay, a nice juicy hamburger for my best girl." But inwardly he wondered if Angela could handle it. Tamara okayed it, he thought. I guess her digestive system is working normally.

Still, he wondered.

Arlington, Massachusetts

I T WAS SNOWING in Massachusetts, too. Snowing hard.

"Where's he taken her?" Lenore asked for the hundredth time. "What's he doing to her?"

She was sitting tensely on the steps leading down to the house's basement, her husband sitting beside her. Agent Hightower stood between the thrumming heater and its fuel tank, his head nearly touching the pipes running along the ceiling, his beefy arms folded across his chest as he stolidly watched a flannel-shirted FBI technician connecting an electronics box to the telephone panel on the wall.

"Where could he have taken Angie?" Lenore repeated.

Turning toward her, Hightower said, "He's probably heading for some medical facility where he can start the treatment he wants to give your daughter."

"Yeah," said Del. "But where?"

"That's what we aim to find out. We're contacting his colleagues, former students, people he worked with."

Del muttered, "Makes sense."

"We're tracking that Dr. Minteer, too," Hightower added. "It's too much of a coincidence, her taking off at the same time."

"You think she's with Angie?" Lenore asked, brightening a little.

Ignoring the question, Hightower said, "If your father phones you, keep him on the line as long as possible. Our people in the van outside will trace the call."

"How long will that take?" Del asked.

"A minute. Maybe less."

The technician straightened up. "Finished."

Del got to his feet and helped Lenore to stand. They all went upstairs into the living room.

"Suppose he calls while we're up in the bedroom?" Lenore asked.

Hightower moved his head from side to side, once. "Doesn't matter. Any phone in the house, we'll pick it up out in the van."

"Good," said Del.

The phone rang, making them all flinch with surprise. All except Hightower.

Del looked up at the agent, who held out a cautioning hand. The technician nodded as the phone rang a second time.

"Okay," Hightower said.

Lenore went to the table at the end of the sofa and lifted the receiver with a trembling hand.

"Norrie," she heard. "It's me, Dad."

Staring at Hightower with wide eyes, Lenore said shakily, "Dad! Where are you? How's Angie?"

"I just want you to know that Angie's fine. She's in good hands."

"Where are you, Dad? I want to come, I want to be with Angie."

A heartbeat's hesitation. "Not now, honey. Not for a while. But she's fine. We're going to cure her."

"Where are you?" Lenore repeated.

"I've got to go," Luke said. "I'll call you again, soon."

The line clicked dead.

Hightower was already on his cell phone. He snapped it shut and slipped it back into his jacket pocket, his mouth curved downward.

"Did you . . . ?"

"We got the area code as soon as you picked up your phone. He thinks he's smart, keeping his call short, but all we need is for you to make the connection."

"Were is he, then?" Del asked.

"He's on the Jersey Turnpike, apparently heading south."

"Can you grab him?"

Hightower went silent for a moment. Then he told them, "We've already got the New Jersey Highway Patrol heading for the place he called from. Of course, if he's on the move they might not get there in time. It would help if we knew what kind of car he was driving."

"But you'll get him."

"Sooner or later."

"Good."

"Will your people in the van stay all night?" Del asked.

"Twenty-four-hour coverage," said Hightower.

"Through the snowstorm and all?"

Hightower said flatly, "Neither snow nor rain nor dark of night . . ." And made one of his rare smiles. "We'll get him, folks. Don't you worry, we'll get him."

L UKE HUSTLED ACROSS the parking lot with a bag of takeout from the nearest fast-food joint. It was snowing harder than ever, and despite his lined windbreaker he felt cold to the bone.

He hated the snow. Oh, sure, it looks pretty, that first snowfall of the year, he told himself. For ten minutes. After that it's just a mess that screws up traffic and encourages skiers to go out and break their legs.

The same young woman was behind the registration counter. He nodded to her as he hurried to the elevator.

Angela nibbled on her thin hamburger while Tamara gobbled hers. Luke took a few bites and put his paper plate on the night table. He couldn't eat; his stomach was in knots.

I shouldn't have phoned Norrie, he berated himself. That was stupid. Suppose the cops have bugged her phone? I didn't stay on the line very long, but what if they traced the call? They might be on their way here right now. Calling from a fast-food joint next to the motel; that was smart, wasn't it?

But I had to call her. I had to tell her Angie's okay. I couldn't leave her totally in the dark.

He saw that Angela had left half her burger and was drifting back to sleep. She looked terribly thin and pale.

Suddenly she started coughing. Tamara dropped her burger and reached for the child. As she lifted her to a sitting position, Angela spit up gooey chunks of burger and bread in a slimy green liquid.

"Water," Tamara snapped at Luke. He ran into the bathroom and fumbled with the plastic-wrapped paper cups on the sink. He could hear Angie gagging and moaning.

By the time he came back into the bedroom with the water, Angie was sitting up, her thin pajamas a foul-smelling mess. But the coughing and upchucking had stopped. Tamara sat on the edge of the bed, gently massaging the child's back.

She looked up at Luke and reached for the water. Holding the cup to Angela's lips she said softly, "Take a sip, Angie. It'll take the sour taste out of your mouth."

Angela sipped. "I'm okay now," she said weakly. "I don't know what happened. I'm sorry."

"Nothing to be sorry about," Tamara whispered. To Luke she said, "You go to your room. I'll clean her up."

Feeling useless and grateful at the same time, Luke went to the door that connected the two rooms. "I'll come back to say good night, Angel."

Angela nodded and tried to smile.

As he fidgeted in his room, unable to concentrate on the movie the TV was showing, Luke heard the squeaky wheels of the chambermaid's cart, then muffled sounds from Angie's room. Changing the bedclothes, he figured. Then the cart squeaked past in the other direction.

At last Luke heard a tap on the door. Pulling it open, he saw that Angie was sleeping peacefully, as if nothing had happened.

"She's all right now," Tamara said as he stepped into the room. The bed was freshly made. Luke wondered what his granddaughter was wearing beneath the covers. We didn't bring that many clothes for her, he realized.

Tamara wiped the back of her hand across her forehead. "I shouldn't have let her have a hamburger. That was stupid of me."

Luke asked, "Should we feed her intravenously?"

Tamara nodded. "For the time being. We can give her broth, gelatin, things that are easy to digest."

"Yeah."

Tamara saw Luke's unfinished hamburger, still resting on the night table. "Are you going to eat that?"

He shook his head.

"Do you mind? I'm starving."

"Go right ahead."

Luke almost grinned at her. Slim as she is, she's a real carnivore, he thought. Must have a high metabolic rate.

"Did you have enough to eat?" she asked.

"Yeah. Plenty." He realized he was very tired. And he felt chilled, achy. "I'm going to bed now."

Tamara nodded. "It's been a long day."

"Tomorrow will be easier."

"Hope so."

He left her chewing on his half-eaten hamburger and closed the door that connected the two rooms. Stripping quickly, he rummaged in his suitcase for the one pair of pajamas he had packed. Prison gray. Could be appropriate, he thought.

Once he stretched out in bed, he still felt cold, even with two blankets over him.

This isn't going to work, he told himself. I'm too old to do this. I'm already falling apart.

Then he realized, I'll have to do something about it. In his mind's eye he saw the mice he'd experimented on in his lab, scampering in their cages youthfully in spite of their advanced age.

If it works for the mice it ought to work for me. Same genes involved. Get me to start producing telomerase the way I did when I
was a teenager. The freaking fountain of youth.

He fell asleep and dreamed of the day he'd met the young beauty
who eventually became his wife.

Lucas Theodore Abramson

YOU HAVE GOT to be the stubbornest SOB I have ever had the misfortune to attempt to educate," his biochemistry professor once told Luke.

Twenty-two-year-old Luke stood in front of the older man's desk and bit back the reply that came to mind.

"You think you're so goddamned smart, you don't give anybody else any credit for having any brains at all," his professor rumbled on. "Including me."

Running a hand through his thick mane of dark hair, Luke protested, "That's not entirely true, Prof."

The professor shook his head disapprovingly. "You've got to stop being so damned stubborn, Abramson. You'll never get ahead unless you learn to get along."

Luke never learned to get along. He went his own way, often bucking his professors, department chairmen, committee heads, university executives. He succeeded because he was brilliant and saw farther and faster than those around him.

Slowly, grudgingly, the scientific orthodoxy surrounding him learned to respect Luke's abilities. Over the years they came to realize that this loner of a cellular biologist was making important strides in basic biomedical research.

Decade after decade, Professor Lucas T. Abramson took graduate students into his laboratory and turned them into award-winning researchers. He won few awards himself. He didn't need them. He wasn't interested in them. All he wanted was to do the work he chose to do with as little interference from the outside world as possible. Stubborn, they called him. Cantankerous. But brilliant.

Luke demanded very little from the establishment: just a lab to work in, a few assistants to help, and the freedom to pursue his own line of thinking.

He steered clear of applied research. Despite his unspoken, bitter war with cancer, he never aimed his work specifically at oncology. Luke went deeper, probing into the fundamental cellular processes of the human body.

He picked up on earlier research on the effect of telomeres on cell biology. It took years of patient, unspectacular experiments, but eventually he was able to show how to rejuvenate aged, decrepit lab mice and make them youthful again—by triggering their telomeres to regrow.

And then his granddaughter was stricken by glioblastoma multiforme. Luke was devastated by the news. But he quickly realized that by inhibiting the growth of Angela's cells' telomeres—rather than accelerating their growth—he might be able to destroy the tumors that were killing her.

The bureaucracies that controlled scientific research refused to allow him to leap from experiments with lab mice to an effort to save his granddaughter's life. So be it, Luke thought.

He went his own way. With his granddaughter. They call you stubborn when what you're doing doesn't work. When it does work they call you goal-oriented.

University of Pennsylvania

V AN MCALLISTER'S EXPRESSION was somewhere between disbelief and curiosity.

"You mean you've taken the child out of the hospital and brought her here?"

McAllister had one of those smiling, bright-eyed faces that still would look youthful when he was Luke's age. But he wasn't smiling now. He was leaning his slim rump on a bench in his campus laboratory, facing Luke, who was perched on a lab stool. No one else was in the lab; the previous night's snowfall had snarled Philadelphia traffic so badly that Luke had been half an hour late for his meeting with his former student, yet still none of the lab staff had shown up

"With her attending physician," Luke said.

"Isn't that . . . unusual?"

"It's all perfectly legal, if that's what you're worrying about."

"What did her parents say about this?"

"That's not important," Luke temporized. "What I need to do is get the necessary enzymes to activate the genes that will suppress her telomerase production."

"For how long?"

"A few days, maybe a week or two. I want to get her to Bartram's facility out in Oregon."

McAllister gave out a low whistle. "Why didn't you fly straight there from Boston?"

Luke waggled a hand in the air. "We're driving. I need to start Angie on the telomerase inhibitors right away. By the time we get to Oregon I expect her to be showing signs of improvement."

"But the side effects . . ."

"Her physician is coming along with us."

McAllister stood up, his youthful face deadly serious. "Prof, telomerase inhibitors? You know what that could do to the kid?"

Luke nodded, tight-lipped.

"You're running the risk of progeria, for God's sake."

"I know. But once we've killed the cancer we can reverse the progeria symptoms."

"You hope."

"I'm going to start taking telomerase inducers," Luke said.

"What?"

"I'm too old to be running across country like this. I need to be younger. Stronger."

"You're not a lab mouse, for God's sake!"

Forcing a grin, Luke said, "Anything those mice can do, I can do."

"That's crazy! You can't—"

Luke pushed himself to his feet. "Van, I can and I will. We're talking about my granddaughter's life. I'll do whatever I have to do to save her."

"Including putting your own life on the line?"

"Yes."

"Your telomerase experiments aren't ready for a human trial. No way!"

"I'm volunteering."

"And you expect me to help you?"

"Nobody needs to know you're involved, Van. This'll be just between you and me."

"We'll have to sign the kid into the hospital."

"No. We'll take care of her in the motel."

"In the motel?"

"Listen to me, Van," Luke coaxed. "We're not talking about surgery or radiation treatment. We don't need big facilities. Just the proper enzymes and a little time. Angie's comfortable at the motel, and her physician is keeping watch over her." With some heat he added, "Hell, they wanted to hand her over to Hospice, for God's sake. Do you think they'd do anything more for Angie than we will?"

McAllister shook his head. "I could get fired for this. You know that."

"I know it. But will you do it?"

The younger man turned away and walked down the aisle between lab benches. Luke stood there, watching, waiting. He saw through the lab's windows that the last clouds from the previous night's snowstorm were blowing away. The sky outside was turning a brilliant blue.

"Nobody else will be involved?" McAllister asked, his back still to Luke.

"All I need is the enzymes, and you can get them without any trouble."

"They're steroids."

"But they're not on a restricted list. It's not like we're going to be doping athletes."

Turning back to face Luke, McAllister said, "I'd be sticking my neck out. Way out."

"I know. I appreciate it."

McAllister heaved a big sigh. "For you, Prof. I'll do it for you."

Before Luke could thank him the phone rang.

McAllister went to his desk, at the end of the lab bench. "Hello," he said into the phone.

Holding a hand over the mouthpiece, he said to Luke, "Department secretary. Probably giving me a tally of who's coming in, who's going to be late."

Then his eyes widened with surprise. "The FBI? Yes, okay, put him on."

Luke sank back onto the lab stool, his heart suddenly racing.

"Agent Hightower," McAllister said. "Yes, this is Professor McAllister. Assistant professor, actually."

McAllister listened, his eyes focusing on Luke.

"You say there's no criminal charges? Then what's the FBI—"

He fell silent again. At last he nodded and said, "Yes, I understand. Yes, certainly. Good-bye."

McAllister hung up the phone and leaned on it with both his hands. At last he straightened up and turned to face Luke.

"That was an FBI agent. They're looking for you."

Luke asked, "He said there weren't any criminal charges filed?"

"Not yet. But once they've satisfied themselves that you've taken the kid outside of Massachusetts, they'll call it kidnapping. That's a federal offense."

Luke thought, Lenore wouldn't accuse me of kidnapping. She knows I wouldn't hurt Angie. But Del would. He's pissed at me. And they're both scared that Angie's in danger.

As if she'd be any safer back in the hospital.

Boston FBI Headquarters

SPECIAL AGENT JEROME Hightower stepped into the office of the director of the FBI's Boston division. The division's chief was standing at the window in his shirtsleeves and bright red suspenders, watching a snowplow pushing mounds of dirty gray snow onto a black sedan parked at the curb on Cambridge Street. His hands were clasped behind his back; Hightower saw that one of them held a yellow travel requisition form.

"Some idiot down there parked right under a no-parking sign last night," said the director. "He'll be snowed in until next April, I bet."

Hightower peered over the director's shoulder. "Nah," he contradicted. "The city will dig him out, then tow him away and impound the car. He'll owe a fortune by the time he gets it back."

The director shrugged. "Must be some politician who thought he could park wherever he pleases."

"Maybe somebody from police headquarters," Hightower said, with a grim smile.

"Have a seat, Jerry," the director said. He was a slim, dapper man who'd been with the agency since he'd acquired his degree in accounting, a quarter century ago. Even in his shirtsleeves and suspenders he looked stylish.

Hightower, wearing a comfortable old suede jacket over his creaseless slacks, settled himself in the only chair in front of the director's desk. The director sat on his swivel chair, which rolled slightly, and placed the travel request on his desk, smoothing it carefully with both hands. He had never been comfortable with Hightower's ponytail, it wasn't the Bureau's style, but he knew Hightower would put in a formal complaint if he tried to get him to cut it off. Native American rights and all that crap.

The director put a smile on his face and asked mildly, "What's going on, Jerry? Are you wasting this office's precious resources?"

Despite the smile, Hightower knew the question was serious.

"Might be a kidnapping," he said.

"Might be?"

Hightower shrugged his massive shoulders. "Child's been taken from University Hospital."

"By her grandfather, I'm told."

"Right. But without the parents' knowledge. Or approval."

"The kid's sick?"

"Terminal. Brain cancer."

"Why'd the grandfather take her?"

"According to the parents, he's some kind of biologist. A research scientist. Claims he can cure the kid."

"Can he?"

"Probably not. The parents don't know where he's taken her. They want to file a kidnap charge."

The director leaned back in his swivel chair and tapped his fingertips together. "Has he taken the kid out of the state?"

"Don't know for sure."

"How'd you get involved in this?"

"Got a call from the hospital's top man. Odom Wexler."

The director nodded and murmured, "He's pretty close to the governor."

"A couple of congressmen, too," Hightower added.

"And what've you done so far?"

Hightower figured that his boss already knew the answers to the questions he was asking. But he went ahead and recited, "Put a tap on the parents' phone, in case he calls them. Checking out his known acquaintances. He's got contacts all over the country. Apparently he's a big shot in the biology field."

Again the director tapped his fingertips together. Then, "So what's your gut tell you, Jerry? Has he taken the kid out of the state?"

"Hell yes. None of the people he's worked with here have seen him since the day before yesterday. He's on the run with his granddaughter—and mostly likely one of the doctors from the hospital, the kid's attending physician."

"So where's he gone?"

"Don't know yet." Pointing to the travel requisition, he said, "I'd like to pop down to Washington, talk to some people at the National Institutes of Health who've worked with him in the past."

The director looked into Hightower's steady brown eyes. "All right. Charge him with suspicion of kidnapping. Send out a nation-wide alert."

"You're okaying my travel request?"

The director nodded. "Let's get this guy before the news media get wind of this and start squawking."

NEW YORK CITY had been spared the brunt of the snowstorm. As he ducked out of his limousine, Quenton Fisk muttered to himself, "Snow doesn't get a chance to stick on the sidewalks. Too many pedestrians stomping on it."

Hunching his shoulders against the cold, he hurried to the glass front door of the Fisk Tower. It opened automatically for him. Once inside he went straight to his personal elevator, where a uniformed security woman smiled a good morning to him. Fisk ignored her as he held his ID card before the elevator's digital reader; the doors slid open immediately. The otherwise empty car whisked him directly to his private office on the top floor.

Fisk was a small, intense man, wiry and still trimly athletic in

his fifties. He hardly ever lost at squash or tennis; if the other play-
ers allowed him to win, he took it as nothing less than what he
deserved. He had inherited millions and spent his life working
tirelessly to turn them into billions. The Fisk Corporation was
heavily involved in the electronics, aerospace, and biomedical in-
dustries. He had the good sense to back cutting-edge research in
each of those areas—especially biomed.

His private office was a masterpiece of understated luxury: taste-
ful oils on two walls, the third a broad window that looked out at
Manhattan's forest of skyscrapers. The fourth wall was a mosaic of
display screens, four of them showing financial news channels,
muted. The rest were dark.

Fisk's executive assistant was waiting for him, of course, a tall
fortyish woman with red hair pinned up sensibly, wearing a con-
servatively dark green skirted suit. As she took his fedora and
helped him shrug out of his cashmere overcoat she said, "You re-
ceived a call from the FBI this morning."

"The FBI?" Fisk's brow furrowed. "Who? Why?"

"He said his name was Jerome Hightower and he was calling
about a Dr. Luke Abramson."

"Abramson? Who's he?"

"I've put his file on your main menu."

Fisk nodded and went to his desk while his executive assistant
tiptoed out of the room. As he slipped into his high-backed black
leather chair and reached for the insulated cup of coffee that was
waiting for him, he saw his reflection in the dark screen of his desktop computer and noticed that his hair was slightly awry. Smoothing it, he thought that getting the implants had been a good
investment: He still looked dark-haired and handsome while other
men his age and even younger were balding.

He took a sip of the hot coffee. Luke Abramson. The name
sounded vaguely familiar. Activating his computer, he saw the scientist's image and realized that he had met the man, more than
once. The last time . . . Fisk thought back and recalled the fund-

raising dinner up in Boston, last August. Abramson had been the after-dinner speaker, talking about his research on reversing aging. He'd apparently made some decrepit old mice young again. Fisk had taken the man aside afterward and offered him a research grant, on the spot. Abramson agreed immediately, complaining that NIH had abruptly dropped his funding a few months earlier.

Frowning at the screen, he saw that the FBI was making inquiries about him. Nothing specific, but the FBI didn't get interested in a person for trivial reasons.

He tapped his intercom key.

"Yes, sir?"

"Nancy, get this Agent Hightower on the phone for me, please."

"Yes, sir."

Fisk dived into his morning's routine until, some fifteen minutes later, his assistant buzzed him. "Agent Hightower, Mr. Fisk."

With a tap of his phone console's keyboard, Hightower's heavy, somber face appeared on the central wall screen.

"What can I do for you, Agent Hightower?" Fisk asked crisply.

After listening to the FBI agent for five minutes, Fisk said, "You mean you don't know whether Abramson has done anything illegal?"

"That's right," said Hightower. "He's only under suspicion."

"Why are you calling me about this?"

"I understand that you're funding some of Abramson's work."

"I'm funding *all* of his work. His research on aging."

"I thought perhaps he might have contacted you."

Fisk made a little grunt. "I haven't seen or heard from the man since he cashed my check, nearly a year ago."

Hightower nodded somberly. "I see. Well, if he does contact you, I'd like you to let me know about it."

"Of course. My assistant has your number."

Another heavy nod.

Fisk cut the connection, then buzzed his assistant.

"Get Odom Wexler for me."

"Yes, sir."

University Hospital

WEXLER WAS IN the midst of a wearying budget meeting with the hospital's treasurer and three accountants when his secretary called him on the intercom.

She knows I don't want to be interrupted, he thought irritably to himself. Still, he was almost glad of it. Budget meetings always made his stomach act up.

"What is it?" he snapped into the intercom.

"Mr. Fisk is on the line."

"Quenton Fisk?"

"Yes. On line one."

To his treasurer, Wexler said, "I've got to take this call. Please wait in the outer office for a few minutes."

As they got up and headed for the door, Wexler punched the button for line one. "Mr. Fisk! What a pleasant surprise."

Fisk's voice was cold, no-nonsense. "The FBI is looking for Luke Abramson."

"Yes, I know."

"What's this all about?"

Wexler explained as much of the situation as he knew.

"You mean he thinks he can cure the child?"

"That's right. He's probably taking her to some medical facility where he can work on her."

"Can he cure her?"

"I don't know. He thinks he can."

"But can he do it?"

Wexler hesitated, then admitted, "If anyone on God's green earth can do it, Luke Abramson can."

It was Fisk's turn to go silent. Wexler wondered if he should say something, but then Fisk asked, "And you don't know where he is?"

"We know he's with his granddaughter, and probably Dr. Minteer, too."

"But where the hell is he?"

"That's what the FBI is trying to find out."

He could hear Fisk grumbling to himself. Then, "I think you'd better cut your hospital's connection to the man."

"Cut our connection . . . ?"

"Fire him! Get him off your payroll. He's a fugitive from justice, for God's sake. A kidnapper. You don't want him smearing your hospital's reputation."

"I see," said Wexler. "But even if we did, he'd still be connected to the university. He's got tenure, and—"

"I'll talk to the university people. He can always be fired for cause."

"But—"

"Keep your skirts clean. Just because Abramson's turned rogue is no reason for the hospital or the university to be tarred with his brush."

Thinking of the donations Fisk had given to both institutions, Wexler agreed lamely, "I suppose you're right."

"Damned right I am," said Fisk.

A S HE HUNG up on Wexler, Quenton Fisk smiled to himself. The perfect opportunity, he thought. With the hospital and the university disowning him, my grant money will be all the support

Abramson has. If his research really pays off, I'll own the rights. If it doesn't, he'll go to jail.

M EANWHILE, LUKE ABRAMSON was toting a heavy black attaché case across the lobby of the Cherry Hill Inn and Suites motel. The middle-aged black man behind the registration desk frowned suspiciously, but Luke ignored him and went to the elevator.

Angela was sitting up in bed, with Tamara beside her, watching television. Luke saw that her IV bag was nearly empty. Tamara popped to her feet as Luke came through the front door.

"Hi, Grandpa," said Angela, with a smile.

"Hello, Angel," he said. "How do you feel?"

"Okay, I guess."

Luke put the case down on the desk by the room's only window. Puffing from the exertion, he said, "That's some shopping list you gave me. McAllister had half his staff running around the campus picking up what you ordered."

Keeping her voice low, Tamara said, "She'd be much better off in a hospital, Luke. Even a clinic—"

"When we get to Texas," he said, his eyes on Angela. The child was watching the TV, ignoring them.

"Texas?"

"San Antonio. There's a facility there that can take care of Angie for a few days."

Tamara shook her head. "This is foolishness. She ought to be under medical care."

Unclasping the attaché case, Luke said, "You're a doctor. Here's all the stuff you asked for. That ought to be good enough for now."

"It isn't."

"I'm not letting her go back to Boston, not until I've had a chance to cure her."

Tamara looked as if she wanted to argue. Instead she pressed her lips into a thin line and started rummaging through the vials and bottles in the bag.

Pulling one vial out and holding it up to the light from the window, she squinted at the label. "What's this?" she asked.

"That's for me," said Luke.

"For you?"

"It ought to help me, make me stronger, give me better endurance."

"Steroids?"

"Not the kind athletes use. It's a telomerase inducer."

"You're going to dope yourself?"

He shook his head. "No. You're going to inject the stuff into me. I hate needles. I don't think I'd be able to stick myself without making a mess of it."

Tamara stared at him. "You expect me to help you experiment on yourself while you experiment on your granddaughter?"

Luke nodded.

"I ought to walk out of here right now," Tamara said. "I ought to *run* out of here!"

Looking toward Angela, Luke asked quietly, "And let her die?"

Tamara stared at him for a long, silent moment. At last she said, "What I really ought to do is have my head examined."

He chuckled softly. "It's a beautiful head. I think it's perfectly fine."

"Now you're sweet-talking me." But she returned to pulling the medications out of the attaché case.

"Tomorrow," Luke said, "we drive down to Washington. It'll be an easy drive, only a couple of hours."

"If it doesn't snow again," Tamara growled.

Washington, D.C.

RAMÓN JIMENEZ HAD never met an FBI agent before. As head of the National Cancer Institute's legal department, his working associates were lawyers and accountants, his "customers" were the institute's biologists and other scientists. His friends were mostly fellow Hispanics.

Jimenez was known to them all as a tight-ass: a stickler for details who aimed for perfection in everything he did. His face was lean, although there were significant pouches beneath his deeply brown eyes. His dark hair was luxuriant, but his mustache was nothing more than a pencil trace over his upper lip. His body frame was small and slight, yet his stomach stretched the fabric of his shirt.

He was self-consciously buttoning his gray suit jacket across that ample stomach as Agent Hightower explained why he was asking about Luke Abramson. Jimenez was somewhat in awe of the man. A special agent of the FBI, he thought. And such a large man. He could be a professional wrestler, with that build. He looks like a Native American.

Hightower was saying, ". . . so since your institute has been Abramson's main source of funding for many years, I thought you could tell me who his associates are, who he might go to for help."

Jimenez said, "You should talk to the scientists about that."

Hightower nodded. "I suppose so. I'll need some guidance about who to contact. Maybe an introduction."

"I can do that." Jimenez tapped on his computer keyboard. "Ah. Dr. Petrone. She was overseeing Abramson's work."

"He reports to her."

"Not exactly," said Jimenez. "The institute provides funding for outside scientists. They send us grant requests, we review them. Those that are approved and given funding are monitored by one of our scientific staff. Dr. Petrone was monitoring Abramson's work."

"Was?"

Jimenez peered at his computer screen, double-checking to make certain he was right. Then he said, "Apparently Abramson's grant was not approved this year. We haven't funded his work since . . ." He glanced again at the screen. "Since April first."

"Why not?"

Jimenez made an elaborate shrug. "You'll have to ask Dr. Petrone about that."

L UKE WAS SITTING in the office of Dr. Yolanda Petrone. She was a comely woman in her early sixties, with light gray eyes and hay yellow hair. When Luke had first met her, some twenty years earlier, he'd been surprised to learn her ancestry was Italian.

"My people come from north of Venice, near the Austrian border," she explained. "Plenty of Germanic blood in my family."

Now, as he sat beside her on the sofa in her office, he realized that there was plenty of gray in the blond hair, and her skin was spiderwebbed. Telomerase injections could help her, he thought. But he kept the idea to himself.

"So what brings you to Washington, Luke? It's not like you to just pop in, unannounced."

He tried to grin and failed. Instead, he confessed, "I'm in trouble, Yolanda. I need your help."

"What's wrong? Is the Fisk Foundation cutting off your funding?"

"No, that's not it."

"You know," Petrone said, "I thought it was a mistake when we refused your grant request last spring. Orders from on high, you know. Something about budget cuts. I couldn't do anything about it."

"It's not that, Yolanda," Luke repeated. "It's my granddaughter. She's dying."

Petrone sat in shocked silence as Luke explained the situation to her.

"So where is the child?"

"At the moment she's in a motel out by the Beltway. I was hoping you could find her a bed. I need to run some diagnostics on her."

"Of course! I'll do anything I can, you know that, Luke."

Petrone had flown to Boston when Luke's wife died. She had been an aid and comfort during those devastating first days after Adele's funeral. Once she saw that Luke was able to stand on his own feet again, she returned to Washington, but only after getting him to promise he'd stay in touch with her. He did, in his own way: They saw each other at meetings and conferences, always with other people around, never just the two of them alone. And now he had come to her for help.

"I appreciate it, Yolanda," he said, with some emotion.

She got up from the sofa and went to her desk. "I'll make the arrangements . . ."

The phone rang before she got there.

She picked it up. "Mr. Jimenez? Oh, from legal. Yes, hello. How are—"

Yolanda Petrone's eyes narrowed as she listened to Jimenez's voice. She turned and stared at Luke.

At last she said, "Yes. I'll see him. This afternoon, after lunch."

She put down the phone. "I'm going to be visited by an FBI agent. He's looking for you."

Kennedy Clinic

THE KENNEDY CLINIC was a small, unobtrusive building set in a residential neighborhood across the highway from the NIH campus.

"We've used the facility for years," Yolanda Petrone explained as she steered her Lexus up the driveway. "Top-flight facility, and very private."

Luke nodded absently.

"Plenty of politicians and media stars have been treated here for various problems," she continued while she parked the sedan in a RESERVED FOR STAFF slot. "Your granddaughter will be in good hands."

"I really appreciate this, Yolanda."

"It's the least I could do for you, Luke."

She led him into the clinic's hushed entryway and down an empty corridor to the administrative office. In half an hour Angela was registered as a "Jane Doe" patient.

"I don't how to thank you," Luke said.

Petrone smiled. "You can let me take you to dinner, once the child is safely tucked in here."

Luke said, "Fine. I'll bring her here, then give you a buzz."

"Wonderful," said Petrone.

A GENT HIGHTOWER WAS waiting in her office when Petrone returned from lunch. As she entered the room he got to his feet, rising like a mountain before her.

His hand engulfed hers as he introduced himself. Petrone went to her desk, and Hightower sat down again. Even seated he looked immense to her.

"You're interested in Professor Abramson?" she asked.

"That's right. We want to talk to him about a possible kidnapping."

"Kidnapping?"

Hightower went through the story, ending with, "So I'll need to know who his associates are, who he might go to for help."

Glad that he hadn't asked if she herself had seen Luke, she replied, "You mean other than the people here at the National Cancer Institute."

"Including your people, ma'am."

The "ma'am" nettled her slightly. He must think I'm some fuddy-duddy grandmother, Petrone said to herself. Suppressing a frown, she said as innocently as she could manage, "Well, his main point of contact here at NCI would be me, of course." Quickly she added, "But Professor Abramson didn't get a renewal of his grant this year, so technically we don't have anything to do with him anymore."

"That's what Mr. Jimenez told me."

"From our legal office," Petrone murmured. "Yes, of course."

Leaning forward ponderously, Hightower said, "But you must know the other scientists in his field of research, the people he works with, consults with. His friends and associates. I need their names."

Petrone said, "Let me think a moment. There's McAllister, at the University of Pennsylvania, of course. He was a student of Professor Abramson's, you know."

Hightower leaned back and patiently allowed her to reel off half a dozen names.

The one name that Petrone did not mention was Shannon Bartram. She felt certain that Luke would try to get to Shannon Bartram and her private clinic in Oregon. She would have all the facilities Luke needed to treat his granddaughter. And she would welcome Luke with open arms, Petrone felt certain. With open legs, too, she seethed silently.

Dinner for Three

I WANT TO DO an MRI on her," Tamara Minteer said to Luke in a near-whisper.

Angela was drowsing in the bed of the private room that Petrone had arranged for her. Luke had been impressed, until he realized that the Kennedy Clinic had nothing but private rooms for its patients. Politicians, news anchors, entertainment stars—they don't want to share a room. They want privacy, secrecy.

"MRI?" he asked. "Is that necessary?"

She nodded, tight-lipped. "To see if the tumors are still growing."

"Can't you do that with a blood sample? Measure the tumor signature?"

"That could tell us if the tumors have metastasized into other parts of her body, but it won't work on the brain tumors themselves. There's no blood marker for a brain tumor. It's not like a PSA. We need an image. Might as well make it a full-body MRI while we're at it."

"Full-body? Why—"

"I need to see her complete physical condition, Luke. See what effect all this traveling has had on her."

Luke looked down at his sleeping granddaughter. She didn't seem much different than she'd appeared back at University Hospital, in Boston. Angela seemed to be in no pain. She looked relaxed, almost smiling in her sleep.

Tamara said, "She'll be all right for now. The staff has her under observation."

The child was wired up like an astronaut. In addition to the IV in her arm, a trio of sensors was plastered to her chest, abdomen, and left arm. A bank of monitors beeped softly along the side wall, and a security camera hung up near the ceiling, its unblinking red eye aimed at the bed.

Tugging at Luke's sleeve, Tamara headed for the door. "Let's get some dinner. I haven't had anything to eat since that crappy breakfast at the motel. I'm starving."

Luke followed her out of Angela's room and down the corridor to the nurse's station. Tamara gave the duty nurse her cell phone number while Luke picked up the phone on the counter and dialed Petrone's number.

THE RESTAURANT THAT Petrone picked was in downtown Washington. Luke followed his GPS's directions and found it, then spent several minutes looking for a parking place. Finally he gave up and let the restaurant's valet take the van.

Petrone was already seated at a table when Luke and Tamara came in. It was a fairly elegant place: white linen tablecloths, heavy drapes across the windows, waiters in dark suits. A miniskirted hostess showed them to the table.

Petrone's welcoming smile faltered when she saw that Tamara was with Luke. He introduced the two women to each other as they sat down.

"Tamara is Angela's attending physician," Luke explained. "She's looking after Angela while we're . . ." He fished for a word. "Traveling," he finally said.

"I see," said Petrone. "And who's looking after the child while you're here?"

Tamara said coolly, "She's in good hands at the clinic. If a problem arises they have my cell number."

"I see," Petrone repeated.

It finally dawned on Luke that Yolanda was annoyed. She's sore that I brought Tamara with me, he said to himself. I told her I'd be bringing Angela's physician. With a jolt of surprise he realized that Yolanda was jealous. She had wanted a quiet dinner for just the two of them. A romantic dinner. Bringing a third party was an intrusion. Bringing a younger woman was an affront.

The dinner was hardly romantic. The two women talked to each other like a pair of Old West gunslingers sizing up each other. They practically ignored Luke as the waiter brought their salads and entrées and busboys removed their emptied plates. Tamara ate like a wolverine, while Yolanda barely touched her food.

Luke saw that Tamara was really quite a good-looking young woman, with her high cheekbones and sparkling eyes. Not that Yolanda wasn't pretty herself, but she was at least twenty years older than Tamara, getting kind of plump and wrinkled.

"Are you sure that dragging the child across the country like this isn't going to harm her?"

Luke started to say, "We'll be checking—"

But Tamara cut him off. "She's in an excellent facility, thanks to you. I'm going to run some scans on her tomorrow. If I see that she's not up to traveling, we'll have to return her to her parents, I suppose."

Petrone smiled coldly. "You can keep her at the clinic as long as you need to. I'll take care of the paperwork."

"And the bills?"

"Part of my discretionary budget."

Luke said, "That's awfully good of you, Yolanda."

Still focused on Tamara, Petrone said, "That's what friends are for, isn't it? To help each other."

Tamara looked down at her plate. Nothing left but crumbs. Gazing up at Petrone again, she said, "You're being a wonderful help. I'm sure Luke is very grateful."

"That's right," Luke said eagerly. "We owe you a lot, Yolanda."

Petrone gave him a displeased look as their waiter came up to the table and asked, "Would you like to see the dessert menu?"

Petrone immediately shook her head. Luke said, "Not me." Tamara hesitated, then reluctantly said, "Me neither."

"Coffee, then?" the waiter asked. "Espresso, perhaps?"

They ordered coffee, and Tamara excused herself.

As she walked away from the table, Luke leaned toward Yolanda. "You know, she's taking a big risk to come along with Angela."

Petrone nodded.

"It's strictly professional. She's Angie's doctor. There's nothing else going on."

Petrone's pale gray eyes narrowed slightly. "Of course there isn't. Why, she's young enough to be your daughter. Maybe even your granddaughter."

Luke just stared at her.

A S LUKE DROVE the SUV back to Bethesda, Tamara said, "She's interested in you."

Keeping his eyes on the traffic in the street, Luke muttered, "I didn't know. Not until tonight."

"I bet she's calling the FBI right about now."

"She wouldn't do that!"

"Hell hath no fury."

He glanced at Tamara sitting beside him in the shadows, profiled against the passing streetlamps.

"We can't take Angie out of the clinic. Not yet."

"Hell hath no fury," Tamara repeated.

Maybe so, Luke thought, but at the moment his most immediate problem was pressure from his bladder. Should've gone to the freaking toilet before leaving the restaurant, he grumbled to himself.

Kennedy Clinic

NGELA WAS SLEEPING soundly when they got back to her room, the monitors alongside the bed showing her heart rate, breathing, and EKG all normal. Low normal, Luke saw, but nothing dangerous. Not yet.

The telomerase inhibitors were flowing into her bloodstream, he knew. Now it would be just a matter of time until they started to show some effect. How long? he wondered. A few days, at least. Maybe we ought to stay here instead of trekking across the country. It'd be better for Angie.

If Yolanda isn't so pissed off that she'll tell the FBI we're here.

Tamara broke into his thoughts. "I'm going to stay here tonight," she whispered.

"Oh?"

"I've made arrangements with the staff. They have guest rooms for relatives right here in the building."

Luke huffed. "Maybe we should let Yolanda know."

"She'll know."

He nodded and headed for the door, Tamara beside him. Out in the empty, silent corridor, he said, "I'll see you tomorrow morning."

"Tomorrow I'm going to put a port in your chest."

Luke's blood ran cold. "A port? I don't want one of those things attached to my chest or anywhere else. It's like having a plastic leech hanging on me."

She gave him a disapproving frown. "It's better than sticking you every day. You'll look like a drug addict, with all the bruises."

His face twisted with revulsion.

"After the first half hour you won't even notice that it's there."

"Yes I will. I don't want it."

"You'd rather be stuck every day?" Tamara argued. "With a port, I just put the needle into the valve, not in your arm."

"But the damned thing is in my chest all the time."

She sighed. "Your granddaughter has one. You don't see her complaining about it."

Luke stared at Tamara, then muttered, with a reluctant nod, "You're the doctor."

"That's right," she said. "I am."

Grousing to himself, Luke went out into the cold night and climbed into the SUV. He poked at the GPS box sitting atop the dashboard to find a gas station. Goddamned van gobbles gas like an Army tank, he thought.

Once he'd filled the van's capacious fuel tank, he went into the station's minimart to pay in cash. And find the men's room. Fill the gas tank and empty the bladder, he mused. At least I don't have to fill the SUV every couple of hours.

As he left the men's room, Luke spotted a display of throwaway cell phones next to the cashier's stand. He took one, paid cash, and bought a hundred minutes on it.

Glancing at the clock on the wall, he thought, They'll be asleep by now. I'll just leave a quick message on their answering machine.

He was surprised when Del picked up on the first ring.

"Del? It's me, Luke. Listen, Angie's doing fine—"

"Luke! Wait a minute, Lenore's getting ready for bed, but I know she'll want to talk to you."

He heard Del calling for his wife. Luke fidgeted uncertainly for a few seconds, then clicked the phone off. I told them Angie's okay.

That's enough. Maybe the FBI can trace cell phone calls, he thought. Nervous, uncertain, he dropped the cell phone in the first trash bin he passed.

Then he drove back to the motel and slept fitfully until daybreak.

Tamara was waiting for him in Angela's room, with a mischievous glint in her eyes.

"Good morning," Luke said softly as he entered the room. "How is she?"

"She's holding her own. We're scheduled for the scans in an hour."

Luke looked down at his granddaughter. She seemed to be sleeping peacefully enough. "Has she eaten anything?"

"Intravenously," said Tamara.

Luke sank into one of the easy chairs.

Her lips curling into an almost impish smile, Tamara said, "It's time for you to get your port."

"Now?"

"You gave me a schedule, and I intend to keep it. Now take off your jacket and unbutton your shirt."

He watched her pull a gray plastic port and a hypodermic syringe out of a case on the table, then a small bottle of alcohol and a wiper pad. All in one neat package, Luke said to himself. The vial of enzymes sat on the table beside the case.

"I've been thinking about Yolanda," he said, as much to keep his mind off the port and the needle as for any other reason. "I don't think we have to worry about her."

"Oh no?" Tamara was filling the syringe with the steroid cocktail that Luke had gotten in Philadelphia.

"If she's as interested in me as you think, why would she turn us in? She'd want to keep us here as long as she could, wouldn't she?"

"Maybe," Tamara half-agreed, as she swabbed a spot on his bared chest with alcohol.

Luke said, "No cops have shown up."

"Uh-huh. A little stick now."

He looked away as the needle stung him. He knew it was silly, but he felt as if some alien creature were attaching itself to him, sucking his blood. Tamara taped the port to his chest, then pushed the syringe into the port's seal, and the hormones rushed into his bloodstream, hot and strong.

Tamara smiled down at him and said, "I ought to get some lollipops to give you after each injection."

Luke smiled back, weakly, glad that the little ordeal was over. But he couldn't work up the courage to actually look at the port, inserted into a blood vessel in his chest.

YOLANDA PETRONE WAS at her desk, staring unseeingly at her morning's schedule on the computer screen. She had called the clinic first thing in the morning, from her home, and learned that the very feline Dr. Minteer had stayed there last night, while Luke had driven back to whatever motel he was staying at.

Good, she thought. They're not sleeping together. Not last night, at least.

Hardly thinking of what she was doing, Petrone fished the card Agent Hightower had given her out of her desk drawer.

If I call him, she thought, Luke might end up in jail. But if I don't, he could very well kill his granddaughter. Then she realized that Dr. Minteer was just as guilty of kidnapping as Luke was.

She picked up the phone.

Boston FBI Headquarters

D R. PETRONE," SAID Jerry Hightower. "How are you?"
Petrone's voice sounded shaky, uncertain, as she said,
"Exactly what are the charges against Dr. Abramson?"

Hightower leaned back in his creaking desk chair. His office was
so small that some of the other agents teased him about it. "You'd
have more room in a teepee," they'd wisecrack. Hightower, who
had spent his childhood on the Navaho reservation in a mobile
home jacked up on cinder blocks, merely smiled patiently at his
colleagues and replied, "Agents work out in the field, not in their
offices."

He cleared his throat before answering. "Actually, Dr. Petrone,
there are no formal charges filed. Not yet. We just want to talk to
Dr. Abramson about bringing his granddaughter back to her parents."

"I see."

Hightower waited patiently for the rest. At last Petrone said,
"He's at the Kennedy Clinic. With his granddaughter and her attending physician."

"Will he be there all day?"

"For several days. Maybe longer."

"All right. I'll fly down this morning."

"Are you going to arrest him?"

"Not if he cooperates."

"And the attending physician?"

"Same deal. Our main interest at this point is the safety of the little girl."

Petrone's voice seemed a little stronger. "All right. He'll be there when you get here."

Hightower said, "I'd appreciate it if you didn't tell him I'm on my way."

"Yes. Of course."

"Thank you, Dr. Petrone."

"You're very welcome."

SITTING IMPATIENTLY IN the clinic's quiet little waiting room, Luke glanced at the mirror on the wall. The port made a slight bulge beneath his shirt. As far as he could tell, his chest wasn't sore. Damn things caused infections, he knew. But Tamara was careful, she had swabbed the area down good.

Still, he felt uneasy about it.

He'd been in the waiting room all morning. For a while he'd paced nervously, like an expectant father. Then he'd read through every magazine in the waiting room. Now he sat, feeling tired and anxious. He remembered other waiting rooms, when Adele was going through chemotherapy and radiation treatments. All in vain.

Only one other person was in the room, an elderly dark-skinned man sitting sour-faced and unhappy on the couch along the far wall. The room was tastefully decorated in cool pastels. A large flat-screen TV showed some idiotic game show, muted.

Elderly man, Luke thought. Who the hell am I to call him elderly? Still, the guy looked like a cheerless grump, lean and disagreeable in a dark pinstriped suit. Luke was in his shirtsleeves. Maybe he thinks I should be wearing a jacket, Luke guessed.

Tamara came in and Luke jumped to his feet.

"How is she?"

"The good news is that the tumors haven't metastasized," she said, her voice low.

"And the bad news?"

Tamara plunked down in the chair next to Luke's. She looked tired, defeated. He sat down, too. "The bad news?"

Shaking her head wearily, Tamara said, "The growths are spreading through her brain. She'll start losing motor function in a few days. Then . . ."

"Then?"

"They'll start to affect the autonomous nervous system. She won't be able to breathe on her own." Bleakly, Tamara concluded, "I don't think she's got more than a couple of weeks left."

Luke knew it was too soon to expect any results from the telomerase inhibitors. I need another few days, he thought. At least. Maybe a week.

"Where is she?"

"They're taking her back to her room. She slept through the whole battery of scans."

He got to his feet slowly, his knees creaking. No results from his own injections yet, he realized. As he and Tamara walked out of the waiting room and into the corridor, a large, bulky man in a suede jacket strode purposefully toward them, pulling a little billfold from the rear pocket of his slacks.

Flipping it open, he said to them, "I'm Special Agent Jerome Hightower, Federal Bureau of Investigation."

Damn! thought Luke. Yolanda finked on us, after all.

Hightower asked, "Where is Angela Villanueva?"

Feeling as if half the world had fallen on his shoulders, Luke replied numbly, "On her way upstairs, to her room."

"Let's go see her."

Silently, Luke led Tamara and Agent Hightower back to Angela's room. The FBI agent looked like a professional wrestler, big in every dimension. His skin was a light tan. Native American? Luke wondered. He's got a ponytail.

Angela was still sleeping, the IV in her arm, the monitors on the side wall blinking steadily.

Hightower took it all in with one sweeping glance, then turned to Luke. "How is she?"

Tamara answered, "Terminal."

"Unless I can save her," Luke interjected.

Hightower sighed heavily. "Her parents want her back."

"They gave up that right when they signed the admitting papers at University Hospital," Luke said, his voice low but firm.

"I've read those papers," said Hightower. "They don't give you the right to transport the child out of Massachusetts."

"They don't say anything about that."

Almost smiling, Hightower said, "Yes, they do. Down in the fine print. Technically, you could be charged with kidnapping. That's a federal offense."

"She's going to die unless I can treat her," Luke said.

Hightower turned to Minteer. "Is that right?"

Tamara looked at Luke before answering. "She's certainly terminal now. Professor Abramson's treatment is new, untested, but it can't do the child any harm at this stage."

"Look," Hightower said, "my job is to get this kid back to the hospital you snatched her from. That's what her parents want."

"Her parents won't let me treat her," Luke snapped. "You'll be killing her."

With a slow, ponderous shake of his head, Hightower said, "You've transported the child across state lines. Her parents want her back with them. If you don't cooperate I'll have to file a kidnapping charge against you. You don't want that."

"I don't want my granddaughter to die!"

Tamara suggested, "Why don't you tell her parents to come here? She's in good hands; this is a first-rate facility."

Hightower blinked at her. "I suppose I could ask them."

Brightening, Luke said, "Call them!"

Pulling his cell phone from his shirt pocket, Hightower flipped it open and tapped out a number. Luke marveled that his thumb could press individual buttons: It looked much too big. The agent's hand engulfed the tiny phone.

"Mr. Villanueva? This is Agent Hightower. I've found your daughter—"

Luke could hear the excited babble coming from the phone. Hightower explained where Angela was. After a pause, Lenore came on the phone; Luke heard the high-pitched exhilaration in her voice.

Hightower handed him the phone. "She wants to talk to you."

"Daddy? How is Angie?"

Luke glanced at Tamara before answering. "She's holding her own."

"Are your treatments helping her?"

"It's too early to see any results, Norrie."

"Bring her home, Daddy. Bring her back to me."

"But—"

"I want her here for Christmas. I want her to be with us for . . . for her last Christmas."

"If you let me treat her . . ." But Luke knew she wasn't listening. Lenore had broken down into wracking sobs.

Del came on the phone, his voice hard, bitter. "You bring Angie back to us, Luke. Now. Today."

Luke told himself, If I do I'll be killing her. Aloud, he pleaded, "Let me treat her, Del. Let me treat her long enough to have some effect."

"Lenore's been a wreck since you kidnapped Angie," Del raged. "It's bad enough our daughter is going to die, but you're killing Lenore, too!"

Seeing the expression on Luke's face, Hightower took the phone from his hand.

"This is Agent Hightower again. Yes, we'll bring the child back." Del's voice chattered angrily. "Kidnapping is a very serious charge, you know." More ranting from Del. "All right. All right. I'll get started on it right away."

He clicked the phone shut and gave Luke a somber stare. "Your son-in-law wants you in jail."

"He's an asshole," said Luke.

Shrugging his massive shoulders, Hightower said, "I'm going to make arrangements to fly all of us back to Boston. Don't try to leave this clinic. I'll post some security at the door."

Luke's shoulders slumped. Tamara looked frightened.

Hightower went to the door. Turning back toward Luke, he said, "For what it's worth, I think your son-in-law is very worked up about this."

"Thanks for the news flash," Luke growled.

Kennedy Clinic

As soon as Hightower left Angela's room, Luke turned to Tamara. "We've got to get her out of here."

"What? You can't do that! You heard what he said, there'll be security at the door."

"Then we've got to get out before the cops come."

"No, Luke. You can't."

"The hell I can't. Pack up everything. I'll grab a gurney. The two of us can handle this."

Without waiting for Tamara to reply, Luke bolted out of the room and hustled down to the nurse's station. He spied a gurney along the wall beyond and went to it.

"Sir?" called the nurse. "Can I help you?"

"I can manage," Luke said as he wheeled the gurney past her station.

The nurse got to her feet. "Where are you going with that? You can't take it, that's not allowed."

"I'm just taking it to my granddaughter's room. We need to bring her downstairs for more tests."

Trotting behind him, the nurse said, "Nobody's told me she's scheduled for more tests."

"Her attending physician's in the room with my granddaughter. She'll tell you."

Luke worked the gurney into Angela's room. The nurse stood uncertainly in the corridor for a few seconds, then turned and headed back to her station.

"She'll be calling security," Luke told Tamara. "We don't have a second to waste."

He saw that Tamara was busily packing medications and IV equipment into one of the suitcases they'd brought with them. She looked doubtful, though, worried.

"Luke, don't you think—"

"Help me move her," Luke commanded.

Angela stirred as they lifted her out of her bed. "Grandpa? Where is this?"

"We're going for a little ride, honey. It'll be fun."

A puzzled-looking security guard in a blue uniform was talking to the nurse as they wheeled the gurney and IV rig out into the corridor.

"Sir," said the guard, walking toward them. "Just what are you doing, sir?"

Tamara answered, "I'm this patient's physician. We're taking her downstairs for further scans."

From behind her station's counter, the nurse said, "There's no tests on the schedule."

"I'll fill out the paperwork when we get there," Tamara said.

"But Doctor—"

Luke got an inspiration. "Call Dr. Petrone, over at NCI. She'll okay it."

The nurse looked uncertain, but she picked up her phone. Luke pushed the gurney past her, toward the elevator, thinking, By the time she gets to Yolanda we'll be out of here.

"I'll help you," said the security guard. He was middle-aged, overweight, and out of condition. Rent-a-cop, Luke thought. Some security.

"That's okay," Luke replied. "We can manage."

The elevator doors slid open and he pushed the gurney inside,

Tamara wheeling the IV stand beside him. Angela was looking around, smiling as if she were at an amusement park and going on one of the rides.

As the elevator doors slid shut, Tamara muttered, "What now?"

"They must have a loading bay in the back of the building. We'll go there and I'll get the van."

There was another security guard sitting at a tiny desk at the loading bay, younger, dark-skinned, in much better shape than the one upstairs. Otherwise the area seemed deserted.

Getting slowly to his feet, the guard frowned perplexedly as they approached the garage-type overhead sliding door.

"What're you doin'?"

"Taking our patient out of here," Luke said. "How's the weather outside?"

"Damn cold. Whyn't you goin' out the front, like regular?"

"No time to explain," Luke said, heading for the glass-paned door next to the overhead.

He heard Tamara talking to the confused guard as he stepped through the door and into the bright afternoon. It was cold, crisp, and clear. Luke sprinted around the corner of the hospital building to the parking lot where he'd left the van.

He tooled the SUV back to the loading dock, swung its rear hatch open, then ran up the steps and inside again. Tamara was still talking earnestly with the security guard, who was shaking his head warily.

"I don't know. This is awf'ly irregular." He pulled his two-way from his shirt pocket.

Luke swung a savage backhand chop at the nape of his neck as hard as he could, and the guard collapsed to the floor.

Tamara looked totally shocked. Angela's eyes went round, too.

"Come on," said Luke, puffing slightly. "We've got to get out of here before all hell breaks loose."

They wheeled Angela down the ramp and lifted her into the make-shift bedding in the rear of the SUV.

"Wow, Grandpa, you really whacked that guy," she said.

Luke made a tight grin for her. "Army training. I wasn't always an old grandpa."

Two more security guards popped out of the door, waving and yelling, as Luke gunned the van's engine and roared out toward the road.

On the Road

"S O WHERE ARE we going?" Tamara asked.

Luke glanced at her. She looked tense, almost angry. Can't blame her, he thought. I'm dragging her into a frigging FBI manhunt.

Then he realized. "I don't know."

They were headed for the Beltway. But after that, where?

"I was planning to get to San Antonio," Luke said, "but if the FBI's looking for us, they'll probably check out all the people I know."

Without an instant's hesitation, Tamara said, "Get the child back to her parents, Luke. You can't go running around the country like a maniac. Think of your granddaughter's well-being!"

"Take her back and let her die? Hell no."

"Then what?"

"Let me think."

Tamara puffed out a disgusted sigh, then unbuckled her seat belt and clambered back toward Angela.

Luke was thinking furiously as he drove through the heavy Beltway traffic. Don't go over the speed limit, he told himself. Don't give them an excuse for stopping you. That's all they'll need.

He wondered if the two rent-a-cops at the clinic got his license plate number. Probably not. I was starting to turn the corner when they came out of the building. Maybe they could make out what state the plate's from, but I doubt it.

Then he realized, Security cameras! Could they read the license plate?

Got to find help! But who? If the FBI got to Yolanda, they'll be contacting everybody else I know. I need to get Angie into a safe facility. But where? How?

By the time Tamara scrambled back into the seat beside him, Luke had hit on the one person he could think of that could help him: Quenton Fisk.

Without being asked, Tamara reported, "Angie's okay. Sleeping again."

"Is she warm enough back there?"

Nodding, she said, "I tucked the blankets around her. She'll be all right." Then she added, "For now."

"I need to call Quenton Fisk," Luke said.

"Who's he?"

"Big-shot industrialist. Financier. He's funding my work on telomerase."

"You think he can help you?"

Luke nodded. "He's got money, connections. Owns factories, research labs. And I don't think the FBI would connect him with me. Not right away, at least."

"But will he help you?"

With a shrug, Luke replied, "We'll find out."

He knew that he couldn't use his own cell phone: The FBI would track any calls he made. Probably Tamara's, too, Luke reasoned. At a rest stop along the highway he pulled in to the minimart and bought another throwaway cell phone and a hundred minutes of calling time. He didn't have enough cash in his trouser pocket and had to sprint back to the SUV, unzip his suitcase, and pull a handful of bills from the wad he had stuffed inside the suitcase's lid.

Tamara's eyes widened. "You shouldn't be carrying all that cash. It's dangerous."

He shook his head. "I can't use credit cards or traveler's checks. Too easy to trace."

"But still . . . if anybody knew how much cash you've got in there . . ."

Tightly, he said, "That's a chance I have to take."

He left Tamara and Angela in the van, the motor still running to keep the heater going, and bought the cell phone.

Opening Tamara's door, Luke said, "You drive. I've got to call Fisk."

"Do you know his phone number?"

Luke replied, "It's in my laptop." Almost grinning, he added, "Right beside my money stash."

She got out of the van, went around, and climbed into the driver's seat. Luke pulled out his laptop and, after a quick glance at his sleeping granddaughter, climbed in beside Tamara.

Off they drove.

Fisk Tower, Manhattan

QUENTON FISK WAS dictating a letter to his computer's voice-recognition program when his desk phone blinked. Gritting his teeth in irritation at the interruption, he killed the dictation program, then tapped the intercom button.

"What?" he demanded.

"Professor Abramson calling, Mr. Fisk," said his assistant.

"Abramson? I'll take the call."

"On line one, sir." Before Fisk could react, his assistant added, "Should I notify that FBI man?"

"No," he said sharply. "Not yet."

Then he lifted the phone from its cradle and leaned back in his comfortably yielding chair. "Professor Abramson. How are you?"

Abramson's voice sounded strained, gritty. "I need your help, Mr. Fisk."

"What can I do for you?"

For several minutes Abramson poured out his troubles. Dying granddaughter. He could cure the child. Parents don't understand. The FBI is after him.

"I need a medical facility where I can treat Angie without the FBI grabbing me."

Fisk wished he could see the man. It was always so much easier dealing with someone face-to-face, rather than a disembodied voice.

Reading a man's facial expressions often told more than listening to his words.

"Where are you now?" he asked.

Abramson replied, "On the road. South of Washington, D.C."

"Heading where?"

"I don't know!" Abramson's voice rose a notch. "I don't know where we can be safe. We need a facility for Angie. I can't keep her in this van forever!"

"Calm down, Professor. I'll be glad to help you."

"You'll be saving my granddaughter's life."

"Of course. Now, exactly where are you? I need to know which highway you're on, and which mile marker you are passing."

Abramson replied, "Interstate 95, heading south. Twenty miles before Richmond."

Smiling to himself, Fisk thought, It all goes so much more easily when you have money and connections. He told Abramson, "I'll set you up with a hotel for the night. I'll call you back in ten minutes or less."

The professor was reluctant to hang up on nothing more than that promise, but the poor chump had no choice.

Clicking his intercom again, Fisk told his assistant to make the necessary hotel reservation.

"Then call Professor Abramson with the information," he ordered.

"Yes, sir. Should I call Agent Hightower now, sir?"

"No. No need to bring him into this. Not yet."

"Yes, sir."

"And when you talk to Abramson, tell him to call me back once he's in the hotel. On Skype. I want to see his face."

"Yes, sir."

L UKE FIDGETED NERVOUSLY in the van while he waited for Fisk to call back.

"You think he's calling the feds?" Tamara asked, her eyes focused on the road.

"He wouldn't do that."

"Neither would your friend Petrone."

Before Luke could reply, the cell phone buzzed. He snatched it.

"This is Mr. Fisk's personal assistant," said a smooth female voice. "I have made the following hotel reservation for you and your party."

T HE HOTEL WAS an upscale Marriott, with its own restaurant and room service. Fisk had reserved them a two-bedroom suite on the top floor.

Angela woke up as Luke lifted her out of the van. "Hi, Grandpa," she said, blinking sleep out of her eyes. Looking around as Luke carried her through the lobby, she said, "Wow, this is super."

Tamara, holding the IV bag as she walked beside them, agreed smilingly. "Top-flight place. I hope you can afford it."

"Fisk's paying for it," Luke replied. "At least, that's what his assistant said."

Sure enough, the room clerk at the desk told Luke everything had been taken care of. A young bellman offered to find a wheelchair for Angela, but Luke kept his granddaughter in his own arms.

"I can handle it," he told the bellman.

The suite was spacious and quiet, with heavy drapes on the windows and thick carpeting. Two bedrooms connected by a tastefully furnished sitting room.

As Luke deposited Angela on one of the double beds, the child said, "I can sit up, Grandpa."

"Fine," he answered, with a smile.

"Can I have something to eat?" she asked. "I'm hungry."

Luke glanced at Tamara, who said, "Some broth. A cup of Jell-O."

"A cheese sandwich," Angela said. "Please? I won't throw up again. I promise."

"Maybe later," Tamara said. "Let's see how you do with the soup and gelatin."

Angela nodded glumly, then turned to Luke. "Where are we going, Grandpa? Can we phone Mommy and Daddy?"

"Not right now, honey," he said, feeling rotten when he saw the disappointment on her face.

Tamara asked Luke, "Do you want an ibuprofen?"

"No, I'm okay."

She gave him a doubting look. "After carrying Angela all the way up here, your back isn't hurting?"

"No," said Luke, feeling slightly amazed that it was true. "No pain."

Tamara shrugged and went to the phone to call room service. Luke clicked on the TV set and fished for a program that would entertain his granddaughter.

Once they finished their late lunch, Angela sat up in bed happily enough, watching a kids' cartoon channel.

Luke motioned Tamara into the sitting room that connected the suite's bedrooms. Sitting on the sofa, his laptop on the coffee table, he told her, "Fisk wants me to call him back."

"It should be safe enough to use the hotel phone."

"On Skype."

"That's even better. You can use your laptop. I don't think they can trace Skype calls, or if they can, it takes longer. Something like that."

Feeling embarrassed, Luke admitted, "I don't know how to do Skype."

Tamara almost laughed, but checked herself just in time. With a smile, she said, "That's okay. I can show you."

Within ten minutes, Luke was talking face-to-face with Quenton Fisk.

———

Fisk was still at his desk when Luke's call came through. He peered at Professor Abramson's image on his wall screen. He had expected the old man to look haggard, weary. Instead Abramson seemed lively, almost energetic.

"I've given your problem considerable thought, Professor," Fisk said, after the usual preliminaries. "I believe I've worked out a solution for you."

Abramson said nothing, but the expression on his face radiated hope.

"I have a friend in Louisiana, near Baton Rouge," Fisk explained. "He has a fine old house down there, a former cotton plantation. You can stay there."

"But we need a medical facility," Abramson objected.

"Not to worry, Professor. If Mohammed can't come to the mountain, we'll arrange to have the mountain come to Mohammed."

Abramson looked doubtful.

"My friend can arrange to have medical people and equipment brought to his mansion. All very quietly, very discreetly."

"He can?" The professor's face brightened.

"And you can stay as long as you like, no problem."

"That's great! But Baton Rouge is at least a two-day drive from here."

"My assistant will set you up with route directions and make hotel reservations along the way. Right through to Baton Rouge."

"Fine," said Abramson. "Wonderful. I don't know how to thank you, Mr. Fisk."

Fisk lowered his eyes in a brief gesture of humility. Then, "We can't let them stop your work, Professor. Your granddaughter's life is at stake."

"That's right. But still, you're being very generous."

"Think nothing of it."

Fisk allowed a few more moments of gratitude, then cut off the professor's thanks with, "I think you ought to know the name of the man you'll be visiting."

"Oh! Yes, of course."

"His name is Lorenzo P. Merriwether. He's quite wealthy."

"Lorenzo P. Merriwether."

"My assistant will give you all the details before the end of the day."

"Thanks again, Mr. Fisk."

Fisk waved the admiration away and clicked Abramson's image off his wall. Then he ordered his assistant to contact Lorenzo P. Merriwether.

I ought to let Lonzo know what I've put him up for, he said to himself.

Nottaway Plantation

NGELA WAS SITTING in the van's backseat as Luke drove the
SUV down the long driveway leading to the plantation's
manor house.

Sitting beside him, Tamara said, "This is like something out of
Gone with the Wind."

"It's beautiful," said Angela. Luke thought her voice sounded
weak, frail.

The driveway ended at a large, three-story house fronted with
tall graceful white columns and decorated for Christmas with holly
and wreaths and candles at every window.

Two young black men were standing at the entrance to the mansion, lean and smiling. Luke had half-expected the servants to be
in livery, but these two youngsters wore dark pullover shirts and
jeans.

"Welcome to Nottaway Plantation," said one of them, as Luke
and Tamara climbed out of the SUV. Luke opened the rear door
and helped Angela out of the van. Her IV was disconnected, but
she still bore the port in her arm. It made Luke remember that he
had one of those plastic leeches attached to his bloodstream, too.

The air felt chilly but soft, even gentle, nothing like the cold farther north. The two young men cheerfully took all the luggage and
packages of medications and equipment, then led them to the front

door. Angela, in Luke's arms, was goggle-eyed as she took in the big house with a huge holly wreath bedecking the heavy oak door.

The front door swung open as they approached, and Lorenzo P. Merriwether beamed a warm, cordial smile to them.

"Welcome to my humble abode," he said grandly, in a deep basso voice, his arms spread wide.

He was well over six feet tall, slim and willowy. Like a basketball player, Luke thought. His skin was a light mocha, his smile brilliant. Merriwether's face was lean, almost gaunt, the skin stretched over prominent cheekbones and a strong jaw that bore a fuzzy dark beard.

As he led Tamara and Luke, who still held Angela in his arms, up the wide, winding staircase to the second floor, Merriwether happily explained, "This was a thriving cotton plantation in the antebellum days. More than a hundred slaves worked here. Now it's a tourist attraction. The old slave huts have been remodeled to accommodate tourists from all over the world."

As they passed a window, Tamara looked out and asked, "Is that the Mississippi?"

Merriwether beamed at her. "Yes indeed. Old Man River, just keeps rolling along."

He led them along the upstairs corridor and into a spacious, beautifully decorated bedroom.

Angela's eyes went wide as she took in the canopied bed. "Is that for me?"

"Yes indeed, little lady," said Merriwether. "All for you."

Luke deposited Angela gently on the bed, then stretched the stiffness from his back. Tamara went to the curtained window, fascinated with the view of the slowly flowing river.

"You and the lady have the next room, through there." Merriwether pointed toward a door in the side wall.

Luke felt his cheeks go warm. "Um . . . we'll need two rooms. Dr. Minteer is Angela's physician."

"Oh!" Merriwether looked surprised, but he quickly masked it with another brilliant smile. "Forgive me. I thought . . ."

Tamara turned back from the window and said, "Our relation-ship is based on Angela."

"I see."

All three of them turned to look at the child, who was sleeping blissfully, half buried in the mound of pillows on the canopied bed.

IN BOSTON, JERRY Hightower stood stolidly in front of his chief's desk.

"Do you mean to tell me you went back to the Washington office and left him there in the clinic, without anyone guarding him?"

Hightower felt like a schoolboy being reprimanded by the prin-cipal. But I deserve it, he thought. I let the guy get away.

"I told the clinic's security head to keep him from leaving the building," he said.

"That worked fine, didn't it?" The chief sneered.

"He's an old man," Hightower said. "I didn't expect him to slug one of the guards and drive away with the kid and the doctor."

The director got up from his squeaking chair and came around the desk. He was barely as tall as Hightower's shoulders, but the agent backed a step away from him.

"Jerry, this is a major screw-up. You let a fugitive get away from you."

"Technically, he's not a fugitive. At least, he wasn't then. That's why I had to go to the office, to fill out the papers—"

"But you let him get away! That's not like you. What's going on?"

Hightower shrugged. "He's not a criminal. He wants to save his granddaughter's life."

The director scowled at him. "The man is wanted for kidnap-ping, for God's sake! You had him and you let him go! By rights, I should ask for your resignation!"

"I'll find him," Hightower said. "I found him once, I'll find him again. There's only a few places in the country that he can run to, only a few places with the facilities that he needs."

The director took in a big breath, then let it out again in a wistful sigh.

"All right. You find him. You find him before the news media gets wind of this and I have to discipline you."

Hightower nodded once, then left the director's office, working hard to suppress an urge to run.

IN HIS OFFICE in Boston's financial district, Del Villanueva paced back and forth as he listened to his wife on the cordless phone he held clamped to his ear.

"Yes, Norrie, I've called the FBI office twice this morning. Same story: They were in Bethesda, just outside of Washington, but they took off."

Lenore's voice was shuddering. "Why didn't they arrest him? How could they let him go?"

Shaking his head, Del replied, "They couldn't arrest him because he wasn't officially charged with a crime yet."

"But he's kidnapped Angie!"

"The charge has been filed," Del said, before Norrie could work herself up into another bout of weeping. "He's now officially a wanted man. The FBI's looking for him across the whole country."

"What if he's gone to Canada? Or Mexico?"

"He'd have to show a passport, and they'd nail him then and there."

"Where is he?" Lenore sobbed. "Where's he taken my baby?"

"They'll find him," Del said, with a confidence he didn't really feel. "The FBI will find him."

Lorenzo P. Merriwether

LUKE WAS STARING out the window of the bedroom Merriwether had given him, watching a barge gliding slowly along the placid Mississippi River. Angela was sleeping again, after finally getting the cheese sandwich she'd asked for at lunch.

Angie's kept it down, Luke thought. That's a good sign.

A tap on his door. He crossed the ornately decorated room and pulled the door open to find Tamara standing there, with a medical kit in one hand.

"Time for your shot," she said, stepping past him into the room.

Suppressing a shudder of distaste, Luke said, "They seem to be helping. I don't feel as stiff and creaky as I did a couple of days ago."

"It could be psychosomatic."

"Yeah," he admitted. "Maybe."

The phone rang. Glad of the interruption, Luke went to the night table and picked it up.

Merriwether's bass voice said cheerfully, "Cocktail time! I'm brewing up a batch of mint juleps in the library. Care to join me?"

Luke glanced at Tamara, then replied, "We'll be there in ten minutes."

The library didn't have a book in it. Instead, the walls were lined with paintings and photographs; some of the photos looked to Luke as if they dated from the Civil War.

Merriwether waved a long arm at a batch of faded sepia-toned pictures. "Mathew Brady," he said. "Nottaway survived the war without being burned or looted. Sheridan's lads weren't so kind to Georgia."

Merriwether led Tamara and Luke through a tall French window out onto the veranda, facing the river. A silver tray sat on a table among the big, high-backed rocking chairs, bearing a huge ceramic pitcher and three tall glasses already adorned with sprigs of mint.

As they sat, Tamara said, "If you don't mind my asking, how did you come to own this place?"

Merriwether chuckled gleefully and hooked a long leg over his rocker's arm, facing her. "You mean, how did a black man acquire this bastion of southern gentility?"

Luke said, "I'd hardly call slavery a sign of gentility."

Sobering slightly, Merriwether said, "You see, I am a product of the American way of life. A success story. Born poor in N'Orleans. Got a basketball scholarship, played college ball. And studied hard. College was an opportunity and I seized it. Went on to the NBA. Not a tremendous star, but I had a few good years."

"Good for you," said Tamara.

He smiled gleamingly at her. "Got myself an MBA at Wharton during the off-seasons. Eventually I became a drug lord."

Startled, Luke gasped. "Narcotics?"

Merriwether tossed his head back and broke into a delighted laugh at Luke's consternation. "No, no. Nothing illegal. When my basketball days were finished, I got a position at Brady & Brady."

"The pharmaceutical firm?" Tamara asked.

"Indeed. Biggest pharmaceutical firm in Louisiana. Also the only pharmaceutical firm in Louisiana." He laughed again.

"And then?" Tamara prompted.

"Eventually the Brady boys gave me a seat on their board of directors. Strictly affirmative action window-dressing. Former basketball star. Black. Up from the slums of N'Orleans." His voice hardening, Merriwether went on. "After Katrina, they had me tour the Ninth Ward to show that ol' B&B *cared* about poor flooded-out black folks."

Then the bitterness evaporated and his eyes twinkled again. "I maneuvered the Brady boys out of their own company! Sent them into retirement and took over as CEO. How's that for affirmative action?"

Luke couldn't help smiling. "Pretty damned good."

"And then I bought Nottaway. Discombobbled some of the old gentry, but there wasn't much they could do about it. Not legally, that is. I survived a few potshots and a fire bomb and here we are, sitting on the veranda and watching Old Man River." He winked at Tamara and took a sip of his mint julep.

Luke cleared his throat, then said, "Well, I really appreciate your taking us in."

"Think nothing of it," Merriwether replied graciously. "Quenton said you needed help, and I'm always glad to help friends of Quenton Fisk's." Then, with another wink, he added, "Who do you think gave me the wherewithal to oust the Brady boys?"

"So that's the connection," said Luke.

"Indeed it is," Merriwether replied. Then he asked, "This treatment you're giving the child, does it have anything to do with the p53 gene?"

Luke shook his head. "Not directly."

"The p53 gene suppresses tumors, doesn't it?"

"When you've got two copies of the gene in your genome, one from each parent. Angela only has one p53. That makes her vulnerable to tumor formation."

"Oh. Too bad."

Tamara said, "Professor Abramson's treatment deactivates the genes that produce telomerase."

"Really," said Merriwether.

Slightly annoyed that Tamara had told more than he wanted Merriwether to know, Luke took up, "Suppress telomerase production and you suppress cells' ability to reproduce."

"And cancer cells reproduce endlessly," Merriwether said.

"So if you suppress telomerase production, the cancer cells die."

Merriwether pondered this information for a few moments, took another sip of his mint julep, then asked, "What effect does the treatment have on the other cells of her body?"

"Same effect," said Luke tightly. "Suppresses their reproduction."

"Doesn't that cause harm?"

"The cancer cells die off more quickly. Then we can make up for the side effect, bring her telomerase production back to normal."

"I see," Merriwether said slowly. "So it's a horse race, then, isn't it?"

Luke glanced at Tamara before answering. "Sort of. But it's a race we intend to win."

Christmas Eve

JERRY HIGHTOWER GLANCED furtively at his wristwatch as he followed the two young men along the main corridor of the University of Texas's cellular biology building. He had an appointment to talk with Professor Hiram Goldstein, and a reservation on the five-thirty flight out of Austin to Phoenix. The timing was going to be tight.

The students brought him to Goldstein's office, but the room was empty.

"Where is he?" Hightower demanded.

One of the kids shrugged his skinny shoulders. "Prob'ly in one of the labs, sir."

The other student went to the desk and picked up the phone. "I'll have him paged. He's around here someplace."

Then they left him in the office, alone. Hightower sat heavily on one of the sculpted plastic chairs and glanced at his watch again.

He wanted to spend Christmas with his brothers and uncles and their wives and kids at their family gathering at the Navaho Reservation in northern Arizona. Fly out to Phoenix after talking with Goldstein, pick up a rental car and drive to Chinle. Get there around midnight, if the traffic wasn't too bad. Christmas was for the family, the whole horde of them.

But if the professor's not here soon, he thought, I'm going to miss my flight. Getting another one on Christmas Eve will be impossible. Might as well try to hitch a ride on Santa's sleigh.

Still, Goldstein had worked with Abramson in the past. He knew the man's habits; maybe he knew where Abramson might have gone to ground.

So Special Agent Hightower sat there and waited, while his chances for having Christmas with his family ticked away.

ARLINGTON, MASSACHUSETTS, WAS aglow with Christmas decorations. Fat white flakes of wet snow were drifting down from the leaden sky, covering the streets and the cars passing by. Carols rang from every storefront as Del Villanueva trudged from the Mass Av bus stop toward his home, his hands dug into his parka pockets, his shoes getting soaked from the wet, fluffy snow he was slogging through, his mood anything but jovial.

For the first time in his life, Del appreciated Ebenezer Scrooge's attitude toward Christmas. His father-in-law had kidnapped his daughter and taken her God knows where. His wife was on the verge of a nervous breakdown, the FBI wasn't doing a fucking thing, and these goddamned shops were playing "Have Yourself a Merry Little Christmas." Bah! Humbug!

He dreaded going home. Dreaded seeing the house all lit up with holiday decorations, dreaded the tree that he and Norrie had dutifully decorated in the vain hope that Angie would be home with them for Christmas. Dreaded Norrie's endless tears that tore at his heart.

If Luke was here right now, Del thought, I'd break his fucking head in.

Angela was speaking delightedly to Luke's open laptop, re-cording a Christmas message for her parents. Luke stood by her bed, alert to catch any hint Angela might give of where they were. He had put the laptop on the bed and angled it so that its camera showed nothing more than the luxurious bedspread and heaped-up pillows behind the little girl.

". . . I'm feeling better, really I am," Angela was saying to an image of her parents that Luke had put on the screen. "Grandpa says I'm coming along fine and maybe I'll be home with you before long."

Standing beside the bed, Luke told himself for the hundredth time that a Skype message to Norrie and Del was safe enough. It wouldn't be traced. He'd arranged with Merriwether to have the message sent from an Internet café coffee bar in downtown Baton Rouge. That'd be safe enough, he tried to convince himself.

Tamara was sitting at the desk in the bedroom's far corner, going over the results of the newest round of X-rays and blood tests Angela had gone through earlier in the day.

Merriwether had been as good as his word. Angela's bedroom had been transformed into a clinical facility, with an IV stand and medical sensors stacked by the bedside.

Angela's message was interrupted by the growl of a diesel engine rumbling outside. Going to the window, Luke saw a semi-trailer rig pull up and huff to a stop in the driveway, its flank emblazoned with BATON ROUGE MEDICAL CENTER.

"What the hell is that?" he wondered aloud.

Angela pulled the bedcovers off and hurried to the window, her eyes wide with curiosity.

Tamara went to the window, too. "The portable MRI rig is here," she announced. "Courtesy of Mr. Lorenzo Merriwether."

"I'll be damned," Luke muttered.

They quickly dressed Angela and led her downstairs, where a pair of medical technicians took her inside the trailer for the MRI scan of her brain.

Merriwether was standing by the door, grinning at them, when they brought Angela back inside the house.

"I didn't realize it'd be so big," Luke admitted. "When you said 'portable' I didn't understand that it needs a semi-trailer to haul it."

"Main thing is it got here," said Merriwether, jauntily, as the truck chugged noisily down the driveway.

That afternoon two uniformed nurses arrived with their equipment and helped Tamara give Angela a complete physical.

By the time Angela returned to her bed and Luke's laptop, her cheerful tone from earlier in the day had faded noticeably. "I wish I could be home for Christmas," she said to her parents' image, "but Grandpa says I've got to stay here for the treatments he's giving me." Brightening, she said, "For Christmas we're going to have turkey with all the trimmings! Grandpa said I can even have some pumpkin pie!"

The child prattled on for several more minutes, then ran out of words. She ended with, "Merry Christmas, Mommy and Daddy. I love you."

Luke patted her shoulder. "That was very good, Angel. Wonderful. Your mom and dad will be very happy."

"I wish they could call me, talk to me."

"They will, honey. In a few days, you'll see."

Luke took the DVD of Angela's Christmas message to Merriwether, who assured him all over again that it would be sent to Norrie and Del that evening without being traced back to Nottaway. He was taking a chance, he knew. The FBI might be able to trace it anyway, and if they did they'd come swooping down on them.

But I couldn't let Angie not talk to her parents on Christmas. That'd be inhuman.

He hoped his decision wouldn't boomerang on them.

Angela looked good, he thought. The telomerase inhibitors were starting to have an effect on her. Her hair seemed thinner than before, not quite as golden as he remembered it. But that might be just a subjective outlook, maybe some guilt feelings working inside his head.

He took the child's hand in his own and patted it tenderly. "You want to watch some TV now?"

"Can I play a game on your laptop, Grandpa?"

"Sure," he said. "What would you like?"

It took half an hour of fiddling with the laptop before Luke finally acquired the computer game Angela wanted: something about a fairy princess in a castle.

Leaving his granddaughter leaning raptly toward the laptop screen, its glow lighting her face, Luke walked across the room to where Tamara was bent over the screen of her own laptop.

"How're you doing?" he asked.

Without looking up at him, Tamara murmured, "The MRI shows the tumors haven't progressed since her last scan."

"That's good."

"But her blood test shows an elevated blood pressure. That's not good."

Luke leaned over her shoulder and peered at the graph on the screen. "High blood pressure," he muttered.

Tamara turned toward him. "It doesn't necessarily mean anything. It's just an uptick in her pressure. But there's no obvious reason for it." She got to her feet and stretched, catlike. "We'll take another look the day after tomorrow."

"High blood pressure," Luke repeated. One of the possible side effects of suppressing Angela's telomerase production was progeria, premature aging. Luke had seen victims of the condition back in Boston: six-year-olds who had atherosclerosis, cardiovascular problems, kidney failure. Preteen kids who looked like bald, wrinkled, dying old dwarves.

Tamara caught the expression on his face. "Luke, what is it?"

"HGPS."

"Hutchinson-Gilford progeria syndrome." Tamara looked shocked. "But it can't be! That's a genetic disorder. She doesn't—"

"One of the effects of suppressing telomerase production is that the somatic cells stop reproducing, as well as the tumor cells. That causes the symptoms of progeria."

They both stared at Angela, busily tapping away at the laptop's keyboard. Luke thought the child's arms looked wrinkled. And her hair was definitely thinning.

Merry Christmas, he said to himself.

Christmas Day

MERRY CHRISTMAS!" LORENZO Merriwether loudly proclaimed as he wheeled a shopping cart piled high with brightly wrapped gifts into Angela's room.

Merriwether wore a fire-engine red shirt, dark slacks, and an elf's fur-trimmed cap. His face radiated good cheer.

Sitting up in her bed, Angela clapped her hands with delighted surprise. Luke, who had been shaving in the next room, stuck his lathered face through the doorway to see what the commotion was all about.

As he rolled the cart up to Angela's bed, Merriwether explained smilingly, "Santa Claus came by last night and left all these gifts for you, Angela."

Luke saw that Angela was beyond believing in Santa Claus, but she laughed as she got up on her knees and leaned into the shopping cart to start tearing open the wrappings.

By the time Luke finished his shave and pulled on a shirt, Tamara had come in from her room down the hall, wearing a forest green sheath decorated with Christmassy red jewelry. Angela was half-buried in torn gift paper, surrounded with digital games, a fully programmed smartphone, beautiful clothes, and a robotic fox terrier that was eagerly wagging its tail.

As Tamara began clearing away the wrappings, Luke said to Merriwether, "You didn't have to do that."

With a dazzling smile, Merriwether replied, "I couldn't let the child have Christmas without any presents. And I knew you weren't going out to do any shopping. So . . ." He gestured toward Angela, who was aglow with pleasure.

"Thank you," said Luke. "I owe you a lot."

"Think nothing of it. As I told you before, any friend of Quenton Fisk's is a friend of mine."

Luke started to say, "We're not exactly friends—"

"By the way, he's coming here. This afternoon."

"Quenton Fisk?"

Merriwether nodded vigorously. "He'll be here in time for Christmas dinner. Says he wants to talk with you."

FISK ARRIVED IN a chauffeur-driven black sedan in mid-afternoon. He was wearing a navy blue blazer over gray slacks. No luggage. Not even a briefcase or a computer.

He bounded up the front steps of the mansion, where Merriwether and Luke stood to greet him, a small, intense man with a luxuriant crop of dark wavy hair and penetrating gray eyes who radiated energetic good health.

"Lonzo," he said, with a big grin, as he took Merriwether's hand. Then, turning to Luke, "Professor Abramson," less warmly.

Luke blurted, "What brings you down here on Christmas Day?"

Draping a hand on Luke's shoulder, Fisk replied, "You do, Professor. I've left my home and hearth to talk with you, face-to-face."

"Really?" Luke felt impressed.

Fisk laughed brittlely. "Actually, Lonzo's more like family to me than any of my ex-wives."

As they walked inside, Merriwether asked politely, "How was your flight, Quenton?"

"Uneventful, thank God. Even though we filed our flight plan at the last minute my pilot got into the Baton Rouge airport, despite all the little creeps buzzing around in their Cessnas."

Luke realized that Fisk had come in his own private jet. Must be nice to have money, he thought. Come and go when you please, where you please.

Christmas dinner was festive, the five of them seated at one end of the long dining room table, by the ceiling-high windows that looked out on the Mississippi. The room was decked with bright green loops of ivy, tinsel dripping from the ornate crystal chandelier, and flickering candles in silver holders at the middle of the table.

Sitting between Luke and Tamara, Angela wilted noticeably as the various courses were served. Just before the pumpkin pie was served, she asked if she might be excused.

"I'm tired, Mr. Merriwether," she said, her voice soft, weak.

"It's been a big day for you," Merriwether said. "I hope you enjoyed it."

"I did. I really did."

Tamara took the child back to her room, and Merriwether promised to have a helping of the dessert sent up to her.

Luke watched them worriedly. He himself had eaten more than he had expected to. And drunk several glasses of the excellent Beaujolais that Merriwether's servants had poured generously. Now the three men sat together over the crumbs scattered across the tablecloth.

Without preamble, Fisk said, "I came here to get a few things straight with you, Professor."

"Luke. Call me Luke."

Fisk nodded briskly. Then, "I want you to sign a privacy agreement."

Surprised, Luke asked, "Privacy agreement?"

"It's strictly routine," Fisk said, with an impatient wave of his hand. "Since the Fisk Foundation is funding your research, you agree not to reveal details of your work to anyone outside the foundation."

"You mean I can't publish?"

"In time, of course you can. Publish in any journal you like. But first we have to go through the legal process of establishing our proprietary claim. That takes some time, I'm afraid."

Luke objected, "But the university—"

"The university has fired you, Professor. You're a fugitive from justice, a hunted man."

"I've got tenure!"

Shaking his head, Fisk said, "Not anymore, you don't."

"This FBI business is all a misunderstanding," Luke said. "I didn't kidnap Angela, she—"

Waving his hand again, Fisk said, "My lawyers will straighten all that out for you. Once you've signed the agreement."

Merriwether, sitting at the head of the table, had been swiveling back and forth like a spectator at a tennis match. Seeing the discomfort on Luke's face, he asked, "This is about your work on aging, Luke?"

"Life extension," Fisk corrected.

"Oh."

"We need to lock up our proprietary claims," Fisk repeated.

Luke saw iron-hard resolve in Fisk's cold gray eyes. "I'm not sure my work is patentable," he said.

"Let my lawyers be the judge of that," said Fisk.

Merriwether seemed puzzled. "And now you're doing aging experiments on your granddaughter?"

"To cure her of cancer."

Fisk tapped a manicured fingernail on the tabletop. "His work will make old people young again, and as a by-product it'll cure cancer! How's that for an investment?"

"It's very preliminary," Luke cautioned. "I'm working on Angela because everybody else has given up on her."

"But you believe you can cure her, don't you?" Fisk asked. The question was almost like an accusation.

"I think so. I hope so."

Merriwether gave out a low whistle. "So that's why you're so interested in his work," he said to Fisk.

With a tight nod, Fisk said, "Luke, I need you to sign the agreement. We'll take care of your legal problems, and you can treat the kid right here at Nottaway until she's either cured or she's dead."

"If she dies," Luke retorted, "then my research isn't worth much, is it?"

Fisk eyed him for a silent moment. Then, "If she dies you could be accused of murder. You'll need my lawyers more than ever, in that case."

Statistical Analysis

THE WEEK BETWEEN Christmas and New Year's is usually a slow time for businesses and government agencies. People take vacation time, or use their available sick-leave days to stay away from the office. Most schools are closed. Across the nation, almost everyone is in a holiday mood, partying and reuniting with families. Hardly anyone expects to be working during the final week of the year.

Hardly anyone.

Yolanda Petrone was surprised when her supervisor phoned her at home and asked her to come in for a meeting with the National Institutes of Health's budget committee.

"Budget committee?" she had asked, into the phone. "Why do you want me to talk with the budget committee?"

The voice on the other end sounded pained, irritated. "It's that report you sent in on Professor Abramson's work."

Petrone felt her brows knit. The report was part of her normal year-end routine, a summary of the work that the Cancer Institute had been funding. In Luke's case, it was a final report, since the agency had canceled his funding.

Feeling confused and more than a little discomfited, Petrone drove the next day to the NIH campus in Bethesda and made her way to the administration building. The traffic was unusually light, the campus quiet in the mid-morning sunshine.

She was even more confused, and surprised, when her supervisor introduced her to the others in the conference room. Only one of the men was from the budget committee. Three others were statisticians with the Department of Health and Human Services, another was from the Department of the Treasury, and the seventh person at the table was a youthful, hard-eyed man who identified himself as a special assistant to the President of the United States.

Lots of firepower, Petrone thought, for an ordinary program review.

Her supervisor sat at the head of the conference table, looking dour. Petrone—the only woman present—was seated on his left. The White House man was at his right, across the table from her. The statisticians, seated down the table, wore comfortably casual open-necked shirts or sweaters. The White House man was in a dark pinstriped suit. Her supervisor wore a suit, too, dreary gray, and a carefully knotted green and red tie that could only have been a Christmas present, Petrone theorized: No one would buy a tie like that for himself.

She was wearing a presentable skirt and sweater. But she got the impression that she should have dressed better.

Her supervisor—gray hair, thick gray mustache almost the same shade as his suit—was actually perspiring, she realized. The various statisticians looked just as curious and perplexed as Petrone herself felt. The White House aide was very serious, all business, and looked to be the youngest man at the table. He was lean, with thinning sandy hair and a stern intensity in his light brown eyes.

Once the introductions had gone around the table, the supervisor said, "Dr. Petrone, you submitted a report summarizing the work of Professor Luke Abramson, of Brighton University, in Massachusetts."

Petrone nodded.

"Your summary included an analysis of the results of his research."

"That was mostly speculation on my part," she said, immediately regretting that she had dabbled in that direction. "I thought that since our program with Professor Abramson had concluded, it was appropriate to examine where his work might lead. In the future."

"Very appropriate," said the Treasury Department representative, seated next to Petrone.

One of the statisticians said, with a youthful grin, "You opened up a can of worms, you did."

"Really?" she asked.

The Treasury Department representative was wearing a sporty checkered vest beneath his dark blue jacket, Petrone noticed. He was the oldest person at the table, from the looks of him: chunky, but faded, tired, resigned to the endless tedium of bureaucracy.

"Do you really believe," he asked Petrone, "that this man's research could extend human life spans?"

She nodded warily. "If he's successful with his work on telomeres, it could lead to greatly extended life spans, yes."

Her supervisor said, "We're not talking life expectancies here, but actual life *spans*, is that right?"

"Yes," said Petrone.

Turning to the Treasury Department man, the supervisor explained. "Average life expectancy has been rising for more than a hundred years. Better sanitation, better nutrition, better health care—they've all contributed to lowering infant and childhood mortality. More people live into adulthood, you see."

"But we're not talking about average life expectancy here," said the White House man, his high tenor voice sharp and crisp. He's from New England, Petrone realized once she heard him pronounce "here" as "hee-yeh."

"Exactly right," said the supervisor. "We're talking about people living well past one hundred. Lots of people."

The White House man shook his head. "We can't have that."

The man from the budget committee blurted, "Why not? Don't you want to live longer?"

The White House man gave him a cold stare. "Do you know what it would mean if most people could live to be a hundred or more? Do you have any idea of what would happen to our economy if we had millions of centenarians living, demanding their Social Security benefits, Medicare, retirement pensions?"

"It would wreck the economy," said the Treasury Department man. "It would bankrupt us."

One of the young statisticians said, "You'll just have to change the laws, then, and—"

"Change the laws?" the White House man snapped, his voice sharp as a whip crack. "When we've got millions of centenarians voting? D'you think they'd vote to cut their own benefits? Get real!"

Petrone finally understood. "That's why we refused to continue Abramson's funding."

One of the statisticians said, "We can't afford to have this work become successful. It would ruin the economy."

"But you'd be condemning millions of people to die before they have to."

"Better than allowing the economy to collapse. They're going to die anyway, sooner or later."

He was young enough to see this as an exercise in statistical analysis, Petrone realized. Old age and death were nothing but abstractions, in his mind. For other people, not for himself. Not yet.

Clasping his long-fingered hands together on the tabletop, the White House man said, "Look, we're not trying to stop scientific research here. Abramson's continuing his work somewhere, we know that."

"The Fisk Foundation is funding him," Petrone said.

Nodding, the White House man said, "Then we'll have to talk with the Fisk Foundation people. Abramson's work has to be controlled very carefully. We can't have this new capability suddenly injected into the national economy. It could be ruinous. It's got to be controlled."

My God, Petrone thought, he makes Luke's work sound like some plague virus.

With a pained expression on his face, her supervisor said, "We're going to have to excise your conclusions from your report on Abramson's work."

Before Petrone could object, the White House man said, "You say he's continuing his work under funding from the Fisk Foundation."

She nodded.

"Then we've got to get to the Fisk people and ask them to cooperate."

"Drop his funding?"

He shook his head. "Control his work. Keep it under wraps. No premature publicity."

"And if the Fisk people refuse to cooperate?" the supervisor asked.

With a careless shrug, the White House man said, "Then we'll investigate the foundation. We'll find corruption, illegal dealing with overseas companies, tax evasion—something, anything, to convince them to see things our way."

The Treasury Department man shook his weary head. "I know Quenton Fisk. He doesn't scare easily."

The White House man smiled thinly. "If he's a practical man, he'll cooperate. Otherwise he'll have to spend a lot of his money defending himself against our investigations. He'll see the light, I'm sure."

Petrone wondered which possibility bothered her more: the idea that the government would take control of Luke's work, or the idea that the Fisk Foundation would simply move Luke overseas, beyond Washington's control, and take him away from her forever.

River Walk

NOT BAD WEATHER for the end of December," said Luke as he, Tamara, and his granddaughter walked slowly along the gravel path that followed the river's edge.

It was a sunny afternoon, temperature in the fifties, a few white puffs of clouds sailing serenely across the blue sky. The Mississippi flowed slowly past; Luke guessed it must be nearly a mile to its other bank.

He was wearing the windbreaker he'd brought with him, but had unzipped it and even thought about removing its zip-in lining. Tamara wore her winter coat, too, and let it flap open in the soft afternoon breeze. They had bundled Angela into the pink quilted coat that Merriwether had brought among her Christmas presents, but Luke thought it might be too heavy for her.

Angela was trudging along between them, peering curiously at the flowering bushes and the low buildings on the other side of the river.

"It's like springtime," she said. Luke thought her voice sounded strained, raspy.

"We're a long way from New England," he said.

The child nodded glumly, and Luke thought, We're a long way from her parents. He wished there were some way he could bring Norrie to be with them. Del he could do without, but he wanted to make his daughter happy.

On the other hand, he thought, Norrie might freak out if she saw how aged and wrinkled Angie looks. But that will change. It's only temporary. Once we've knocked out the tumors, we'll reverse the progeria symptoms.

"Look! A bunny!"

Angela darted out from between them and ran toward a small rabbit that had popped out of the shrubbery that lined the walk. The rabbit bolted back into the shrubs, frightened by the child's approach.

Luke started after his granddaughter. "Angie, wait!"

Angela half-turned at the sound of his voice, stumbled, and fell forward. She put out both arms to break her fall.

"Ow!"

Luke reached his granddaughter and scooped her up in his arms, Tamara a scant step behind him.

"Are you okay, Angel?"

"My arm . . ." Angela clutched her left forearm with her right hand.

Tamara started to push the child's coat sleeve up the arm, but Angela yowled with pain.

"Let's get back into the house," Tamara said.

Luke nodded agreement and headed back, the little girl in his arms. Angela began sobbing. "It hurts."

"We'll take care of it," Tamara said, soothingly. "We'll make it all better."

ONCE THEY GOT Angela back to her room and removed her coat, they saw that her left wrist was swollen.

"Might be a fracture," Tamara said.

"She just tripped," said Luke.

"Brittle bones are a symptom of HGPS, aren't they?"

"Oh, for the love of God."

Tamara wheeled the X-ray machine to Angela's bedside and confirmed it: hairline fracture of her second carpal bone.

"That's not so bad," Tamara told Angela, her voice a gentle purr.

"It hurts," Angela whimpered.

"We'll take care of that right away."

In less than an hour Tamara had injected a painkiller into the port in the child's arm and encased her hand and forearm in a tightly wrapped plastic cast that she improvised from the box that the robot dog had come in. Angela could wiggle her fingertips but not flex her wrist.

"She'll sleep now," Tamara whispered to Luke, who had stood by the whole procedure, feeling helpless, blaming himself for the accident, for Angie's brittle bones, for this whole stupid business.

"She'll be all right for tonight," she went on. "I'll ask Lonzo to send a specialist here tomorrow and put a proper cast on her arm."

Looking at his half-asleep granddaughter, Luke murmured, "You did a good job. A great job."

"She'll be all right," Tamara repeated. "I'll stay with her. You go down and tell Lonzo what's happened."

Luke nodded. "I'll bring up some dinner for you."

Glancing at her wristwatch, Tamara said, "It's almost cocktail hour. I could use a drink."

"You and me both," he said fervently.

Boston FBI Headquarters

J ERRY HIGHTOWER HAD been nettled when he returned from his brief Christmas vacation with his family in Arizona. His chief had taken him off the Abramson case, just told him to fold up the dossier and get on with his other cases.

It bothered Hightower that a university professor, a scientist, had somehow eluded him. He kicked himself mentally for underestimating Abramson and letting him get away when he had found him in Bethesda. The guy had gone to ground somewhere, and Hightower was determined to find him. It was a matter of personal pride and professional responsibilities.

But the chief had decided not to waste any more time or effort on what was, after all, a very minor case.

"We've got better things to do than spend our time hunting for some damned runaway scientist," the chief had said, quite firmly. "We've alerted all our field offices to his case. He'll show up sooner or later and they'll nab him."

Hightower had left his chief's office feeling annoyed, frustrated. I can find Abramson, he complained to himself. I can run him down.

Now, though, not even a week later, Hightower could hardly contain his surprise as he sat in front of the chief's desk once again.

"You're back on this Abramson business." The dapper little man looked far from pleased.

Hightower said nothing, but the chief caught the expression on his normally impassive face.

"Orders from Washington," the chief grumbled. "Apparently somebody in the White House has taken an interest in Abramson."

"How come?" Hightower asked.

The chief shook his head unhappily. "Washington didn't deign to enlighten me. They just want Abramson found."

"Hmph."

"So what are you going to do about it? Just sit there and make grunting noises?"

"No," said Hightower, lumbering to his feet. "I'm going to talk to the people who're funding his research. The Fisk Foundation, in New York."

"You think they know where he is?"

"Even if they don't, they must know his contacts, his friends and colleagues."

The chief heaved a discontented sigh. "Go find him, Jerry. Make the White House happy."

CURIOUSER AND CURIOUSER, Hightower said to himself as the polished, stylishly dressed young blonde led him into the private office of Quenton Fisk.

"Agent Hightower," said Fisk, rising to his feet from behind his massive desk. It looked as big as a house trailer.

The blonde left the office, quietly closing the door to leave the two men alone.

Hightower had been surprised when the first flunky he had talked to immediately picked up the phone and called Fisk himself. And even more surprised when Fisk quickly told the man to bring him up to his private office.

"Mr. Fisk," Hightower said, walking across the thick carpeting toward Fisk's desk. The office was big enough to house a hockey rink, almost.

"I understand you're making inquiries about Professor Luke Abramson," Fisk said, as he gestured to one of the armchairs in front of the desk. It was upholstered in bottle green leather.

Easing himself into the chair, Hightower began. "Professor Abramson is wanted in connection with the abduction of his granddaughter."

"Really?" said Fisk, all innocence.

Hightower had seen that act before, on dozens of others he had interviewed over the years.

"Really," he said. "I thought that since your foundation is funding his research, you might have some idea of where he might be."

Leaning back in his high-backed swivel chair, Fisk said, "I'll instruct my people to cooperate with you fully."

"That's good."

"But you've got to understand, the foundation only hands Professor Abramson checks to support his work. We don't dictate where he goes."

"But your people know who his associates are, where he might be."

Fisk cocked his head to one side. "Possibly."

"I'd appreciate it if they told me all they know."

"By all means! I'll give them the word right now."

While Hightower watched, Fisk went through the motions of instructing his underlings to cooperate fully with the FBI. It was too easy, Hightower thought. Much too easy. *The man is trying to get rid of me by smothering me with cooperation.*

On the other hand, he thought as he got up from the comfortable armchair, *maybe the blonde will escort me through the building. That would be pleasant.*

Fisk watched the FBI agent shamble out of his office. *He walks like Frankenstein's monster,* he thought. *Big man. But not terribly bright.*

Leaning back in his desk chair, Fisk said to himself, Well, let him talk with my people. They can tell him everything he wants to know, be completely honest with him. He smiled. None of them knows where Abramson is. There's nothing to connect him with Merriwether and Nottaway. Only me and my personal assistant, and she certainly won't do any talking.

He reached for his private phone. Better tell Lonzo to make sure Abramson doesn't leave Nottaway. Keep him there, where the FBI can't find him and he can do his work without interference.

New Year's Eve

I T's BETTER IN New Mexico," Luke said.

He was sitting with Tamara and Merriwether in the spacious living room of the Nottaway manor house. A beautifully decorated Christmas tree scraped the high ceiling, off in one corner. Over the huge fireplace, the gigantic wall-screen TV showed the New Year's Eve countdown in Times Square. It looked cold out there, but the place was thronged with revelers bundled in heavy coats, parkas, hoodies, woolen caps, tooting horns and shouting greetings to one another.

"New Mexico?" Merriwether asked.

With a nod, Luke replied, "My wife and I used to go out there for the holidays. We could sit up and watch the ball go down in Times Square, and when they were screaming 'Happy New Year' in New York it was only ten P.M. We could go to bed and get a good night's sleep."

"Real party animals," Merriwether teased.

Tamara said nothing, but she gave Luke an odd gaze. She was sitting on one end of the deep, long sofa that faced the TV screen and the fireplace beneath it, her legs tucked beneath her. Luke sat a few cushions away from her. Merriwether was in a big armchair that looked to Luke more like a monarch's throne than a piece of living room furniture, his long legs stretched out on a carved wooden ottoman.

The coffee table in front of the sofa was laden with a tray of desserts and a bottle of Armagnac, which Merriwether touted as being much superior to Cognac. Luke had poured snifters for Tamara and himself: The liqueur was smooth and warming, true enough.

Merriwther sipped at a tall glass filled with something dark and somehow sinister looking. Rum, he had answered when Luke asked him what he was drinking.

"This used to be pirate territory, you know," he explained. "Jean Lafitte and all that."

Glancing at her wristwatch, Tamara got up from the sofa and said, "I'm going to check on Angela. I'll be back before the ball drops."

Luke nodded wordlessly. In the past week Angie's condition had worsened noticeably. The brain tumors seemed to be shrinking, but the symptoms of progeria were more obvious with each passing day. The child's blood pressure kept climbing; her hair was whitening and falling out; she was becoming a bald, wrinkled, wizened little gnome.

Ignoring the festivities blaring from the TV screen, Luke stared into the fireplace. The treatment's killing her cancer, but it's also killing her, he thought. We're in a race.

If Angie dies, he told himself, I'll turn myself in to the FBI. Let them arrest me for murder. What difference would it make?

But then he thought: She's not going to die. I won't let her die!

"Three minutes to go!" the TV screen shouted. The camera focused on the glittering ball at the top of the pole.

Tamara came back into the living room and sat beside Luke. "She's fine," she said, before Luke could ask. "Sleeping peacefully."

"Good," he said.

Very casually, Merriwether said, "My butler told me you asked him about borrowing a car."

"Thought we'd drive into Baton Rouge," Luke replied.

"I need some clothes," said Tamara.

"It'd be good to get around a little," Luke added.

His smile dimming just a fraction, Merriwether said, "That's not such a good idea, Luke. You can do your shopping right here. I can get the best stores in town to send some people and a selection of clothes. Just tell me what you're looking for, Tamara."

"It's not that easy," Luke objected.

"You'd be better off staying here, where you're safe," Merriwether said. His voice was gentle, but quite firm.

"One afternoon in town won't hurt."

"You never know, Luke. You never know. Quenton tells me the FBI came to see him, in his office in New York."

"That doesn't mean—"

"You stay right here, man," Merriwether said softly. "Better all around."

Luke saw iron-hard determination in Merriwether's eyes. "Is this your idea or Fisk's?" he asked.

Widening his smile, Merriwether said, "Come on, Luke. Is it so bad here? You've got everything you want, don't you? You can treat Angela and even carry on your research, can't you?"

Luke nodded grudgingly. "I guess so."

"Thirty seconds to go!" shouted the TV screen.

Tamara said to Merriwether, "I need to get my hair done. Can you recommend a beauty parlor?"

Instead of answering, Merriwether pointed to the TV.

"Five . . . four . . ."

Despite his misgivings, Luke stared at the screen. A year was ending. A new year beginning. The ball was sliding down its pole, lights flashing madly as the crowd below roared.

"Happy New Year!"

The din from the TV was nerve-rattling. Tamara leaned toward Luke and, placing a hand on his shoulder, kissed him on the lips. Totally surprised, Luke found himself grasping her waist and kissing her back fervently.

"Hey!" Merriwether yelled from his armchair. "What'm I, chopped liver?"

With a laugh, Tamara got her feet and went over to Merriwether and pecked at his lips.

"Happy New Year," she said, returning to the sofa to sit beside Luke.

And Luke realized that this was the first time in at least five years that he'd stayed up late enough to see the new year in. I'm not even sleepy, he marveled.

Nottaway Plantation

THERE WAS A small but well-equipped gym in the house, and Luke began to use it daily. *The telomerase is working,* he told himself as he worked with the barbells. It felt good to be sweating, to feel the exertion as he exercised. *I'd rather play tennis,* he thought, *but this gym is better than nothing. Besides, it's kind of cold outside for tennis.*

But then he thought of Angela. Her progeria symptoms were progressing too rapidly, overwhelming her. In the past two weeks she had lost all her hair, and her body was wasting away. The MRI scans showed the brain tumors were almost gone, but Luke wasn't sure he trusted the portable equipment that Merriwether's people brought to the house.

We need to get Angie to a proper hospital and run her through a complete physical, Luke thought. *But Merriwether won't let us leave the frigging house. We're like prisoners in here.*

Moving to the treadmill, Luke realized that Merriwether's fears were probably well grounded. *If the FBI's looking for me, it's best to stay here. Fisk will protect me, now that I've signed his damned privacy agreement. He can have the results of my research as long as I can treat Angie. It's a bargain with the devil, but what the hell else can I do?*

The door to the compact gym opened and Merriwether stepped through, loose and lanky, wearing a gray sweatsuit.

"Using the equipment," he said to Luke. "Good. That's what it's for."

Puffing as he ran on the treadmill, Luke said, "We ought to send a video to Fisk, show him how youthful and vigorous I'm becoming."

"I'm sure he'd be pleased," Merriwether said, grinning, as he swung a long leg over the saddle of the weight machine. Then he added, "Are you keeping up-to-date on the reports you're supposed to be writing?"

Luke nodded. "Yep. Both Angie's treatments and my own. E-mail them to Fisk every day."

"That's good. Quenton wants everything down on paper."

Changing the subject, Luke said, "I need to get Angie to a facility with a full-up MRI system and complete diagnostic equipment."

Grunting as he pulled at the weights, Merriwether said, "You tell me what you need and I'll have it brought here."

"I need a regular MRI unit. The portable doesn't give fine-enough resolution. I've got to get the kid to a real hospital."

Merriwether shook his head. "Too dangerous, man."

"We can do it at night, in and out with no paperwork. You can pull enough strings for that, can't you?"

Merriwether halted his workout. "Maybe. We'll see."

Luke understood his unspoken message: He has to check it out with Fisk. And Fisk will veto the idea.

WE'RE PRISONERS HERE," Luke muttered to Tamara. After his workout and a shower, he had dressed and popped into Angela's room. He hardly recognized his granddaughter. She was sleeping, her frail little chest rising and falling fitfully. She looks like a hundred-year-old crone, Luke thought.

Standing by the bed, Tamara asked, "Prisoners?"

"Fisk wants to keep us here, and Lonzo does what Fisk tells him to."

Her sculpted face pinching into a frown, Tamara said, "You mean he'd keep us here even if we want to go?"

"That's exactly what I mean."

"What do you intend to do about it?"

Glancing around the room, realizing that a hundred listening bugs could be hiding among the elaborate furnishings and decorations, Luke said, "Nothing much we can do. Just enjoy Lonzo's hospitality, I guess. As long as it lasts."

Tamara gave him a puzzled look. Taking her by the arm, Luke said, "Let's go outside and watch the river."

Clearly uncertain, Tamara allowed Luke to lead her to the French window that opened onto a little veranda.

Once outside, Luke closed the glass door and said in an undertone, "I don't think they have any bugs planted out here."

"Bugs?"

Motioning for her to keep her voice down, Luke said, "They might have our rooms bugged. That's what guards do to prisoners."

"Isn't that a little paranoid, Luke?"

"Even paranoids have enemies," he muttered. "They could have planted the bugs when they were cleaning our rooms."

"What do you intend to do?" Tamara half-whispered.

"Something. I don't know what. Not yet." He leaned over the railing and looked down at the grass below. "I think I could make it down to there. Climb over the railing, hang full length, and then drop to the ground. I could do that."

"And break every bone in your legs."

"No, I'd be okay. I could do it."

"And what about me? What about Angie?"

As if he hadn't heard her, Luke conjectured, "Then you could wrap Angie in a bedsheet and lower her to me. And then you climb down the sheet afterward."

"Luke, this isn't some fraternity house escapade."

"Then we could get to the garage and get our van and get the hell out of here."

"And go where?" Tamara asked, halfway between disapproving and intrigued.

"Oregon. Shannon Bartram's place. She'd take us in."

Tamara shook her head. "With the FBI hunting for us? And Fisk will probably come after you, too."

"They don't know about Shannon. It's been years since I talked to her."

"Luke, you can't do it. You can't put Angela through an ordeal like that. She'd never make it."

He glared at her. "You have any better ideas?"

Returning his stare, Tamara said, "Let me think about it."

Escape Plan

THE FOLLOWING MORNING, Merriwether tiptoed into Angela's room as Tamara injected another dose of telomerase inhibitor into the port on the child's arm. Angela was sleeping soundly, but she looked very frail, emaciated, totally bald, wrinkled—*old*.

As Tamara straightened up, Merriwether whispered, "How is she?"

With a shake of her head, Tamara replied, "Not good."

Merriwether gazed down at Angela. "Poor little kid."

"We need to get a complete diagnostic workup on her. We're working half in the dark here."

"I know." Merriwether nodded. "Luke told me yesterday. I'm working on it. We can take her out to Mercy Hospital tonight. But we'll have to bring her back here before the morning shift comes in."

"That's great!" Tamara said. "That's wonderful. Thank you, Lonzo."

As they walked away from the bed, Merriwether said, "You know, you could use a little break from all this. You've been under quite a strain, haven't you?"

Tamara admitted, "It hasn't been easy, that's true enough."

"Maybe you and I could have a quiet dinner together one of these evenings. Do you good to get away from all this, at least for a little bit."

Warning signals flashed across Tamara's mind. He's coming on to you! Be careful: You don't want to turn him off, but you don't want to turn him on, either.

"That'd be very nice," she said.

Merriwether flashed a bright smile at her. "Tomorrow night, then."

Tamara nodded mutely, thinking, We've got to get away before tomorrow night.

M ERRIWETHER LEFT, AND Tamara checked the monitoring equipment. Satisfied that if anything changed in Angela's condition, the beeper she carried in her skirt pocket would alert her, she went to the door that connected to Luke's room and rapped on it.

"It's unlocked," came Luke's muffled voice.

He was on the sofa, she saw, bent over the laptop that Merriwether had loaned him, writing another daily report to Fisk. Can the FBI tap e-mails? she wondered. Luke's not using his own computer, but might they be watching Fisk?

Looking up from his screen, Luke asked, "How's Angie?"

"Sinking. It's slow, but she's getting worse."

"We need to get a high-resolution scan of her brain. See if the tumors are really gone. If they are, we can stop pumping the inhibitors into her."

Sitting on the sofa beside him, Tamara revealed, "Lonzo said we can go to Mercy Hospital tonight."

"Tonight?" Luke brightened.

"He's greased the wheels," Tamara said. "They'll be ready for us tonight."

"Good. Wonderful. If we can stop the inhibitors her progeria symptoms will begin to clear up."

"You hope."

"If they don't we can give her telomerase inducers, bring her back to normal."

"And activate the tumors again."

He shook his head. "No, once they're dead, they're dead." Before Tamara could object, he added, "I've been thinking, once we're in Oregon, we could even do some genetic engineering, give Angie a full complement of the $p53$ gene, protect her against tumor formation."

"If you can get us out to Oregon."

Luke's enthusiasm collapsed like a pricked balloon. "Yeah. Big if."

Tamara pointed to the French window that led out onto the veranda. "Let's get some fresh air."

Luke understood. "Let me shut down the computer first."

She watched him save the report he'd been writing, then close the laptop. As they got to their feet, Tamara motioned for Luke to bring the laptop with him.

Once they were out on the veranda, where a cool breeze was wafting in from the river, she said, "I've been thinking about how we can get away from here."

"Me, too. We've got to make the break tonight, from the hospital."

Nodding, Tamara said, "And rent a private jet to fly us out to Oregon."

"Rent a . . . How the hell can we do that?"

"How much money do you have in that wad of yours?"

"About fifty thousand, a little more."

"In cash?"

"Yeah."

"Look up aircraft rentals. On Google."

"Okay," Luke said uncertainly. "How do you do that?"

With a disapproving "Tsk," she sat on one of the wicker chairs and reached for the laptop in his hand. "May I?"

Within minutes Tamara connected with Bayou Air Services and

rented a private jet for a flight to Portland, Oregon, using a credit card to hold the reservation.

"You have that kind of money in your account?" Luke asked.

"The bank is happy to loan me the money," she replied, with a bitter smile. "At twenty-some percent interest."

"Oh," said Luke.

"I figure you can pay the actual bill out of your cash supply when we get to the airport. That way there won't be any record of my credit card actually being used."

"Smart. But what about clothes and stuff?"

"I'll pack a suitcase. You do the same. Then you can put them in the van when we drive to the airport."

"Yeah," he said. "Now all we have to figure out is how to get from the hospital to the airport without Merriwether's people stopping us."

Mercy Hospital

"THEY'RE GONE!" TAMARA said, her face bright with excitement. "Not a trace of a tumor."

"You're sure?" Luke asked.

"See for yourself."

It was nearly four A.M. They were sitting together in a small office off the MRI lab at Mercy Hospital, in a suburb of Baton Rouge. Merriwether had insisted on personally driving Luke, Tamara, and Angela in his own sleek snow white Lamborghini convertible. He kept the car's metal roof up while Angela slept in the rear seat, with Tamara beside her, and Luke rode in front with Merriwether, who promised them that the hospital staff had been well paid to allow them to use the equipment without filing any paperwork.

But Luke knew that their suitcases were still in his SUV, parked in the Nottaway garage. They were going to arrive in Oregon with nothing but the clothes on their backs and the two laptops Tamara had brought with her. Assuming we make it to Oregon, he told himself.

At least I've got my money with me, he reminded himself as he patted the bulging wallet he'd slipped into his jacket pocket. Merriwether didn't notice the gesture; he was fully focused on driving his pride and joy.

Now Luke and Tamara hunched together as they stared at the display screen showing the results of Angela's brain scan.

"No trace of the tumors," Tamara murmured, almost as if she were afraid to say the words too loudly.

"They're gone," said Luke. His voice was shaky, too.

Running a lacquered fingernail along the screen, Tamara observed, "But these arteries have thickened."

"Atherosclerosis," Luke muttered.

"One of the symptoms of HGPS."

"Like we need a scan to tell us she's got progeria."

Tamara straightened up, rubbed her eyes. "We can stop the inhibitor treatment."

Luke shook his head. "Not yet. Give it another week."

"Another week?"

"I want to make sure the damned tumors are dead."

"But the progeria!"

"Another week," Luke said, with a firmness he didn't really feel.

Tamara sat silently for several moments, her fingers working the laptop's keyboard to record the test results. Luke thought he could see the wheels turning inside her head as she typed.

At last she looked up and said, "Stop the treatment now, Luke. Don't let the progeria advance any further."

Before he could object she went on. "If the tumors reappear we can put her back on the inhibitors."

It was Luke's turn to fall silent. He sat there, turning over the possibilities in his mind. At last, "You're right. We'll stop the inhibitors and give her a chance to recover."

Tamara breathed out a relieved sigh. "Good," she said. "Now, how do we get out of here?"

"Merriwether's downstairs, in the waiting room," said Luke. "So we go out the back way. I'll carry Angie; you phone for a cab."

They went to the recovery room where Angela lay sleeping and wrapped her in several blankets. The two nurses on duty helped; then one of them pushed a wheelchair to the child's bed. Tamara stuffed her laptop and Luke's, together with a case full of medications, into her tote bag while Luke tenderly lifted Angela into the wheelchair. She stirred and muttered something incomprehensible.

"Thanks," Luke told the nurses as he wheeled Angela toward the elevator. "We can handle her from here."

The nurses looked uncertain but didn't try to stop them. As the elevator doors closed, Luke grinned at Tamara. "Next stop, the airport."

Angela stirred and murmured sleepily, "Mommy?"

"I'm right here, Angel," Luke said.

"I feel tired," the child said weakly. "Can we go home now?"

"Soon, honey," Luke said, hating himself for lying to his granddaughter. "We'll have you back home real soon now."

But when the elevator doors slid open, Merriwether was standing there, waiting for them with a sly grin on his face.

"Goin' somewhere?" he asked.

Luke nodded. "To the airport. You've been very good to us, Lonzo, but we've got to get Angie to a first-rate medical facility."

Spreading his long arms, Merriwether said, "You're in one right here."

Luke said, "We're leaving."

"No you're not. You thought you were pretty fucking clever, doing your talking out on the verandas, where we couldn't hear you. But you weren't clever enough. I know what you're up to."

"Let us go, Lonzo," Tamara pleaded.

He shook his head. "Fisk wants to you to stay at Nottaway." His smile widening as he focused on Tamara, he added, "And that's what I want, too."

Luke let his shoulders slump and began pushing the wheelchair with Angela half asleep in it.

"Down this way." Merriwether pointed in the opposite direction. "My car's parked at the main entrance."

Luke saw that the corridor was empty of other people at this time of night. Probably security cops at the entrance, he thought. If I'm going to make a move it's got to be now.

Lorenzo Merriwether was more than a head taller than Luke, maybe thirty years younger. He's in good physical shape, Luke thought. Former athlete, he's still trim and fit, works out in his gym.

Luke's brief career in the Army had been as a very junior lieutenant in an intelligence unit in Tokyo. ROTC had paid his way through college, and in return he'd pulled a tour of duty in Japan during the Korean War. He'd taken a routine course in hand-to-hand fighting, nothing more. And that was a lot of years ago.

Surprise counts for a lot, he remembered from his training. He heard the grating growl of his drill instructor's voice. "Catch 'em by surprise, get the first shots in, and make 'em count."

Luke sucked in a deep breath, then swerved Angela's wheelchair into Merriwether's legs. He stumbled, grabbed the back of the wheelchair for support.

Luke smashed a karate chop at Merriwether's neck, but the man was quick enough to partially block it with an upraised arm. He slid to the floor, but before Luke could get around the wheelchair to kick him he bounced to his feet.

Grinning, Merriwether crouched as he faced Luke.

"I was wondering why an old fart like you was working out in the gym," he said. "Give it up. There's no way a guy your age is gonna get past me."

Knees, Luke remembered. Knees are vulnerable, and exposed. He edged closer to Merriwether, who stood his ground, waiting for him. Luke feinted a punch at Merriwether's head, and when the man's hands came up reflexively to block it, Luke kicked at his left kneecap as hard as he could.

Merriwether yelped in pain and collapsed to the floor, but he grabbed at Luke's leg, pulling him down to the tiles beside him.

"Motherfucker," Merriwether growled as he rolled over on top of Luke, his fist raised like a hammer.

Tamara swung her oversized handbag at him. It hit Merriwether's head with a loud *clunk*! His eyes rolled up; then Luke hit him under the chin with a cupped hand and his head snapped back. Tamara clouted him again and he slumped to the floor, unconscious.

"What the hell do you have in that bag?" Luke asked as he scrambled to his feet.

"The kitchen sink," she replied tightly.

Luke realized she had both their laptops in the bag, along with God knows what else.

"Come on," he said, "the taxi ought to be waiting for us at the rear entrance."

Airborne

YOU'RE DAMNED LUCKY I was available," said the twin-jet's pilot. Luke was surprised when the pilot stuck his head through the open hatch and invited him to come up and sit with him in the cockpit's right-hand seat.

"Yeah," the pilot said as he leaned back in his chair with a pleased, relaxed smile on his face, "most guys would've wanted a copilot to make the flight with them. With me, you only need to pay for one man."

Luke, Tamara, and Angela had made it to the airport just as the sky began to turn milky white. Don't have to worry about being late for the flight, Luke told himself. We're chartering our own business jet, and it'll wait for us to show up.

He was surprised that the general aviation terminal was busy so early in the morning. A smiling executive of Bayou Air Services greeted them curbside and took Tamara's weighty tote bag from her shoulder.

"No other luggage?" he asked.

Luke was carrying the sleeping Angela in his arms. Shaking his head, he replied, "Nope. Just us."

The executive looked nonplussed, but he led them into the company's office, off the terminal's main room. He was wearing an open-necked sports shirt and a white blazer that bore the company's logo.

His eyes went wide when Luke pulled a bulging billfold from his own jacket and peeled off three hundred one-hundred-dollar bills.

"Cash?" he squeaked.

"You don't take cash?" Luke asked.

Recovering some of his composure, the executive said, "Oh, sure we do. But it's usually from young punks in the drug business."

Luke grunted. "We're flying my granddaughter to Oregon for medical treatment. And we're in a hurry."

"Certainly, certainly. We've laid out our best plane for you, it's spanking new. And our best pilot to fly it."

The pilot's name was Jason Kleiner, a skinny youngster with long, sweeping blond hair and a cocky grin, wearing Levi's and a leather jacket over a white T-shirt. Luke wondered how good a pilot he really was until he asked about the golden wings clipped to the breast of his windbreaker.

"Navy pilot, man," said Kleiner. "You haven't lived until you've tried to land an F-18 on a carrier at night."

They settled Angela comfortably on the padded bench that made up the last row of the passenger compartment, with Tamara sitting next to her. Takeoff was smooth, and they were soon at cruising altitude. Then Kleiner had invited Luke up to the cockpit.

"Yep, you're lucky I was available," Kleiner repeated as the jet flew high above an unbroken layer of silken white clouds.

"I had the day off," he explained. "Was going down to New Orleens for a night of fun and games. Then the office called and asked me to take this last-minute job."

"There weren't any other pilots available?" Luke asked.

"None as good as me."

Luke let the guy talk for a while, then said, "I'm going back and take a snooze. I've been up all night."

Kleiner laughed. "I was planning to be up all night myself, until your job came through."

Luke unbuckled his safety belt and got up from his seat.

"I'll call you when we land at Rapid City."

"Rapid City?"

"Refuel," Kleiner explained. "We'll only be on the ground for half an hour or so."

Luke nodded and headed back into the passenger compartment. Tamara had cranked her seat back and was sleeping soundly. As was Angela.

He didn't realize he had fallen asleep until the sudden noise of the plane's wheels being lowered startled him awake. Tamara was sitting tensely in the seat across the aisle.

"This doesn't look like Portland," she said, with a worried frown.

"It's Rapid City, South Dakota," Luke told her. "We need more fuel to get to Oregon."

"Oh."

The plane landed smoothly and taxied to the terminal, where a fuel truck stood waiting. Kleiner ducked through the cockpit's hatch, smiling happily.

Pointing to the hatch at the rear of the passenger compartment, he said, "There's sandwiches and coffee in a cooler back there. Soft drinks, too. Compliments of the company."

Then he got a good look at Angela, who was stirring from her sleep.

"Jesus! What's wrong with her? How old is she?"

Tamara answered sternly, "It's a condition called progeria. We're taking her to Oregon for treatment."

Kleiner stared. "She looks like she's a hundred years old, for chrissakes."

"She's eight," said Luke.

Looking at the cast on Angela's wrist, Kleiner asked, "What happened to her arm?"

"She fell. It's nothing serious."

With a visible effort, Kleiner tore his eyes from Angela and went back to the main hatch, at the front of the passenger compartment. Once the ladder unfolded, he clattered down the steps and into the cold morning air. It was cloudy outside, and piles of dirty gray snow were banked along the edge of the tarmac.

Luke saw Angela stir and wake up, peering with bloodshot eyes out the plane's window.

"How do you feel, Angie?" he asked.

"Tired," the child replied.

"Are you hungry?"

She shook her head slowly, as if it were too much of an effort to speak.

"I'll get a nutrient preparation for her," said Tamara, reaching into her capacious tote bag.

Angela went back to sleep before the plastic bag was half emptied. Tamara and Luke munched on the limp sandwiches and drank lukewarm coffee.

She appraised him with narrowed eyes. "Have you done anything to your hair?"

"Anything?" Luke asked, sitting sideways on the plane's chair, his legs in the aisle. "What?"

"It looks darker."

He shrugged. "Fountain of youth."

She smiled. "You took on Lonzo like a superhero."

"Some superhero. He'd have beaten my brains out if you hadn't slugged him."

"Conked him with our laptops," Tamara said. "I hope I haven't damaged them."

"I'll buy you a new one."

Kleiner ducked through the hatch. "You guys warm enough in here?"

Nodding, Luke said, "It's not bad."

His face totally serious, Kleiner said, "Could you come up to the cockpit for a minute, sir?"

Luke glanced at Tamara, then got up and headed forward, suddenly worried. What's he want?

Kleiner gestured to the right-hand seat and, as Luke slid into it, closed the hatch. Then he sat in the other chair.

"Something wrong?" Luke asked.

"The flight dispatcher back in Baton Rouge told me you're toting around a big wad of bills."

Tensing, Luke said, "So?"

"So here in Rapid City one of the clerks watches those TV reality shows about cops tracking down crooks. She tells me the FBI has a bulletin out for a Professor Abramson, who's traveling with a sick child and a Dr. Minteer. They want him on suspicion of kidnapping."

Luke couldn't think of anything else to say except to repeat, "So?"

"That's you, isn't it?"

His pulse thudding in his ears, Luke said, "It's no business of yours."

"Yes it is," said Kleiner.

For a long moment the two men stared at each other wordlessly, practically nose to nose.

Then Kleiner smiled thinly. "Hey, I've flown crooks and runaway husbands. I've taken tax evaders to Mexico. No skin off my nose, as long as they pay the fare."

"I've paid for this flight," Luke said tightly.

"Narcotics guys pay best. They carry suitcases full of money, you know that?"

Luke saw where Kleiner was heading. "How much?" he asked.

"How much you got on you?"

"None of your damned business."

"Hey, don't get hissy with me, man. You ain't getting to Oregon unless you pay the bill."

Trying to hold on to his temper, Luke repeated, "How much?"

"Twenty thou?"

"Ten."

Kleiner smiled easily. "Let's meet in the middle. Fifteen thousand and I'll fly you to Portland quick and clean and keep my mouth shut."

Luke nodded. "I'll have to go back to my seat and get the money."

"Sure."

Luke went down the aisle to where Tamara and Angela were waiting. Keeping his back to the open cockpit hatch, he reached into his jacket, pulled out his billfold, and counted out fifteen thousand dollars worth of bills. He didn't want Kleiner to see how much was left. Then he realized that there was less than ten thousand remaining. I'm going broke, he said to himself.

Tamara, watching him, asked, "What's going on?"

"Highway robbery."

Luke went back to the cockpit and handed the bills to Kleiner. "Don't spend it all in one place," he growled.

The pilot laughed.

Once they were airborne again, heading for Portland, Luke wondered if Kleiner was an honest extortionist. Would he stay bought?

Fisk Tower

H E GOT AWAY from you?" Quenton Fisk bellowed.

In the wall screen's view, Lorenzo Merriwether seemed to be sitting in bed, with some sort of white medical horse collar around his neck.

"The two of them jumped me. I got a concussion, man. And a herniated disk!"

Fisk demanded, "A seventy-five-year-old man and a woman beat you up?"

Merriwether's expression hardened, but he said nothing.

"Where'd they go?"

"To the airport."

"Where did they fly to?"

"I'm not sure."

His anger mounting, Fisk fairly shouted, "You just let them get away from you?"

"No sense hollering, man. You want them, you're gonna have to go find them."

"Thanks to you." Furious, Fisk slammed a fist on his desktop phone console, cutting off Merriwether's call.

For several minutes he sat there, feeling his heart pounding beneath his ribs. Abramson got away. He's on the loose. Where is he? Where'd he go?

Then he asked himself the ultimate question: How can I find him?

The FBI's looking for him. Maybe I should call that agent, whatever his name is. But then I'd have to admit that I was hiding Abramson, protecting him.

He's signed the privacy agreement. With that and the funding contract he agreed to, I own his work. He can't publish anywhere unless I permit it, and he can't go to work for anyone else.

But then Fisk realized, The man's a wanted criminal! Do you think a couple of scraps of paper are going to hold him to you? He's on the loose; God knows where he's gone.

I'll have to get my own security people to chase him down, Fisk concluded.

Then he brightened. Maybe I can use the FBI to help, after all.

Almost smiling, he tapped his intercom and told his assistant to get the FBI agent on the phone.

"Agent Hightower, sir?"

"Yes, Hightower." That's his name, Fisk recalled. The big redskin.

As he waited for his assistant to reach Hightower, Fisk began to compose the story he would tell the FBI agent. Stick to the truth as much as possible, he reminded himself. But don't let him know that you were deliberately hiding Abramson.

JERRY HIGHTOWER WAS in Minneapolis, talking with a former student of Abramson's, when his phone buzzed. He ignored the call, not willing to interrupt his interview with the scientist. Not that he got much out of it. Yes, the man knew Professor Abramson. He was even fairly current on what Abramson had been working on.

"Telomerase," said the redheaded geneticist. "He's done some truly startling work with lab mice, you know."

Hightower nodded. "He's a fugitive now. He's been charged with kidnapping."

"Kidnapping! Professor Abramson?"

Making a reassuring gesture with both his big hands, Hightower explained, "It's a family matter. He's taken his granddaughter away from the kid's parents, without their permission. Now we've got to find them."

The scientist looked puzzled. "That doesn't sound like Professor Abramson."

"His granddaughter is dying from cancer. The professor thinks he can save her, but nobody else agrees with him—including the child's parents."

"I see. Well, he hasn't contacted me recently. I haven't seen him since the Triple-A-Ess national conference, in October. Or was it November?"

"Do you have any idea of where he might have gone, who he might turn to?"

The scientist shook his head. Hightower realized he wasn't going to get anything more from the man, whether he knew Abramson's whereabouts or not.

He rose from the bare wooden chair he'd been sitting on, pulled one of his cards from his wallet, and handed it to the scientist.

"If you hear from him, let me know. The man's a wanted fugitive."

"Sure," said the scientist. "Of course."

Fat chance, Hightower thought.

In the taxi headed for the airport and his next interview, Hightower pulled out his cell phone and checked his messages. Quenton Fisk. He grunted with surprise.

FISK WAS WALKING a quartet of potential investors out of his office when his assistant stepped beside him and said, almost in a whisper, "Agent Hightower is calling, sir."

Fisk nodded to her, then said to the departing men, "Thanks so much for coming by. I'm sure we're going to make an indecent profit on this deal."

They laughed and nodded agreement. Fisk went back to his desk and picked up his phone.

"Agent Hightower," he said pleasantly. "Good of you to return my call." To himself, he added, Four hours after I called you.

No video, Fisk realized. From the sounds coming through the phone, Hightower must be in a car, he thought.

Hightower's deep voice rumbled. "You said you have some information about Professor Abramson."

"Yes," Fisk replied, leaning back in his desk chair and loosening his tie with his free hand. "It's almost embarrassing, actually."

Hightower said nothing.

"You see, a friend of mine has been hosting Abramson at his home for the past couple of weeks. I just heard about it today."

He waited for Hightower's response but heard nothing except the traffic noise.

"He's been in Louisiana, at Nottaway Plantation, just outside of Baton Rouge."

"You say he *has been* there?"

Fisk felt uncomfortable, as if the FBI agent knew he wasn't telling the entire truth. He wished he could see the man's face, but then realized that maybe it was better that Hightower couldn't see his.

"Yes, he's gone."

"Where?"

"I don't know. Apparently there was some sort of scuffle. Abramson took off with his granddaughter and her doctor. He headed for the airport, I believe."

Another stretch of silence. Fisk squirmed uncomfortably, waiting for the agent to say something, anything.

Finally, "Nottaway Plantation, you said."

"Yes. In Louisiana."

"I'll have to go there and talk to your friend. What's his name?"

"Lorenzo Merriwether. I'll tell him to cooperate with you fully."

"Uh-huh."

"My assistant can give you directions. I'll tell Merriwether that you're coming and he's to cooperate with you fully."

"Good. Thank you."

"You're entirely welcome," Fisk said, struggling to keep his self-control, to keep from babbling.

"Good-bye."

"Good-bye."

Fisk hung up after passing Hightower on to his assistant. Then he punched his speed-dial key and hit Merriwether's number. We've got to get our stories straight, he told himself. Lonzo's got to tell the same tale to Hightower that I just did.

Oregon

LUKE GLANCED AT the clock on the airport terminal's wall for the tenth time in the past two minutes. Angela sat between him and Tamara, a soft blue blanket wrapped over her clothes, fully awake and staring with her owlish eyes at the people striding through the busy terminal.

"Shannon said she'd have a car out here in less than an hour," he muttered, more to himself than anyone else.

Luke had called Shannon Bartram from a pay phone in the airport terminal. She sounded totally surprised that he was in Portland, but once Luke explained about Angela she had immediately agreed to let him use her laboratory facilities to treat the child.

"It's been just about an hour since you called her," Tamara said.

"I have to go to the bathroom," said Angela.

Tamara asked, "Can you walk?"

Angela shot a disapproving frown from her old woman's face. "Sure I can walk."

The three of them got to their feet; Luke removed the blanket while Tamara held Angela's frail right arm.

"The ladies' room is right over there," Tamara said to the child, pointing. "Just lean on me."

"Okay."

Luke watched them go, haltingly, painfully slowly. Tamara bent slightly to keep an arm around Angela's shoulders. People stared and moved out of their way to allow them to pass.

Where the hell is Shannon? Luke asked himself again. She should be here by now. Then he realized that she'd have to park her car and make her way through the terminal to find him.

He sat down again. And realized that he didn't have to use the men's room. Hell, he thought, I haven't peed since we were in the plane, more than three hours ago. That's a new record, I think.

A short, blocky Hispanic-looking man in a dark suit walked by, bearing a small sign that read ABRAMSON.

Luke jumped to his feet. "Hey, that's me!" he called.

The man peered at Luke's face. "You look younger than your picture."

"You're from Bartram Labs?"

"Yes, sure. Mrs. B. herself sent me to pick you up. She said you had a woman and a kid with you." The driver was young, with a full head of dark hair and a thick mustache.

"They're in the ladies' room."

"Hah. Women."

Once Angela and Tamara reappeared, the driver led them through the terminal toward the exit that led to the roadway.

"I thought you'd be over in the luggage pickup area," he said to Luke. "That's where we usually meet our passengers."

"Oh."

With a laugh, the driver said, "Good thing you're in the general aviation terminal. If you came in on one of the airlines I'd have had to call for a posse to find you."

"Yeah," Luke said, "good thing." He was watching Angela. The child seemed to be walking all right, although very slowly, hesitantly, as if she couldn't quite trust her own legs.

They waited just inside an exit door while the driver went out into the chilly gray afternoon and retrieved his car from the parking lot.

"How do you feel, Angel?" Luke asked.

"Okay," she replied shakily. Pointing to the row of chairs farther inside the terminal, she asked, "Could I sit down over there?"

"Sure, sure. Tamara will go with you. I'll wait here for the car."

The car came at last: a spacious, comfortable silver-gray Infiniti sedan. In less than a quarter hour they were speeding up the highway that ran along the Columbia River.

Even in the gray, misty day the valley looked beautiful, with green hills and the majestically flowing river, broad and smooth. They passed a fountain spraying water high into the air on the other side of the river. The sun broke through the overcast, and suddenly a rainbow arched brightly before their delighted eyes.

"Look!" Angela cried.

Tamara said, "Rainbows are supposed to bring good luck."

Luke had never heard that one before, but he hoped she was right.

The sedan turned onto a side road that climbed up into the hills. Perched on top of the highest hill in the area sat the cluster of square white concrete buildings that was the Bartram Research Laboratories.

As they rolled up the driveway to the main building, Luke saw that Shannon Bartram was standing at the entrance, waiting for them.

SHANNON BARTRAM HAD been one of Luke's graduate students, more than fifteen years earlier. The daughter of a Wyoming cattle rancher, she had surprised herself in undergraduate school by falling in love with biochemistry. She had thought she'd put in the four years of college that her father insisted on, then return to ranch life in Wyoming.

But one of her professors changed all that. Luke Abramson's undergraduate course in biochemistry opened her eyes to a fascinating new world filled with possibilities she had never before dreamed of.

When she graduated, she convinced her somewhat dubious father to allow her to go on to graduate school. She became one of Professor Abramson's grad students. She had not only fallen in love with biochemistry, she had fallen in love with Luke Abramson.

He was more than thirty years her senior, and happily married. To him, she was merely another bright young kid, a willing pair of hands to work in his laboratory for the usual grad student's pittance. She never let the professor know her inner feelings, never came on to him the way some of the other young women did. Not that it did them any good; the professor was blind to their advances.

Shannon never returned to Wyoming to live. Once she got her PhD she moved to California and won a position with a start-up biotech company. She spent Christmases and holidays with her father, of course. But she married Carter Bartram, the dynamic young CEO of a rapidly growing biotech firm.

She still kept in touch with Professor Abramson, distantly, professionally. She met him at scientific conferences, and once in Washington, D.C., where he won an award for his groundbreaking research.

When Abramson's wife died of cancer, Shannon was tempted to fly to Massachusetts. Instead, she sent a sympathy card and a large donation to the National Cancer Society. Then her husband was diagnosed with prostate cancer. It took several years, and they tried every treatment known to science, but in the end the cancer killed him.

Shannon used the money she inherited to build the Bartram Research Laboratories, on a hilltop in her late husband's native Oregon. By now she was a handsome woman in her late forties, with a generous figure and short-cropped hair that was kept golden blond by her stylists. She dressed well. She personally directed the work of the Bartram Labs, following the published research of Professor Abramson and other leaders in various fields of biochemistry.

And now Luke Abramson was stepping out of the sedan she had

sent to fetch him. She stood on the top step of the main entrance to her laboratory facility, resisting the urge to rush down and greet him.

Luke looked trim and fit. His hair seemed darker than she remembered it. He looked almost like the man she had fallen so girlishly in love with, all those years ago.

Then she saw Luke help a little girl out of the car. And behind the child came a slim young woman with high cheekbones and glossy dark shoulder-length hair.

Nottaway Plantation

JERRY HIGHTOWER FELT tired. And exasperated. The story that Lorenzo Merriwether was telling smelled like a dead prairie dog to him, but he couldn't shake the man out of it.

They were sitting in Merriwether's so-called library. It looked more like a picture gallery to Hightower. The owner of Nottaway Plantation was trying to look relaxed, but Hightower sensed an inner tension. Merriwether was wearing a soft maroon velour pullover shirt over a pair of chinos. And an osteopathic white plastic collar around his neck.

For the tenth time, Hightower asked, "How did Abramson come to this place? You said you'd never met him before he arrived at your door."

Merriwether had a phony smile painted on his face as he leaned back in the wing chair he was sitting on and crossed his long legs carefully. Hightower thought the man was stalling for time to think up an answer.

"So?" he prodded.

"A friend phoned me and asked me to take him in."

"A friend? Who?"

"I'd rather not say."

"Would you rather be arrested for obstructing an investigation?"

Hightower said it softly, gently, almost as if he were asking about the weather. But the threat was there.

Merriwether's smile dimmed a fraction. "Look. My friend heard that Abramson was traveling with his sick granddaughter and needed a place to stay for a week or so. That's all there is to it."

"How'd your friend know Abramson?"

Merriwether spread his arms in a gesture of helplessness. "Don't ask me."

Hightower stared at the man for several moments. Pointless, he told himself. This guy has his story down pat and he's not going to budge from it.

"All right," he said, trying to switch from bad cop to good cop. "Why did Abramson leave and where did he go?"

"Something spooked him. Maybe he was afraid to stay in one place for too long. Maybe he was afraid you'd catch up with him."

Smart, Hightower thought. Put the blame on me.

Pointing at the collar, he asked, "Does your neck injury have anything to do with his leaving?"

Merriwether chuckled faintly. "This? This comes from playing basketball with kids twenty years younger than me."

"Where'd Abramson go?"

"Don't know. He and the woman doctor with him were clever enough to do their talking out on the verandas of their rooms, where we couldn't pick up their voices."

"You mean you had their rooms bugged?"

Suddenly uncomfortable, Merriwether nodded mutely. And winced at the motion.

"Why?"

"All the guest rooms are bugged. It's kind of a hobby of mine."

"Like a Peeping Tom."

"Listening, not peeping."

"And you don't want to tell me who your friend is, the one who asked you take Abramson in?"

"Rather not."

"Then let me have the CDs from your bugs." Before Merriwether could object, Hightower went on. "Maybe the tech guys at our lab can get more out of them than you can."

"Maybe they can," Merriwether agreed. Reluctantly.

HIGHTOWER FELT DEAD beat as he drove through the gathering darkness of night, down Interstate 10 toward New Orleans, skirting the edge of Lake Pontchartrain. He'd started the day in Minneapolis, had to switch planes twice before finally landing at Baton Rouge for his frustrating late-afternoon interview with Merriwether, and now was heading for the FBI office in New Orleans.

Sleep can wait, he told himself. Dinner can wait. The CDs in his jacket pocket might be important. He'd phoned the New Orleans office and alerted them that he was coming in with evidence that had to be examined immediately. The clerk he talked to complained that it was almost quitting time for the lab, but Hightower promised to get overtime pay for whoever checked out the CDs. The clerk agreed to find a technician who would wait up all night if he had to, under those terms.

It was well past eight P.M. by the time he parked in the fenced-in lot behind the bank building that housed the FBI office. Hightower's last meal had been the miserly snacks offered on the last leg of his flight from Minneapolis, early in the afternoon. He felt hungry, tired, and angry at himself for not being able to shake the real story out of Merriwether. There's more going on here than a runaway grandfather, he realized.

At the root of it all was a sick eight-year-old child, probably scared half to death, far from her mother and father. Hightower thought of his own nieces and how frightened they would be under the same circumstances.

If the New Orleans office can't find anything on the CDs, I'll have to send them to Washington. I'll find a motel after I drop these discs off at the local office.

He'd heard tales in his childhood of Navaho warriors of old and their initiation rites, enduring hunger, thirst, privation in the burning sun of the desert. All I've got to do is postpone dinner for a few hours. And then get some sleep. It's been a long day.

L ORENZO MERRIWETHER SAT on the cushioned sofa in his living room, his long arms stretched across the sofa's back, his longer legs propped up on the glass-topped coffee table. The collar chafed his neck, and the mint julep on the coffee table didn't seem to be helping any.

Quenton Fisk's chiseled features glared at him from the display screen above the fireplace. Merriwether wished he were watching the Chicago Bulls game, but he realized with an inward sigh that business had to come before pleasure—even when he had a fair-sized bet riding on his former team.

"And you gave him the CDs?" Fisk asked, like a district attorney grilling a hostile witness. He was in his shirtsleeves and a set of dead black suspenders.

Keeping himself from shrugging because of his neck, Merriwether said, "Wasn't much else I could do. I kept your name out of it, though, just like you said."

"Those CDs are my . . . eh, your property. He had no right to take them."

"You try saying no to the FBI."

His stern expression relaxing a little, Fisk mused, "Well, maybe he can get something out of them that we can't."

"Maybe."

"The real question is, where has Abramson gone? And how can we get him before the FBI does?"

"If I were you," Merriwether said slowly, "I'd put a man on Hightower's tail. That way, the FBI'd be working for us, sort of."

Fisk nodded minimally. "Might be a good idea. At least we ought to cover that base."

"Yeah."

Bartram Laboratories

S HANNON BARTRAM WATCHED Luke carry his granddaughter up the steps to the entrance of her domain. The child looked like an eighty-year-old.

Behind them, this sleek younger woman stood tall and smiling, a heavy tote bag slung over one shoulder.

Shannon wondered what she should say. As Luke came to a stop before her, with the child in his arms, she heard herself proclaim, "Welcome, Luke. Mi casa es su casa."

He broke into a guarded smile. "Thanks, Shannon. Thanks a million."

"Come on in," Shannon said. "I've set up a room in the clinic for your granddaughter."

As they stepped through the glass doors of the entrance, Luke introduced Tamara, ending with, "She's Angela's personal physician."

"How do you do?" Shannon said.

Without waiting for an answer, she led the three of them into the building, through its central corridor, and along a covered walkway to the small clinic in the rear. The main building was humming, Luke saw. Through open doors along the corridor he could see white-smocked men and women bent over the tools of their trade, microscopes and spectrometers, centrifuges and computer screens.

Shannon chattered away as they came to the room prepared for Angela. Two nurses in starched white uniforms were already there, waiting for them.

"I think you'll find everything you need for Angela right here," Shannon said. "And if there's anything we don't have, I'll see to it that we get it right away."

"That's great," Luke said, laying Angela gently on the bed.

Shannon eyed the child for a moment, then turned to Luke. "Progeria?"

"It's a side effect of the treatment I'm giving her: telomerase inhibitors."

"Ah. To kill off the tumors."

"It's working. I think the tumors are gone."

Tamara interjected, "But we need a high-resolution MRI to make certain."

"Of course," said Shannon. "We have one of the best in the country here. Is her wrist broken?"

"Hairline fracture," Tamara said.

"I'll call a local osteopath and have him look at it."

"Good," said Luke.

Once they got Angela comfortably settled, Shannon gestured to the nurses. "I've set up round-the-clock care for her. What's her feeding schedule?"

Tamara started to give her the details, but Shannon said, "Tell the nurses, why don't you? They'll enter it into the computer schedule."

With a glance at Luke, Tamara stepped over to talk with the nurses.

Shannon said to Luke, "This is the first time in years that you've been here."

"I came for the dedication ceremony," he remembered.

"Eight years ago."

He nodded.

Looking at him curiously, Shannon said, "You seem . . . well, younger than you did then. Your hair's darker, longer."

"I haven't had a chance to get a haircut the past few weeks."

"And your skin isn't as wrinkled."

He admitted, "I've been taking telomerase accelerators."

Shannon's breath caught in her throat.

Luke explained, "A seventy-five-year-old coot can't go barging across the country they way we've been. I'd have collapsed from arthritis or asthma or a heart attack."

"But accelerators can lead to tumor growth, Luke. You know that."

"I know. But it's a risk I've got to take."

With a sigh, Shannon said, "Come on, let's get some dinner into us."

Luke called to Tamara, "You hungry?"

"Starved."

"Come on, then."

After promising Angela that they'd come back to say good night to her, Luke allowed Shannon to lead them through a small but gleamingly immaculate cafeteria and into a still smaller dining room behind it. The table was already set for two; Shannon told the white-coated Hispanic waitress, younger than her overweight body suggested, to put another setting in place.

"Executive dining room," Luke said, looking around. The room was tastefully decorated with paintings of the Columbia River valley. "Nice."

"I like my comforts," said Shannon.

Another Hispanic, male, dark-skinned, joined the chunky young woman to serve the three of them a passably fair dinner. Shannon ordered a bottle of wine.

Luke recognized the label. "Still drinking the local stuff."

"They make a very drinkable sauvignon blanc," Shannon said, as she poured for them all.

As dinner progressed, Luke filled Shannon in on all the details of Angela's case and their trek across the country.

"So here we are," he concluded, with a cheerfulness he didn't really feel.

"And the tumors are gone?" Shannon asked.

Tamara replied, "To the best resolution of the equipment we had available in Louisiana."

"We'll get you the best resolution available anywhere, tomorrow."

Luke nodded as he raised a forkful of poached salmon to his mouth.

"But what about the progeria?" Shannon asked.

"Angie's been off the inhibitors for less than twenty-four hours. If her body doesn't start producing telomerase at its normal rate, we'll have to give her accelerators."

"And risk new tumor growth."

"I was thinking of injecting a second set of p53 into her, too. She only has one."

Shannon nodded. "We can do that here. It might help."

Tamara spoke up. "So we'll hold off on the accelerators until we give her the p53?"

They discussed that back and forth right through dessert. At last they got up from the crumb-littered table.

"I've put you in a room in the clinic, right next to Angela's, Luke," Shannon said. Turning to Tamara, she added, "I hadn't expected another person, so you'll be sleeping in a guest suite upstairs, on the top floor."

"Fine," said Tamara.

Feeling somewhat embarrassed, Luke confessed, "Look, Shannon, we left Baton Rouge with nothing but the clothes on our backs."

"And our laptops," Tamara added.

"We'll need to do some shopping . . ."

"Of course," said Shannon. "I'll put Jesús at your disposal tomorrow. He can drive you into Portland, all the shopping malls."

"After Angela's MRI," said Tamara.

"Certainly. After the MRI."

The Oval Office

S HE SEEMS TIRED, thought Paul Rossov.

The President of the United States sat behind her massive desk in the Oval Office, frowning worriedly at the three people sitting before her. She wore a softly draped pearl gray dress that disguised her figure. Some women lose weight when traveling; she tended to gain, and she had just returned from nearly a week of campaigning. Her short blond hair was freshly coiffed, though, and while her eyes were puffy, they looked alert, almost angry.

She didn't like what she was hearing, Rossov knew.

This was a "for your ears only" meeting. No one was recording what was being said. The only people in the room were the President, Rossov, the Attorney General, and the Secretary of the Treasury. The electronic equipment that normally took down every word spoken in the Oval Office had been switched off by the President herself.

She had acceded to the highest office in the land when the incumbent had suddenly and ingloriously died in bed with his mistress. So far, that detail of his death had been kept quiet. As far as the news media and the public knew, the late President had died alone in his sleep, of a heart attack, while his wife was attending a feminist convention in Chicago.

Although the next presidential election was more than a year away, the woman behind the desk was already campaigning up and down the nation to be elected in her own right. She had just returned from a tour of the western states and was obviously suffering from jet lag, lack of sleep, and the tremendous anxiety that is the inevitable companion to tremendous drive.

And now this.

"It will wreck the economy," the Secretary of the Treasury was saying, his deep voice dolorous, like the crack of doom.

Incredulous, the President asked, "One man's work?"

The Treasury Secretary was an old friend and backer, bald and portly, as if he'd never bothered to read any of the government's many publications on the dangers of obesity.

He nodded hard enough to make his wattles jiggle. "Social Security and Medicare are in bad enough shape as it is. If people start living past a hundred—"

"That won't happen for years," scoffed the Attorney General. "Decades."

The AG was an almost painfully thin black woman with a thick mop of dark spiky hair, flinty eyes, and a hard lantern jaw. She was wearing a burnt orange sweater over her blouse and skirt. Rossov and the Treasury Secretary were both in standard D.C. uniform: gray three-piece suits, although Rossov's ensemble was stylishly enriched with hair-thin silver pinstripes.

Sitting between Treasury and Justice, Rossov said, "It's going to happen a lot sooner if this man Abramson isn't brought under control."

"It could drive the nation into bankruptcy," Treasury moaned.

"We mustn't allow it to happen," said Rossov, with iron in his tone.

"Never?" the President asked.

Treasury answered, "Not until we've got Medicare and Social Security firmly funded."

The President said sourly, "Those wingdings on the Hill have been kicking that can down the road for twenty years and more."

"Giving people the ability to live to a hundred, a hundred and fifty . . . that would break those programs, blow the budget apart," Treasury repeated. "And the insurance industry! Private pension plans! We can't let that happen. We just can't."

"How can we stop it?"

Casting a glance at the Attorney General, Rossov said, "This man Abramson has got to be found and tucked away someplace where he can't do any harm."

"Wait a minute," said the Attorney General. "From what you've told me about his work, it can also cure cancer?"

"Could be."

"I've had breast cancer," the AG said. "They caught it in time, thank God. But what if it comes back? This man's work could save my life."

Leaning back in his chair, Rossov replied, "That's just what we're talking about. If we let this man go on, just about everybody will want to take advantage of his work. Nobody wants to have cancer! Nobody wants to die!"

Staring at him, the Attorney General said, "So you're saying that you'd rather let people go on having cancer, go on dying?"

"The economy can't stand having people live twice as long as they do now. It'll ruin the nation!"

With a grim smile, Treasury said, "Do you know why they set the retirement age at sixty-five, back when Social Security was started? It was because the average life expectancy was only sixty. Now you're talking about doubling that! Maybe tripling it!"

The AG shook her head stubbornly. "Can't you change the economy? Fix it so that this won't ruin things?"

The President let out a short, humorless bark of a laugh. "*You* try getting any meaningful changes through Congress."

"But—"

"I'm not going to let this issue swamp my re-election campaign," the President said flatly.

Rossov repeated, "Abramson has got to be found and put away

someplace where he can't have a destabilizing effect on the economy."

"But . . . cancer," the Attorney General whimpered.

"I know," said Rossov. "My father died of cancer. Chances are I will, too."

Treasury leaned forward and whispered like a conspirator. "Of course, we could let the man carry on his work in a suitably protected facility. Just because we can't release his discoveries to the general public doesn't mean certain people in privileged positions can't avail themselves of his results."

The President's expression turned thoughtful.

But the Attorney General asked, "So you want my people to find this Abramson. Okay. We find him. Then what?"

"He's got to be put someplace where we can control him," said Rossov. "Let him keep on with his research, but don't let it get out to the public."

The AG shook her head. "That's illegal."

"No, it's not," Rossov countered. "People have been held incommunicado before. Detained indefinitely."

"Terrorists," said the Attorney General. "Mob bosses. This man's just a scientist."

"A scientist who could blow the economy apart," the Treasury Secretary growled.

"He's wanted for kidnapping," Rossov pointed out.

Folding her skinny arms over her meager chest, the Attorney General insisted, "I can't tell my people to do something like this." Staring at the President, she added, "Not without an executive order."

The Oval Office fell absolutely silent. At last the President nodded and said, "See to it, Paul."

Rossov nodded back, knowing that his signature would be on the order and, if things blew up, the President could plausibly deny she knew about it, while he would obediently fall on his sword.

Ruefully, he remembered another Vice President who rose to the top through the death of his President. When Harry Truman occupied this office he kept a sign on his desk: THE BUCK STOPS HERE. The sign was nowhere in sight now.

Bartram Laboratories

"Y OU KNOW, THIS is the first almost-normal day I've spent since we left Massachusetts," said Tamara Minteer.

She and Luke were riding back to the Bartram Labs after an afternoon of shopping for clothes. Luke had insisted on paying for everything out of the diminishing bankroll he carried in his wallet. Tamara wanted to at least buy their lunch, but that would mean using her credit card, and Luke balked at that.

The MRI scans of Angela's brain that morning had been very positive. No trace of tumors. Luke had let out a whoop of victory that startled the lab technicians and made Angela laugh at her grandfather's antics.

"Now if the progeria reverses . . . ," Tamara had said.

"If it doesn't," Luke had countered, "we'll put her on telomerase accelerators and bring her back to normal."

Tamara nodded without pointing out that the accelerators might lead to new tumors. She didn't have to say it; Luke knew.

But for a few hours they left all that behind them as they traipsed from one shop to another at the biggest mall in Portland and bought everything from underwear to winter hats.

Sitting in the back seat of the Infiniti, with Jesús driving up front, Luke said, "Let's have dinner at a top-grade restaurant."

"I'm still full from lunch," Tamara said. "Besides, we're halfway to the labs now."

Luke nodded, disappointed. It would have been fun having a quiet dinner, he thought. Just the two of us. Then he realized that he was thinking of a quiet *romantic* dinner. And why not? he asked himself. Tamara's a wonderfully good-looking woman, and I . . . Lord, I haven't felt this way about a woman in years. Ages.

Tamara broke into his thoughts. "How many women are in love with you, Luke?"

Startled, he blurted, "In love with me?"

With a mischievous smile, she said, "There was Petrone in Bethesda, and now Bartram here in Oregon. How many other women do you have stashed away someplace?"

Luke stared at her. "What're you talking about? Shannon was a student of mine. We never had anything going on between us."

"Maybe you didn't, but she did."

"Nonsense."

"If I wasn't around to protect you . . ." She let the thought dangle.

Luke saw the curve of her lips. "Listen," he said. "I never had anything going with either one of them, or anybody else, for that matter. I was a faithful husband. If you'd known Adele, you'd know why."

More seriously, Tamara said, "I'm sure you were, Luke. But she's gone, and Shannon is interested in you."

"Bullshit."

"For real. Keep your guard up."

"Bullshit," he repeated. Then he added, "Besides, if I was going to get interested in a woman, it'd be a good-looking chick like you."

It was Tamara's turn to go wide-eyed with surprise.

THERE WAS NOTHING more stupefyingly boring than listening to other people's conversations. All morning long, Hightower sat in the audio technician's cramped little booth and strained to hear a clue, a hint, a whisper that might tell him where Abramson had fled to.

The young technician had worked all through the night to amplify the weak voices on the CDs. Now—baggy-eyed and listless, with four emptied cardboard mugs of coffee littering his worktable—he was playing them for Hightower to hear.

The booth was the size of a casket stood on end, Hightower thought. Windowless, airless. The only chair they could find for him was a rickety three-legged stool. Hightower planted himself on it without complaint, so close to the young technician that he could smell the kid's body odor. Little geek didn't shower this morning, he told himself.

Nothing. Nearly two hours of nothing. Most of the chatter between Abramson and Dr. Minteer was about the condition of their patient, Abramson's granddaughter. Several times they left whichever room they were in and went outside, where the microphones couldn't pick up their voices.

Hightower shook his head. Amateurs. Merriwether was an amateur at bugging his guests' rooms. A pro would have included those verandas.

Or maybe, Hightower thought, Merriwether had installed the listening devices suddenly, on the spur of the moment, when he'd learned that Abramson would be coming to stay at Nottaway.

The tech running the machines was a bushy-haired kid; looked like he was still troubled with acne. Knew his business, though. He slouched in his wheeled swivel chair, earphones clamped to his head, and tweaked the knobs on his equipment to keep the sound as clear and intelligible as possible.

Hightower's thoughts drifted as he sat there, stuffed into the stifling booth beside the tech, listening to the man he was supposed to be finding.

Got to check Merriwether's phone records, he told himself. Find out who his "friend" is, the guy that sent Abramson to him. And get the Washington office to pull up a record of all Abramson's graduate students; they're the people who'd be helping him, no doubt.

He wished the law weren't so tough about hacking into e-mails. He was certain that Abramson must be calling his daughter every now and then. After a couple of messages too brief to be traced, he'd stopped phoning her. Must be using e-mail or Skype or something. I'll need a judge's order to go after that, and no judge is going to sign off on a case that boils down to a family squabble.

"You hear that?" The technician's sharp-toned voice broke into his thoughts.

"Hear what?" Hightower asked.

"Listen." The kid fiddled with the knobs on his console, and Hightower heard the squawking gibberish of rewind.

Then he heard Abramson's voice. "I've been thinking, once we're in Oregon, we could even do some genetic engineering, give Angie a full complement of the p53 gene, protect her against tumor formation."

Oregon! Hightower felt a flash of hope.

Minteer's voice replied, "If you can get us out to Oregon."

He strained to hear more, but their talk focused on the granddaughter's condition. Not another word about where they were going.

"Oregon," Hightower muttered.

Lifting the earphones from his head, the tech said, "That's the only mention of a destination in all their gabble."

"What's in Oregon that would attract them?"

The kid spread his hands. "Hey, I'm only an audio geek. You're the detective."

Hightower nodded. "So they went to the airport and flew to Oregon. No record of them on any of the airlines, though. We've checked that already."

"Private plane?" the tech suggested.

"Or they rented a car at the airport and they're driving to Oregon."

"With a sick kid?"

"Hmm." Hightower thought it over. He pushed himself up from the stool he'd been sitting on. "I'm going to check the charter plane companies. You make a copy of those CDs and send it to my office in Washington. The originals go back to Merriwether, at Nottaway Plantation."

Fisk Tower

QUENTON FISK ALWAYS felt uncomfortable when he had to talk with the head of his security department.

A veteran New York Police Department detective, Edward Novack was not a particularly large or imposing man. His job with the Fisk Corporation was mainly administrative: He oversaw the security guards and electronic systems that protected Fisk's employees and offices.

But there was something about Novack, something unsettling. Maybe it was the way he moved, like a lean, prowling cat, always on the balls of his feet, always ready to spring at you. He had retired from the NYPD in the midst of a scandal about police brutality against homosexuals.

Fisk knew that Novack was capable of violence, bone-breaking, blood-letting violence. The realization made him nervous in the man's presence.

As he explained the Abramson situation to Novack, the security chief's lean, hard face remained expressionless. His eyes were half closed, as if he were drifting to sleep. Yet Fisk knew the man heard every word he said. And understood.

"So you want me to have somebody tail an FBI agent?" Novack said, in his heavy, rasping voice. It almost sounded as if he were sneering at the idea.

"I don't think the FBI would be willing to allow a private security employee to team up with one of their agents."

Novack cocked his head to one side. "If the private security employee had something to offer to the FBI . . ."

"Some information, you mean," said Fisk.

Novack nodded.

Fisk thought, What could I tell them? That I knowingly hid Abramson away at Lonzo's place? That I helped and abetted a fugitive wanted for kidnapping?

The buzz of his intercom broke into his musings.

"Agent Hightower calling you, sir," came his assistant's voice.

Novack made a grim smile. "Speak of the devil."

"Tell him I'm not available. I'll call him tomorrow morning. Get his number."

Novack's smile turned cynical. "Saying no to the FBI. Gutsy."

"I'll talk to him," Fisk replied, annoyed, "once I've got a story worked out to tell him."

LUKE AND TAMARA had dinner with Shannon in her private dining room at the Bartram Labs complex.

Shannon wants to come on to me? Luke asked himself as he spooned up some French onion soup. Barely tasting it, he realized, She's going out on a limb to take us in like this. Is it because she's interested in me? I'm a seventy-five-year-old man, for chrissakes. I'm not some romantic hotshot; never have been.

But there she was, sitting at the head of the table, with Luke at her side and Tamara across the table from him. What would be going on if Tamara weren't here? Shannon was wearing a sensibly comfortable pink sheath with a pearl necklace draped over her V-shaped neckline and more pearls at her wrists and earlobes. And perfume: some sort of musky scent.

As the main course was being served, Shannon said very evenly, "I want to do a complete workup on you."

Luke sputtered into the wine he was drinking. Coughing, gagging, he croaked, "You what?"

Tamara started to get out of her chair, but Luke waved her back down, swallowed hard, and regained his breath.

Ignoring his distress, Shannon replied, "A complete physical. You've been taking telomerase accelerators for a couple of weeks now; it's time to check on how your body is reacting."

"He looks younger," Tamara said. "His reflexes are awfully good for his age."

"Reflexes?" Shannon snapped.

"I slugged a security guard," Luke explained.

"And knocked down a former basketball star."

"Yeah, but you knocked him out."

Shannon said, "You can't just keep on flying by the seat of your pants, Luke. You need an organized program of therapy. And I have the equipment and the people here to handle that."

"I'm here to make Angela well," he began.

"We're doing that," Shannon interrupted. "She's getting the best care possible. But you need care, too, Luke. You're running a terrible risk with those accelerators, you know."

"I know," he murmured.

Tamara said, "The accelerators could lead to tumor growth."

"That's right. The fountain of youth doesn't come for free. We've got to see what's going on inside your body."

Luke realized he'd been avoiding such a test. He'd started using the accelerators because he couldn't take Angie across the country without them. But he didn't want to face up to the possibility that the side effects could kill him.

"I'm all right," he said. "My skin's smoothing out. My reflexes are sharper. Even my hair is darker. No symptoms of tumors."

"Not yet," said Tamara. Luke glared at her.

Patiently, Shannon said, "Luke, you know as well as I do that most cancers don't show any symptoms in their early stages. If you wait until you're symptomatic it could be too late."

"I'm all right," he repeated stubbornly.

"You're taking a complete physical tomorrow," Shannon said.

Tamara added, "No ifs, ands, or buts."

New Orleans FBI Headquarters

ORNING WAS GRAY and cold in New Orleans. Smoke from chimneys seemed to congeal in the still, gelid air. Hightower awoke with the sun, as usual, and quickly showered, shaved, dressed, and made his way to the local FBI office, a few blocks' walk from the motel where he'd spent the night. Despite the chill snap in the air, he wore only his usual suede jacket.

He picked up coffee and a greasy croissant on the way, longing for the fried bread and chilis of his native Navaho territory. The arid high desert was so different from this reclaimed swampland. Hell, he thought, half this city is below sea level.

The local office manager had permitted Hightower to use a private cubicle that belonged to an agent who was on the road on an assignment. It was a small compartment, but at least it had a window that looked onto a parking lot, a wheeled desk chair that groaned under Hightower's weight, and a first-rate computer/communications system, with a high-definition display screen taking up most of one wall.

If ever I've seen a phony smile, Hightower thought as he looked at Quenton Fisk's image on the screen, that's it.

"What can I do for you, Agent Hightower?" Fisk asked, with

forced cordiality. "I'm sorry I wasn't available yesterday, but I'm all yours this morning."

Hightower went straight for the jugular. "You can stop the tap dance you've been doing and tell me the whole truth about your relationship with Professor Abramson."

"Tap dance? Relationship?"

"You didn't tell me you're Abramson's sole funding source."

"I didn't realize that would be important to you," said Fisk.

"Or that you told Lorenzo Merriwether to take in the professor, his granddaughter, and Dr. Minteer."

For an instant, Fisk looked shocked. Then he forced his smile again. "You've been poking into my phone records."

Hightower nodded once.

"Don't you need a court order for that?"

"Never mind. What is your relationship with Professor Abramson? Where has he gone?"

Fisk looked away for a moment, as though gathering his thoughts. Then, "My *relationship*, as you put it, is strictly financial. The Fisk Foundation is supporting his work. The foundation is a charitable organization and funds cutting-edge research in a number of fields."

"Where's Abramson gone?"

"I wish I knew," Fisk answered. "He bolted out of Nottaway quite suddenly. I think he was afraid you'd discovered his whereabouts."

Blame the hunter for the prey's actions, Hightower thought. Aloud, he asked, "Why did you get Merriwether to take the professor in? You knew he was a fugitive from justice."

"Now wait a minute," Fisk countered. "When you first talked to me you said Abramson was suspected of kidnapping. From what the professor himself told me, it sounded like a family squabble."

"With a little girl's life hanging in the balance."

"Exactly. Abramson convinced me that his granddaughter would die unless he could treat her. I decided to give him a safe haven for a little while and see what he could do for the child."

"Yet you knew he was a fugitive."

"He's not a mass murderer, for God's sake. I knew exactly where he was, if and when the time came to turn him in."

"But he skipped out on you."

"Sadly, yes."

"And you have no idea of where he's gone?"

"None whatsoever."

Hightower studied the man's face on the high-def screen. The phony smile was gone. Fisk looked concerned, almost worried.

"I'm not the only one who's after him, am I?"

Suddenly puzzled, Fisk asked, "What do you mean by that?"

"Abramson's an important investment of yours. You want him found just as much as I do."

"I suppose that's right," Fisk admitted.

"So it's important that you be completely forthcoming with me. Where's he gone?"

With a helpless shrug, Fisk said, "Believe me, if I knew I'd tell you."

Hightower didn't believe the man for an instant.

Fisk put on an earnest face and said, "Agent Hightower, I'd like to make a suggestion."

"What is it?"

"I'd like to have the head of my security department work with you. He'll have clear access to all my foundation's files, all the records of Abramson's work, his associates, the meetings he's attended. That would help you, wouldn't it?"

"It might."

Nodding vigorously, Fisk said, "His name is Edward Novack. Top-flight man. I'll tell him to fly to Washington to meet you in person."

Hightower thought it over swiftly. He wants to plant a spy in my operation, he realized. But if I say no, he can complain to his politician friends that I turned down his offer of help.

Putting on his own phony smile, Hightower said, "That would

be fine, Mr. Fisk. I'm in New Orleans at present, but I'll be back in my office in Boston bright and early tomorrow morning. I'll tell the receptionist to expect Mr. Novack. In Boston."

"Good."

"And thank you, Mr. Fisk."

Hightower cut the connection, thinking about the tribal wisdom of his people, and the old days when white men gave blankets freely to the red men. Blankets that were infected with smallpox, of course.

Bartram Laboratories

S HANNON WENT WITH Luke every step of the way through his physical exam. While Tamara stayed with Angela, Shannon led Luke to the basement of the clinic and a set of rooms that varied from a mini-gymnasium to the MRI lab where Angela's brain scans had been done.

Luke submitted to stress tests, jogging along on the treadmill, and gritted his teeth when a nurse took a blood sample. Two vials' worth. Then he stripped down to his skivvies and an MD poked and prodded him from his scalp to the soles of his feet.

The doctor was a young man, totally unembarrassed when he asked Luke to drop his drawers and bend over the examining table.

Prostate exam, Luke knew. Painless but humiliating.

He looked across the room at Shannon, who gave him an impish smile. "I'll wait outside," she said, before Luke could ask her to leave.

But as she opened the door, she said, straight-faced, "Don't take too long." Then she broke into a giggle as she left the room.

Finally Luke spent nearly an hour in the cavernous MRI machine, as the table he lay upon slowly slid through the tunnel while the machine took images of his innards.

At last, dressed and on his feet once again, he stepped out into the area's little waiting room. Shannon was the only person there. She immediately popped to her feet.

"Have you been sitting out here all this time?" Luke asked her.

"Of course not," she replied. "They called me when they were finishing up with you."

"Well, they have enough data on me now to keep them busy for a few hours. I'm going upstairs to see how Angela is doing."

"It's past one o'clock. Don't you want some lunch?"

"After I look in on Angie."

"Dr. Minteer's with your granddaughter," Shannon said, with a slight edge in her voice. "Come on, Luke, let's have a bite of lunch."

He spied the telephone on the corner table. "Let me call her."

"Dr. Minteer?"

"Angie."

Luke steered clear of using his cell phone. Might be traced, he thought. Over the past few days he'd agonized over letting Angie call her mother, back in Massachusetts. How to get a message to Norrie without the freaking FBI tracing it back to where I am? He'd come to the conclusion that he'd have Angie make a CD voice recording, send it by FedEx to Van McAllister in Philadelphia, and have Van forward it to Norrie and Del. Van will do that for me. He can just drop the package in a FedEx depository someplace; that way it won't be traced back to him. Or me.

Tamara picked up the phone in Angie's room.

"How's she doing?" Luke asked.

"Not bad," came Tamara's tawny voice. "She's doing a crossword puzzle. Wait a minute . . ."

Angela's higher-pitched voice came through. "Hi, Grandpa."

"Hello, Angel. How're you feeling?"

"Okay, sort of."

"Sort of?"

"My back hurts. Just a little."

"Maybe you need to walk a bit, get some exercise."

"I guess."

"Is your wrist bothering you?"

"No. Tamara says the cast can come off in another two days."

"That's wonderful," Luke said. "Put Tamara back on, will you, honey."

Tamara agreed that a little exercise would be helpful. "But not too much. She's pretty frail, still."

"I know," said Luke. He had though about sending a DVD to his daughter but immediately realized that one look at Angela's skeletal condition would send Norrie into convulsions. A CD recording of her voice would be enough, he thought.

Angela came back on the line. "Can I go outside, Grandpa?"

"It's pretty chilly out there," he said.

"I'll dress warm. I'd like to go outside. I'm tired of staying in this room."

"Okay. You ask Tamara about it. She's your doctor. She knows what's best for you."

"Uh-huh."

"Love you, Angel."

"Love you, too, Grandpa."

Luke hung up and allowed Shannon to lead him to her private dining room.

BEFORE LEAVING THE FBI office to go to the airport, Hightower started calling the private air services in Baton Rouge, looking for a flight Abramson might have chartered. The second company on his alphabetically arranged list was Bayou Air Services.

A young woman answered his call. Once Hightower identified himself as an FBI agent, she bucked his call to the office manager.

"Sir," the man asked politely, "no offense, but how do I know you're really from the FBI?"

Hightower sighed inwardly. Can't blame the guy for being careful.

"Call the New Orleans FBI office and ask for Agent Hightower," he said. Then he hung up and waited.

It took nearly ten minutes, but at last his phone rang. The Bayou Air Services manager was on the line.

"Hello again," said Hightower. "I hope you're convinced now."

The man was very apologetic. Hightower cut to the chase as quickly as he could and, to his delight, learned that Luke Abramson had indeed booked a flight two days earlier. With a very sick-looking little girl and a very good-looking young woman. And paid in cash.

Bingo! Hightower exulted silently.

"Where'd they fly to?" he asked.

"Let's see . . . Portland."

"Portland, Maine?"

"No. Oregon."

L UKE WENT THROUGH lunch as quickly as he decently could, talking with Shannon mostly about inconsequential matters, old reminiscences, the work of Bartram Laboratories.

"The university fired you?" Shannon asked, indignant. "But you have tenure!"

"Being accused of kidnapping is enough cause to break tenure, apparently," he said, a little ruefully.

"Without a hearing?"

Shrugging, Luke replied, "They didn't know where to find me."

"Well . . . ," she said. "You could stay right here. We have all the facilities you need."

"Shannon, you're harboring a man being hunted by the FBI."

With a wave of her hand, she replied, "Oh, you'll get that straightened out." Then she asked, "Won't you?"

"I hope so," he said. "I really hope so."

Boston FBI Headquarters

HIGHTOWER WAS LOOKING forward to a night's sleep in his own bed, but once he retrieved his car from the long-term parking lot at Logan Airport, instead of heading for his apartment he drove through the Ted Williams Tunnel and the growling, honking late-afternoon traffic to his office in downtown Boston.

No sooner had he slid into his desk chair and turned on his computer than the chief appeared in his doorway, looking his usual elegant self in a charcoal gray three-piece suit.

"We have a visitor," the chief said, before Hightower could even say hello. He looked very serious, almost grave.

"A visitor?"

"In my office," said the chief.

Hightower got up from his chair and followed him. Can't be Fisk's security man, he thought as they made their way along the corridor. I told Fisk I wouldn't be here in the office until tomorrow morning.

Sitting in one of the cushioned chairs in front of the director's desk was a youngish man with thinning dirty blond hair and probing gray eyes. Thin nose, pointed chin, long slim fingers, like a pianist's. The gray pinstriped suit he wore told Hightower he was a bureaucrat of some sort.

"This is Mr. Rossov," said the director as he stepped behind his desk and sat down. "He's from the White House."

Hightower started to extend his hand, but Rossov remained sitting, eying him almost suspiciously.

"Mr. Rossov," Hightower said as he lowered himself into the chair beside the White House official.

"Agent Hightower." Rossov's voice had a hard edge to it.

"Mr. Rossov has an interest in the Abramson case," said the director.

"What's the White House want with Abramson?"

"We want him found and brought in," Rossov said.

"For kidnapping?"

"That's what he's charged with, isn't it?"

Hightower grunted an affirmative, then went silent. He'd learned over the years that often enough people he was talking with would feel uncomfortable with silence and start talking just to fill in the void. Sometimes they told things they hadn't meant to.

But Rossov merely said, "This case is of interest to the highest levels of government. You can have the full cooperation of the Justice Department and the entire executive branch, anything you need to find Abramson."

The director said, "I think the Bureau has enough firepower to get the job done."

Rossov's expression was almost a grimace. "The Department of Justice will back you. Wiretapping, hacking into computer files, Skype, whatever—don't waste time waiting for court orders. This man must be found as quickly as possible."

"And the department will protect us?" the director asked.

Rossov said, "Completely. And I'm here to tell you that if you need more, I can provide it for you."

What's he saying? Hightower wondered. Does he expect us to need a SEAL team to bring in one lousy college professor?

"I'd like a briefing on where you stand on this case," Rossov said.

"Certainly," said the director, nodding toward Hightower.

Hightower ran through what he'd accomplished so far. He saw Rossov's eyes glint at the mention of Quenton Fisk's name.

"So he left Louisiana and went . . . where?" Rossov demanded.

Hightower was about to tell him about the Bayou Air Services flight to Oregon. But he hesitated.

"We're working on that," he said.

Rossov stared at him for a stony moment, then said, "Find him. It's important."

O NCE LUNCH WAS finished, Luke hurried up to Angela's room. Neither the child nor Tamara was there. She's taken Angie outside, Luke realized.

Going to the window, he saw them walking slowly along the stone pathway between buildings. They were both bundled in winter coats, with scarves over their heads. Angie's coat looked a couple of sizes too big for her. She looked so small, so frail, walking slowly, like an old, old woman. Tamara kept pace with her. Luke could see that she was talking to Angie.

Briefly he debated going down to join them. Instead, he went to his own room, opened his laptop, and started working up a report on his work of the past few days.

I THINK I'M getting better," Angela was saying.

Tamara had to trudge along slowly beside the child; her long legs could easily outpace Angela in a few strides.

"I'm sure you are," she said. "When we do your next workup tomorrow, we'll see how far you've come along."

"Grandpa says I can send a CD to my mommy and dad."

"You must miss them, I know."

"I do miss them. But Grandpa says once I'm all better I'll go home and they'll be terrifically happy."

"You bet they'll be."

Angela fell silent for a few paces. The brick path they were following wound between two of the facility's buildings. As they passed the end of them, a chill damp wind sliced along the crosswalk. Tamara shivered, despite her heavy coat and the scarf she'd wrapped around her head.

Frowning, she said to Angela, "We'd better go back in now, Angie."

"Okay." Glumly.

This kind of weather isn't good for you, Tamara said to herself. Wet cold, the kind that cuts right through you. You can feel colder here at fifty degrees than you do in Massachusetts when it's near zero.

As they neared the door to their building, Angela turned her eyes upward toward Tamara and asked, "I'm not going to die, am I?"

Surprised, Tamara answered, "No, honey. You're going to live. You're going to get all well again."

Angela said, "My grandpa won't let me die."

Tamara smiled. "That's right, Angie. He won't let you die."

She hoped it was true.

Bartram Laboratories

ONCE ANGIE HAD fallen asleep, Luke took Tamara down to the cafeteria for a late dinner. The place was practically empty; most of the staff had gone home, and half the cafeteria's counters had shut down for the night. They picked from what remained available: tomato soup, cold cuts, and cookies.

"We should have come down earlier," Luke said, half apologetically, as they unloaded their trays onto one of the long, deserted tables.

"It's all right," Tamara said. "I had a good lunch with Angie. Her appetite seems to be coming back."

Before Luke could reply, he spotted Shannon at the cafeteria's entrance. She quickly scanned the nearly empty room, then made a beeline for their table.

"What are you doing here?" she asked as she sat beside Luke. "Why didn't you go to the executive dining room?"

Luke grinned ruefully. "I didn't think they'd let us in without you."

"I waited for you," Shannon said.

Tamara said, "We stayed with Angela until she fell asleep."

As if she hadn't heard that, Shannon said, "I've been going over the results of your physical."

"Am I ready for the Olympics?" he joked.

Totally serious, Shannon said, "Your muscle tone is like a fifty-year-old's. Your reflexes are very good, too."

Luke nodded.

"Telomeres are longer than any seventy-five-year-old's I've ever seen," Shannon went on. "And your dermal pliability is excellent."

"Great. The fountain of youth is working."

"It is," said Shannon. "But . . ."

"But what?" Tamara challenged, her voice tense.

Shannon said, "PSA is elevated. Not a lot, but it's higher than normal range."

Luke frowned. "My proctology exam was okay."

"You have an enlarged prostate."

"Yeah, but I've had that for years. It's normal at my age. No nodules, no sign of cancer."

"Your blood test shows a PSA higher than normal," Shannon repeated.

Tamara asked, "How much higher?"

"A few percent above the upper limit for normal."

"Damn," Luke muttered.

"The accelerators are affecting your prostate."

"Not necessarily," said Luke. "This might be normal for a man my age."

"But you're not 'your age,'" Shannon argued. "All the other indicators show your physical age is much less than your calendar age."

"Tumors grow faster than normal cells," Tamara said, almost as if to herself.

Shannon said, "Luke, you've got to stop the accelerators."

"No," he said.

Very patiently, Shannon said, "The accelerators are extending your telomeres, but they could also be causing tumor growth. You've got to stop the treatment."

"Not yet."

"Why not, for God's sake?"

With a glance at Tamara's apprehensive face, Luke said, "I don't want to be old again. I'm going to continue the therapy."

"But the tumor growth!"

Luke clasped his hands together on the edge of the table, like a schoolboy. It was a technique he used to calm himself. Fold your hands like a good boy. Take a deep breath. Sit up straight.

At last he said, "The PSA results might be just a coincidence, nothing to do with the telomere accelerators. And my MRI didn't show any tumors, did it?"

"No," Shannon admitted. "But I want you to have another MRI tomorrow. Specifically of the pelvic area."

Luke grinned at her, sardonically. "Give me enough radiation to start tumors growing?"

"Don't be sarcastic!" Shannon snapped.

He nodded. "Okay. I'll take another MRI tomorrow. But I'm not stopping the accelerators. I want to see how young I can get."

"It's dangerous," Tamara said.

"Maybe. But you don't understand, do you? I want to find out what happens! I started this experiment and I want to see it through. I want to know how it works out."

"Even if it kills you?"

"It's not going to kill me. Besides, finding out how it works is worth the risk. I've got to know! I'm going to keep on going until I do."

Tamara shook her head. "Luke, you're doing the reverse of Angela's therapy. You've killed her tumors but made her age prematurely."

Shannon jumped in. "While you're making yourself physically younger but growing tumors."

"Maybe," Luke said stubbornly. "Maybe not. We'll just have to wait and see."

"You're being foolish," Shannon insisted.

"No, I'm being curious," Luke retorted. "That's what science is all about, isn't it? Curiosity."

"Which killed the cat," Tamara pointed out. "And a lot of people, too."

Boston FBI Headquarters

HIGHTOWER GOT INTO the office before eight A.M. and immediately started running down the list he'd obtained from the university of Professor Abramson's graduate students over the past ten years.

He was looking for someone from Oregon. But he drew a blank. Not one of the grad students hailed from the so-called Beaver State. He ran the list through his computer sorting program again. Still no joy.

The office was quiet, nearly empty this early in the morning. The secretary he shared with two other agents wasn't in yet, so Hightower got up from his desk and went to the coffee urn that the housekeeping staff kept on the hot plate in the supply closet. Whichever staffer came in earliest made it his or her first duty to start the coffee perking.

The hot plate was technically a fire hazard, Hightower knew. The director had told the staff to find a safer place for it, but he never had followed through to see that his command was obeyed. As long as his personal assistant brought him steaming hot coffee when he wanted it, he didn't investigate where the stuff was brewed.

Got to call the university and get updates on where all those grad students are, Hightower told himself as he headed back to his office, his mug of coffee in one meaty hand. Checking his wristwatch, he saw that it was too early to expect the university's offices to be open. The early bird might get the worm, he thought, but most of the worms aren't up early enough to get caught.

He was surprised to see a lean, almost stringy man standing in front of the secretary's empty desk. The visitor's face was hard, his head shaved down to a silver-gray fuzz, and he was wearing a dark blue jacket buttoned over a sports shirt and lighter slacks. He's carrying a gun, Hightower realized.

The man turned as Hightower approached. "You're Hightower?" he asked, in a low, rasping voice.

Hightower nodded once. "You must be Novack. Come on into my office."

Hightower was three times Novack's size, but he got the impression that the man could take care of himself in a brawl, despite his smaller stature. Hightower gestured to the chair in front of his desk as he went around and settled himself into his comfortable swivel chair.

"Quenton Fisk sent you," Hightower said, without preamble.

"Yeah," said Novack. "I told him you wouldn't be happy with a civilian at your elbow, but Fisk is the boss."

"And you follow orders."

"That's right." Novack's expression said that he was no happier about the situation than Hightower himself was.

"So what can you do for me that I can't do for myself?" Hightower asked.

Novack broke into a bitter smile. "You don't mince words, do you?"

"Not when I don't have to. So what can you do for me?"

"The Fisk Foundation keeps close track of the people it's funding. Names, associates, meetings they've attended, research papers they've published, that sort of thing. That might be helpful."

"I can get that kind of information with a couple of phone calls."

"Yeah, but we already have it."

Hightower made a little grunt. "Okay. I'd like to see what meetings Abramson's gone to, what papers he's published."

"You've got it."

Straight-faced, Hightower countered, "No, I don't got it. That's why I'm asking you for it."

Novack grinned again, wider this time. "Point taken. I'll get the poop to you before the day is out."

"Fine. Any idea on where Abramson's gone?"

Shifting slightly in his chair, Novack replied, "I had a conversation late yesterday with the pilot that flew him out of Baton Rouge. Fellow named Kleiner."

"And?"

"Apparently he took a bribe from Abramson to keep his mouth shut."

"And?" Hightower repeated.

"I convinced him that it would be better for his health if he told me where they'd flown."

Hightower realized that one advantage Novack had over him was that he didn't have to follow the Justice Department rules of procedure on interrogating suspects.

"How rough did you have to get?"

Novack spread his hands, palms up. "Not rough at all. Just the suggestion worked fine. He flew Abramson to Portland, Oregon."

So he knows as much as I know, Hightower thought. Does he know more?

"Why Portland?"

"He didn't know."

"You're sure?"

Nodding, Novack said, "He was almost crapping in his pants. I'm sure."

"So we need to see who Abramson knows that lives in Oregon," said Hightower.

"Yep. Like I said, I can drop that info in your lap before the day is out."

Hightower studied the man's hard-cast face. Looks like I've got a partner working with me, he told himself. He was not happy about it.

The White House

PAUL ROSSOV'S OFFICE was little more than a cramped cubicle in the basement of the West Wing. Surrounded by men and women who measured their prominence in the executive chain of command by the size and sumptuousness of their offices, Rossov was content with his trappings.

He remembered from history earlier men who had worked in the White House and achieved greatness. In particular he was fond of Averell Harriman, a man who served half a dozen Presidents and never worried about the size of his office or the title of his job description. As long as he had his President's ear he had power.

The important thing in this rat race, Rossov knew, was to have power. And power was found by being as close to the President of the United States as possible. And you got close to POTUS by accomplishing what she wanted done.

Rossov had convinced the President that Professor Luke Abramson was dangerous. Once convinced, the President had told Rossov to deal with the problem. She did not want to know how he dealt with it, only that the task had been accomplished. If things turned sour, her skirts would be clean. Rossov took the risks, and Rossov was determined to please her and reap the rewards.

He had the Treasury Department's bean counters worried that

Abramson's work could destroy Social Security and Medicare. Good. He had the Justice Department's promise of using all their muscle to find Abramson. Even better.

The question now was what to do with Abramson once the FBI found him. Jail him for kidnapping? That would mean a trial and publicity. Too risky.

The man's a scientist, Rossov mused. Maybe he'd be content to continue his research in some top government facility—under our control, of course.

How to work that? How to make Abramson *want to* work for us? We'll have to keep his results secret, certainly. Can't release the news that old age could be countered, that elderly people could be made young again.

At the same time, though, we should allow Abramson to continue his research. The Treasury Secretary had hit the nail on the head: Just because Abramson's results can't be released to the general public doesn't mean that a few selected men and women should be deprived of eternal youth.

Eternal youth. Rossov leaned back in his desk chair and pondered the possibility.

That would put me very close to old POTUS. She'd want that, and I'd be the one who could give it to her.

And to myself, of course.

But how to get to Abramson? How to make him cooperate with us?

Rossov pulled up the Abramson file and spent a good part of the morning studying it. His phone rang and he ignored it. A fellow worker popped her head into his cubicle and he waved her off. What makes Abramson tick? he asked himself. And then it all suddenly clicked together.

His granddaughter. Abramson has kidnapped the child because he refused to allow the medical profession to give up on her. He's on the run with her, trying to use his scientific expertise to save the kid's life.

Rossov smiled to himself. Control the child and you control her grandfather.

It's not Abramson I want, he realized. It's his granddaughter.

Still smiling, he reached for his phone and called the Boston FBI headquarters.

L UKE ABRAMSON KEPT as still as he could manage while the MRI machine hummed away. He lay on a white-sheeted table that trundled slowly through the machine's tunnel. He felt nothing, but he saw in his mind's eye the sculpted magnetic fields producing images of his innards.

Prostate cancer.

At my age the tumors will grow so slowly that I can pretty much ignore them, he told himself. But then he thought, Wait. That's what happens to men at my *chronological* age. I'm not seventy-five physically anymore. The tumors will grow faster. They'll kill me— and put me through a lot of pain first.

Stop the telomerase accelerators? Go back to being a creaky old man with arthritic knees and high blood pressure and asthma? End the experiment before you see how far you can go?

He started to shake his head, then remembered that he had to keep still as long as the frigging MRI equipment was at work.

Maybe I can get selective, he thought. Maybe I can keep on taking the accelerators for my general body and tailor a set of inhibitors for the goddamned prostate.

Tailored telomerase treatment. Is it possible? Maybe. Why not? I'll have to take samples of the prostate tissue, identify the particular telomeres, then develop a set of inhibitors to inject specifically into the prostate.

That could work, Luke decided. I've got everything I need right here. Shannon's given me free run of her facility. I could push telomerase therapy to a new level!

He didn't realize that his scan had finished until the technician—a seriously overweight black woman—announced cheerily, "All through! You can get up now, Professor Abramson."

I'm not all through, Luke thought as he sat up on the table. I'm just beginning.

WHEN HIGHTOWER TOLD his chief that he was being saddled with an outsider in the Abramson investigation, the director frowned at the news. When Hightower told him that the outsider was from the Fisk Foundation, the chief's frown morphed into a more pensive look.

"Quenton Fisk?"

"Quenton Fisk," Hightower confirmed.

"He's got friends in high places."

"We've already got that White House guy looking over our shoulders."

"He's on the phone every damn day, asking how we're doing." The director drummed his manicured fingernails on his desktop for a few moments, then said, "Let me make a few phone calls."

Toward the end of the afternoon, the director called Hightower to his office. Before he could take a chair the director grumbled, "Looks like the senior senator from New York wants us to 'accommodate' Mr. Fisk."

"Are we going—"

"And both senators from Massachusetts," the director added.

"Friends in high places," said Hightower.

The director pulled in a deep breath. "Okay. Be nice to the guy. Let him think he's helping you. But don't let him know anything about internal FBI procedures. Got that?"

It was about what Hightower has expected: milk Novack for whatever information he could provide, but don't let him in on the action.

"Got it," he said. Then he stood up and went back to his own cubicle.

When he passed his secretary's desk, the woman looked up at him, phone pressed to one ear. Covering the phone, she whispered, "A Mr. Novack. Calling from New York."

Hightower nodded and went to his desk.

Novack sounded almost jovial. "We went through Abramson's graduate students for the past fifteen years. There's a Shannon Reese who is now the widow of Carter Bartram and is living outside of Portland, Oregon."

Hightower scribbled the name on his desk pad.

"And get this," Novack continued. "She owns the Bartram Research Laboratories. They specialize in biomedical research."

"A good place for Abramson to light in."

"You bet!"

"Thanks. That could be an important lead."

"When do we go out there?"

Hightower's first instinct was to retort, "What's this *we*, white man?" But instead, he said, "This is FBI business. I can't take a civilian along."

"The hell you can't!" Novack flared. "You wouldn't know about Bartram if I hadn't told you."

"I would've found out sooner or later."

"But I helped you find out sooner."

"That's true, but I can't take you along. My boss won't approve it."

"*My* boss will fry my jeeblies if I don't go. And yours, too!"

When in trouble or in doubt, Hightower told himself, buck the problem upstairs.

"Let me talk to my boss. I'll get back to you."

"Make it quick," Novack said. "I've already booked a flight to Portland."

Arlington, Massachusetts

DEL VILLANUEVA OPENED the front door. Agent Hightower was standing out in the late-afternoon cold, wearing nothing heavier than a suede jacket that strained across his muscular shoulders. He had parked his black Ford sedan at the curb.

"Come on in," said Del, standing aside to let Hightower get through the doorway.

Lenore was sitting tensely on the black Danish rocker in the living room. Del gestured Hightower to the sofa, but the agent shook his head.

"I can't stay long," he told them. "I'm on my way to the airport."

Del stayed on his feet, too. He was accustomed to being the tallest person in just about any social gathering, but Hightower topped him by a good two inches.

"You said you had something for us when you called," Del prompted.

Hightower nodded once. "We have a lead. I think it's a pretty good lead, but I might be wrong. It might turn out to be a false alarm."

Lenore had obviously lost several pounds since Hightower had first met her. Her face was lined, strained.

"Then why . . . ?" she started to ask.

"I want you to know that we're still working your case. We haven't put it on a back burner. We're trying to find your daughter."

"And you think you know where she is?" Lenore asked, her voice trembling slightly.

"Maybe. Don't get your hopes up too high."

"Was that CD that Luke sent us any help to you?" Del asked.

"Not really. We couldn't trace where it was sent from. He was too smart for that."

"But couldn't you get a court order or something?"

Hightower stared at Del. The man watches too many cop shows on TV, he thought. He was lying to the two of them, and he didn't like it. FedEx had cooperated reluctantly, just enough to reveal to him that the CD package had originated in Salem, Oregon. Not Portland, but close enough to add strength to Novack's information about the Bartram Research Laboratories. He had no intention of telling the parents more than he had to.

Yet he felt sorry for the miserable, bewildered couple. This visit was intended to give them some hope, not to let them in on the details of his investigation. The chief would go ballistic if he found out I'd dropped in on them like this, Hightower knew.

He lifted his arm and peered at his wristwatch. "I've got to go," he told them. "Plane to catch."

Lenore rose to her feet. "Thanks for coming by, Mr. Hightower," she said slowly. "Thanks for helping us."

"We'll find your daughter," Hightower said. Then he turned to leave.

Del grabbed at his arm. "I'm coming with you."

Hightower shrugged him off. "No you're not."

"Yes I am, dammit! This is my daughter. I have a right to go with you."

"Your place is here with your wife. This is FBI business. We can't have civilians involved."

"It's my daughter! I have a right—"

"Mr. Villanueva," Hightower interrupted, "if you try to follow me I'll have to arrest you for hindering an official investigation. You don't want that, and neither do I."

And he made his way to the door, leaving Del Villanueva standing in the middle of the living room beside his wife, looking angry and frustrated.

As he ducked into his sedan, Hightower wished he didn't have Novack hanging on to his coattails. Civilians shouldn't be involved in a Bureau investigation, he told himself. But what can you do about a civilian who has powerful U.S. senators on his side?

L UKE AND TAMARA were sitting side by side in the room Shannon had given him. It was an efficient little bed/sitting room, like something out of a modestly priced hotel chain: bed, dresser, TV set, desk, sofa, one cushioned chair with an ottoman and one wheeled desk chair.

They sat next to each other on the sofa, with the images from the morning's MRI scan spread across the little coffee table.

"I can't see anything that looks like a tumor," Tamara said.

"Good."

"The body generates tumorous tissues all the time," she went on, "and the immune system destroys them."

"Most of the time," said Luke.

She nodded, tight-lipped. "You don't show any symptoms."

He made a sardonic grin. "I'm peeing easily enough. And not as often as I used to, before starting the accelerators."

"But you're not having any difficulties urinating?"

Luke shook his head. It seemed just the tiniest bit odd to be discussing his pissing habits with a dark-haired, good-looking young woman.

"Well," said Tamara, "the PSA results might be anomalous. We'll take another shot tomorrow."

"No," Luke countered. "Tomorrow we start Angie on the p53 gene therapy."

"Tomorrow?"

"No sense waiting. She's improving. She's stronger than she was a few days ago. Her hair seems to be coming back in."

Tamara nodded slowly, but Luke knew what was behind her silence. Angie still looked old, wrinkled. Her blood pressure was still high. At least the tests showed her kidney function was still okay. And her fracture was healing nicely. Thank God for small mercies, he thought.

And then he grimaced. Thank God, yeah. Thanks for the kid's brain cancer, big guy. Thanks for killing my wife. Thanks for all the crap you throw at us.

"What is it?" Tamara asked.

"Huh?"

"You look . . . you look like somebody ready for a fight, almost."

Luke forced a smile. "We're in a fight, Tamara. A life-or-death battle."

She nodded. "Yes, I suppose we are."

In Flight

WHEN YOU FLY on Uncle Sam's dime you fly coach, Hightower reminded himself. It was uncomfortable for a man his size to squeeze into the tight little seat, especially with Novack sitting beside him. At least Fisk's man took the middle seat; Hightower was on the aisle. Every time the flight attendants went by with their cart he had to lean away or get bumped.

Novack opened his iPad as soon as they reached cruising altitude and busily scrolled through reams of information. Hightower asked for a cola when the cart brushed by and sat quietly, grateful for the silence from his so-called partner.

But the silence didn't last long. Novack closed his notebook, then said, "Should we phone this Bartram woman from the airport, tell her we're coming?"

Hightower looked down at him. "And give her an hour or more to stash Abramson someplace? I don't think so."

Novack agreed. "So we'll just drive up there and spring a surprise on her."

Still unhappy about the "we," Hightower said, "I'll do the talking. I'll show them my ID and they'll assume you're with the Bureau, too. Keep your mouth closed and don't let them know otherwise."

Novack grinned carelessly. "Right, chief."

Hightower wondered if the "chief" was a play on his Navaho background.

I N MASSACHUSETTS, DEL Villanueva had spent the hour since Hightower's departure phoning people he knew in the travel business, trying to find out where the FBI agent was flying to.

It wasn't easy, but at last a friend whom he regularly played golf with came up with, "American Airlines has a J. Hightower booked to Portland, Oregon. Through Chicago."

Del flashed a triumphant smile. "Thanks, Bernie! I owe you one!"

"You didn't hear it from me," his friend said. "This could cause big trouble if anybody found out."

"Mum's the word." Del hung up, then phoned his sister and asked her to come and stay with Lenore while he was away.

His ear ached slightly, he'd been on the phone so long. But as he finally hung up he looked across the living room to his wife and announced, "I'm going to Oregon, honey. I'm going to get Angie and bring her home!"

Lenore had stayed in the rocker through all his telephone calls, rocking slowly back and forth, staring at nothing. Now she focused on her husband.

"You've found Angie?"

"I think so." He got to his feet and headed for the stairs. "Got to pack. Maria's coming over; she'll stay with you while I'm away."

S HANNON BARTRAM FOUND Luke in his granddaughter's room, along with Dr. Minteer. Angela was sitting up in bed, eating halfheartedly from a dinner tray.

Shannon insisted that Luke and Tamara have dinner with her. "You don't want to eat in the cafeteria," she said.

Luke bantered, "It's good enough for your staff, isn't it?"

"You're not staff," Shannon said firmly. "You're friends."

"Okay," Luke said. "We'll meet you in your dining room after Angie's finished her dinner and is all tucked in for the night."

"Fine," said Shannon. Looking across at Angela, who had pushed her tray away and slumped back tiredly on the pillows, she suggested, "Seven o'clock?"

"Seven should be fine."

Once she had left, Angela said, "Why can't I have dinner in the cafeteria, Grandpa?"

Luke's brows hiked up. "Don't you like having dinner in bed?"

"It's boring. The same old thing every day. Can't I go out with you two?"

Luke glanced at Tamara. "If you'd like to, honey," he answered. "That'd be okay, wouldn't it?"

Nodding, Tamara said, "I don't see why not."

"Okay," said Luke. "Tomorrow you eat out, with us."

"Good," Angela said, smiling as she snuggled down into her pillows. She fell asleep within a few minutes.

Softly, Tamara said, "Maybe I should stay here with Angie."

Luke shook his head. "I don't want Shannon to get any ideas."

"You want me for protection?" Tamara asked, seemingly amused at the thought.

Frowning, Luke muttered, "Yeah. You can be my bodyguard."

Tamara said nothing for a few moments. Then, "You know, Shannon might get the idea that you and I are involved."

"You and me? That's crazy. I'm too old for you."

"Chronologically."

He blinked, thinking, She's just a kid. A very attractive kid, but there's nothing between us. She's here for Angela's sake; she's not interested in me.

Slowly, he said, "You've taken an enormous risk to come with Angie and me, haven't you? I've probably ruined your career."

She tried to give a careless shrug. "My first duty is to my patient."

"University Hospital has probably fired you by now."

"They can't do that. Not without a hearing."

"You could go back right now and try to patch it up with them. I know Wexler, he'll try to be fair. You can blame the whole thing on me."

Glancing at Angela, sleeping peacefully in her bed, Tamara asked, "And what happens to Angie?"

"We're in a good facility here. Plenty of help."

"You don't need me anymore?"

"No! That's not what I mean. I don't want you to go, but it might be the best thing for you to do."

Tamara looked at him coolly. "So I got back to Boston and the FBI starts asking me where you are."

"You tell them you don't know."

"And they'll believe that, won't they?"

"They can't force you to tell them anything."

"Luke, they can arrest me for helping you. What do they call it? 'Aiding and abetting' a kidnapper, isn't it?"

It was Luke's turn to fall silent. Finally he muttered, "I've really messed up your life, haven't I?"

"No," she replied. "I've messed it up for myself."

For the first time, Luke realized how totally fouled up everything was. But then he looked over at Angela, a helpless little child.

We've done this for her, he told himself. We've saved Angie's life. And thrown away our own.

THE DIRECTOR OF the Boston FBI office felt uncomfortable talking with Rossov. He didn't like the idea that someone from the White House was looking over his shoulder. And now the young snot was giving him orders.

Rossov's face looked pleasant, almost cheerful, in the screen of the director's desktop phone. But his words were far from congenial.

"And just where is Abramson?"

Trying to keep from squirming like a little kid, the director said, "We're not certain yet, but it appears he might be at a private research facility in Oregon."

"When will you be certain?"

"One of my top men is on his way out there right now."

Rossov considered this for a moment. "I want to know the instant you find him. If he's not there, I want you to report that to me, just as well."

The director nodded. "We'll keep you informed."

"If he is there," Rossov said, his face hardening, "he's to be kept there until I can fly out and meet him face-to-face."

"That's not our normal procedure," the director said.

"This is not a normal case. I want to meet Abramson as soon as you get your hands on him."

The director nodded. He had already spoken to his Justice Department superiors in Washington about Rossov's interest in the Abramson case—and been told to cooperate fully with the White House man. Fully.

"Keep me informed," said Rossov.

The director suppressed an urge to say, "Yes, sir." Instead, he merely replied, "Right."

The phone screen went blank. With a sigh, the director told his secretary to get the head of the Salem, Oregon, office on the phone. Standard operating procedure. The Salem office covered the entire state. You don't send a man into someone else's territory without informing them first. He doubted that Hightower would need backup in dealing with Abramson, but just in case . . .

O'Hare International Airport

NOVACK LOOKED AROUND at the bustling crowds in the O'Hare terminal.

"Two-hour layover," he said to Hightower. "We might as well grab something to eat. My treat."

Hightower grunted an assent. As they made their way to the food court, he thought that it was easy for Novack to pick up the tab: He was on a Fisk Foundation expense account. Generous with his boss's money.

But something was prickling the hairs on the back of Hightower's neck, something bothering his peripheral senses. Del Villanueva. The kidnapped girl's father had wanted to come along on this search for Professor Abramson. Hightower's experience in judging men and their intentions told him that Villanueva would not give up on that quest just because he risked being arrested for hampering an investigation. That was a paper-thin threat, and both men knew it.

Novack led him to a hamburger joint, but Hightower felt edgy, uneasy, like an old-time brave being tracked through the arroyos by an enemy or an invisible skinwalker.

He's here, Hightower realized, just as surely as if the man were standing before him. The sonofabitch hopped a later flight out of Boston and he's here in the airport, searching for me. He didn't have to settle for the lowest-fare flight to Chicago; he's not working for the government.

"Don't you like the burger?" Novack asked, half his sandwich already devoured.

"It's all right." Hightower munched it down. Novack paid the check with an American Express card, and the two men went down the busy terminal corridor to the gate from which their flight to Oregon would leave.

"Still got damned near an hour to wait," Novack complained as he plopped into one of the plastic chairs.

Hightower remained standing, scanning the crowd hustling along the corridor.

And there he was, Delgado D. Villanueva, tall, lanky, pulling a roll-along bag, his face set in a determined scowl, his eyes scanning back and forth like twin radar dishes.

Their eyes met. Villanueva's lips twitched, as if he wanted to smile. He headed straight for Hightower.

"I told you to stay home," Hightower said by way of greeting, almost growling the words.

"It's a free country," said Villanueva. "You can't keep me off this flight."

Novack, looking puzzled, got to his feet. He was much shorter than either of the other men.

Grimly, Hightower introduced, "This is Del Villanueva, Angela's father."

Novack frowned puzzledly for a moment, then recognition dawned.

"And who are you?" Del asked, almost truculently.

"He's with me," said Hightower. "Ed Novack."

Novack looked back and forth between the two men. "You're heading to Portland, too?"

"I'm going to find my daughter."

"This is FBI business," Hightower said. "You'll be in our way."

"Don't hand me that crap," Del snapped. "She's my daughter, for chrissakes. I have every right to be with her."

Novack said, "I'm going to get myself a Coke. You guys want anything?"

Surprised, Hightower said, "Nothing for me."

"Me, either," said Del.

"I'll be right back," Novack told them. And he practically sprinted away from them.

Some partner, Hightower thought, mildly disgusted. First sign of trouble, he disappears.

Del eased himself into the seat Novack had vacated. "I didn't know if I'd be able to catch up with you. I could only get a standby seat on this flight to Portland."

Sitting ponderously beside him, Hightower said, "You'd be better off going back to Boston. This is an official FBI investigation, and you are *not* part of it."

"You can't keep me out of it," Del insisted.

"I can have you arrested for hampering an official investigation."

"You do that and I'll bring you up on charges of illegal arrest."

Hightower stared at Villanueva. What I ought to do, he thought, is break your goddamned neck. Take you into the men's room and pulverize you.

Yeah, he told himself. Beat up a private citizen. Father of the kidnapped girl. Great career move.

Novack came back, sipping a drink through a straw. He looked around for an empty seat near the other two, but there weren't any.

"Guess I'll have to stand," he said, almost cheerfully.

"There's seats over there," said Hightower, pointing.

"Naw. I'll stand here with you guys."

Del glared up at him. Hightower glowered.

Two uniformed airport security guards shouldered their way through the crowd streaming through the corridor and came right up to the three of them. The younger of them was black, thin almost to the point of being skinny. The other was chunkier, a Hispanic with a thick dark mustache and a somber expression.

Pointing, the Hispanic asked, "Del Villanueva?"

Warily, Del answered, "Yes."

"Would you come with us, please?"

"Why? What for?"

"We need to ask you a few questions." Wiggling a finger, the guard indicated that Del should get up.

"What's this all about?" Del demanded. But he rose to his feet. Hightower got up beside him. Novack stood beside the two guards, sipping and trying to look concerned.

"Airport security," said the Hispanic. "Strictly routine, but you'll have to come with us. Bring your bag, sir, we'll have to inspect it." He rested a hand on the butt of the gun holstered at his hip.

"I don't understand this," Del said. But with one guard on either side of him, he gripped his roll-on and left the gate area. The crowd in the corridor parted to make way for them.

Del looked back over his shoulder at Hightower, his expression halfway between confusion and anger.

Hightower turned toward Novack, who broke into a satisfied grin.

"They'll hold on to him until our flight has left," Novack said.

"That's illegal!" Hightower exclaimed. "You can't detain a man for no reason."

Pursing his lips, Novack said, "Apparently somebody tipped off the guards that a guy answering Villanueva's description was trying to smuggle drugs to Portland."

"Somebody? You!"

"It's a reasonable story," Novack said. "They'll ask him some questions, search his bag. When they don't find anything they'll apologize and let him go."

"After he's missed his flight."

Shrugging, Novack said, "He was only on standby anyway."

"And those guards believed your cockamamie story?"

"Maybe. But they believed the fifty bucks I handed each one of them a lot more."

Hightower glared at him, fists on his hips.

"Come on, man," Novack coaxed. "You couldn't do it, so I did. There are some advantages to having a freelancer working with you."

Shaking his head, Hightower muttered, "If this ever gets back to my director . . ."

Ten minutes later the ticket clerk announced that their flight was ready for boarding. As he stepped into line Hightower thought, Villanueva can take a later flight. But what's he going to do once he's landed in Portland? Search the whole city for us?

He followed Novack into the access tunnel that led to the plane.

Love, Maybe

D INNER WITH SHANNON was pleasant enough. Luke talked about his plans to take samples of his prostate tissue and identify their telomeres, then develop a specific inhibitor to stop the tumors.

"But you don't know if there are any tumors," Shannon objected, over her bowl of French onion soup. Tamara thought the soup came from a can, but she said nothing about it.

Luke waggled a hand in the air. "Even if there aren't any, the inhibitors ought to shrink the prostate gland itself."

Shocked, Shannon objected. "You can't run experiments on yourself! You'd be operating in the dark, Luke."

"Besides," Tamara pointed out, "the accelerators you've been taking seem to have reduced the prostate to what it must have been when you were fifty or so."

Luke frowned at both of them. "You want me to wait until the tumors are full-blown?"

"At least wait a week for another PSA test."

He glanced at Tamara, who nodded and said, "That makes sense."

Luke replied, "Maybe. But in the meantime we can take some tissue samples, so I can identify the telomeres."

"You'll be urinating blood for several days," Tamara said. "Are you ready for that?"

Luke shrugged as nonchalantly as he could manage and shifted the conversation to Angela's condition. By the time the waiter had cleared the soup bowls and set out the grilled trout entrée, the three of them had agreed that the child's brain was free of tumors.

"But the damned progeria is still dogging her," Luke complained.

"She's improving," Tamara said.

"Maybe I should start her on accelerators," he mused.

Shannon said, "And run the risk of starting fresh tumor growth?"

Luke huffed. "The p53 implant should help there."

"Be patient, Luke," Tamara said, placing a hand on his arm. "Don't rush things."

"I thought I could cure her in a couple of weeks," he muttered.

"You did, but now we've got to deal with the side effects."

Shannon said, "You're welcome to stay here as long as it takes, Luke. You know that, don't you?"

"Yes, I do. And I appreciate it," Luke said. "But I wonder how long we really have."

"What do you mean by that?"

"The FBI."

"Oh, they won't find you here," Shannon said. But then she added, "You don't think they could, do you?"

"It's the mother-loving FBI, Shannon. They're good at finding people who don't want to be found. That's what they do for a living."

Her chin rising a notch, Shannon said, "Even if they come here, I won't allow them into the facility. They have no right to search my laboratories."

"They could get a court order," Tamara said.

"Not from any judge in this county," Shannon boasted. "I know them all."

Luke glanced at Tamara, who shook her head just the slightest bit. Neither of them said anything to contradict their hostess.

———

Aᴼᴛᴇʀ ᴅɪɴɴᴇʀ, ᴛʜᴇ three of them looked in on Angela, who was sleeping peacefully.

"She looks noticeably better," Shannon whispered. "Her skin looks much healthier."

Luke said noncommittally, "Maybe."

The three of them stepped back into the hallway, and Luke softly closed Angela's door.

"How about an after-dinner drink?" Shannon suggested.

"Not for me," Luke said. "I'm going to hit the hay."

"Oh. All right. Well . . ." She finished reluctantly, "Good night, then."

"Good night, Shannon."

Luke and Tamara watched her go down to the end of the hall and through the door to the outside, glancing back at them just before she shut the door.

"She doesn't like leaving the two of us alone with each other," Tamara said.

Luke shrugged. "Then she shouldn't have given us rooms in the same building."

"The same building with Angie."

"Yeah. Right."

She started down the hallway. Luke kept stride beside her.

As they started up the stairs, Tamara asked, "Luke, what happens after Angie's cured?"

"We fly back to Massachusetts and return her to Norrie and Del."

"And the FBI?"

Their footsteps echoing slightly on the concrete stairs, Luke replied, "How can they prosecute a kidnapper who's returned the kid to her parents?"

"You think it'll be that easy?"

"Should be."

"I hope you're right."

They reached the top floor and went down the corridor to Tamara's room.

She stopped at the door, then turned back to Luke. "Well, good night."

He tried to smile. "We should have taken Shannon up on that offer of a drink. I could use one."

Tamara shook her head. "She offered *you* a drink. She never even looked at me."

"She meant both of us."

"Did she? She thinks of me as competition."

Feeling uncomfortable, Luke groused, "Don't start that again."

"Why not?" Tamara asked, her expression almost impish. "You're getting younger every day. You're a handsome, intelligent, accomplished man. She's willing to stiff the FBI over you."

"You're crazy."

"And she's a wealthy, good-looking woman. Just about your age, somatically. A little plump, maybe, but I think she's started working out in the gym."

"Look," said Luke, "if I were going to get involved with anybody, it wouldn't be with Shannon."

Tamara said nothing.

"It'd be with you."

Her eyes went suddenly wide, and Luke felt just as surprised as she looked.

He slipped a hand around her waist, pulled her to him, and kissed her soundly on the lips. Tamara didn't resist. She clung to Luke for a long, breathless moment.

"Uh . . . good night," Luke stammered.

"Good night," Tamara whispered.

And he stomped down the hallway and the concrete stairs to his own floor, thinking that the freaking fountain of youth brings all kinds of complications along with it.

Portland

THE THREE-HOUR TIME difference between Boston and Oregon made Hightower's day twenty-seven hours long. Even though the clocks in the airport terminal read 9:22 P.M., he felt as though it were time to call it a day and get some sleep.

Novack seemed chipper, though, as they threaded their way to the rental car counter, his cell phone clapped to his ear.

"Okay, okay," he was saying. "Airport Marriott, good. Adjoining rooms. Fine. And the car'll have a GPS? Fine. Good work. I'll call Mr. Fisk tomorrow morning."

Smiling as he snapped the phone shut, he told Hightower, "Car and hotel reservations. My office's travel agency has set it all up for us."

"Good," was all that Hightower responded. But he thought that his own office could have done the same thing. Probably. But the accommodations would be cheaper, using Uncle Sam's dime.

The car waiting for them at the Avis counter was a shiny maroon Chevrolet Malibu. Novack drove it to the hotel; they checked in and went to their adjoining rooms.

"See you in the morning," Hightower said.

"Right. And then we go to the Bartram Labs."

Hightower nodded and entered his room. Flicking his carryall onto the king-sized bed, he pulled out his phone and called his chief's home number.

The director answered on the first ring. "Been sitting up all night waiting for you to check in."

"Just got to the hotel," Hightower reported.

"Any problems?"

Hightower told him about Villanueva and Novack's little ploy.

The director chuckled. "He's a slick sonofabitch, isn't he?"

Hightower said, "I think Villanueva will come out here anyway. He'll be pretty damned sore, you know."

"What's he going to do, search the whole city by himself?"

"If it was me," Hightower replied, "I'd grab a phone book as soon as I got off the plane and look for scientific research establishments."

The director was quiet for a moment. Then, "You give him too much credit, Jerry. Besides, phone books don't have listings like that."

"Yahoo does. Google. A dozen search engines."

"Yeah, maybe, but how'd he know which place to go to?"

Hightower shrugged. "He's stubborn. And he's pissed off. He won't give up easily."

"Well, if he gets in your way, arrest him for hampering your investigation. You'll have my complete support. And the White House's backing, too. I've notified the Salem office; they'll be able to give you a hand if you need it."

"I ought to be able to handle this by myself," Hightower said. Then he added, "With my little sidekick."

The director let the sarcasm pass. Instead, he said, "Now listen, Jerry. This White House guy wants you to hold Abramson wherever you find him. Just keep him on ice and notify me immediately. I'll tell the White House and he'll fly out to you. He wants to confront Abramson himself."

"That's not our regular routine."

"I know. But this comes from the White House, Jerry. I've checked with the Bureau in Washington. Do it their way."

Hightower felt uneasy. But he said merely, "If that's the way you want it, chief."

"That's the way it's got to be."

LUKE SLEPT FITFULLY that night, his dreams filled with visions of his wife, Adele, alive and vibrant and happy. But he couldn't reach her; every time he fought his way through crowds of strangers to be near her, she slipped away, out of reach, out of touch.

Yet she spoke to him. "You're getting younger every day. You're a handsome, intelligent, accomplished man." And he realized she spoke with Tamara's voice.

His eyes snapped open. It was starting to get light outside. He sat up, swung his legs off the bed, and stepped to the window. Pushing the curtains back, he saw another gray, cloudy dawn rising. How do these people stand it? he asked himself. This bleak climate. Their suicide rate must be way higher than Massachusetts's.

Padding his way to the bathroom, Luke realized that he had slept the night through without needing to urinate. He shook his head. If my prostate is still enlarged, and maybe even growing a tumor, how come I don't have to piss every couple of hours?

I'll have to ask Tamara about that; she's a physician, she ought to know.

Tamara. He looked down and saw that he had the beginnings of an erection. "Fountain of freaking youth," he muttered. "Next thing, you'll start breaking out with acne."

Shaking his head, he did his business at the toilet while mentally reviewing his plans for the day: Shannon had set him up with a surgeon to take tissue samples from his prostate. Tamara was going to run Angie through another physical, then take the kid outside for a walk—if the weather wasn't too cold or wet.

Angie's starting to complain about being cooped up in her room all the time. That's good. That means she's feeling stronger, antsier.

And so are you, he told himself. Coming on to Tamara like that. You must be going nuts.

But as he looked into the mirror over the bathroom sink, Luke had to smile at his image: skin smoother, hair darker, jawline firmer, eyes clearer.

And your brain's getting just as stupid as it was when you were a kid, he admonished himself. Freaking fountain of youth is making an idiot of you.

Then he remembered what it had felt like to kiss Tamara. And have her kiss him back.

Forget it! he commanded himself. But he couldn't.

DEL VILLANUEVA AWOKE slowly, groggily. For a few moments he didn't know where the hell he was. Blinking at the unfamiliar surroundings, he slowly remembered: Portland, Oregon. Airport Marriott Hotel.

He sat up and, on a sudden hunch, reached for the bedside telephone. Ignoring the automated instructions, he dialed for the operator.

After a half-dozen rings, a human voice answered, "Front desk."

"Connect me with Mr. Hightower's room, please."

"You can dial that for yourself if—"

"I don't know his room number."

"Oh. Let me look it up for you." A pause. Del fidgeted impatiently. Then the voice came back, "I'm afraid Mr. Hightower checked out about half an hour ago."

Damn! Del thought as he put the phone down. He was right here in the same fucking hotel all night!

He threw the bedcover back and went to his carryall to dig out his laptop. Still naked, he sat on the sofa and booted up the computer.

Luke would go to some medical facility, he reasoned. A hospital or a laboratory somewhere in the area.

Doggedly, he started searching for the hospitals and research institutions in and around Portland. There were tons of them.

Bartram Laboratories

S HANNON BARTRAM MARCHED herself down to the reception
lobby. A pair of FBI agents had arrived, asking about Luke
Abramson.

The reception area was small, since the labs didn't receive that
many visitors: just the receptionist's desk and a pair of curved
couches for waiting salesmen and such. Shannon saw through the
floor-to-ceiling windows that the gray overcast outside was thinning. We might see some sunshine before the day's over, she
thought.

The two men got up from the couch by the windows as she approached them. One of them was big, massive; his black ponytail
made him look like a Native American. He wore a tight-fitting
suede sports jacket and chinos. The other was shorter, not much
above Shannon's own height. Wiry build, but his face looked as if it
had been carved out of granite. Grayish hair cropped down to a
military buzz cut.

Extending her hand to the big man, she said, "I'm Shannon Bartram. What can I do for you gentlemen?"

Hightower reached into his back pants pocket, pulled out a
leather wallet, and flipped it open. "I'm Special Agent Jerome Hightower, ma'am." Turning his chin a bare inch, he added, "And this is
Edward Novack."

"What can I do for you?" Shannon repeated.

"We're searching for a Professor Lucas Abramson. He's wanted for kidnapping."

"He's not here," Shannon lied.

Hightower looked pained. "Ma'am, would you mind if we looked through the building?"

"I certainly would mind. This is a research establishment, and I can't have my staff disturbed. Besides, there are five buildings altogether and—"

"We know that," Novack said. "And we know that Abramson came here a few days ago."

"Nonsense. In any case, I can't have my staff upset by your poking into our facilities."

Hightower said, "Ma'am, we could get a court order."

"Go ahead and do that, then. Good day."

Novack started to say something, but Hightower silenced him with a heavy hand on his chest. "Ma'am, it's like this. Abramson kidnapped a little girl. We're trying to find the child and return her to her parents."

Shannon almost blurted that the "kidnapped" child was Luke's granddaughter, but she caught herself just in time.

"If we have to get a court order," Hightower went on, looking pained, "we'll come back with a squad of police officers who'll be authorized to turn your place upside down. You don't want that, do you?"

Standing her ground in front of the oversized FBI agent, Shannon said stubbornly, "You go ahead and do what you have to do. I won't willingly allow you to search this facility."

"We know he's here," Novack said, in his rasping, almost snarling voice. "If you're hiding him, that makes you an accessory to kidnapping. We could arrest you right here and now."

"Arrest me?"

"That's right. Put the cuffs on you and take you downtown to be arraigned."

Shannon blinked several times. "You're trying to frighten me," she said, her voice fluttering slightly. "You're bullying me."

"Ma'am," said Hightower, playing the good cop, "we just want to find that little girl and return her to her parents."

"You can't do that. She's under treatment."

Hightower glanced down at Novack, then said, "You mean she's here."

"I didn't say that."

"She's here," Novack snapped. "And that means Abramson's here, too."

Shannon looked from Novack to Hightower, her mind churning.

Before she could think of what to say, Hightower explained, almost gently, "Look, ma'am, we're not going to take him away from here."

"You're not?" Novack snapped.

"No. If the little girl is under treatment here, we won't move her. But we've got to see Abramson for ourselves and make sure that he'll stay here until we can get this situation straightened out."

Shannon wavered. "You're not going to arrest him?"

"My orders are to keep him here. Somebody from Washington wants to talk to him."

Trying to sort it all out in her head, Shannon asked, "Can you wait here for a few minutes?"

Hightower nodded. Novack looked as if he wanted to object, but he remained silent.

Shannon turned and hurried back toward her office. Hightower sat down on the curved couch.

Plopping down beside him, Novack demanded, "What the hell's this business about keeping him here?"

"Orders," said Hightower. "From the top."

"Washington?"

"Yeah. Washington."

Novack's brows knit. Then he turned from Hightower to look at the door Shannon Bartram had gone through.

"Ten to one, she's going back to tell Abramson we're here," he grumbled. "He'll scram out the back door while we're sitting here like a couple of chumps."

Hightower almost smiled. "If you feel that way, go out to the car and watch for anybody trying to leave. There's only one road up here."

Novack gave him a sour look, but he didn't move.

L UKE WAS LYING on his stomach, his pants and briefs removed, while a male surgeon and his two female nurses bent over his bare buttocks. To get a tissue sample from his prostate, they were going to insert a plastic catheter into his anus.

Luke made no secret of his distaste for the procedure, but the surgeon—a youngish man with a pale blond pencil-thin mustache, an air of self-confidence, and a seemingly endless supply of urinary tract jokes—assured him the job would be practically painless.

"Not like the old days, with those hard catheters," he said cheerfully, as he slipped on his mask. "Patients would crap blood for a week afterward."

Luke grit his teeth. At least the nurses seemed quite professional. And serious.

Shannon burst into the little room, looking distraught.

"Luke, the FBI is here!"

The surgeon straightened up, his eyes glaring at her over his mask. "Mrs. Bartram, you're not scrubbed or gowned."

Luke wanted to throw a towel or something over his bared butt.

"I'll stay here, by the door," Shannon said, paying no attention to the view. She closed the door and leaned against it. "Luke, they know you're here."

"They're guessing," he said.

"They know!" Shannon insisted. "They threatened to arrest me!"

The surgeon threw the catheter to the floor. "I can't work like this! We'll have to reschedule." To the nurses, he commanded, "Clean him up." And he stamped out of the room, past Shannon, and into the hallway beyond the door.

"What should I do?" Shannon asked, her voice edgy.

She looked distraught, Luke saw, not at all the woman who last night had confidently promised to protect him.

"They want to search the place," she went on. "They said they'd bring a squad of police who'll turn everything upside down!"

"They'll need a court order. That'll take a little time."

"They said they won't take you away. You can stay here. They just want to talk to you."

"They didn't come all the way out here just to talk to me," Luke said.

"But they'll arrest me! They threatened to handcuff me and drag me away!"

Luke recognized defeat when he saw it. "Okay," he said, pulling himself up to a sitting position while keeping both hands cupped over his groin. "Let me get my pants back on and I'll go out and see them."

"I'll go tell them that." And Shannon bolted out of the room. One of the nurses handed Luke his underpants and trousers.

A S SHE WALKED back toward the lobby, Shannon tried to compose herself. I should call my lawyer, she thought. I can't let the FBI bully me.

But when she reached the lobby and the two men rose to their feet, she said to them, "Professor Abramson will see you in my office. In a few minutes."

Hightower nodded. "Thank you."

"Please wait here. I'll send someone to bring you to my office once Professor Abramson is ready."

Another nod. "Okay," said Hightower.

They sat down again as Shannon left the lobby.

"We shook her up," Novack said, almost smirking about it.

"Yeah." Hightower pulled his cell phone from his jacket pocket.

"Who're you calling?" Novack asked, fishing for his own phone.

"The kid's mother. She'll be happy to hear we found her daughter."

"What about the father? He's in Portland someplace."

Hightower shrugged. He recalled how distraught Mrs. Villanueva had looked, back in her home in Arlington. Tight as a bowstring, worrying herself half to death about her daughter.

He saw Novack peck a single key on his phone. "Who are you calling?"

With a sardonic smile, he said, "The man who pays the bills."

Hightower wasn't surprised. Quenton Fisk would want to know that they'd found Abramson, just as badly as his own chief and the big mucky-muck from the White House did.

Shannon Bartram's Office

Luke sat down gingerly; even though they hadn't gone through with the procedure he felt vulnerable.

They were sitting around the circular conference table in a corner of Shannon's office: Luke, Shannon, and the two FBI agents. Hightower's partner, sitting next to him, was wiry, high-strung. Hightower had introduced him as Edward Novack. They made an odd couple. Hightower looked as imposing and impassive as a monumental statue. Novack was narrow-eyed, suspicious, somehow crafty-looking.

Shannon appeared outwardly calm, but she seemed paler than Luke had ever seen her before, and her sea green eyes darted from Hightower to Novack to Luke and back again.

"I did not kidnap my granddaughter," Luke said, by way of starting the discussion. "I legally checked her out of the hospital."

"And took her across the country," Novack countered, "without telling the kid's parents."

Hightower looked down at the smaller man. "The charge is kidnapping," he said to Luke. "You can argue about it with a judge. Our job is to find you."

Shannon spoke up. "You said Professor Abramson could remain here."

"For the time being."

"My granddaughter's undergoing treatment. She shouldn't be moved."

"The treatment has killed off the child's brain tumors," Shannon said, forcing a smile.

Hightower nodded. "That's good. I'll have to see the little girl."

"Certainly."

"And there's a Dr. Minteer involved, too, isn't there?"

Luke said, "I dragged her along with us. She's Angela's physician. She's been looking after Angie since before we left Massachusetts. You can't charge her with anything except taking care of her patient."

Hightower studied Luke. The professor looks a lot younger than he did a few weeks ago, he realized. Maybe he's dyed his hair, but his face looks younger, tighter, as if he's had a really good plastic surgery job.

Carefully, he said, "It seems this case has attracted the interest of the White House. One of their people is on his way here to talk with you, Professor."

"The White House?" Luke asked.

Novack looked surprised, too. "Not the Justice Department?"

"The White House," Hightower repeated.

For a moment they were all silent. Then Luke asked, "So what do we do now?"

"You go on treating your granddaughter," said Hightower. "I'm going to ask the Bureau office in Salem to send a few men here to make sure you don't try to leave."

"I won't," Luke said.

With a nod and an utterly serious expression on his face, Hightower murmured, "Trust, but verify."

Shannon seemed to have recovered her spirit. "I can't have policemen barging in here."

Hightower said, "They'll stay outside. I just need to make sure that the professor doesn't sneak away from here."

Luke snorted but said nothing.

"Now I'd like to see the child," Hightower said.

A NGIE WAS OUTSIDE, walking in the wan sunlight with Tamara. Luke led Hightower and Novack to them. The sky was more than half covered with gray clouds, and the slight breeze felt nippy, but the little girl seemed happy enough, walking alongside Dr. Minteer.

Hightower was taken aback when he got his first good look at Angela. The kid was supposed to be eight years old, but beneath her woolen cap her face looked *old,* wrinkled skin stretched over bones, eye sockets big, prominent. Then he saw that there was a cast covering her left wrist.

"What happened to her arm?" he asked as they approached Angela.

"Hairline fracture of the wrist," Luke explained. "She fell down chasing a rabbit."

Novack looked skeptical, Hightower sympathetic.

Luke dropped into a squat beside his granddaughter and introduced the two men. Angela squinted up at Hightower.

"How tall are you?" she asked.

Hightower grinned at her. "Just tall enough so that my feet reach the ground."

Angela laughed. Tamara, standing beside her, looked him up and down, then pronounced, "Six-four, I'd say."

"And a half," Hightower added.

"You're big," said Angela.

"How do you feel?" Novack asked her.

"Pretty good. My grandpa says I'm getting better every day."

"That's good," said Hightower.

"The brain tumors are gone," said Tamara.

"That's good," Hightower repeated.

They chatted for a few minutes more, then Tamara said, "We'd better be going back now."

Angela nodded glumly, and they all started back toward the building.

After they saw Angela and Tamara back to her room and started for the reception lobby, Luke explained, "Angie's suffering from progeria, premature aging."

"That's what it is," Novack said. "I was wondering."

"It's a side effect of the treatment I used to kill her cancer. She's recovering from it, coming back to normal."

Hightower wondered how true that was, but he said nothing. He left Abramson in the reception lobby and headed back to the parking lot and the rental Chevy, with Novack yapping at his heels.

"What's this White House guy? You didn't tell me about that."

"My boss back in Boston told me the White House wants to talk with Abramson. That's as much as I know about it."

"The White House?" Novack wondered out loud. "What the fuck do they want?"

"We'll find out when he gets here."

Hightower drove partway down the winding road that led back to the highway, then pulled over onto the shoulder and killed the engine.

"If Abramson tries to skip out, he'll have to come past us."

"So we sit here freezing our butts till your office sends in reinforcements?"

Hightower gestured to the sky. "Sun's trying to come out. It'll warm up soon."

Novack grumbled and reached for his cell phone.

QUENTON FISK BARKED into his phone, "The White House? What's the White House's interest in Abramson?"

Novack's voice rasped, "Don't know. But I guess you've got better contacts there than I do."

"That's for damned certain." He cut off the phone call and told his secretary to get the head of his Washington office on the line.

D EL VILLANUEVA WAS not in a happy mood. He had tried three different hospitals this morning, all with zero results. None of the administrators he'd talked with would acknowledge knowing a Professor Abramson. None had an Angela Villanueva on their admissions lists.

This is stupid, Del told himself as he headed for his rental car. They could be hiding Angie from me. She could be in any one of these hospitals and I'd have no way of knowing.

He thought about going to the police for help, but figured that would be a waste of time.

Where the hell is Hightower? He knows where Angie is.

But he didn't have Hightower's phone number, and the FBI agent had threatened to have him arrested if he didn't go home.

Home. His cell phone had buzzed half a dozen times this morning, but he'd ignored the incoming calls while he was talking with the hospital people. Probably Norrie, he thought, wanting to know what I've accomplished. Which is zilch.

Sliding in behind the steering wheel he pulled out his cell phone and, sure enough, there were six calls from his wife.

Hating to admit he'd failed, Del deleted the messages. But as he reached for the car's ignition, he relented and called Lenore.

"Del!" Norrie's voice was bursting with delight. "They found her! That Agent Hightower called this morning and told me they know where Angie is!"

Del listened to his wife's eager babble, half joyful that they'd found his daughter, half resentful that he'd been such a miserable failure at doing the job himself.

Paul Rossov

I T WAS NEARLY noon when Rossov's flight landed at Portland International Airport. He was met by a professional chauffeur, as arranged by his office back in the White House. Surprisingly, the chauffeur was a young woman, fairly good-looking, with creamy dark skin, tightly kinked strawberry hair, and strangely hazel eyes.

A lot of crossbreeding there, he thought. Generations of miscegenation. Smiling inwardly he thought, *E pluribus unum.* She'd make a great poster girl for the nation's motto. Especially in the nude.

The chauffeur stowed Rossov's overnight bag in the limousine's trunk, then drove unerringly to the Bartram Research Laboratories complex.

Once he told the cute receptionist who he was, Shannon Bartram herself came to the lobby to greet him. She was younger than Rossov had expected, a bit on the blousy side but basically good-looking despite the extra weight.

"It's been a busy day," Mrs. Bartram said as she led Rossov back to her office. "First the FBI and now you."

"Agent Hightower was here," Rossov said.

"Oh, yes. This morning. He and his partner met with Professor Abramson. It was a good meeting."

"Abramson's here."

"Yes, he's been here for several days, with his granddaughter and Dr. Minteer."

She walked him past a secretary and into her own office. Rossov took it all in with a glance; desk by the window, conference table in the corner, bookshelves. Everything neat as a pin.

As he took one of the chairs in front of the desk, he said, "I need to talk to Abramson. In private."

"Of course," Mrs. Bartram said, settling into her desk chair. "He's busy at the moment, having a tissue sample taken, but he'll be available in an hour or so."

"And the little girl?"

"She's either in her room or out on the grounds, taking a walk. Dr. Minteer is with her, wherever she is."

"Can I see her?"

Mrs. Bartram's face contracted briefly into a frown, but she quickly forced a smile. "Wouldn't you like some lunch first? I'm sure the airline food wasn't all that satisfying."

"I'm fine," said Rossov. "I'd like to see Angela Villanueva." He spoke the words pleasantly enough. No need to get tough with her, he thought, unless she puts up some resistance.

Bartram picked up her desk phone. "Let me make sure where she is."

After a few words into the phone, she got to her feet. "She's in her room with Dr. Minteer."

As she led him out of the office, Rossov realized, "You haven't had your lunch yet, have you?"

Bartram managed a smile. "Oh, that's all right. I'm trying to slim down a little. I can afford to skip a meal."

When they got to Angela's room, Luke Abramson was there as well, together with a tall, slim, attractive brunette. The child was sitting by the window, bent over a digital game that emitted faint beeps.

Rossov went straight to Abramson and stuck out his hand. "I'm Paul Rossov, special assistant to the President of the United States."

Abramson looked surprised. "You work in the White House?"

"I do. But I flew out here to meet you, Professor."

"I guess I should be flattered."

Rossov smiled thinly. "I think your work is tremendously important."

"That's . . ." Abramson fished for a word. "Good," he finished lamely.

"And this must be Angela." The child looked up from her game, and Rossov's breath caught in his throat. Angela Villanueva didn't look like an eight-year-old child; she looked like a geriatric midget.

The brunette broke the sudden silence. "I'm Angela's physician, Tamara Minteer."

"Hello," he said, his eyes still on Angela.

Angela said, "Hello."

Turning to Abramson, Rossov asked, "What's wrong with her?"

Abramson's face turned stony. "Progeria. It's a side effect of the therapy that eliminated her brain cancer."

"She recovering nicely," Minteer added, moving to Angela's side. "Soon she'll be completely back to normal."

"I'm going home pretty soon," Angela said.

Rossov thought, Maybe not, kid. Maybe not.

To Abramson, he said, "We have to talk. The highest levels of government have taken an interest in your work."

The professor forced a tight smile. "That's good. I've been fired from the university, you know."

Wrapping an arm around Abramson's shoulder, Rossov said, "Not to worry. We can take care of that."

Shannon Bartram said, "Why don't we go to my office? We can talk it all out there. And I'll have some snacks sent in."

H EY, WE GONNA sit out here all day?" Novack grumped.
Hightower had cranked the driver's seat back to where he

felt reasonably comfortable. "Did you see that limo come up the road?"

"Yeah."

"I imagine that's the White House guy."

"Okay," said Novack. "So your backup from Salem has arrived and they're watching the road. The White House guy is inside, talking to Abramson. Let's get back to the hotel and get something to eat, for chrissakes."

"Aren't you curious about why the White House is interested in this case? I am."

"And we're gonna find out about it while we're sitting here in the cold?"

"I don't feel cold," Hightower said.

"I sure as hell do."

Thinking it over for a second, Hightower started up the Chevrolet's engine. "Okay. Let's go back up to the labs. It'll be warmer inside."

Fisk Tower

QUENTON FISK GLARED at the image on his wall screen. It was the chief of his Washington office, the man he paid handsomely to know what was going on in the labyrinths of the federal government.

"We know there was a meeting in the Oval Office last week," said Neville O'Connor, "with the Secretary of the Treasury and the Attorney General. Apparently they were discussing Abramson's work."

"Apparently?" Fisk snapped.

O'Connor, a large, round, perfectly bald man replied blandly, "We don't have the White House bugged, Mr. Fisk."

Fisk let the irony pass him by. "Somebody from the White House is out in Oregon right now, talking with Abramson."

O'Connor pursed his lips. "Probably a result of that meeting last week."

"Why would the White House be interested in Abramson's work?"

"Beats the hell out of me," O'Connor replied. Before Fisk could explode, he quickly added, "But we'll find out. Give us a couple of days. We'll find out."

"You do that," Fisk said coldly. He tapped a button on his phone console and O'Connor's image winked out.

Why would the White House be interested in Abramson's research? he asked himself again. I can see the Justice Department's interest: The FBI is part of that department. But why Treasury? What's the Treasury Department's interest?

Steepling his fingers and leaning back in his comfortably yielding desk chair, Fisk stared up at the ceiling and tried to think it out.

Abramson's working on life extension. He's made old lab rats young again, and he wants to try the same trick on chimps. And then humans, eventually.

If he can rejuvenate old people, his work is worth a fortune and a half. And it's *mine*. I'm his sole source of funding, and he's signed a privacy agreement. He's tied to me, tied tightly.

But the government could step in and upset the apple cart. Somebody in Washington could find some legal reason to take Abramson away from me.

He made a mental note to get his legal department to check on the Abramson agreements.

Then it hit him. Abramson's granddaughter. She was dying of cancer, and he kidnapped her so he could treat her. Has he succeeded?

Abruptly, he sat up straight and banged on his desktop intercom. "Get Novack on the line," he commanded his secretary. "I don't care where he is or what he's doing. I want to talk to him *now*."

A S SHANNON LED Luke and Rossov back toward her office, the White House man asked, "Is there a conference room someplace, where Professor Abramson and I could speak in private?"

Shannon stopped, frowning slightly. "Why, yes. Of course. This way."

They turned a corner and went past several doors. Through one of them Luke saw a middle-aged man sitting at a desk, staring into space. Thinking, he figured. Or daydreaming. He noticed the whiteboard behind the man, covered with chemical equations. Not daydreaming. Thinking.

Shannon opened a door and ushered them into a small conference room: round table, six cushioned chairs, sideboard bare except for a telephone, cabinets, no windows.

"Will this do?" she asked.

"Fine," said Rossov, with a nod.

"I'll be in my office," she said, gesturing toward the phone on the sideboard. "Extension one."

"Easy to remember." Rossov smiled as Shannon left the room and quietly closed the door.

"Have a seat," he told Luke. It was more of a command than a suggestion.

Luke pulled out one of the chairs, and Rossov took the one next to him, turning it to face Luke.

"You look younger than your photographs," Rossov said, with a smile that was meant to be disarming.

Luke studied his face. It was narrow, bony, with probing gray eyes and thin sandy hair combed straight back off his high forehead.

"I've been taking telomerase accelerators," he admitted.

Rossov's pointed chin went up a notch. "And it's working, isn't it?"

"So far."

"Your granddaughter's really cured?" His voice was sharp, eager. Luke got the impression of a rat that had just discovered a sizable morsel of cheese.

"Her brain tumors are gone. Now we've got to get her past the side effects."

"Progeria, it's called?"

Luke nodded.

Rossov stared hard at Luke. At last he said, "Professor, we think your work is incredibly important."

"We?"

"The highest levels of government. The very highest."

"NIH doesn't," Luke said. "They dropped my funding."

"That was a mistake."

Luke said nothing. What's he after? he asked himself. What's he fishing for?

Rossov said, "I understand that the Fisk Foundation is funding your work now."

"That's right."

"We would like you to work under federal sponsorship again. We'll provide you with the finest laboratory facilities and staff. You'll have everything you want."

"And the Fisk Foundation?"

"We'll take care of them. Your work is too important to be monopolized by a private organization."

"But Quenton Fisk—"

"Is no match for the President of the United States," Rossov said, as if he had just pulled a rabbit out of a hat.

Despite himself, Luke whistled softly. "The President?"

With a sly grin, Rossov said, "As I told you, the very highest levels of government are interested in your work."

"That's . . . very good to know," Luke said.

Clasping his long-fingered hands together, Rossov said, "Okay. We'll have to set up a facility for you. Someplace where you won't be bothered by outside pressures. You and your granddaughter and Dr. Minteer."

"You know that the FBI wants me on a kidnapping charge."

"Oh, that will be dropped. You just leave everything to me."

"And Dr. Minteer—you'll need to restore her credentials."

"No problem. Anyway, she'll work with you and your granddaughter for the time being."

A tiny voice in Luke's head was telling him that this was all too good to be true, but he heard himself ask, "Could you arrange for Angela's parents to come out and see her? They're pretty upset about all this, you know."

Rossov's almost jovial expression soured a bit. But he said, "Sure. Certainly. Not right away, of course. But we'll get word to them, let the little girl talk to them on Skype, that sort of thing."

Luke nodded uncertainly.

Reaching out to pat Luke's knee, Rossov said, "You just leave everything to me. I'll take care of all of you."

Bartram Research Laboratories

U H-OH," SAID HIGHTOWER.

He and Novack were sitting in the lobby, waiting for the White House man to come out. Novack had his cell phone plastered to his ear; Hightower could hear a loud angry voice yammering at him.

And then Del Villanueva pushed through the glass door and stalked up to the receptionist's desk, striding past Hightower and Novack without noticing them.

Loud enough for Hightower to hear him clearly, Villanueva demanded, "I'm Delgado Villanueva, Angela's father. I've come to see my daughter."

The receptionist looked startled. "Angela Villanueva?" she asked.

"That's right. She's here, and I want to see her, right now!"

Hightower pushed himself up from the couch and started toward the reception desk. Novack, still on the phone, watched him.

"I'll call Mrs. Bartram," said the receptionist.

"I don't want to see Mrs. Bartram or anybody else. I'm here to see my daughter!"

"But—"

"Mr. Villanueva," Hightower said, in a soft, friendly tone.

Villanueva whipped around. "So you're here," he said. "You can't stop me from seeing Angie!"

Shaking his head slowly, Hightower said, "I have no intention of stopping you from seeing your daughter. Who do you think phoned your wife and told her Angela was here?"

"Well, I want to see her. Now."

Hightower flashed his FBI credentials at the receptionist. "I'm Special Agent Hightower."

"I remember you from this morning," the young woman said.

"I can vouch for this man. He is Angela Villanueva's father."

Nodding, the receptionist repeated, "I'll call Mrs. Bartram."

Villanueva burst out, "I told you I don't want—"

Hightower laid a placating hand on his shoulder. "It's all right. We're going to see your daughter."

Novack came up to them. Hightower introduced Villanueva while the receptionist phoned Bartram.

Calming somewhat, Villanueva asked Hightower, "How is Angie? Is she okay?"

"The doctors say that her cancer's gone."

"Thank God!"

"There are some side effects, though."

"Side effects? What?"

Shannon Bartram came through the door that led into the building. She looked tired.

Hightower introduced Villanueva to her.

"Where's my daughter? I want to see her."

"Certainly," said Bartram, although her voice sounded less than enthusiastic to Hightower.

She led the three men into the building's central hallway, telling them, "We ought to pick up Professor Abramson along the way. He can explain about Angela's condition."

"Condition? What condition?" Turning to Hightower, Villanueva said, "You told me she's been cured."

"Side effects," Hightower murmured.

Bartram stopped at a door marked CONFERENCE ROOM C and tapped on it.

After a few seconds, Paul Rossov opened the door.

"Mrs. Bartram, what a sense of timing you have," Rossov said, with a plastic smile. "We were just about to phone you."

Luke got to his feet, his expression somewhere between pained and resigned. "Hello, Del," he said, walking to the doorway.

"Luke. Where's Angie?"

"She's all right. She's going to be fine."

"What the hell have you done to her?"

"Cured her. She's cancer-free."

"But what else?"

Luke pushed between Del and Hightower, out into the hallway. As he started toward Angela's room he began to explain about progeria. The others stayed silent while Luke talked.

"It's temporary, Del. She's already improving."

"Like an elderly person? Is she crippled? Sick?"

"No, her body's just reacting to the treatment that killed the tumors. She looks old. Somatically, she is old. Like me."

"You don't look so old."

"That's another story."

They reached the door to Angela's room. Shannon hesitated, then turned to Hightower and the others. "I think it would be best if Professor Abramson and the girl's father went in without the rest of us. No sense turning this into a mob scene."

Rossov glanced up at Hightower, then said, "You're right. Let's wait in your office."

Bartram looked less than happy about that but nodded agreement.

Hightower laid a heavy hand on Luke's shoulder. "You ought to know that there are a couple of Bureau cars out along the road. If you try to skip out, they'll stop you."

Luke almost smiled at him. "I'm not going to skip out on you. My running days are over."

"Good." Hightower turned to Bartram and said, "Let's go to your office."

Luke watched them walk down the hallway. It looked as if Shannon were being escorted by a contingent of guards.

"Well, come on," Del urged.

Luke grasped the doorknob, hesitated. "Remember, she's going to look old."

"You already told me that."

"And, uh, she's got a cast on her left forearm."

"A cast?"

"She broke her wrist, chasing a rabbit."

"What?"

"She'll be fine, Del. The bone is healing normally." Silently, Luke added *almost*.

"I want to see her."

"Right."

Pulling the door open, Luke ushered Del into the room. Angela was sitting by the window, bent over her smartphone. Tamara Minteer was on the other side of the room, tapping on a laptop.

Rising to her feet, Tamara called out, "Angie! Look who's here!"

Angela turned. Her eyes went wide and she jumped up from the chair she'd been sitting on, her smartphone falling to the carpet.

"Daddy!" She flew to Del's arms.

Del saw his daughter, but she looked like an eighty-year-old, wrinkled and painfully thin. And there was a cast on her left wrist.

"Angie!" he gulped, wrapping his arms around her. "My little Angel."

Luke stood in the doorway and watched the two embrace. Don't squeeze her too tightly, he warned mentally. Her bones are still pretty brittle.

Tamara came to Luke's side, her eyes glistening with tears.

Breathlessly, Angela told her father, "I'm getting better, Daddy, I really am. Grandpa says I'll be able to go home soon."

Del glanced up at Luke, then said, "We should call your mother. She'd like to hear your voice."

"Good idea," said Luke.

Del whipped out his cell phone and punched a speed-dial key. In a moment, he said into the phone, "Norrie, it's me. I'm with Angie. She's right here."

Then he handed the phone to Angela, who began chattering into it, happy as only an eight-year-old could be.

Luke said to Tamara, "I'm going to Shannon's office and try to get things straightened out. Do you mind staying here with Angie?"

"Not at all," Tamara replied. "She's overjoyed."

But Luke saw the expression on Del's face. He looked bitterly angry.

Plan of Action

THE SECRETARY OUTSIDE Shannon's office looked up as Luke came into the anteroom.

"Mrs. Bee said she didn't want to be disturbed."

"I'm the guy they're talking about," Luke said, without stopping. "I won't be disturbing them."

Before the secretary could say anything more, he opened the door to Shannon's office and went in. She was at the round conference table, with Rossov, Hightower, and Novack.

". . . so it's open and shut," Rossov was saying. "We find a suitable facility for Abramson and his grand—"

They all turned to look at Luke as he entered the room.

"You find a suitable facility for me and Angela," he echoed, "and then what?"

Rossov tilted his head slightly. "Then you do your research without any hindrances."

Shannon gestured to one of the unoccupied chairs, but Luke remained standing.

"And once Angie's finished with the progeria, she can go home." Luke said it flatly; it wasn't a question, it was a statement.

Rossov put on a smile and answered easily. "Sure."

Shannon said, "I don't see why they can't stay right here. We have the facilities and the staff Luke needs."

"No, we need a secure facility," Rossov said. "A place where Professor Abramson can work without any outside interference."

"Wait a minute," said Novack. "The Fisk Foundation is funding the professor's work. Mr. Fisk himself is very interested in what he's doing."

Rossov's smile froze in place. "I'll meet with Mr. Fisk and explain the situation to him. I'm sure we can work something out."

Novack hmmphed. "Lotsa luck."

"So for the time being," Luke said, "we stay here."

Shannon nodded and Rossov said, "For the time being."

"What about Dr. Minteer?"

"Her credentials will be restored."

"She can go back to Massachusetts, then?"

"Once the little girl is fit to return home. Until then, the three of you ought to stay together."

"Makes sense, I suppose," Luke murmured.

The intercom on Shannon's desk buzzed. Frowning, she got up from the conference table and hurried to her desk.

"I told you I wasn't to be disturbed," she said sharply into the phone console.

Her secretary's voice sounded agitated. "It's Mr. Villanueva! He says he's taking his daughter home and he's not stopping for anybody or anything!"

Del Villanueva

T AMARA MINTEER STOOD defiantly between Angela and her
father.

"You can't take her out of here," she said to Del, half tena-
cious, half pleading.

"You can't stop me," Del said. "Not you, not Luke, not the whole
fucking FBI."

"But—"

Dropping into a crouch, Del held his arms out to his daughter.
She stepped to him and let him embrace her once more.

"You want to go home, don't you, Angie?"

"Yes," in a tiny, almost mournful voice.

"Well, Daddy's going to take you home. Today. Mommy's waiting to see you."

"I miss Mommy."

"You'll be back home tonight." Looking up at Tamara, he said,
"Help me pack her things."

Luke entered the room, followed by the two FBI agents, Mrs. Bartram, and a slick-looking guy in a three-piece gray suit.

"Del, you can't take Angie away," Luke said.

"The hell I can't."

"She's still under treatment, for God's sake!"

"You can treat her in Boston."

"I'm afraid that won't be possible," said the slick guy, stepping up beside Luke.

"Why not? And who the hell are you to tell me I can't take my own daughter back to her mother?"

Very deliberately, Rossov answered, "My name is Paul Rossov. I'm a special assistant to the President of the United States."

Del straightened up. He towered over Rossov. "I don't give a damn if you're God Almighty. I'm taking Angie home."

"There's more involved here than you realize, Mr. Villanueva. Professor Abramson is doing some very complicated research. He can't go back to Boston, not just yet."

"She can go with us," Del said, pointing to Tamara. "She's Angie's doctor; she's been taking care of my daughter all along."

Rossov shook his head and started to say, "You don't understand—"

Novack came up to Del with an easy smile on his face. "Let's all stay calm. I'm sure we can work this out. Mr. Villanueva, would you step outside with me, please?"

Suspiciously, Del asked, "What for?"

"Just a little talk, one on one. Before everybody gets too excited." Nodding in Angela's direction, he added, "You don't want to upset the little girl, do you?"

Del glared suspiciously at them all: his father-in-law, the big Indian with his ponytail, the chubby woman who apparently owned the place, Angie's doctor, the guy who claimed he was from the White House. All their eyes were on him. Then finally he looked at Angela herself. Angie seemed almost frightened, her eyes wide in her old woman's face.

"Come on," Novack coaxed. "Just you and me. We can work this out."

"Okay, I guess," Del replied warily. To Angela, he said, "I'll be right back, honey. You help Dr. Minteer pack your clothes."

And he walked uncertainly out into the hallway with Novack.

Luke watched them go, thinking, Novack must be a snake charmer.

Angela stood in the middle of the room, her eyes fixed on the door that her father had gone through.

Tamara knelt beside her and said softly, "He'll be back in a few minutes."

Angela nodded silently.

"Come on," Tamara coaxed, "let's get your suitcase and start packing."

Luke wanted to tell her not to do that, but he said nothing.

Shannon sat on the bed, looking perplexed.

"I've never had such a crazy day," she muttered, as if talking to herself.

Luke turned to Hightower. "I thought you were his boss."

Hightower shook his head slowly. "He's not with the Bureau. He works for the Fisk Foundation."

"I thought—"

"I'm pretty sure he works directly for Fisk himself."

Looking toward the open door to the hallway, Luke wondered, "Then what the hell's he doing with Del?"

NOVACK SAUNTERED SLOWLY along the hallway, with Del beside him, trying to keep his long legs from outpacing the shorter man.

"I'd like you to consider the big picture here," Novack said.

Del snapped, "The only picture I want to consider is seeing my daughter reunited with her mother."

They came to the end of the hallway and a steel door marked EXIT TO ROOF. Novack pushed it open. "Well, that will happen, don't worry about it. It just isn't going to happen today."

"The hell it's not."

Novack started climbing the bare concrete stairs, his footsteps echoing hollowly. Following behind him, Del demanded, "Where the fuck are you going?"

"No place special," Novack answered easily. "It's just easier to talk here in the fire escape. Nobody else but us two. No snoops."

"Listen," Del snapped, "I'm taking my daughter home and not you or the whole FBI is going to stop me."

They reached a landing between floors. Novack turned to Del and said, "I can give you five thousand reasons to back off."

"What the fuck are you talking about?"

"Five thousand bucks."

"Five thousand dollars?"

"Five thousand in your hand today," Novack said smoothly, "and another five thou for every week the kid's kept away from home."

"You're trying to bribe me! An FBI agent offering me a bribe! I'll report you."

Novack made a shushing motion with one hand as he said, "Take it easy. I'm not with the FBI. I work for Quenton Fisk."

"Who the hell is Quenton Fisk?"

"One of the richest men in the country. And he can make you rich, too, if you'll play along."

"That's my daughter we're talking about. Keep your fucking money!"

"I'll make it ten thousand. Ten now and ten for every week the kid's away from home."

"Go shove it up your ass."

Del started toward the stairs, but Novack had maneuvered himself between Del and the steps. Del tried to push him aside; Novack brushed his arms away.

Del looked down at this wiry little guy. He was smiling, sort of, as he blocked access to the stairway.

"I don't want to hurt you," Del said, clenching his fists.

"I wouldn't at all mind hurting you," Novack said, his grin widening. His arms remained at his sides. He looked relaxed, at ease.

Del grabbed for his shoulders, intending to push the smaller man out of his way. Novack ducked under his reaching arms and planted a solid right fist in the pit of Del's stomach. The air gushing from his lungs, Del staggered back against the bare concrete wall. Novack drove two more punches into Del's midsection. The pain was incredible; Del's legs began to fold.

"Not yet," Novack muttered, pinning Del against the wall. He grabbed a fistful of hair and smashed the back of Del's head against the concrete. Del's vision blurred.

Dragging Del's half-collapsed body to the edge of the stairway, Novack rammed a vicious punch into his right kidney, then kicked Del's legs out from under him. Del went tumbling down the bare concrete steps and sprawled unconscious on the landing below.

Novack stepped lightly down the stairs, stooped to check Del's breathing, then went out into the hallway, heading back to the kid's room.

L UKE WATCHED TAMARA and Angie placing the child's clothes in the suitcase they had bought for her during their brief shopping spree in Portland. Women, he thought. They fold each piece just so, and lay it in the suitcase like it's made of crystal. The clothes will get all rumpled during the trip, but they still have to be so neat, so precise.

Shannon was still sitting on the bed, looking weary. It's been a hell of a day for her, Luke realized. The FBI, this White House guy, and now Del.

"I still don't see why Professor Abramson can't stay and continue his work here," Shannon was saying.

Rossov, sitting beside Luke, shook his head. "We need a secure facility, Mrs. Bartram. A place where the professor can work without distraction."

"Like where?" Luke asked.

"I have people checking federal research facilities," Rossov said. "I don't know which ones, off the top of my head."

Hightower stood by the door, arms folded across his chest, like a cigar store Indian. Silent and still. But his eyes were alert. He doesn't miss anything, Luke thought.

The door burst open and Novack stepped in, looking flustered. "There's been an accident."

Luke jumped to his feet. "What?"

Novack said, "Your son-in-law, he fell down a flight of stairs."

"Daddy?" Angela bleated.

"It's all right," Tamara said, placing a restraining hand on the child's shoulder. "Your grandfather will take care of it."

Luke headed for the door, Hightower and Rossov right behind him. Over his shoulder, he told Tamara, "Stay with Angie."

The four men hurried down the hallway. Novack was explaining, "We went into the fire escape, for privacy. He got all excited and started swinging at me. We scuffled, and he fell down the stairs."

Luke opened the fire door and there was Del, semiconscious, moaning, a gash on his forehead bleeding down his face.

Kneeling beside his son-in-law, Luke muttered, "He might have a concussion."

Rossov said, "Good thing we're in a medical facility."

Pointing to the intercom phone on the wall out in the hallway, Luke commanded, "Phone Shannon—Mrs. Bartram. Extension one." He figured that Shannon's secretary would know the number of the phone extension in Angie's room.

Rossov dashed to the wall phone. Hightower knelt beside Luke, then looked up at Novack, his face like a carving made of ice.

The White House

PAUL ROSSOV FELT grungy. He had flown from Portland to Seattle, bumping a disgruntled businessman off the flight, then taken the redeye from Seattle to Washington, D.C.

Years earlier he had taught himself the knack of sleeping on an airplane: put a pillow behind your neck, crank the chair as far back as it will go, close your eyes, and think of erotic fantasies. So he was reasonably fresh by the time his plane landed.

But his clothes were wrinkled and sour-smelling. He needed a shower and badly needed a shave. Still, he told the chauffeur that was waiting for him at the Baltimore/Washington airport to drive him directly to the White House.

I can shower and shave there, he told himself as the limo weaved through the morning traffic. I've got a couple of fresh shirts in my office.

By nine A.M. Rossov was at his desk, showered, shaved, wearing a crisply clean shirt, and on the phone with Quenton Fisk.

Fisk's image in the phone's console screen looked wary, scowling.

"Abramson works for me," he said, once Rossov explained what he wanted. "I fund his work, and he's signed a privacy agreement."

"Of course, of course," Rossov said, as placatingly as he could manage. "But Professor Abramson's work has some important national implications."

Fisk huffed. "If he's cured that child of brain cancer, I'll say it has national implications."

"Look, Mr. Fisk," Rossov said smoothly, "this is too important to discuss over the phone. I'd like to talk with you face-to-face, if it's all right with you."

Fisk's eyes shifted away. He's checking his calendar, Rossov thought. Good.

"How about the day after tomorrow?"

"Don't you have any time free today? I can get up to New York in a couple of hours."

Shaking his head, Fisk said, "Today's impossible." Before Rossov could reply he added, "Unless you want to have cocktails. Say, around five?"

"Five o'clock. That's fine."

"Here in my office," Fisk said.

"I'll be there."

A S ROSSOV'S IMAGE winked off from his wall screen, Fisk bellowed into his intercom, "Get Novack on the phone. And get me a dossier on a Paul Rossov. He's some sort of aide in the White House."

Within minutes Novack's face appeared on the wall screen. He looked grim.

Without preamble he said, "We've got to get Abramson out of here, Mr. Fisk. Too many people butting in."

Then he explained about the White House aide and Del Villa-nueva.

"The girl's father?" Fisk hadn't expected that. "How did you handle him?"

With a smirk, Novack said, "The poor slob had an accident yesterday. Fell down a flight of steps. He's in bed with a concussion. He won't be taking the kid anywhere for a couple of days."

Fisk accepted that without comment. "I'm meeting with the same Paul Rossov this afternoon."

Novack looked impressed. "He gets around."

"I want to find out just what the White House's interest in Abramson might be."

Novack nodded.

"You make certain that Abramson stays where he is until I tell you where to move him. And the little girl, too. Control her and you control Abramson."

"What about the kid's doctor? She's hot."

"Keep her with Abramson and the kid. I don't want her loose and blabbing this story to anybody."

"Check," said Novack.

THE DEEPER HE got into this case, the less Jerry Hightower liked it. At first it looked like little more than a family spat, but then his boss insisted on filing a kidnapping charge against Abramson, and now he was telling Hightower to keep the professor where he was.

"Don't let him get away from you again." His director's voice sounded urgent in Hightower's cell phone. He sounded almost scared.

"He seems okay with staying here at the Bartram labs," Hightower reported.

"Good," said the director. Then he repeated, "Don't let him get away from you again."

The "again" made Hightower wince.

LUKE STOOD BY his son-in-law's bed. Del's head was swathed in bandages, but his eyes seemed clear enough. Shannon's medical people had diagnosed a concussion right away, but when Del urinated blood they ran him through an MRI. His right kidney was swollen to twice its normal size.

"He beat the crap out of me," Del was mumbling. "And then he threw me down the stairs."

Luke wondered how much was true and how much was hallucinations from the painkillers they had pumped into Del's veins.

"Why did he do it?" he wondered aloud.

"Didn't want me to take Angie home," said Del, his words slightly slurred. "Offered me big bucks to let her stay with you."

Luke felt his brows knitting in puzzlement. "And you say he works for Quenton Fisk? He's not with the FBI?"

"That's what he told me." Del's eyes closed briefly, then he muttered, "Used me for a fucking punching bag."

The door opened and Tamara stepped in, with Angela beside her. The child's eyes went wide when she saw her father's bandaged head.

"Daddy!" She ran to Del on pipestem-thin legs, Tamara within arm's reach every step of the way.

He held out his arms to her, even though the motion cost him a sharp stab of pain. "Angie baby."

"You're hurt, Daddy." Angela's eyes filled with tears.

"Nah, it's nothing, Angel. Just a bop on the head. I'll be okay in a day or two."

And Luke realized, In the meantime we're all going to stay right here. Nobody's leaving this place, not for a few days, at least.

I CAN GIVE YOU half an hour," said Quenton Fisk, as he reached across his desk to shake hands with Paul Rossov.

Rossov nodded. He had arrived at Fisk's office ten minutes before five, and cooled his heels by the secretary's desk until precisely five P.M. No cocktails, he thought ruefully. Just as well, I'll need a clear head to deal with this guy.

"So what about Professor Abramson?" Fisk asked.

Rossov settled himself in the upholstered chair in front of the desk before replying. "We need to find a secure federal facility where he can continue his research."

"Under your watchful eye," said Fisk.

"That's one way to put it."

"I'm paying for his work. The government isn't going to screw me out of it."

"We have no intention of doing that," said Rossov. Then he added, "But his work has got to be controlled, controlled very carefully."

Fisk leaned back in his swivel chair, his face radiating suspicion. "Tell me why."

"Do you have any idea of how Abramson's work could affect Social Security, Medicare, retirement programs, the insurance industry?"

"His work could make a lot of money for me. More tax income for you people."

"Yes, but what good would that do you if the economy collapses? Take away cancer as a major cause of death, let just about anybody live to be a hundred or more—the economy would be wrecked. It'd make the Great Depression look like a Christmas holiday."

Fisk stared at him without speaking. Rossov could sense the wheels in his head churning.

Finally Fisk said, "You can't keep breakthroughs like this from the public."

"Not indefinitely, I agree," said Rossov. "But we can control their effects. Let the new therapies enter the marketplace gradually, not in a big, uncontrolled thump."

"Gradually."

"Keep Abramson busy with human trials. Make sure there are no harmful side effects, that sort of thing. That'll take years. Once we've ascertained that the treatments work the way they should, we allow a few selected people to benefit from them. Keep things under control."

"And how do I make money out of that?" Fisk snapped.

Rossov smiled thinly. "Two ways. The government will grant you patents on the new therapies."

"You can't patent a therapy."

"Oh yes you can," Rossov shot back. "I've checked with the Patent Office. You can patent a new medical method, a set of unique steps that lead to a previously unobtainable outcome."

"Really?"

"Really. You'll have the patents, and the full protection of federal law."

"A monopoly."

"A monopoly," Rossov agreed. "For as long as the patent laws allow. More than ten years, I believe."

For the first time, Fisk smiled. "I see," he said. "And you allow this treatment for a selected few people."

"Who will pay just about whatever you want to charge them."

"I'd make a lot more profits if the therapies were made available to the general public."

"Yes. And a year or so later the stock market would collapse and the whole economy go down the drain. Where would you be then?"

Fisk went silent again, steeping his fingers and staring at Rossov. Don't blink, Rossov told himself. Stare him down.

"What if I don't go along with you?" Fisk asked. "You can't force me, you know."

Nodding, Rossov said, "You don't want to have the federal government against you. There's a thousand ways we could tie you up, make your life miserable."

"You're threatening me?"

"I'm asking for your voluntary cooperation."

Fisk went silent, looking grim. But at last he asked, "I'd have a monopoly on the treatment?"

"For as long as the patents allow."

"And we bring the new therapies to the marketplace gradually."

Rossov nodded again.

"But we do bring the therapies to the marketplace," Fisk insisted.

"Of course. In time."

"I'll probably need cancer therapy myself in a few years," Fisk murmured. "It runs in my family."

"You'll get it," Rossov promised.

Fisk drew in a big breath, then let it sigh out of him. "All right. I'll go along with you. I'll tell my legal people to start work on a patent application."

"I'll see to it that it's given top priority by the Patent Office."

"And I want a legal piece of paper about this agreement between us."

"It'll have to be classified secret, of course."

"With the President's signature on it."

Rossov hesitated a moment, then said, "That can be arranged."

Fisk nodded back at him. "Now all you have to do is get Abramson to go along with you."

"That can be arranged, too," said Rossov.

Bartram Research Laboratories

"IDAHO?" LUKE BLURTED. "Why Idaho?"

Paul Rossov smiled at him. "It's a secure facility. You'll be able to work there without being bothered."

It was four days after Del's "accident." Luke's son-in-law was almost fully recovered and itching to get out of bed. Hightower seemed to be standing watch over them all, a massive presence, silent but seemingly omnipresent. Novack had faded into the background; Luke thought that Hightower felt better off with Fisk's man some distance away.

Luke had left Angela speaking through Skype with her mother, who was still back in Boston. Angie was looking better, good enough so that her appearance didn't seem to unsettle Norrie. At least she didn't look upset. She was all smiles and happiness to be talking with her daughter.

Leaving Angie in Tamara's care, Luke had gone out to the lone tennis court behind the main laboratory building for a game with one of the lab's staff researchers. They couldn't round up two more people, so they played singles, the first time Luke had done that in years. Decades, actually.

The White House executive had appeared unannounced at the tennis court. Luke had broken off the game he'd been playing to talk with him. Just as well, he thought: The guy's beating me damned easily. Should have stuck to doubles.

Now Rossov and Luke were walking down the hallway that led to Del's room, Luke in shorts and a sweat-stained T-shirt, Rossov in his usual precise three-piece gray suit.

Shaking his head, Luke said, "I don't know of any facility in Idaho that has the equipment or the staff that I need."

"It's there, believe me. And whatever equipment or staff you need, I'll see to it that you get them."

"Idaho," Luke muttered.

"Good ski country," Rossov coaxed.

"Good way to break a leg," Luke grumbled.

Rossov laughed. "I thought you'd be interested in skiing, considering how much your physical condition has improved."

"Not me. Tennis is challenge enough."

They came to Del's room. Luke rapped once on the door and opened it. His son-in-law was sitting up in bed, with Angela beside him, both of them bent over a laptop. Tamara was standing at the foot of the bed. As Luke entered, she turned and smiled at him. Luke could hear Norrie's voice coming from the computer.

I DAHO?" TAMARA LOOKED totally surprised.

"That's what Rossov tells me," said Luke.

They had left Del's room and gone to the cafeteria. Now they were sitting at a small table, heads bent together so they could talk low and still hear each other over the babble and clatter.

"Me, too?" she asked.

"For the first few weeks," he said.

Tamara's green eyes shifted away. Luke knew what she was thinking: She'd put her entire career in jeopardy by following him on this desperate trek across the country; now he was asking her to stay with him a while longer, keep her career on hold to continue taking care of Angela.

"I know it's a lot to ask," he said.

Tamara shrugged. "Like I've got a lot to go back to in Massachusetts."

"Think of it this way," he coaxed. "You'll be the only physician in the world who's actually participated in this new therapy. You're the attending physician in a case where glioblastoma multiforme's been cured."

She smiled wanly. "I'm also the physician of record in the first case of human age reversal."

"You'll be able to write your own ticket."

"I wonder."

"Of course you will!"

"Luke . . ." She hesitated.

"What?"

"What about us?"

"Us?"

"You and me," she said, her voice low. Barely looking at him across the table, Tamara said, "Is there a future for the two of us? Together?"

There it is, Luke thought. Out in the open. With a shake of his head, he replied, "I hope so."

"So do I."

He reached across the table and took both her hands in his. "Tamara . . . I'm an old man, you know. Old enough to be your father."

She smiled impishly. "Yes, Daddy."

Luke wanted to reach across the table and kiss her. But instead he simply sat in place, holding her hands, staring into her gleaming green eyes.

At last he said, "It might not be so bad in Idaho. The two of us, I mean."

Tamara nodded, but her smile faded. "What about this place in Idaho? It sounds almost like a federal prison."

"No," he said. "Rossov assured me we'd have a top-flight staff and all the equipment we want."

"Would we be able to leave?"

He shrugged. "You want to go skiing?"

"I don't want to be kept under lock and key in some federal facility in the middle of nowhere."

Luke's brows knit. So much for romance, he thought.

"Look, Tamara," he said, "we've got the opportunity to carry Angie's treatment to its conclusion. And my own. Top staff, no interference from asses like Wexler. You'll be coauthor on all the papers I'll write."

Looking askance, she asked, "They'll allow you to publish?"

Luke felt shocked. "They can't stop me from publishing! For God's sake, that's what science is all about: to do experiments and publish them."

Tamara nodded. But she did not look convinced.

N OVACK WAS SITTING in his motel room, making his daily report to Fisk. On his laptop's screen, Fisk looked calm, almost pleasant. But Novack knew that was only skin deep.

"The arrangements for transferring them to Idaho are almost complete," Fisk told him. "Another couple of days and off they all go."

"The kid's father, too?"

Fisk replied, "I've talked that over with Rossov. Yes, bring the father along with you. Hightower is going to fly out to Boston and offer Mrs. Villanueva the opportunity to be reunited with her daughter."

Novack grunted. "Family reunion, huh?"

"Yes. One big, happy family: grandpa, daddy, mommy, and baby."

"Maybe we can get them a puppy."

Fisk smirked. "Not an altogether bad idea."

"What happens when Poppa finds out that he can't leave until we're ready to let him go?"

"You contain him. Treat him with kindness. Make sure he's not lacking for any creature comfort." Fisk's expression hardened. "But he won't be allowed to have any communication with the outside world. Once his wife gets there, the whole kit and caboodle of them are going to *stay* there until we're damned good and ready to let them go."

Novack understood. "Which might be a long time."

"It might be a very long time indeed," Fisk agreed.

Novack said to himself, So I'll take them to Nowheresville, Idaho, me and Hightower and a team of federal marshals.

And that Dr. Minteer, he thought. Might not be so bad in Nowheresville with her around.

Moving Day

Y OU JUST PASSED the turnoff for the airport," Tamara said.
She and Angela, Del, and Luke, plus their luggage, were
bundled into a government-issue black Ford Expedition SUV.
Before the federal marshal who was driving could reply, High-
tower, sitting beside him, turned slightly and said over his shoulder,
"We're not going to the commercial airport."

"We're not?" Luke asked.

"Air Force base," said Hightower. "A plane will take us direct to
Spokane; from there we go to the Idaho facility."

"Huh." Luke settled back in his chair. Angela sat beside him,
Tamara on the child's other side. Del sat behind them, grumbling
as the SUV thrummed along the highway. Rossov and Novack were
in the white Chrysler 300 sedan following them.

Those two make a good combination, Luke thought. Glad they're
not in this wagon with us.

"I want to file assault-and-battery charges against that Novack
guy," Del said loudly.

Hightower said, "That's not a federal matter. You'll have to talk
to the local police about that."

"But we're leaving the area."

With a shrug, the FBI agent said, "Well, maybe you'll be able to
call them from where we're going."

Luke asked, "You don't know where we're going?"

"Not the final destination. Our orders are to get you aboard that Air Force jet."

"Babysitters," muttered the marshal driving the car. He was a youthful-looking African American.

Luke leaned back and tried to enjoy the ride. Their route down the Columbia River basin was spectacular, even in midwinter. Some of the trees were bare, but there were plenty of firs standing dark green against the distant snow-capped mountains. The sun was shining brightly, for a change, and the river sparkled as it coursed toward the sea.

Luke didn't see the name of the Air Force base as they drove up to a guard gate. Funny, he thought: They usually have a big sign telling you the base's name.

Their driver showed the white-helmeted Air Policeman his identification papers, and the guard handed him a little map.

"Stay on the route indicated in red, sir," the AP warned. "Otherwise you'll be stopped."

The marshal nodded his understanding, and they drove past several rows of nondescript barracks, finally arriving at the airfield, with Novack and Rossov close behind them.

They pulled up in front of a hangar where a sleek, low-winged, twin-engine jet stood waiting. Luke got out of the car, hunching against the cold wind, and helped Angela out. He zipped up her wool coat and made sure her hat was snug and covered her ears. Hightower popped out of the front seat and opened Tamara's door, then gave her a hand getting down from the SUV.

"Thank you," she said, smiling at him.

"De nada," he replied, smiling back at her.

It was cold but dry, and the sunshine felt good. The wind was blustery, though. Looking down at Angela, Luke saw that she didn't seem to mind the weather at all. She looked happy to be out in the open.

Rossov and Novack pulled up behind them. A pair of Air Force enlisted men toted the baggage from the SUV to the plane, and the whole group of them went to the stairway built into the hatch at the front of the plane. Novack clambered up the steps first.

Luke could feel the tension as soon as his son-in-law climbed into the plane's cabin. He glared at Novack, who had taken the first seat by the hatch. Novack returned the angry look with an amused smile.

"I'm filing assault-and-battery charges against you," Del said, leaning over Novack's seated form.

"It's a free country," said Novack.

Del stared at him for another moment, then stomped down the plane's narrow aisle and took a seat behind Luke and Angela. Luke let Angie have the window seat and helped her click her safety belt in place. Tamara sat across the aisle from him.

"Will we be flying real high, Grandpa?" Angela asked.

"Over the clouds," Luke replied.

"Wow."

Angie didn't look frightened about flying. She's been on planes before, Luke remembered. She'll be okay.

When Hightower ducked through the hatch, Luke thought he felt the plane tilt from his weight. The FBI man sat across the aisle from Novack without saying a word to him. Or anyone else. Rossov came aboard last, looked up the aisle, then came down and sat himself beside Del.

As the plane's engines whined to life, Rossov said to Del, "I can understand that you're upset about Novack—"

"Upset?" Del snapped. "I'm going to get him thrown in jail!"

"For assault and battery? Not likely. Besides, if you got before a judge it would boil down to an I-said and he-said case. There weren't any witnesses."

Luke half-turned in his seat and pointed out, "There's the MRI showing injury to Del's kidney."

Rossov nodded. "Yes, I know. Those records are on board with us."

"You took them out of the Bartram labs?"

"Of course. You'll want them with you when we get to the facility in Idaho, won't you?"

"We could have phoned the labs and asked them to e-mail the scans to us. No need to carry them along."

Rossov pursed his lips. "That might not be so easy. The base where we're going is buttoned up pretty tight. They don't want e-mails coming in from unauthorized senders."

"Base?" Luke asked. "I thought it was a medical facility."

"Oh, it's a medical facility, all right. On an Army base."

The pilot's voice crackled over the intercom. "We're ready for takeoff. Please make sure your seat belts are fastened."

THE FLIGHT TO Spokane was quick and smooth, although they landed not at the commercial airport but at another Air Force installation.

And instead of going into another SUV, Rossov led them to a big helicopter that was waiting on the tarmac, its huge rotors drooping almost to the ground. Several Air Police were standing by, with heavy pistols strapped to their blue uniforms.

As they approached the chopper, Angela walked beside Luke. Tamara, on the other side of the child, nodded toward Novack, who was at the end of their little procession.

"We're under guard," she said to Luke.

"Important persons," he said.

"More like prisoners."

ANGELA KEPT HER nose pressed against the window as the helicopter lifted off and headed east, toward the mountains. Luke had never been in a helicopter before, and found he had an innate distrust of a flying machine that had no wings. But he kept his feelings bottled inside him. People have been flying these things for damned near a century, he told himself. Still, he would have felt better in a fixed-wing aircraft.

The flight was surprisingly smooth, though. Even over the snow-clad mountains the copter chugged easily past the peaks, with none of the bumpiness Luke expected. And the cabin was well insulated, acoustically: The roar of the jet engines was muted, and the swooshing sound of the rotors practically inaudible.

Tamara was sitting alone across the aisle from Luke, with Rossov in the seat behind her. Novack sat by the main hatch, reading from his iPad, while Hightower sat across the aisle from him, seemingly dozing.

Tapping a fingernail on the window glass, Tamara asked, "Is that where we're going?"

Rossov nodded. "Yep. That's the place."

Luke unbuckled his seat belt and slid into the chair beside Tamara's. Past her shoulder he saw a cluster of small, low-roofed buildings. Didn't look like much. This is a first-rate biomedical facility? he asked himself.

Angela called out, "I want to see, too."

Rossov tapped Luke's shoulder. "I'll get her. You stay put."

And the White House executive got up as Angela unbuckled and slid to the aisle seat.

"Come on, Angela," he said, in a surprisingly gentle voice, "you can sit with me, right behind your grandpop."

Angela clambered to the window seat. Luke started to tell her to fasten her safety belt, but she did it by herself without prompting, then gave Luke a self-satisfied little smirk.

The chopper was getting lower. Luke saw that most of the buildings down there were two-story wooden structures; they looked like barracks. Paved roads and walkways between them. Parking lot only partly filled with cars, many of them Army green with white stars painted on their hoods.

And a helicopter pad, he saw, off to one side of the buildings.

Then he realized that the entire complex was surrounded by a high wire fence topped with coils of razor wire.

"By God," he whispered to Tamara, "it does look like a prison."

A QUARTET OF SOLDIERS helped them out of the helicopter and carried their luggage to a waiting Army truck.

Luke looked around. The area seemed barren, not a tree anywhere. Hardly any grass on the bare, dusty ground. Snow-covered mountains in the distance. We're a million miles from anyplace, he thought.

A heavyset officer in an unzipped tan windbreaker walked briskly up to him. His short-cropped brown hair was starting to turn silver; it made him look quite distinguished.

"Professor Abramson?"

"That's me," said Luke.

A quizzical smile spread across his pudgy face. "I had expected an older man, from the photos in your dossier."

My dossier? Luke thought.

"Well, anyway, I'm Colonel Dennis," he said, sticking out his hand. "Welcome to Y-18."

Luke took the man's hand warily, noting the silver eagle on one shirt collar and the snake-entwined caduceus, symbol of the Army medical corps, on the other.

"Y-18?" he asked.

With a sweep of his hand, the colonel explained. "That's the designation for this base. But don't let its looks fool you. We're doing some top-level work here."

Colonel Dennis, it turned out, was the commander of this godforsaken base in the wilderness. He insisted that Luke and the others call him Frank as he led them to a pair of olive green Army sedans waiting for them.

"We're in the rain shadow of the mountains here," he explained cheerily to Luke as they piled into the cars. "Semiarid, you know. But we don't get those bleak gray skies like they do on the other side. Lots of sunshine here!"

Luke sat in the rear of the sedan with Angela and Tamara, wondering how Del was going to behave in the other car with Rossov and Novack. At least Hightower's with them; he'll keep the peace, Luke thought.

Colonel Dennis took the seat beside the driver, a corporal young enough to still have acne spotting his lantern-jawed face.

"I can't tell you how glad we are to have someone of your caliber staying with us, Professor," said Colonel Dennis, turning halfway around in his seat to face Luke. "The whole research staff is eager to meet you."

"What kind of research do you do here?" Luke asked as they drove away from the helicopter.

"Biological warfare, mainly."

Tamara blurted, "Biological war—"

"Not weaponry," the colonel quickly interrupted her. "We don't work on bioweapons."

"Then what?"

"Countermeasures. We look at possible biological warfare agents and try to come up with countermeasures against them."

"Terrorists," Luke muttered.

"Exactly right," the colonel agreed. "Most security people worry about planes crashing into skyscrapers, or some nut case trying to bomb a nuclear reactor. But one fanatic pouring a vial of anthrax bacteria into a city reservoir could kill thousands of people. Tens of thousands."

"I guess so," Luke said.

"And there are new potential threats all the time," the colonel went on. "Genetically engineered viruses, plague bacilli, not to mention the H5N1 avian flu virus. The government should never have permitted the scientific community to lift its moratorium on that."

"And you try to find countermeasures for all that," Tamara said.

Nodding vigorously, Colonel Dennis replied, "Vaccines, anti-dotes . . . We're kept pretty damned busy. There aren't enough resources to cover everything, so we have to pick our targets care-fully."

Luke wondered, If his staff is stretched so thin, how's he going to find the people to work with me?

As if he could read Luke's mind, the colonel said, "But we're very glad to have you on board, Professor Abramson. Mr. Rossov is making arrangements for a half-dozen new personnel to assist you."

"Oh. That's good." Then he said, "I'd like to recruit some of my grad students from back in Massachusetts. They've worked with me and know what they're doing."

Looking a little shamefaced, the colonel replied, "I'm afraid that won't be possible, Professor. Security clearances and all the paper-work, you know. The people we'll bring in will be top-rate, I prom-ise you."

Luke said nothing, but he thought, Great. Now I'll have to break in a new crop of assistants.

The car pulled up in front of one of the two-story wooden build-ings.

"Well, this will be your home sweet home for the time being," said the colonel as he opened the car door.

Luke got out and surveyed the building warily. It looked brand-new, as if it had just been put up.

Standing beside him in the cold clear sunshine, Colonel Dennis said, almost shyly, "Um, I've set up a dinner for you this evening with a few of my key staff people. We're all anxious to hear about your work."

Luke nodded absently and helped Angela out of the car. "Here she is," he said brightly. "This little girl is going to become very fa-mous someday soon."

Colonel Dennis nodded. "Someday," he said.

The Staff

DEL CLIMBED OUT of the sedan he'd ridden in like a man trying to escape a life insurance salesman. He looked sullen, disgruntled, almost angry.

Having him ride with Novack wasn't such a hot idea, Luke said to himself. Rossov must've had to referee between them. More likely Hightower did.

The building they stood before was indeed newly constructed, Luke saw once he and the others stepped inside. He could smell the paint that had just been applied, and the faint odor of sawdust that still hung in the air.

"Welcome to the Abramson Laboratory," Colonel Dennis said grandly, sweeping the bare room with his outstretched arms.

Luke blinked with surprise.

"This first floor will be your work area," the colonel explained, standing in the middle of the empty space. "Equipment's not here yet, but it's on its way."

Leaving Novack, Rossov, and Hightower on the first floor, Luke, Angela, Tamara, and Del followed Dennis upstairs. Four bedrooms, two baths. Decent furniture: nothing spectacular, but adequate, Luke thought. We're not going to be here that long, he told himself.

Standing in the hallway that bisected the upper floor, Colonel

Dennis said, "I thought the two ladies could take the rooms on this side"—he pointed—"and share the bathroom between them. You two men can take the other two and share that bathroom. Will that be okay?"

Luke glanced at Tamara, who nodded, then said, "Fine." Del said nothing.

The colonel smiled broadly. "Good. Great. Now about dinner tonight. Seven P.M." Turning to Tamara, his face turned apologetic. "I'm afraid dinner is going to be strictly stag. You can eat in the base mess hall, if you don't mind."

Tamara looked almost amused. "I don't mind. Do you, Angela?"

Angie looked surprised to be asked. But she replied, quite seriously, "I don't mind. Do they have any pies? I like peach pie."

Colonel Dennis beamed at her. "I'll see that the cooks bake you a peach pie."

Del managed a smile. "I like peach pie, too."

YOU ACTUALLY DESTROYED the brain tumors by restricting the patient's telomerase production?" asked one of the scientists at the dinner table. Like almost all of Colonel Dennis's research staff, he was a civilian: middle-aged, wiry, intense, wearing a flannel shirt and a bushy beard that made him look like a frontiersman. Appropriate, for this place, Luke thought.

Luke nodded patiently. He had heard the same question, in one form or another, at least four times during the course of the dinner.

They were seated at a long table in a room off the main mess hall area. The officers' club, Colonel Dennis had called it. The only other military officer at the table was a crisply uniformed captain who had not said a word all evening.

"How do you know the tumors won't start growing again?" asked another civilian.

Luke shrugged. "We'll keep the patient under careful observation, of course. But so far, so good."

"Cancerous cells grow spontaneously in the body all the time," said another of the men. "The immune system destroys them before they get big enough to cause trouble."

"Usually," said Colonel Dennis, "but not always."

"The patient," Luke said, lapsing into the impersonal style of medical reports, "was born with only one p53 in her genome. We've inserted a second p53, to bring her immune system up to normal."

That led to a dozen questions on how the gene was inserted into the patient's cells. By the time dessert was finished, Luke was feeling very much at home with these researchers.

Except for one, a broomstick-thin man with a wild thatch of black hair and an impressive mustache. The colonel had introduced him as Nicholas Pappagannis, a biochemist.

Shaking his head dolorously, Pappagannis said, "You may think you've beaten the cancer, but the disease is insidious, you know."

"I know," Luke agreed.

"It will find a way to beat you, wait and see."

The table fell silent. Luke felt a sudden flare of anger. "That's what we're doing now," he said tightly. "Waiting and watching."

"Don't take Nick too seriously," Colonel Dennis said lightly. "He's our resident pessimist."

Pappagannis forced a smile. "That's right. I try to keep all these optimists from thinking too highly of themselves."

O UT IN THE mess hall, Tamara, Angela, and her father were sitting at one end of a mostly empty long table, enjoying fresh-baked peach pie for dessert. Angie was picking up the last crumbs from her plate between her thumb and forefinger.

"You must have enjoyed that," said Tamara, smiling at the child.

"Could I have seconds?" Angela asked.

Del frowned at his daughter. "You know the rule, Angel."

Tamara thought otherwise, but decided not to contradict the child's father. Very gently, she said, "I don't think it would be a good idea, Angie."

Looking disappointed, Angela said, "I guess not."

Edward Novack pulled up a chair next to Tamara and sat down, uninvited. "Good-looking woman like you shouldn't be dining alone," he said, with a grin.

"I'm not alone," Tamara said coldly, nodding toward Angela, at her other side, and Del, across the table. "Besides, we're finished." To Angela, she said, "Come on, Angie, let's go back to our place."

Novack got to his feet alongside her. "That's not very sociable."

Del rose, too, glaring at him.

She turned away from him, but Novack grasped her wrist and made her face him. "You're going to be here for a long time, lady. You're going to get pretty damned lonesome."

Tamara gave him a withering stare. "If you were the last man in the world," she hissed, "not even then."

Del came around the table, but before he could reach Tamara, Novack released her wrist and put on a knowing smile. "That's what you think."

"That's what I know." Tamara took Angela's hand and started toward the door, with Del on the child's other side.

"Better bundle up," Novack called after them, still standing at the table. "It's pretty damned cold out there."

Tamara ignored him, but glanced down to make certain Angela's coat was zipped.

"I'm supposed to be finding the professor," Novack said, "but that jerk of a colonel has him bottled up behind locked doors. Not to be disturbed. Typical Army bullshit."

A couple of the civilians at the other tables nodded and smirked.

"You can see him tomorrow," Tamara said over her shoulder.

"Yeah. I just wanted to let him know that he's going to have a visitor tomorrow."

"A visitor?"

"Quenton Fisk."

Tamara stopped short of the door. "From the Fisk Foundation?"

"Yeah. Fisk's coming all the way out here just to see him and make sure he's all snug and comfy in his new home."

"I'll tell Professor Abramson," she said.

"Yeah. Do that. And anytime you want to get snug and comfy, here I am."

Tamara didn't dignify that remark with an answer. She pushed through the door, out into the frigid night, holding Angela's hand, Del following behind them. Novack stood there, smirking.

Quenton Fisk

H E'S COMING HERE?" asked Luke.

"Tomorrow, according to Novack," Tamara replied.

The two of them were standing in the empty first floor of the building that Colonel Dennis had assigned them, by the stairs. Angela and her father had gone upstairs together, preparing for bed. The big bare room was bathed in shadows. Not even ceiling lamps had been installed; the only light came through the windows, from the far-spaced lamps lining the lonely, unoccupied street outside.

Luke huffed. "Maybe he can light a fire under these Army people and get us the staff and equipment we need."

Even in the shadowy lighting, Luke could see the frown on Tamara's face.

"You don't like it here, do you?" he asked her.

"There's not much to like."

"It'll be better once we get everything in place, all the people we need. Then we can get to work."

"I suppose so," she said.

"In the meantime, the colonel said we can use the facilities he's already got here. He wants to show me through the place tomorrow."

"I'd like to check out their medical facility," said Tamara. "I want to do complete workups on Angela and you."

"Me? I don't need another physical."

"Your PSA count, remember?"

"That can wait."

"It can wait until I check out the medical facility here. Then you're going to get a physical. Period."

Luke stared at her for a heartbeat, then broke into a rueful grin. "Harkening and obedience, O master."

Tamara smiled back at him. "And don't you forget it."

IT WAS MIDAFTERNOON before Fisk showed up, arriving in an Air Force helicopter that clattered over the base and raised billows of dust as it settled onto the chopper pad.

Standing on the edge of the landing area with Colonel Dennis beside him, Luke wondered if the only way to get in and out of Y-18 was by helicopter. He thought he remembered seeing a road leading out from the base's main gate, but he wasn't sure about that, and he certainly didn't know where the road led, if it existed.

Fisk clambered briskly down the copter's ladder and strode directly toward Luke, an energetic figure in a long cashmere overcoat flapping open and a dark fedora that he held on his head with one gloved hand. Two taller men came out of the helicopter and hurried along behind him. Flunkies, Luke thought.

Still tightly holding the brim of his hat, Fisk came right up to Luke and peered intently at him.

"It's true!" he exclaimed. "You're younger than you were a few weeks ago."

"It's true," Luke replied tightly. He was wearing a windbreaker, no hat. The day was chilly but sunny and dry.

Fisk was shorter than Luke had expected him to be, considerably smaller than he had seemed in their Skype communications. Then Luke remembered that Fisk was always behind an impressive desk in those conversations; this was the first time he'd seen the man on his feet.

"I'm Colonel Dennis." The colonel broke into Fisk's unabashed stare at Luke. "I'm the base commander."

As if snapping out of a trance, Fisk turned to the colonel and offered his gloved hand. "Glad to meet you, Colonel."

Turning, Fisk introduced, "This is Dr. Marlo Gunnerson, and Dr. Basil Holmes. They'll be working with Professor Abramson."

Gunnerson was tall, broad-shouldered, and pale-skinned, with the ice blue eyes and straw yellow hair of a Viking. His hairline was receding, though, and his shoulders seemed stooped. Holmes looked younger. He was almost the same height as Gunnerson, but thin, with dark hair, deeply brown eyes, and an imperious hawk's nose. Both men wore expensive-looking topcoats; both were hatless.

Before either Luke or Colonel Dennis could say anything, Fisk added, "These are two of the top cellular biologists in the Fisk Foundation's laboratories. Absolutely first-rate research scientists."

Luke reached for Gunnerson's hand. "Haven't seen you since the cellular biology conference last year, Marlo." Turning to Holmes, "I've read a couple of your papers. Good to meet you."

Colonel Dennis gestured toward the buildings. "Let's go to the commissary and get something to eat."

"I'll join you there," said Fisk. Grasping Luke's arm, he went on. "I need to speak with Professor Abramson in private for a few minutes first."

Dennis's round face frowned for an instant, but he quickly put on a smile and said, "Of course, Mr. Fisk." Pointing, he added, "That's the commissary building, down the street. We'll meet you there."

And he walked off with Gunnerson and Holmes, chatting amiably.

Fisk followed them with his eyes for a moment, the expression on his face disdainful, almost sneering. "Scientists," he muttered. He turned to Luke. "Show me where you'll be working."

It wasn't a request, Luke thought. It was a command.

As he led Fisk toward the building he'd been assigned to, Luke felt the man's eyes boring into him.

"I can't get over it," Fisk said. "You actually look ten, maybe twenty years younger."

"The telomerase accelerators are working," Luke muttered.

"I'll say!"

Raising a cautioning finger, Luke added, "But we don't know what the side effects might be. We've got a long road ahead of us."

Fisk laughed. "Maybe so, but you'll have all the years you need to go down that road, won't you?"

Abramson Lab

FISK'S HAPPY SMILE disappeared once Luke showed him into the bare first floor of the building.

Scowling as he turned a full circle, he snapped, "This is it? One lousy room? And it's empty!"

"Colonel Dennis says—"

"Screw Colonel Dennis! You're supposed to have a first-rate facility here. And a first-rate staff. I've brought you Gunnerson and Holmes, for chrissakes! What're they going to do *here*, in this goddamned barn?"

"Welcome to the Abramson Laboratory," Luke said sardonically.

"Typical goddamned government shit," Fisk grumbled as he yanked out his smartphone. "I'll have that Rossov's hide pinned to the wall for this."

"He's right here," said Luke. "You can talk to him in person."

But Fisk wasn't listening. He pecked at his cell phone, glared at it, shook it, and jabbed it with his index finger again. "Goddamned phone's dead," he grumbled.

"Maybe its battery is—"

"The damned battery's fine," Fisk snapped. "Charged it on the flight here."

As if on cue, a jeep squealed to a stop outside. Through the window by the front door, Luke saw Rossov and Colonel Dennis climb out. Novack was also in it, sitting beside the driver. He stayed in the jeep while the colonel and Rossov came up the front steps.

Fisk saw them, too. He went to the door and yanked it open as the colonel raised his chubby fist to knock.

"Rossov?" he barked. "What kind of a godforsaken dump have you stuck Abramson into? You've got some explaining to do."

Luke thought he could see steam spurting from Fisk's ears. Waving an arm at the empty room, Fisk demanded, "Is this the first-rate facility the professor's supposed to work in?"

Dennis looked cowed, almost frightened, but Rossov said calmly, "The equipment is on its way. In a day or two everything—and everybody—will be humming smoothly."

"In a day or two?" Fisk barked. "Why isn't everything in place *now*?"

Almost whining, Colonel Dennis replied, "We only had two days' notice that Professor Abramson would be coming here. These things take time. They can't be done overnight."

"*You* can't get them done overnight," Fisk snarled. "I can."

Smiling thinly, Rossov said, "I'm sure you could, Mr. Fisk. But the colonel here has to go through official channels."

"Procurement," said the colonel, as if that explained everything. "We've pushed the paperwork through, but you can't expect miracles."

Still fuming, Fisk said, "I agreed to let you set up Professor Abramson in a first-rate research facility. I'll be back here next week, and if his laboratory isn't fully equipped and fully manned, I'll take the professor away with me."

"No you won't." Rossov said it softly, flatly. It was neither a threat nor a boast. Merely a statement of fact.

Fisk glared at him.

Rossov didn't flinch. "You've been allowed to visit this top-security installation because of your interest in Professor Abramson's work. If you attempt to interfere in that work, you will not be allowed back on this base."

"Says you," Fisk snapped.

"Says the President of the United States, whom I represent."

Fisk glowered at Rossov for a long moment, obviously straining to find a retort. At last he turned to Colonel Dennis.

"I want you to phone me the instant this laboratory is up and running. The very instant!"

"I'd be happy to," said the colonel. Luke saw beads of perspiration above his upper lip.

Then Fisk turned to Luke. "And I expect you, Professor, to let me know if there are any delays in getting your lab running."

Before Luke could reply, the colonel said, "But Professor Abramson's cell phone won't be able to get through the shielding."

"Shielding?"

Looking suddenly self-conscious, the colonel mumbled, "Electromagnetic shielding. Every building in the base is shielded. No cell phones or digital devices can communicate with the outside world." He finished lamely, "It's, uh, one of our security measures."

"I can't call outside the base?" Luke asked.

"Oh, sure you can," said Colonel Dennis. "But you'll have to use one of our landlines."

"Which are guarded, I presume," said Rossov.

"They're monitored, yes."

Fisk nodded. "I see. But you won't prevent the professor from calling me, will you?"

"Oh, no, of course not," the colonel said.

Luke wondered if he was telling the truth.

State of Siege

FISK STEPPED OUT of the so-called Abramson Lab into the nippy late-afternoon sunshine, leaving Luke, Rossov, and the sweating Colonel Dennis in the bare and empty room.

Novack was still sitting in the jeep, chatting amiably with the driver, a young corporal.

Fisk summoned his security chief with a crook of his finger. Novack sprang out of the jeep and walked swiftly to his boss, eyeing Fisk with a scornful grin on his bony, stubbled face.

"Like what you see?" he asked.

"Decidedly not," Fisk answered. "I never liked dealing with the government, and this dump hasn't improved my attitude at all."

"The sooner we get back to civilization the better," said Novack.

"You're not going anywhere."

Novack's normally imperturbable visage cracked with a surprised frown. "I'm not? But—"

"I want you right here for the time being. Report to me every day."

"My cell phone doesn't work. There's no reception in this area."

"Not even satellite?"

Novack shook his head. "They must have it jammed or something."

"Army security," Fisk muttered.

"It's like a state of siege around here. Buttoned up tight."

"That's good," said Fisk. "We want Abramson to stay right here."

"But why do I have to stay? The Army's got Abramson covered; he's not going anyplace."

"I want you around to remind that lard-assed colonel that I'm watching him."

"Christ."

"It should only be a few days. Just until Abramson's lab is up and running."

"But what about things in my office? I've been away long enough; I oughta get back to New York and make sure my office is running right."

Fisk shook his head. "Your office is humming along smoothly enough without you. You've done a good job organizing your people."

Novack tried to hide his disappointment and failed. Another few days in this frontier outpost, he said to himself. And my office is getting along fine without me. Great. Sooner or later he's going to get the idea that he can do without me altogether. Life can stink sometimes.

But then he thought of Tamara Minteer.

She's been playing the cold-shoulder game. But maybe in a few days out here she'll warm up a little. Or I'll warm her up.

SPECIAL AGENT JEROME Hightower was surprised to find his cell phone didn't work, not even outdoors. Impressed by the Army's security measures, he went to Colonel Dennis's office to ask for an available landline.

The colonel wasn't in, but once Hightower identified himself and showed his FBI credentials to the colonel's aide—a middle-aged woman who somehow looked frumpy even in a sergeant's uniform— she smilingly pointed him to an unused office two doors down from the colonel's.

"You can use the phone in there," she said, in a strangely girlish, high-pitched voice. "Just dial nine to get an outside line and then give them the security code: five-five-five."

Hightower's director back in Boston was in a conference, the director's secretary told him. Hightower explained the difficulties of putting through his call.

"I'll tell him," said the secretary. "Hold on."

I've got nothing better to do, he said to himself.

It took a couple of minutes, but the director finally came on the line. To his impatient questions, Hightower gave a terse report on where he was.

"Abramson's going to be kept here indefinitely," he said. "Looks like my job is done. He's in the hands of the Army and this Rossov guy."

For a moment the director said nothing. Then, "Okay. You're right. Our part of this operation is over. Come on home."

Nodding, Hightower said, "I've got two weeks of vacation time coming—"

"I can't spare you for two weeks!" the director shrilled into the phone. "Bad enough you've been traipsing across the country. I need you back here!"

"Just a couple of days, boss. A long weekend. I want to hop down to see my family."

"A long weekend?"

"Yeah. I'll be in the office next Tuesday. Okay?"

Another pause. Then a reluctant, "Okay."

"Thanks."

"Bright and early Tuesday."

"Depends on the airline schedules," Hightower negotiated.

"Tuesday," said his director. Then he hung up.

Hightower carefully replaced the phone in its cradle and got up from the desk, thinking, I can get a kachina doll and send it to little Angela. The kid can use all the spiritual help she can get.

Family Reunion

THE NEXT THREE days were a blur of activity. Helicopters arrived and took off again constantly; the base was awash in the growling thrum of their rotors and the billows of dust they kicked up as they ferried in the equipment for Luke's laboratory, including a diesel-fueled emergency generator that was installed behind the lab building. More helicopters brought half a dozen lab technicians. Luke spent the time supervising the construction of his lab and getting to know his new team of researchers.

There were eight of them altogether, including Gunnerson and Holmes, who were the only scientists among the crew. The others— all men—were young civilian employees of the Army. But they seemed eager to work with Luke, aware of his reputation, and full of energy.

The empty first-floor room quickly filled with soldiers wheeling in heavy crates while the technicians pried them open and set up the sparkling new sets of equipment on lab benches that had just been nailed together, sanded, and painted by other young soldiers.

Luke was in the midst of his bustling lab, supervising the installation of a high-definition atomic force microscope, when a voice from the door called, "Dad?"

He whirled to see his daughter standing in the doorway, one

hand grasping a roll-along suitcase, the other clutching her hand-bag. Lenore looked slightly disheveled, a little bewildered, but she was smiling cheerfully.

"Norrie!" Luke ran to her and wrapped his arms around her tiny form.

"Daddy," she said, breathlessly. "Where's Angie?"

Luke laughed with delight. "I don't know. She's around here someplace. Probably out taking a walk with Tamara—Dr. Minteer, her physician." He felt glad that Angela's wrist had healed and the cast had come off the day before.

Del came thumping down the stairs from the second floor and dashed to his wife, clasping her in his long arms. Luke stepped aside, smiling at the sight of the two of them: Del was a good foot taller than Lenore; he had to bend over like a weeping willow to hold her.

"Angie's fine, hon," he told Lenore before she could ask. "She's out behind the building, playing with some of the other kids."

Other kids? Luke felt surprised, then realized that of course plenty of the personnel on this base would have their families with them. He just hadn't paid any attention to that, until now.

Lenore left her suitcase by the door and went out with Del to find their daughter. Left standing there, Luke debated going after them, but decided not to.

Leave them alone with Angie; no sense butting in. Besides, I've got plenty of work to do here.

T HAT EVENING, THOUGH, they had a family reunion dinner in the base's mess hall. Angela sat between her parents, laughing happily as she gobbled her dinner. Her face still looked gaunt, with wrinkles at the corners of her eyes, but Lenore didn't seem to no-tice. Or maybe she doesn't care, Luke thought. At least Angie's hair is growing back in.

He and Tamara spent most of the dinner explaining the child's condition to his daughter, with Del listening intently.

"But the cancer's gone?" Lenore asked, over and again.

Sitting beside Luke, Tamara assured her each time she repeated the question that the tumors were gone.

"And we've inserted a second p53 gene," Luke added. "That'll help her immune system fight off any new cancerous cells that might arise in her."

Del summed it up. "She's going to live, hon. Our little Angie's going to be all right."

In that instant, Luke forgave all his son-in-law's anger and insults. It was fear, he realized. Del was frightened that Angie was going to die.

"And she'll be . . . normal again?" Lenore asked.

Tamara said, "The progeria symptoms are fading."

"Her telomeres are coming back to normal," Luke explained. "She's going to be fine."

Lenore's eyes went misty. She turned to Angela and hugged the child. Angie put up with it, but was more interested in the peach pie dessert that the camp's cook had personally carried to the table.

Across the mess hall, Novack sat alone, picking at the lousy Army food while watching Luke and his family. And Tamara.

L UKE WALKED WITH Tamara through the chilly darkness back to their building, watching his daughter and her family strolling contentedly several paces ahead of them.

"We'll have to change our sleeping arrangements now that Norrie's here," he said.

"She can bunk with Angela tonight," Tamara said. "Then tomorrow your son-in-law can move to my room and I'll move to his."

Luke felt his eyebrows go up a notch. "We'll have to share the bathroom."

In the darkness, Tamara's silky voice sounded amused. "Does that bother you?"

"Norrie and Del might get the wrong impression."

"Or maybe the right impression."

Luke's brows hiked up toward his scalp.

But then Tamara said, more seriously, "Your PSA count is still rising."

"Yeah, I know," he replied, feeling almost nettled at being forced back to reality.

"You really should have your prostate removed."

"No," he said flatly. "I'll treat it the same way we knocked out Angie's tumors."

"With telomere inhibitors? Luke, that can be dangerous for you."

Thinking of the incontinence and impotence that often followed prostate surgery, Luke muttered, "Not as dangerous as the side effects from surgery."

"Do you have the tissue samples that they took back in Portland?"

He nodded. "I packed them in with our other stuff when they moved us here."

She hesitated, then said, "Luke, I don't like it. You're taking telomerase accelerators, and now you want to take inhibitors?"

"Just for the prostate."

"But you have no idea what the results will be. You'll be messing with your cellular chemistry too much."

Luke said flatly, "No surgery. Surgery is an admission that you don't know how to cure the condition."

"Your 'cure' could be worse than the disease."

Still thinking of impotence, Luke replied in his best John Wayne intonation. "Not hardly."

Welcome to the Gulag

ONCE HIS LABORATORY was up and running, Luke settled into a happy routine. Gunnerson and Holmes were top-notch researchers, and although neither of them seemed totally happy working under Luke's direction, rather than independently, they got along together without too much friction.

God knows how much Fisk is paying them to work under me, he mused. They're both giving up a lot to stay here.

His PSA count was still climbing, despite the telomerase inhibitors Luke had one of the camp medics inject into his prostate. No discernable reaction after nearly two weeks. Luke tried to shake off his concern. Needs more time, he told himself. The effect of the accelerators is still dominant.

At least, he thought, I've got plenty of material for a paper. He spent most of his evenings writing a research report for Fisk's people. As it took shape, he began to think of publishing it in *American Cellular Biology*.

But when he tried to query *ACB*, which had published most of his earlier papers, he found that neither his laptop nor his cell phone could send a message out of the base.

Luke marched off to see Colonel Dennis.

Sitting behind his Army-issue steel desk, the colonel listened patiently to Luke's complaint, then spread his arms in a gesture of helplessness.

"No one can communicate with the world outside this base," he said, "unless it's through our monitored landlines. Army security, you know. What we're doing here is top-secret work."

"But that's not what *I'm* doing," Luke protested. "My work has nothing to do with what the rest of you are doing."

Another spread of arms. "My orders are that you're not allowed to communicate with anyone except Mr. Fisk," said the colonel.

The freaking privacy agreement, Luke realized.

"But this is a scientific research paper," he countered. "The Fisk Foundation will be fully credited as the funding agency for my work."

Dennis shook his chubby head. "You can ask Mr. Fisk to allow you to publish," he suggested.

"How can I ask anybody anything if my phone and my laptop can't get through?"

"You can place authorized messages through the base communications center."

"Authorized?" Luke snapped, feeling nettled. "Who gives the authorization?"

"I do."

"And you won't authorize my query to *American Cellular Biology*?"

"I'm afraid I can't. Orders."

"Orders? From who, Fisk?"

The colonel stiffened. "I don't take orders from Mr. Fisk. My orders come from my superior officers."

"Who take orders from the White House, eh?"

"Ultimately," said Colonel Dennis.

Rossov, Luke thought. He stared at the colonel for a long, silent moment. A middle-aged, overweight nobody in a soldier suit with silver eagles pinned to his shoulders. Career Army man, just following orders.

Without another word, Luke got up and strode out of the colonel's office.

I'll stop working, he said to himself, zippering his windbreaker as he stepped out into the brisk, bright morning. I'll go on strike, that's what I'll do. See how much Fisk and his mother-loving lawyers like that!

But by the time he'd walked halfway back to his own building he saw Angie playing with a bunch of other kids while Lenore and Tamara stood off to one side, chatting like old friends. The kids were running around an open area, kicking up dust on the bare ground, tossing a ball back and forth and shrieking happily.

I can't stop working, Luke realized. I've got to monitor Angie's condition. And my own.

He turned around and headed toward the mess hall. When in doubt, he reminded himself, sit down, have a cup of coffee, stay calm, and *think*.

The mess hall was almost empty, with only a handful of civilians and a couple of women in uniform at the tables. Luke went to the big gleaming coffee urns, poured himself a cup of regular, and headed for an unoccupied table.

Almost as soon as he sat down, Nick Pappagannis came over, holding a mug in both hands, and sat next to him.

"Do you mind?" he asked.

"No," Luke lied.

Pappagannis sipped at his coffee, then put the mug down carefully on the wooden tabletop.

"You've got the look," he said.

Luke stared at him: dark, unhappy eyes and bushy black mustache.

"The look?"

"We all get it, sooner or later." Pappagannis glanced up at the ceiling briefly, then asked, "Ever been to the Sistine Chapel?"

Luke shook his head.

"There's a fresco on one of the walls. By Michelangelo. Everybody gapes at the ceiling, of course, but this painting always gets to me." Pappagannis tapped at his chest with a clenched fist.

"Why?"

"It's supposed to be Judgment Day. God's deciding who goes to heaven, who goes to hell. There's this one guy, he's just been sent to hell. Damned for eternity. The look on his face—that's the look you just had."

Luke didn't know what to say.

"We all get it," Pappagannis repeated. "Once a guy realizes what this base is all about, what he's in for, it's like being condemned to hell."

Luke scoffed. "That's pretty dramatic."

"Yeah, I know. But look at us. We all signed an employment agreement, a security agreement, all kinds of paperwork. Signed our lives away. So now we're stuck here in the middle of nowhere—for years on end."

His brows knitting, Luke asked, "You mean you can't leave this base?"

"Not for the length of our employment agreement. For me, that's five years."

"That's not eternity."

"Seems like it. The only way I can talk to my mother back in Chicago is through one of the secure phones, with some Army officer listening to every word we say. Listening, and recording!"

"Security," Luke mumbled.

"And we can't leave the base. We're locked in here, unless Colonel Dennis gives permission to leave. The only way out of here is on one of those damned helicopters. And even then we have to provide a detailed itinerary and stick to it. If you're half an hour late getting back, they send out the MPs to track you down."

"Like prisoners."

"Like prisoners," Pappagannis agreed. "They say it's for security. Antiterrorism and all that shit. I say it's just to keep us here under their thumbs, and make sure we're working hard for them."

"You mean everybody here?" Luke asked. "Even the Army personnel?"

"All buttoned up like a high-security prison."

Luke stared at the man. He was totally serious.

Suddenly angry, Luke shot to his feet and stormed out of the mess hall, heading back to Colonel Dennis's office.

And he saw Novack coming the other way, heading for him.

"Where you going?" Novack asked, pulling up alongside Luke.

"To see the colonel."

"You been talking to the Greek, huh?"

Luke stopped in midstride. "You people have been watching me?"

"Sort of."

"Is it true that I can't leave this base if I want to?"

Novack hunched his shoulders slightly. "This is a very secure area. People can't just come and go as they please."

"I can't leave?"

"Not without permission."

"And who gives permission? Dennis?"

Novack almost laughed. "The colonel's a career Army man. He takes orders."

"Who gives the goddamned orders?"

"In your case, it's that slicker from the White House."

"Rossov? Not Fisk?"

"Rossov."

"So where's Fisk come into this?"

"He made a deal with Rossov. You're working for Fisk, but you work where Rossov wants you to be."

"And my daughter and her family?"

"Same deal. They all stay here."

Luke started for the colonel's office again. "I'm not putting up with this bullshit."

Novack stopped him by placing a hand on Luke's chest. "Yes you are. You and me both, we work for Fisk. And Fisk wants us right here, same as Rossov does. We're stuck here until they're ready to let us go."

"You mean we're prisoners," Luke growled.

Novack almost smiled. "Welcome to the gulag, buddy."

Plan of Inaction

LUKE STOOD THERE in the crisp, clear morning, the sky above him a cloudless blue, the wooden buildings on every side looking new yet somehow already drab, dreary. Men and women walked along the dirt streets, some in uniform, others not, each of them bundled in a heavy coat or windbreaker. A jeep puttered by. And out at the perimeter of the base was that ten-foot-high wire fence. Bet it's electrified, he thought.

Welcome to the gulag.

Novack was eying him, a sardonic grin on his bony face.

"For what's worth," Novack said, "I'm stuck here, too. And I don't like it any better than you do."

Luke said, "Yeah." Then he turned and headed back toward his own laboratory.

Got to think this through, he told himself. I've gotten myself into this pickle, I'll have to figure out how to get out of it. And get Norrie and Angie out of it. And Tamara.

ONCE BACK IN his lab, Luke allowed the familiar routine of his work to fill the rest of his day. But even as he examined the latest scans of Angela's brain and the results of her most recent physical exam, he was thinking, thinking, trying to figure out what to do and how to do it.

Fisk and Rossov both want to keep me here. Novack's here to watch me, and the whole freaking base is designed to keep people in, not let them out.

Fisk wants the results of my work. That's why he's tied me up with that privacy agreement. But what's Rossov after? Is he working for Fisk? He said he's a special assistant to the President. Has Fisk bought him out?

By the end of the day, he had come to no conclusions. One thing seemed clear, though: In another week or two there'll be no reason to keep Angela here. She'll be back to normal, just about. She can go home, with Norrie and Del.

But Luke wondered if Colonel Dennis, or Fisk, or Rossov, was going to allow that.

As THE DINNER hour approached, and most of his staff left for the day, Luke climbed the stairs from his laboratory to the living quarters on the second floor. Briefly he looked in on Lenore and Del and Angela. They seemed happy enough, gathered around a television set that was showing a DVD of a children's movie.

He tapped on Tamara's door, across the hall. After a moment's wait, she opened it.

"Hi," she said.

"Hello," said Luke. "May I come in?"

"The room's a mess, but yes, sure." She swung the door wide.

Luke stepped in and saw that the bed was neatly made, although there was a stack of freshly laundered clothes atop it. Through the half-open door to the lavatory he saw a pair of pantyhose draped over the shower stall door.

"This is a mess?" he asked, smiling at her.

"Sort of."

"You hungry? Want to go to dinner?"

"It's a little early," she said. "I thought we'd wait for Angie and her parents."

"They can find the mess hall on their own." He extended his hand to her. "Come on."

Looking pleased but slightly puzzled, Tamara went to the closet and pulled out her long winter coat. "Only thing I've got," she half-apologized.

Luke grabbed his windbreaker from his closet, then went across the hall and stuck his head through the half-open door of his daughter's room. "We're going to dinner," he announced. Before they could reply he added, "See you in the mess hall."

And he led Tamara down the stairs, through the now-deserted lab, and out into the lengthening shadows of the chilly evening.

Once they had gone a dozen paces along the street, Tamara asked, "What's going on?"

Luke glanced at her. "Going on?"

"You've got the same look on your face as you did back at Nott-away, when you wanted to talk without being overheard."

He nodded. "Same reason."

"So what's going on, Luke?"

"We're being kept prisoners here."

"I told you that before we ever arrived," Tamara said.

"They won't even let me send a query to *ACB*."

Tamara said nothing.

"I don't think they intend to let Norrie and her family leave this base."

Her brows knitting, Tamara said, "They can't do that. It's illegal." Then she added, "Isn't it?"

"It's only illegal if you can get somebody to pay attention to it. As long as they have us bottled up here in this camp, there's not much we can do."

"But why are they doing this to us?" Tamara wondered.

Luke shook his head. "Must be something big. Big enough for

the White House to get involved. Big enough to get Fisk to go along with it."

She thought that over for a few strides. Then, "Maybe it's all Fisk's idea."

Luke shook his head. "Nah. If Fisk had his way, we'd be at one of his labs."

"You think so?"

"I'm pretty sure."

They turned the corner, and there was the mess hall standing halfway down the block. A few early birds were already going in.

"So what do we do about it?" Tamara asked.

Luke shrugged. "Nothing much we can do. They hold all the cards. For now."

"What do you mean?"

"We just wait and watch. And learn."

"Learn? Learn what?"

For the first time that day Luke smiled. "Learn what we need to know," he said.

Learning Curve

THE NEXT MORNING Luke phoned Colonel Dennis's office and asked to see him. The female sergeant who answered the phone checked the colonel's schedule and told him that four o'clock was the earliest available time.

"Four o'clock," said Luke amiably. "Fine."

He spent most of the morning working on the report that Fisk wanted, thinking of it as the draft of a paper he would submit to *American Cellular Biology*. Using telomere inhibitors to cure cancer: That ought to get some attention, he thought.

Angela, her mother, and Tamara came down the stairs from their quarters upstairs, heading for the front door. Luke got up from his desk and threaded his way through the lab benches toward them.

"Going out?"

"We're going to play softball!" Angela announced, her face alight with excitement.

Luke looked at Tamara, who said, "She's up to it."

He returned his gaze to Angela. The child looked eager, happy. With her winter cap on, it was impossible to see if her hair was fuller, but her face looked smoother, her eyes brighter, than just a few days earlier.

Lenore seemed just as happy, a huge smile on her face.

"Where's Del?" Luke asked.

"He's over at the communications center, talking to his office back in Boston," Norrie told him.

They let Del get through, Luke thought. But I'll bet there's an Army guy listening to every word he says.

"Go have fun," he said to Angie.

The three of them trooped out the front door. Luke noticed Novack sitting in a jeep out by the sidewalk. He hopped out and spoke briefly to Tamara, gesturing toward the jeep. Tamara shook her head, and the three females started walking up the street. Novack returned to the jeep, watched them for a few moments, then gunned the engine and peeled off in the same direction.

Luke headed back toward his desk, unhappy with the expression on Novack's face. The man looked grim, almost angry.

Maybe I should go out to the playground with them, he thought. Then he shook his head and returned to his desk. Tamara can take care of herself, he told himself. Still, he felt uneasy.

B ASE SECURITY IS very important," Colonel Dennis was saying. "Extremely important."

Sitting in front of the colonel's gray steel desk, Luke replied, "But I don't understand why it has to be so tight. I mean, I can't even phone a scientific journal about my work."

Leaning forward earnestly, both his chubby hands flat on his desktop, Dennis said, "It's got to be this way, Professor. There are dozens of possible biological threats that terrorists might try against us. Hundreds. We don't have the manpower to work on all of them, so we have to prioritize our research. If a terrorist organization got wind of which threats we're working on, and which we've put on the back burner, what do you think they'd do?"

Luke straightened in his chair. "They'd concentrate on the threats you're not actively working on."

"Exactly," said the colonel, a pleased smile breaking across his round face.

"And that's why you have to maintain such rigid security."

"Precisely." Dennis seemed very satisfied.

With a puzzled frown, Luke said, "But I don't understand how this all works. Why won't my cell phone work?"

"To begin with," the colonel said, "there isn't a cell phone tower within a hundred miles of here."

"But satellite reception? My laptop can't connect to the Internet."

"We have some rather sophisticated jamming equipment at work 24/7. That's why you can't get any television reception here, except for the local Missoula stations. We had to run a cable all the way out to Missoula; that's nearly seventy miles away!"

"So that's why I can't send my research report to Mr. Fisk."

"Fisk is very anxious to hear from you," Dennis said. "But anything you send to him has to go through Army security clearance first."

"And that Rossov fellow, in the White House?"

The colonel shrugged. "I'm pretty sure that somebody in the White House chain of command gets into the act, in your case. But my orders are to route your communications requests through Army security."

"I see," Luke said. "I understand what's involved now."

Colonel Dennis put on a more serious face. "I'm hoping that, now that you understand what's involved, you'll cooperate with us."

"Oh, sure. Of course." Silently, Luke added, Up to a point.

THAT EVENING, LUKE took Tamara for an after-dinner stroll.

"I saw Novack offer you girls a ride this morning," he said.

"He's a pest," said Tamara.

"You don't like him?"

"No. Not at all."

With a grin, Luke said, "That's good."

She grinned back at him. "I'm glad you approve."

"Stay away from him." Thinking of what he did to Del, Luke added, "He can be dangerous."

Tamara said nothing, but they were passing a lamppost and Luke saw a curious expression on her face. He felt an urge to take her in his arms and kiss her, but he fought it down. Not now, he told himself. Not here. Later, when we get out of this place. If we get out of this place.

They walked in silence out past the last of the buildings, to the perimeter fence.

Luke reached for the wire, but Tamara pulled his hand away.

"It could be electrified," she warned.

"It's not."

"How do you know?"

"Nick Pappagannis told me. Besides, government regulations would require warning signs every so many feet if the fence was electrified."

He closed his fingers around the wire and shook the fence as hard as he could. It barely budged.

"It's climbable," he said.

Tamara looked shocked. "You're not thinking . . ."

He looked up to the top of the fence and the coils of razor wire.

"Luke, a man your age can't bounce around like a teenager."

"Maybe."

"Besides, what would you do once you got over the fence?" she insisted. "There's nothing out there for twenty miles or more."

"Forty-seven miles," he corrected. "Pappagannis has seen the maps."

"What are you thinking of?"

He shrugged. "Nothing. I'm just taking a walk through the moonlight with the best-looking woman on the base."

They heard a jeep rumbling toward them, then saw its headlights approaching.

An MP in a white helmet and a black holster pulled up alongside them. A sergeant, Luke saw.

"Sir, you're not supposed to be this close to the fence, sir."

Luke put on a surprised expression. "We're not? I didn't know that. Nobody mentioned it to me."

"Base regulations, sir," said the sergeant. "For your own safety. Please stay on the other side of the perimeter street, by the buildings, sir."

"Okay," Luke said. "We were just taking a walk."

"Would you like a lift back to your quarters, sir?"

Shaking his head, Luke said, "No, that's okay. We'll walk back." He took Tamara by the arm and started back toward their building.

"They must have cameras looking over every square inch of the base," he muttered.

Tamara pointed to the top of the nearest lamppost. "I could have told you that." Luke saw a slim, unobtrusive camera pointed toward the fence.

"Thanks," said Luke.

She laughed, and they headed back to their quarters together.

The Key

THE NEXT MORNING, as he was dressing, Luke realized he needed a haircut. His hair—dark brown now—was nearly reaching the collar of his shirt.

He heard a tap on the bathroom door. "Can I come in?" came Tamara's muffled voice.

"Sure," Luke said, bending down to pull on his shoes. "I'm decent."

Tamara entered his bedroom and went to the desk chair to sit. She looked quite serious.

"I've been thinking about last night," she began.

Still sitting on the edge of his unmade bed, Luke said, "What about last night?"

Instead of answering him, Tamara hiked a thumb toward the bathroom door. Luke nodded understanding, got up, and went with her into the little room. It felt crowded with both of them in there; no place to sit except on the toilet. He felt the warmth of her body, so close, smelled the flowery scent of her perfume.

Luke grinned at her. "Want to shower together?"

An impatient frown flashed across her face. She reached past him and turned on both of the sink's faucets.

"That ought to scramble their microphones," she whispered.

"You're learning," Luke whispered back.

"You're thinking about jumping the fence and getting away from here, aren't you?"

He nodded.

"That's crazy!" Tamara hissed. "Even if you get past the fence, where are you going to go?"

"That's not the important question," he whispered back to her.

"You'll just be killing yourself."

"I have no intention of killing myself."

"Then why are you doing it?"

He grasped her shoulders, gently, and looked into her troubled emerald eyes.

"I don't intend to spend the rest of my days here in this glorified rat trap," he whispered urgently. "And I certainly don't want you or Norrie and Angie to be stuck here, too."

Tamara frowned at him. "But there's nothing you can do about it. You can't go traipsing out in the wilderness like a Boy Scout. They'll find you and bring you back. If you don't get yourself killed first."

"I got you into this. I'm going to get you out of it." Before Tamara could reply, he went on. "But first I've got to know why they're doing this to us. What do Fisk and Rossov want? Why have they locked us away like this?"

Tamara had no answer.

"What do they want? That's the key to everything. Once I find that out, then I can figure out what to do."

"Don't do anything foolish," she warned.

He grinned at her. "Foolish? Like standing in a bathroom almost cheek to cheek and whispering secrets to each other?"

NICK PAPPAGANNIS WAS a font of knowledge about the base and its environs.

At lunchtime that day, Luke trudged alone to the mess hall,

looking for the biochemist. He spotted Pappagannis sitting with Marlo Gunnerson and a trio of other researchers. Carrying his tray to their table, Luke pulled out an empty chair.

"Mind if I join you?" he asked.

"The more the merrier," Gunnerson said.

"We're discussing possible vectors for anthrax," said Pappagannis.

"Pleasant lunchtime conversation," Luke said.

"Shop talk," one of the other researchers replied, with an uneasy smile.

Luke listened to their discussion, grisly as it was: how a terrorist might maximize the deaths caused by unleashing anthrax bacilli in a crowded city. This is what they're interested in, he said to himself. This is the work they're doing. Shop talk.

One by one the others finished their lunches and left the table. Finally only Luke and Pappagannis remained.

"Your work is really important," Luke said.

Pappagannis seemed in no hurry to return to his lab. "So is yours," he said, leaning back in his chair.

"I guess," said Luke, mopping up the last crumbs of his cheese sandwich. "Apparently even the White House is interested in what I'm doing."

"That's why you're here," Pappagannis said, with a cynical smile. "Your reward for being brilliant."

"I don't understand it," said Luke, with a shake of his head. "All I'm trying to do is save my granddaughter's life."

"By curing her of cancer."

"Glioblastoma multiforme," Luke murmured. "Why would the White House be interested in that? I mean, I'm supposed to be working for the Fisk Foundation, not Washington. Hell, the National Cancer Institute dropped my funding last year."

Toying with the end of his mustache, Pappagannis asked, "The Fisk Foundation? And you wound up here?"

Luke nodded unhappily. "Why would the Fisk people want to keep me isolated like this?"

Pappagannis's heavy dark brows knit in concentration.

Luke continued. "They won't even let me contact *ACB*, for God's sake."

"They don't want you to publish," said Pappagannis. "That means they want to keep your work secret."

"But what good would that do Fisk?" Luke asked. "I've already signed a privacy agreement. Do they intend to keep me from publishing?"

With a knowing smile, Pappagannis said, "Fisk wants to keep your work in his hands. He wants a monopoly on your cure for cancer."

"You think?"

"Of course. He'll have your cure for cancer in his hands, and anyone who wants to be cured will have to pay his price. That's capitalism, pure and simple."

"But why is the White House involved?" Luke wondered.

"They're in cahoots with Fisk, naturally."

"I don't understand."

Like a patient teacher explaining something to a backward student, Pappagannis said, "The people in the White House want to make sure *they* get your cancer cure when they need it."

Luke shook his head. "Sounds like one of those nutso conspiracy theories to me."

"Some conspiracy theories are right," said the biochemist. "And anyway, look at how Washington handles health care. The politicians nearly shut down the government a couple of years ago because they couldn't agree on a budget, remember?"

"That's got nothing to do with this."

"Doesn't it? Once you get politicians involved, head for the hills."

Silently, Luke retorted, That's just what I intend to do. Head for the hills.

Action

FOR TWO DAYS Luke went about his business as usual. Except that he bought a handful of granola bars, several packets of trail mix, and a six-pack of bottled water at the base's Post Exchange. Then he zipped his stash into the capacious pockets of his windbreaker. He couldn't fit all six water bottles, though; he had to settle for three.

He transferred the report he had written for Fisk from his laptop to his cell phone, then checked twice to make certain the entire paper was stored in the phone's memory. Finally he stripped the blanket off his bed and wrapped it into a bulky roll.

From his moonlight stroll with Tamara a few nights earlier Luke recalled it had taken four or five minutes for the MP to get to them in his jeep. I'll have to get over the fence in four minutes or less, he thought. He nodded to himself. I can do that. I'll have to do it.

He tried to go through the next day perfectly normally. But as he sat in the mess hall that evening with Tamara, Lenore, Angela, and Del, Luke felt nervous, jumpy.

"Are you okay?" Tamara asked.

"Sure," he snapped.

From across the table, Lenore asked, "Are you coming down with something, Dad?"

His brows furrowing, Luke said, "What makes you think that?"

"Your hand's trembling."

Luke looked down and, sure enough, the spoon in his hand was shaking noticeably.

"It's a little chilly in here, that's all."

"Finish your soup," said Lenore. "That'll warm you up."

"Eat it all up like a good boy," said Angela, grinning at him.

"Yes, Mama," Luke said meekly.

When they returned to their quarters, Luke checked his overstuffed windbreaker and the rolled-up blanket, then went into the bathroom and tapped on Tamara's door. She opened it immediately, as if she had been expecting him.

"Uh . . . I'm going for a walk," he said.

"I'll come with you."

He shook his head. "Better not."

"It's cold out there."

"I'll be okay."

She looked up at him, worry clearly etched on her face. "You're sure?"

"Positive."

She said nothing. Luke grasped her slim waist, pulled her to him, and kissed her soundly. She clung to him and whispered hurriedly in his ear, "Don't do it. Please. Stay here. Stay with me."

It took every ounce of self-control that Luke possessed to disengage from her. "I'll be back. It's just a little stroll, that's all."

Tamara said nothing, but tears filled her eyes.

He pulled on an extra shirt, then took his windbreaker and the blanket and almost ran downstairs. Outside in the night, it was cold. A sharp wind was keening down from the mountains. Even the half-moon riding over the crests looked icy, chilled.

Luke wrapped the stuffed windbreaker over his shoulders and toted the blanket roll under his arm. The streets were practically deserted; he saw only one couple—both in army khakis—strolling away from the mess hall.

A jeep puttered by, and Luke's heart thumped. The soldier driving it paid him no attention and turned off at the next intersection.

Luke stopped in the shadows of the last building before the fence. No one else in sight.

All right, wise guy, he said to himself. It's now or never.

Quickly he stepped across the street, pulled the windbreaker off his shoulders, and tossed it over the fence. It didn't quite make it. The windbreaker hit the coiled razor wire at the top of the fence and bounced back to the ground with a thump. Cursing himself, Luke grabbed it up and heaved with all his might. The windbreaker sailed over the razor wire, empty arms flapping, and landed on the fence's other side.

Good thing the water's in plastic bottles, he thought. Now comes the tough part.

Swinging the blanket around his neck, he backed away from the fence a half-dozen paces, then ran to it and jumped as high as he could. His fingers clutching the wire fence, his shoe tips finding some purchase, he clambered to the edge of the razor wire.

Hanging there by one hand, he yanked the blanket off his neck and threw it over the sharp prongs of the coiled razor wire. It wasn't much help; Luke felt stinging cuts on the palms of his hands as he struggled over the coils. He heard his pants rip and felt a slash of pain on his inner thigh. Missed the balls, he thought gratefully.

But he was atop the wire. Without hesitating to think, he swung over the coils, grabbed the wire beneath and hung his full length, then let himself drop to the ground.

He landed with a thud and collapsed onto the dusty ground. His right ankle flared painfully. It's not broken, he told himself, hoping it was true. It's just a sprain. I just twisted it.

He was breathing hard, and both his hands stung nastily. In the pale light of the moon he saw his hands were bloody. Then he heard the coughing rumble of a jeep approaching.

Scrambling to his feet, he scooped up the windbreaker and

awkwardly stuck his arms through its sleeves while he hobbled away from the fence. The ankle really hurt; so did his hands and thigh.

Over his shoulder Luke saw the headlights of the jeep. He limped as fast as he could toward a fair-sized rock and huddled down behind it.

He could hear the voice of the MP in the jeep, but not make out his words. His tone was clear, though. He was phoning back to his headquarters, telling them that somebody'd been at the fence. Luke realized his blanket was still wrapped around the razor wire. A dead giveaway, he thought. They'll come out searching for me.

Sure enough, a flashlight beam swung across the dusty ground, past the rock he was hiding behind and on to his right. It switched off, and he heard the jeep drive away.

They'd be back, Luke knew. With reinforcements.

He struggled to his feet and went lurching painfully into the cold night, trying to put as much distance between himself and the base as he could.

Into the Woods

I f this didn't hurt so much it'd be funny, Luke thought as he hobbled farther from the base, into the darkness of the empty desert. Who the hell do I think I am? Kit Carson? Clint Eastwood?

The desert wasn't completely empty, he saw in the wan light of the moon. It was bare and parched, but there were trees up ahead, maybe a mile or so. Must be a river or a stream up there. Plenty of rocks all over the place, strewn around like toys scattered by a careless child. Like pictures of Mars, he thought. Rocks and more rocks. Don't stumble on them. The last thing you need is another bad ankle.

Looking back over his shoulder, he could see lights playing back and forth in the distance. The MPs. But they seemed to be inside the wire fence, so far. They hadn't sent out a search party yet. Good.

He staggered on, his ankle flaring painfully every time he put some weight on it.

Ignore the pain, he told himself. Keep pushing on. Once you're in those trees up there you can ease up, see if the cell phone works.

What if it doesn't? he asked himself. Then you push on, was the only answer he could come up with.

It was cold, and getting colder. He unzipped his windbreaker pockets and fished in them for his cap, but his cut-up hands hurt and were slippery with blood, and the pockets were stuffed with granola bars, trail mix, and plastic bottles of water.

Push on, push on, he urged himself. You'll get there. Somehow he remembered reading years earlier that spiderwebs could stem the bleeding from a cut. The foreign DNA of the spider's silk activated clotting factors in human blood.

Great. Where am I going to find a spider's web in this blasted desert? In the dark, yet. In the cold. No self-respecting spider within a hundred miles of here, I bet.

He heard the distant rumble of jeeps. Maybe trucks.

They're coming out after me!

He hurried ahead, hurting, limping, bleeding, but still moving forward, toward the trees.

He got there at last, staggering in among their dark boles, stumbling in the bushes between them. He could hear the soft gurgle of a stream off somewhere in the darkness. Gratefully, he slid to the ground and rested his back against one of the tree trunks.

He sat there puffing. The cold *hurt*. Every part of his body hurt. I ought to get deeper into these woods, he told himself. Painfully, he hauled himself to his feet and lumbered on.

Sure enough, there was a little stream tumbling over the rocks a few dozen feet deeper into the trees. I didn't need to bring the water bottles, he thought. Then he fished in his shirt pocket for his cell phone.

Damn! It's in the first shirt, underneath this outer one.

His hands smarting painfully, he fumbled with the buttons of his outer shirt and eased the cell phone out of his pocket. It slipped out of his blood-slicked fingers and dropped to the mossy ground. For an instant Luke feared it would tumble into the water, but it stayed at his feet.

Thank the gods for small mercies, he thought as he bent slowly to pick it up. At least my back doesn't hurt the way it used to. Now if only everything else felt okay.

The cell phone was still useless, he saw. NO SIGNAL, its little screen proclaimed. Damned jamming works all the way out here, Luke fumed to himself. He sucked in a deep breath and started moving farther into the woods, thinking, Pappagannis said the jamming peters out a couple miles from the base. Hope he knows what he's talking about.

After what seemed like an hour Luke sank down to the ground and leaned his back against a tree. He was puffing from the exertion, and every breath he took in stung with cold. He tried the phone again. Nothing. Got to move on, he told himself. Follow the stream, stay in the trees.

But his legs ached, his hands stung, the cut on his thigh hurt. He leaned forward and felt his injured ankle.

Yep, it's swelling. All you need now is to be struck by lightning.

The moon was sinking behind the mountains, but the sky was crystal clear, spangled with bright twinkling stars. Luke could even make out the pale stream of the Milky Way. But why's it have to be so freaking cold? he complained to himself.

He pulled out one of the granola bars, unwrapped it clumsily, then munched it down. Dessert, he told himself. He carefully balled up the wrapper and stuffed it back into his pocket. No littering.

Maybe I ought to take a little nap. Be good to rest a bit. But then he remembered that when a person freezes to death he goes to sleep first. It's not *that* cold, he told himself. I'm not going to freeze. Still, he realized that his whole body was shivering.

He heard an eerie yowl from far off. A wolf! he thought. No, more likely a coyote. Either way they eat meat.

And then he saw lights flashing back and forth in the distance.

They're coming after me!

Night

L UKE SCRAMBLED TO his feet, sending a shock of pain through his bad leg. There were several lights swinging back and forth among the trees. A search party, he realized. Come out, come out, wherever you are.

The hell I will.

He staggered off along the side of the stream, pain flaring with each step. Despite the cold he was sweating.

The ground was rising, he noticed. The moon was down, and the only light he had was from the stars. And that damned coyote or wolf or whatever it was started howling again. The moon's gone, dummy, Luke snarled silently. Shut up and go to sleep.

He lumbered on, fighting a growing urge to urinate. What the hell, he thought at last. When you gotta go, go. He unzipped his fly and went against one of the trees. Good stream, he noticed. Then he zipped up again and plunged on through the woods.

It'd be good to sleep, he thought. To sleep, to dream . . . He almost laughed. Quoting Shakespeare. You're getting delirious, man.

The lights seemed to be farther away, a little. That's good. Keep on moving. Put as much distance between them and yourself as you can.

In the dimness he didn't see the tree root snaking across his path. He tripped ingloriously and fell flat on his face with a resounding thud and a crack that he thought was a breaking bone. His nose was bleeding, and his face felt raw, scraped.

Pulling himself to his knees, Luke wondered what the hell else he could do to himself. Maybe fall in the stream and drown, he thought wryly. No. Too cold. Besides, I wouldn't give them the satisfaction.

He struggled to his feet and lurched on. Maybe there's a cave or some hole in the ground where I can hide, he thought. "Yeah, sure," he muttered. "Find a nice hole in the ground; that's where the snakes hide. Rattlers." He stumbled away from the stream, up the sloping ground, peering into the darkness. This is useless, he told himself. Can't see a damned thing.

But he kept on going.

Suddenly the clattering roar of a helicopter shattered the night's silence. Looking upward, Luke saw a bright searchlight swinging back and forth between the trees.

They really want to find me, he thought. Colonel Dennis must be going apeshit. The White House tells him to keep me confined and I bust out like Jimmy Cagney in an old jailbreak flick.

The copter's searchlight was getting closer. Luke realized that he'd be easier to spot if he was moving along among the trees, so he flattened himself against one of the trunks, his head turned upward to watch the approaching searchlight.

It flicked down between the trees, swinging this way and that. Luke was suddenly glad that his slacks and windbreaker were both dark brown. He saw the trees' boughs bending under the downdraft of the chopper's rotors, felt the blast of wind on his upturned face. Then it moved on. The swooshing roar dwindled; the light probed farther away.

Luke sank to the ground, completely spent. He was numb, all his adrenaline used up. Don't fall asleep! he commanded himself. It did no good. His eyes closed, his chin slumped to his chest, and everything went completely dark.

H E WAS AWAKENED by a beam of sunshine piercing through the canopy of trees, bathing his face with brightness. He was shivering with cold, his teeth chattering. His whole body was stiff, the way it had been every morning before he started his telomerase treatment. Only worse. The fountain of youth has its limits, he thought.

But as he lay there blinking into full wakefulness, he broke into a crooked grin. I made it, he said to himself. I got through the night without killing myself or letting the MPs find me.

He saw that his right ankle was swollen to three times its normal size. The cuts on his hands had clotted, and apparently the slash on his inner thigh had, too. The sunlight on his face felt warm and bright.

Not so bad, he thought. Now if only the goddamned phone is working.

It wasn't. NO SIGNAL, the tiny screen insisted stubbornly.

Christ, how far away from the base do I have to get? I must have gone at least two miles by now. Pappagannis doesn't know what he's talking about.

He ripped open one of the trail-mix packets and gulped the stuff down, then drank half a bottle of water. And realized he had to urinate again.

Struggling to his feet, Luke wondered if the MPs were still out there looking for him. Be easier to spot me in the daylight, he knew.

As if in answer, he heard the roar of another helicopter and, over it, an amplified voice bellowing, "Professor Abramson, show yourself. You can't get far and we have teams of trackers searching for you. Come out from under the trees and give yourself up."

Trackers? he asked himself. With bloodhounds and shotguns,

like in old movies? He stayed still until the helicopter rattled off some distance, then started limping doggedly farther upslope, away from the stream, cursing himself for not being bright enough to bring a compass.

Edward Novack

A S HE WALKED toward the mess hall, Novack could see something was going on. Three big Army trucks were rumbling toward the main gate, filled with soldiers in khaki fatigues. A small helicopter was descending onto the chopper pad, swirling a mini-whirlwind of dust across the area, while another, larger chopper sat nearby, its rotors swinging lazily, as if waiting for the order to take off.

Frowning with curiosity, Novack changed his direction and walked briskly to the base's three-story administration building and Colonel Dennis's office.

The dumpy female sergeant who served as the colonel's aide looked distraught. "The colonel can't see you now, Mr. Novack. He's very busy."

From the half-open door to the colonel's office he heard Dennis yell, "Connie, get Rossov on the phone. Top priority!"

Novack watched the aide reach for her phone console. As she did so, he simply walked past her desk and into Dennis's office.

The colonel looked distraught, disheveled, his eyes bloodshot as if he hadn't slept all night. Two young lieutenants were standing before his desk, looking anxious.

"What's going on?" Novack asked.

Dennis gaped at him, and the two shavetails turned at the sound of his voice.

"This is Army business," Colonel Dennis said, his voice pitched high, nervous. "I don't have time to talk to you now." He jabbed a finger at one of the lieutenants. "Night-vision goggles. Round up all the night-vision equipment you can find."

"I don't think we've got anything like that on the base, sir."

"Then find out where it might be and get it here! Pronto!"

"What's going on?" Novack repeated, louder.

Dennis's round face went red with anger. "Do I have to get the MPs to throw you out of here?"

Folding his arms across his chest, Novack said, "Yeah. Do that."

The two lieutenants fidgeted uncertainly, glancing back and forth from Novack to the colonel. Dennis slowly rose from his swivel chair, clenched his fists—then plopped down on the chair again.

"It's Abramson," he admitted, his face miserable. "He . . . he's escaped."

Novack's jaw dropped open. "Escaped?"

"During the night," Dennis said, in a choked voice. "He got over the fence. He's out there somewhere. We're trying to find him."

Suppressing an urge to laugh, Novack thought, The colonel's let a seventy-five-year-old man make a jailbreak. Rossov's going to be pissed as hell.

As if on cue, Dennis's aide called from outside, "Mr. Rossov on line one, sir!"

I T WAS JUST past ten A.M. in the District of Columbia. Rossov had barely slid into his desk chair when the call from Colonel Dennis came through.

"Escaped?" he blurted at the colonel's image on his phone console's screen. "What do you mean, he escaped?"

"During the night," Dennis muttered, his voice weak and miserable. "He got over the fence. We've got a couple of dozen men searching for him."

"You let him get away?"

"He can't get far," the colonel whined. "There's nothing out there for forty-some miles. Not a house, not a barn, no buildings at all."

"So he'll freeze to death out there," Rossov growled.

"No, it's not that cold. It didn't go down to freezing overnight."

Anger rising inside him like hot acid, Rossov said, "You find him. You find him right away."

"We will. We will."

"Do that."

Rossov cut the connection, but the vision of Colonel Dennis's rueful face seemed burned in his mind like a bad afterimage.

On an impulse he banged on the speed-dial key for FBI headquarters.

NOVACK WAS STILL standing in front of Colonel Dennis's desk with the two lieutenants as the colonel put down his phone. Scowling at the younger officers, he snarled, "You heard the man. Find him!"

The two shavetails scampered out of the office. "And get that night-vision equipment!" Dennis shouted after them.

"I'll need to tell Fisk about this," Novack said.

Dennis shook his head. "No. This is an Army matter. No outside communications."

"But you just talked to Rossov."

"He's in the chain of command. He's at the top of my chain of command."

"Well, Fisk is at the top of *my* chain of command," Rossov said. "I've got to tell him about this."

"No. No outside communications."

Rossov stared at the sweaty, rumpled, uncombed colonel. He's protecting his ass. If Fisk finds out Abramson's gone over the wall he'll have Dennis's hide nailed to his office wall.

Without another word he turned and left the colonel's office. Once outside, squinting in the morning sunshine, he tried to figure out how he could get some kind of message through to Fisk. He realized, If Abramson really gets loose, Fisk'll have *my* hide nailed to his office wall.

But then he thought about Tamara Minteer. Wonder how she'll take the news that the professor's cut loose and left her here by herself.

He smiled. She won't be by herself for very long, he thought.

Publish or Perish

A T LEAST I don't hear any bloodhounds baying, Luke thought as he limped painfully through the trees. It felt reasonably warm with the sun up; even in the mottled shadows of the woods he felt comfortable enough to unzip his windbreaker.

Then another damned helicopter roared overhead. It seemed to hover right above him. Luke froze and clung to a tree trunk, wishing he could find a cave or some hole in the ground to hide in. The damned chopper wouldn't go away.

They've got their search strategy figured out. The helicopters can't see me through the trees' foliage, but they're pinning me down, keeping me from moving past the trees and out into the open. And the guys on the ground are beating the bushes, looking for me. They know I'm in these woods; it's only a matter of time before they find me.

He was nearly at the far edge of the woods. In the distance he could see clear ground. Bet the phone will work out there, he told himself. But as soon as I go out in the open the choppers will spot me. And what if the mother-loving jamming is still working out there? What if I go out and the stupid phone's still no good? Then it's all over.

His plan was to send the report he'd written for Fisk to every

Web site he could think of, including *American Cellular Biology* and a half-dozen university sites. Fisk and Rossov, he reasoned, are holding us at this damned Army base to keep me from telling the outside world about my work. Once I squirt the information to the Internet sites, there's no reason for them to hold us anymore.

That's the plan, he said to himself as he squinted up through the tree branches at the helicopter slowly angling away from him. That's the plan. Publish or perish.

Luke grunted to himself. Maybe it'll be publish and then perish.

No sign of the ground troops, he realized. The MPs aren't trained for this kind of thing. Hope they're all city kids. Hope they don't have some Mississippi coon hunters among them.

The damned copter was moving back his way again. Luke hunkered down, his back against the tree's rough bark, his ankle throbbing and feeling hot. With nothing better to do, he pulled a granola bar from his jacket pocket and waited for darkness.

If I can keep away from them until it gets dark, then I can go out in the open and try to get the phone to work.

Publish or perish. He laughed softly at the ridiculous irony of his situation.

SOMEHOW HIGHTOWER COULD tell before lifting his phone's receiver that the call was from his division chief. The ring seemed to be more insistent, more urgent. He knew it was nothing but his imagination but, sure enough, when he put the receiver to his ear he heard his chief's high-pitched voice:

"Jerry, come in here."

Insistent. Urgent.

The chief was pacing from his desk to his window, in his shirt-sleeves. Dapper as ever, his suspenders were decorated with a Stars and Stripes motif. Very patriotic, Hightower thought as he quietly closed the office door behind him.

Turning to face him, the elegant little man said, "Rossov's sending an executive jet to Logan to take you out to Idaho again."

"Why—"

"Abramson's escaped the base out there. He's on the loose, and Rossov's spitting nails."

"Abramson's escaped?"

"Yes!"

"Can't they get Army people to find him?" Hightower asked.

Pointing thumb and finger like a pistol, the chief barked, "Rossov wants you out there! I've been told by the deputy director at headquarters in Washington that you are to get your butt out to that base and assist in the search! So move it!"

Hightower made a barely perceptible nod. "You know that by the time I get there they'll probably have picked him up."

"I know that," the chief admitted. "And you know that. And probably the deputy director knows it, too. But Rossov is from the White House and he wants you in Idaho."

Suppressing an urge to shake his head, Hightower murmured, "I'm on my way."

T HE SUN WAS sinking toward the distant mountains. The air was turning noticeably chillier. Luke still sat at the base of the same tree he'd been under most of the day, bent over his phone, pecking away painfully at a foreword to his paper. He wanted it to be transparently clear, so that anybody could read it and understand what he'd accomplished.

Looking up at the reddening sky, he thought, Another cold night coming. Well, the sooner the better. Let me get out from under these trees and make my goddamned phone call.

Helicopters had been droning back and forth all afternoon. At one point a team of soldiers came whacking at the underbrush within a few hundred yards of where he'd been hiding. Luke hunkered down and froze. Like a rabbit, he thought. They can't see you if you don't move. The searchers passed by, then an hour later came back from the other direction.

City boys, Luke figured. No real hunters among them. They sounded tired and dispirited as they trudged by, heading back toward the base.

Wait for night, Luke repeated silently. Hello darkness, my old friend. Who sang that? James Taylor? No, I think it was Simon and Garfunkel.

As the shadows deepened and the wind sweeping down from the mountains turned colder, Luke chewed on his last granola bar, thinking, This is pretty ludicrous. Camping outdoors night and day. What I wouldn't give for a decent hotel room and a nice, hot shower.

Nobody in sight. Even the choppers have gone away. Maybe I could walk out there and try the phone without waiting for night. Then I could phone Tamara and ask her to tell Colonel Dennis where I am.

He shook his head. No. Wait for night. Don't throw everything down the toilet because you're tired and antsy.

So he waited.

In the distance he heard a helicopter droning, but it didn't seem to be coming his way.

He waited.

Closing the Ring

THANKS TO THE three-hour time difference between the East and West Coasts, the executive jet carrying Hightower arrived at Fairchild Air Force Base, just outside of Spokane, a few minutes after four P.M.

A pair of local FBI men escorted him to a big, sausage-shaped Army helicopter. Neither of them had much to say. Hightower figured that they resented being ordered to babysit an agent from the other side of the country. I'd be a little ticked, too, he thought, having some stranger invade my territory.

The chopper was comfortable enough, even though most of the seating area was filled with sealed boxes. The only passenger aboard, Hightower tried to make sense of the labels stenciled on them. Army gobbledegook, he figured. Specialized equipment.

It was starting to get dark by the time he landed at Base Y-18. A grizzled sergeant, paunchy and sour-faced, stood at the base of the ladder as Hightower descended from the helicopter, his suede jacket hanging open.

Looking puzzled, the sergeant asked, "Where's your luggage?"

Hefting his slim briefcase, Hightower said, "This is it. I guess I should see Colonel Dennis before anything else."

With a knowledgeable nod, the sergeant said, "Yeah. The colonel wants to see you right away."

———

IT'S DARK ENOUGH, Luke thought, looking at the moon smiling lopsidedly down at him. Enough light to get around without breaking my neck. But then he realized, That means there's enough light for them to spot me.

He didn't hear any helicopters, though. And he hadn't seen any soldiers searching for him since that halfhearted squad had passed him a few hours earlier.

Okay, Luke said to himself. Out of the woods and keep on going until the phone connects.

Wincing on his bad ankle, he started out toward the bare desert, his cell phone in one hand.

Should've gotten a smartphone, like Tamara has. All this little piece of crap can do is make phone calls.

But maybe that's enough.

NO SIGNAL, the minuscule screen flashed. Cursing under his breath, Luke trudged on.

COLONEL DENNIS WAS clearly miserable, Hightower saw. The man appeared to have aged ten years. His fleshy face looked pale, his eyes frightened. He seemed to be hunkered down in his swivel chair, using the desk as a protective barrier.

"The men I have here aren't trained for searching the woods," he grumbled. "My men are clerks, lab technicians, not commandos."

"Maybe he's not in the woods," Hightower suggested.

"He's got to be in the woods!" Dennis snapped. "That's the only cover for miles around. If he was out in the open, the choppers would've spotted him."

Hightower agreed with a nod. "I'm not sure what I can do to help you." Smiling gently he added, "I hope you don't think that I'm some sort of native tracker."

Shaking his head hard enough to make his cheeks wobble, Dennis said, "Bringing you out here was Rossov's idea, not mine."

"I'll do whatever I can, of course. But I don't what it might be."

Casting an eye at the lengthening shadows of sundown, Colonel Dennis answered, "Let my quartermaster find you a place to sleep. That chopper you came in on has brought us a load of night-vision equipment. We'll get him tonight."

"Good," said Hightower. But he wondered if it was true.

SITTING IN THE mess hall, Novack saw Tamara come in for dinner alone. He waited while she loaded her tray and found a seat, then left his own dinner and went to sit across the table from her.

"Where's the kid and her parents?" he asked, by way of a greeting.

"They ate earlier," Tamara said. "Too early for me."

Take it easy with her, Novack counseled himself. Let her relax.

"You mind if I bring my tray here? I hate to eat alone."

Tamara tilted her head slightly. "So do I."

Within a few minutes they were talking about Luke's escape.

"This is going to make me look real bad," Novack said. "Fisk is going to blame me for letting him get away."

Tamara almost smiled. "He's locked us into an Army base in the middle of nowhere with whole squads of soldiers to guard it, and he's going to blame you?"

Novack shrugged. "That's the way the cookie crumbles. The Army'll blame the colonel, but Fisk's going to come down on me. Hard."

"You mean you could lose your job?"

"Maybe."

She shook her head. "That's not fair."

He shrugged again.

Tamara looked past him. "I'm worried about Luke, out there in the cold all by himself."

She calls him by his first name, Novack realized. Is there something going on between them?

"If the soldier boys haven't found him by now," he said to her, "he must be halfway to Canada."

Tamara said nothing.

"And he left you holding the bag. Left his granddaughter, too."

"Angela's almost fully recovered. She'll be fine."

"Yeah, but he took off by himself, looking out for numero uno."

Scowling, she challenged, "How do you think he could manage to get all of us out of here? He did what he had to do."

"Numero uno," Novack repeated.

Suddenly Hightower's massive form loomed over them, carrying a tray that looked almost toy-sized in his big hands.

"Mind if I join you?"

"What the hell are you doing here?" Novack yelped.

Sitting down wearily next to him, Hightower said, "I've been drafted."

Moonlight Encounters

NO SIGNAL, THE phone still said.

Luke stared up at the half-moon hanging above the crest of the mountains. Enough light to let me walk out here without breaking my neck, he thought. Also enough light to let a helicopter spot me.

Maybe I should've waited until the moon's down. No, he decided. There aren't any helicopters buzzing around, I would've heard them. But the farther I get from the woods, the harder it'll be for me to hide if any choppers come over.

Trudging along doggedly, he zipped up his windbreaker and pulled his wool cap from its now-empty pocket. His hands still stung when he tried to grip something, but at least they weren't bleeding anymore.

Okay, he told himself. Keep going until the phone gets clear of the jamming.

Far off in the distance he heard a coyote howl. And beyond that, the faint throbbing rumble of an approaching helicopter.

HIGHTOWER WAS STILL munching his way through a sizable dinner when Tamara finished her coffee.

Pushing back from the table, she said, "I've got to get back."

"Sure," said Novack, getting up from the table also. "I'll walk you home."

She gave him a cold stare. "I don't need any company."

"It's on the way to my room," Novack said easily. Raising both hands as if to show he wasn't carrying any weapons, he added, "Honest."

Wordlessly, Tamara turned and headed for the row of pegs by the door, where people had hung their coats. Novack went with her.

Hightower looked up from his bowl of chili and watched them go.

THE HELICOPTER WAS hovering over the trees. And there was more than one of them, Luke realized. If they head this way they'll spot me easily.

He looked down again at the phone in his fist. Time and date!

"It's working!" Luke shouted into the night. He squatted on the dusty ground and punched up his paper and its foreword. Tap. To *ACB*. Tap. To his university. Tap. Tap. Tap. To three blogs that he followed.

The helicopters were still down by the trees. He could see searchlights flicking back and forth from them.

Twitter, he thought. Send the foreword to Twitter. Too long. Chop it in half and send it in three pieces.

The searchlights winked off. Luke stared up into the moonlit sky. Why'd they do that?

Never mind them. Send the foreword to the university's Facebook site. And the whole paper to the AAAS. And *Science News*.

One of the choppers was definitely heading his way. Luke ignored its approach as he bent over his phone, sending his paper and its foreword to one Web site after another.

TAMARA WALKED ALONGSIDE Novack, never letting him get close enough to touch her. He chatted amiably enough, though. Maybe he doesn't have any ideas about me, she thought.

But then he stopped and pointed at the nearest building, a two-story wood frame structure identical to the building where she and the Villanueva family were housed.

"That's my place. I've got a bottle of pretty good Scotch in my room. Practically untouched."

"No thanks," she said, and started walking toward her own quarters.

She only got two steps away before Novack gripped her arm. "Come on, don't be so antisocial."

"I said no."

In the moonlight she could see his face harden. And his grip on her arm along with it. "One lousy drink. It won't kill you."

"No." Tamara tried to pull loose.

"You think you're better than me? You got the hots for the professor? Well, he's flown the coop, babe, and I'm all you've got."

"Let go of me!"

He pulled her to him and twisted her arm behind her back. Tamara was pinned to him. She opened her mouth to scream, but he clapped his hand over it.

"You just keep quiet and you won't get hurt."

Tamara kicked him in the shin as hard as she could. Novack yelped with pain, and she broke free of his grip. She started to run away, but a sudden blow to her back knocked her sprawling on the dusty sidewalk.

Novack loomed over her. "You open your mouth again, bitch, and I'll break your fucking face."

Tamara tried to get up, but Novack was on top of her, pinning her to the ground.

He slapped her face, hard. "Come on, bitch. You're going to get it, whether you like it or not."

Suddenly he was lifted up and off her. Tamara saw that High-tower, massive as an avenging angel, had hauled him up in the air by the scruff of his neck and the seat of his pants and was shaking him like a terrier shaking a rat.

Novack yowled and struggled, arms windmilling and legs thrashing at the empty air, unable to get at the bigger man. Hightower raised him high over his head, still shaking him mercilessly, then slammed him to the ground. Tamara heard a resounding thump and a sharp crack as the man's head hit the pavement.

She raised herself up on one elbow. Novack was sprawled face-down on the ground, his limbs twisted, his eyes half closed. But he was breathing, she saw. Gasping for air, actually. Unconscious, not dead.

Hightower offered her a hand, and she got shakily to her feet.

"He . . . he . . ."

"He's not going to do anything for a while," Hightower said, as calmly as if discussing the weather. "Come on, I'll take you to your building."

P ROFESSOR ABRAMSON." THE loudspeaker blared over the thrumming of the approaching helicopter. "STAND WHERE YOU ARE. WE'RE GOING TO LAND AND PICK YOU UP."

Luke watched the chopper settle onto the ground, kicking up a whirlwind of dust. No searchlight, he said to himself. They must have an infrared detector.

He got slowly to his feet and raised his arms above his head, like a prisoner who's been caught by the guards. In one hand he still clutched his cell phone.

You got me, he said silently to the chopper crew, but not soon enough to stop me.

Viral

WHEN THE HELICOPTER crew brought Luke into the little wooden shack that served as a control center for the helipad, Tamara was there, standing between Colonel Dennis and Hightower. She looked anxious, Dennis tense and angry, Hightower as imperturbable as a mountain with his beefy arms folded across his chest.

She ran across the tiny room to him. "Are you all right?"

"Yeah," he answered, with a crooked grin. "I'm fine. Now."

"You look terrible," she said. He saw that there were tears in her eyes.

"Cut my hands a little." He showed them, palms up.

"Your face is bruised. And your nose has been bleeding. Clotted blood."

"Tripped in the dark." He glanced down at his ripped trousers. "Cut my leg, too."

"My God. We've got to get you to the infirmary."

"Not so fast." Colonel Dennis came between them. "You've got some explaining to do, Professor."

But Luke noticed that Tamara's cheek was bruised. "What happened to you?"

Hightower stepped up and answered, "Novack."

"That sonofabitch!"

Placing a massive hand on Luke's chest, Hightower said, "It's all right. He's in the infirmary. Couple of cracked ribs and a concussion."

Luke stared at the FBI agent.

Dennis tried to reassert his authority. "All right, I want to know just what the hell you were trying to do out there. Where did you think you were going?"

"No place," said Luke.

"What do you mean, no place?"

Luke looked around the crowded little room. The two men of the helicopter crew were standing in the doorway, and a trio of tech sergeants, seated at their consoles, had swung their chairs around to watch their colonel and the civilians.

Luke explained. "I just wanted to get far enough away so I could put through a couple of phone calls."

"Phone calls?"

Luke dug out his cell phone and brandished it in front of the colonel's face as if it were a magic wand. "Yep. The news is out, Colonel. My work's been published on the Internet."

Dennis's face went pale. "Ohmigod."

D ENNIS FLED TO his office while Tamara took Luke to the infirmary, with a pair of MPs and Hightower accompanying them. Luke saw Novack lying on one of the beds, asleep or unconscious. The other three beds in the minuscule sick bay were empty.

Tamara fussed over his hands, washing them thoroughly, then swabbing disinfectant over his cuts and bandaging them carefully.

"That's the longest time we've ever held hands," he said to her, grinning foolishly.

She gave him a tight-lipped look. "You could have killed yourself out there."

"Maybe. But I didn't."

She led Luke to the examination table. He sat on its edge, and she helped him pull off his pants. Luke wanted to laugh, thinking this would be much more enjoyable if the MPs and Hightower weren't watching.

"You must have a guardian angel watching over you," she said as she cleaned the clotted blood from his thigh. "Another inch and your femoral artery would have been ripped open. You would've bled to death out there."

Luke said nothing, but he thought that he did indeed have a guardian angel watching over him at this particular moment. An angel with green eyes.

With Tamara holding one arm and Hightower the other, Luke shuffled to the nearest empty bed and sank down on it.

"You must be tired," she said.

"Yeah. I didn't get much sleep out there."

She bent over and kissed him lightly on the lips. He closed his eyes and, smiling, fell asleep.

WHEN LUKE AWOKE it was bright morning. Novack's bed was empty, he saw. Nobody else was in sight.

Then Hightower pushed through the door, carrying a breakfast tray.

"You're awake. Good."

Luke pulled himself up to a sitting position as Hightower put the tray on the swinging table next to the bed.

"Colonel Dennis has been on the phone most of the night. Rossov is on his way here. So is Fisk."

Jerking a thumb at the mussed bed, Luke asked, "Where's Novack?"

"They took him to Spokane late last night."

"How'd he get the concussion?"

Hightower swung the table in front of Luke. "He was bothering Dr. Minteer. He fell and hurt himself."

"With a little help from you, huh?"

Smiling minimally, Hightower replied, "An FBI agent doesn't rough up people. That's against our rules, even if the little jerk is attacking a woman. He just fell and hurt himself."

"If you say so."

Luke looked down at the breakfast tray: cup of fruit, scrambled eggs, toast, and coffee. Picking up the fork, he asked Hightower, "No breakfast for you?"

"I had mine two hours ago."

Luke speared an apple slice just as the door opened again and a blur raced to his bedside. "Grandpa!" Angela said, reaching for him with both arms.

Luke hauled her up beside him and saw Lenore and Del at the door, both of them wreathed in smiles.

"Grandpa, we're going home!" Angela cried happily. "Tomorrow!"

"That's great," he said, looking past the child to his daughter and her husband. "Wonderful."

Hightower burst the bubble, though. "I'm afraid you'll have to stay until Rossov and Fisk decide what to do about you."

Luke's elation dimmed. "When will they be here?"

"Later this afternoon," said Hightower. "They're flying to Spokane on one of Fisk's jets, and Colonel Dennis has arranged for a chopper to bring them here."

Luke nodded. Shootout at high noon, he said to himself.

Then he realized that Hightower was smiling broadly.

"I'm glad you're happy," he said, absently hugging Angela.

"You should be, too," said the FBI agent. "Whatever it was that you sent out on your phone last night, it's gone viral on the Internet. Dennis has been talking to Army brass and White House people all morning. He's sweating bullets. Probably lost five pounds already."

Viral, Luke thought. Good. The word is out. Angela is fine. Everything's fine. Well, almost everything.

Lead, Follow, or Get Out of the Way

DO YOU REALIZE what you've done?" Rossov snarled. Luke saw anger in the White House man's face. Anger, tension—and fear.

They were sitting in Colonel Dennis's office. The colonel sat entrenched behind his desk, looking very flustered. Quenton Fisk sat beside Rossov, quiet, cold, his expression unreadable.

Luke answered calmly. "What I've done is show the world that telomerase therapy can be used to kill cancerous tumors."

"You signed a privacy agreement!" Fisk snapped.

"And you agreed to locking me up in this glorified prison. Sue me and I'll countersue you."

"The hell you will."

"The hell I won't!"

Shaking his head, Rossov said, "I don't think you understand what you've let loose. Curing cancer. All sorts of people living past a hundred. It's a disaster."

"It's a revolution," said Luke. "What the hell are you so spooled up about? This is the best news the human race has had since . . . since Watson and Crick unraveled DNA."

Rossov moaned. "Death rate going down. Lifetimes doubling. That's a disaster, Abramson! A fucking disaster!"

Genuinely puzzled, Luke asked, "What the hell are you talking about?"

"You've ruined Social Security. We're already going broke with Medicare. And the whole insurance industry, too. You've wrecked the American economy."

"Bullshit."

Jabbing a finger at Luke, Rossov insisted, "The economy can't survive having a nation full of centenarians! It'll break the bank."

Luke felt growing anger simmering inside him. These chowderheads don't understand, he realized. They don't understand anything at all.

He rose slowly to his feet. "You just don't get it, do you? You can't stop this. You can't put a cork in scientific knowledge. What I've done is just the tip of the iceberg. We have the knowledge, the power, to transform the human race."

"And ruin the country."

"*Change* the country. Change the world." Luke started to pace across the office, but his ankle flared and he sank back onto his chair. Still, he continued. "We're going to be able to extend human life spans indefinitely, sooner or later. Prevent genetic diseases like cancer, Alzheimer's, Parkinson's. Stem cell therapies will repair failing hearts, rebuild nerves and any other tissue that's been damaged, regrow limbs that have been lost—"

"By killing fetuses," Rossov growled.

Luke waved the thought away. "We don't need fetal stem cells. We can take stem cells from your own body. Or regress skin cells to become stem cells."

"I've read reports on that," said Colonel Dennis.

Turning in his chair to face Rossov squarely, Luke said, "You think we're going to have a country full of pathetic, creaking old geezers. Well, that's wrong. Look at me! I'll be seventy-five in a couple of months, but somatically—physically—I'm like a forty-year-old. And I'm going to stay this way for a long time."

"That's the fucking problem," Rossov muttered. "Millions of people living to a hundred and more. My Christ."

"It's not a problem," Luke countered. "We're entering a new era. The first transhuman beings are with us now. My granddaughter's one of them. There are going to be plenty of others."

Fisk said, "So what you're telling us—"

"What I'm telling you," Luke interrupted impatiently, "is that people will be healthy and vigorous all their lives. So they live to be a hundred and fifty, two hundred, so what? They won't *need* Social Security or Medicare. They'll be working, going back to school, starting new careers for themselves."

Fisk's eyes narrowed. "They'll continue to be consumers."

"Damned right," said Luke. "They'll continue to buy cars, homes, take vacations, overseas trips—"

"Have babies," said the colonel.

"You just don't understand," Rossov repeated. "You think your transhumans are going to give up their Social Security benefits, their Medicare, their pensions just because they're feeling spry and healthy? In your dreams! This is going to destroy the economy."

"No," Luke replied. "It's going to *change* the economy. And you politicians are going to have to make some real changes to Social Security and Medicare and the rest."

"Change them? That's impossible. Political suicide."

"Then we're going to have to find political leaders who can make it possible."

Rossov glared at him.

"Besides," Luke went on, "this isn't going to happen all at once. We've still got a lot of work to do. You won't start to see any major effects for another five, ten years."

"The President will be out of office by then," Rossov mused. "Even if she wins a second term."

Turning back to Fisk, Luke said, "You thought that by keeping me bottled up here you could prevent news of my work from getting out."

"We wanted to control the situation," Fisk admitted.

Shaking his head, Luke pointed out, "But I'm not the only one working in this area. Sure, I'm ahead of all the others, but sooner or later some bright researcher would hit on the same idea. You can't control everybody. You can't stop people from thinking, learning."

Rossov muttered, "And you can't drop a bombshell like this without dislocating the economy. We're having a tough enough time keeping Social Security and Medicare properly funded. Now . . ." He sank his head into his hands.

"Now," Luke took up, "you're going to have to get those egomaniacs in Washington to do the jobs they were elected to do. You've got at least five years to do it, maybe ten. Instead of trying to stop this transformation, get to work and prepare for it."

"You've never tried to work with the Congress," Rossov moaned. "You've never tried to move the bureaucracy."

Luke snapped, "Then get out of the way, buster, because the change is coming, whether you like it or not."

Fisk broke into a tentative smile. "He's right, Paul," he said to Rossov. "You know, if you play your cards right, you and the President could come out of this smelling like roses."

Rossov looked dubious, but Fisk went on grandly. "Transhumans. It's exciting. People staying young, vigorous past a hundred. Active."

"Buying your products," Luke said.

Fisk tried to glare at him, but broke into a tentative smile instead. "You're still under contract to me, you know."

"Where does Marlo Gunnerson work?" Luke asked.

"In the Fisk Laboratories, in Cincinnati."

Luke nodded. "That's where I'll go. I like Gunnerson. He and I could work well together."

Fisk's tentative smile widened into a happy grin.

"So you peddle your fountain of youth to the masses," Rossov growled.

"That's right," said Fisk. "And you start getting the government ready for the changes that are coming."

Rossov shook his head wearily.

"I'll talk to the President about this," Fisk said happily. "She'll see the sense of it. It'll win her that second term. And I'll put in a good word for you while I'm at it. Deal?"

"What choice do I have?" Rossov said bleakly.

"No choice at all," said Luke. "The change is coming. Either you take credit for it and try to lead the country or you'll get rolled under by it."

"It's impossible," Rossov muttered. "You have no idea how impossible it is."

Luke shook his head at him. "Listen, pal, you either lead, follow, or get out of the way."

Fisk nodded briskly. "Professor Abramson, how would you like to explain this prob—this *opportunity* to the President of the United States?"

T HAT EVENING LUKE met Tamara, Angela, Lenore, and Del in the mess hall.

"We're going home tomorrow," Angela enthused. Lenore looked happier than Luke had seen her in a year or more. Even Del seemed relaxed, pleased.

Luke smiled back at them and said, "I'm going to the White House, to meet the President."

"You are?" Lenore gasped.

Reaching for Tamara's hand, Luke went on. "Yep. Rossov is setting it up. Him and Fisk."

"Can I come?" Angela asked.

Laughing, Luke replied, "Sure, why not? All of us."

"The President of the United States," said Lenore. "I hear she's very sweet."

"She's very smart. She knows which way the parade is heading, and she's going to see to it that she's at its front."

O NCE DINNER WAS finished, Lenore and Del took Angela back to their quarters.

"We have to finish packing," Lenore said, almost apologetically.

Luke took Tamara by the hand, and together they strolled along the quiet dark street, out toward the fence.

"You're not thinking of going over it again, are you?" Tamara teased.

He chuckled softly. "Hell no. Once was enough."

"You've changed the world, Luke."

"With your help. I couldn't have done it without you."

"Yes, you could have. And you would have. I just came along for the ride."

He stopped and turned toward her. "Do you want to continue the ride?"

In the shadows between the lampposts Luke couldn't make out the expression on her face. But he heard the uncertainty in her voice. "Do you want me to?"

He replied instantly. "I sure as hell do."

She stepped closer to him and they kissed.

"Maybe we can get married in Washington. Get a Supreme Court justice to do the job."

"You're fantasizing!"

"Yeah, but not about a Supreme Court justice. My fantasies center on you, Tamara."

And they kissed again.

But then Tamara said softly, "Luke, about your biopsy."

"What about it?"

"You've got cancer. It's early, but it's definitely prostate cancer."

He nodded. "I figured." With a stubborn snort, he said, "We'll have to do something about that."

And, hand in hand, they headed back toward their quarters. And Washington. And a long life together.